# Lost in Tuscany

A Novel

by

Sophie Sinclair

Lost in Tuscany


Print Edition

Editors: Michelle Morgan, www.fictionedit.com
Holly Ingraham, www.hollyingraham.com
Copy Editor: Michelle Morgan
Book Cover Design: Carrie Guy, Shawna Montague
Formatting: BB eBooks

*This book is dedicated to the dreamers who are still searching,
still wandering, and still hoping.*

# Content Warning

Dear readers, this book contains content that may be sensitive. While fun, the story includes elements of alcoholism and alcohol use. Readers who may be sensitive to this, please take note.

*La famiglia è tutto.*
Family is everything.

# Chapter 1

I PEEL MY eyes open, hissing like a vampire against the sunlight streaming through the open blinds. Dried drool cakes across my cheek as I ease myself up on the couch, rubbing the crick in my neck. A chocolate-chip cookie hiding in the folds of my sweatshirt drops to the carpet, and for a split second, I contemplate picking it up and eating it. *Nasty, Summer. You're better than a stale sweatshirt cookie on the floor.*

Groaning, I pick up the empty bottle of wine on the coffee table, my head throbbing to the beat of my pulse. It's not a habit of mine to plow through a bottle and a half of wine by myself on a Friday night, but guys like Kevin will do that to you.

I close my eyes and flashbacks from last night unwillingly play like a bad Netflix movie in my head. I met Kevin at a local sports bar called Lucky's after swiping right on the dating app, *The One*. There was nothing lucky about that place. One look at the LED lights drooping from the Styrofoam ceiling like a limp bra strap should have been my first clue. The dried ketchup stains on the faux-wood tables and the busty server wearing a tank top made for a nine-year-old were my second and third clues to how this date was going to go.

Kevin, who is most definitely not *the one*, prattled on about how many reps he did at the gym that morning. I didn't even blink when he told me he maxed out at 395 pounds on a bench press.

His nostrils flared in irritation. "That's a big deal, Susan."

My eye twitched. I couldn't help but stare at the small glob of ranch dressing clinging to his goatee. My finger automatically edged up to my chin as I subliminally pointed it out.

"Wow, that's—"

"Gary couldn't believe it. He said it's the highest he's seen in months."

I couldn't even get a word in to pretend like I was interested in the conversation. All I could see was the ranch dressing stuck in his beard. I moved my limp lettuce doused heavily in garlic dressing around with my fork, annoyed he kept calling me by the wrong name, even though I'd corrected him twice.

After twenty more minutes of lackluster conversation about all his achievements at work, and Gary's reps at the gym, I had to pull the plug. I took out my credit card to cover my side salad and glass of cheap wine. Kevin got a plate of fire-breathing chicken wings, a cheeseburger with an extra side of onion rings, and three beers. When the server came over with the check, he had the nerve to ask her to split it equally between us and then he winked at me and said, "You look like the Gloria Steinbeck type who insists on paying her own way."

I gave him a flat stare. "I assume you mean, Gloria Steinem."

"Yeah, whatever. You feminist chicks are all the same."

I tilted my head and smiled. "I'm shocked you're still single, Kevin."

"Yeah, well, I like playing the field. Why buy the cow when you can drink the milk for free?"

After spending more than I wanted on dinner and wasting an hour of my life I'll never get back, I left Lucky's and came home to two chilled bottles of white wine in the fridge, a roll of cookie dough, and serious thoughts of never dating again.

I rub my eyes and blindly reach for my phone. One missed call from my best friend, Cara. I stumble to the kitchen and throw the empty bottle of wine in the trash while eyeing the half-eaten tub of melted ice cream and the baking sheet of cookie crumbs. I've hit an all-time low if I indulged in all three last night. Fucking Kevin.

I start the coffee, hoping a good douse of caffeine will rejuvenate me, and rummage through my cabinets for some blessed ibuprofen while I wait for the coffee to percolate. From the couch, my computer dings with a new message.

The heavenly aroma of freshly brewed coffee permeates the air. I pull a mug down and pour a good helping of cream into my coffee. Easing back down on the couch, I take a sip before picking up my laptop. I have a new Facebook message from someone named Monica Morelli. Curious, I open up the message and almost spit coffee all over the couch.

> *Ciao Summer, we're so glad you decided to join Tuscan Bike Tours, LTD.! My name is Monica Morelli and I run the social media for the tour. We can't wait to meet you!*

*There's a Facebook page for TBT if you would like to join. If you have any questions, please email us at tuscanbike-toursltd@gmail.com. Buona giornata! Monica*

The pounding in my head increases two-fold as I pull up my email. I have three emails from Tuscan Bike Tours that came in overnight. I open the first one, which confirms my reservation for the June 5th tour. I press my fingers to my eyes. What the hell is going on? I don't even remember signing up for this. There must be a mistake. There *has* to be a mistake. I don't even *like* bike riding!

The second email is a welcome letter.

*Dear Ms. Andrews,*

*Congratulations on signing up for a ride through Tuscany! Here at Tuscan Bike Tours, LTD., we pride ourselves in our commitment to making our customers' trip a once-in-a-lifetime event. Our bikes are state-of-the-art, and our tour guides are trained in the art of hospitality to make your tour of Tuscany unforgettable. You can trust our guides to handle all the logistics and give you tons of background on each place you visit on tour. Our staff handpicks hotels to give you the utmost comfort on your journey. Meals are also included and will feature local staples and specialties. You'll get to know your fellow travelers at our welcome dinner and come together throughout your tour to celebrate and share stories.*

*Your reservation is for the June 5th–June 14th Singles Only Tour—Paid in Full.*

*We booked your Delta Airlines itinerary as well as the transportation from Florence to Tuscany. You'll be sent a follow-up email with that reservation. Please be advised you will need a valid passport. We look forward to meeting you!*

*Ricardo Filloni,*
*Director of Tuscan Bike Tours, LTD.*

My fingers shake as I open the flight itinerary and receipt for payment. Why do I have no recollection of this? Did Kevin slip something in my drink? What in the hell possessed me to book this trip? I don't even speak Italian! I hastily email the address Ricardo left me for the sales department and tell them there must be a mistake and I need to cancel this trip ASAP. I'm about to check my credit card statement when I hear a key turn in my front door. There's only two people who have a key to my townhouse—Cara and my mother, Barbara.

"Knock-knock, anyone home?"

*And that's definitely not Cara.*

With a groan, I flop an arm over my eyes, hoping to miraculously blend into the couch cushions.

The last person I want to deal with right now is my mom.

She sits down in the chair next to me, huffing. Her signature scent of Obsession and cigarettes pervading the air. "What's wrong now? I thought you'd be up mopping the floors and singing with the birds."

"I'm having a rough morning," I tell her.

"Are you hungover?" I can hear the smile in her voice. "This is a delightful surprise. Perhaps the little birdie didn't fall too far from the nest, after all?"

Barbara and I have never seen eye to eye on anything. Growing up, she was in and out of my life—mostly out of it. When she was around, it was because she needed money or a place to stay, and my grandmother always took her in.

"What do you want, Barbara?"

"Can't I come by on a beautiful Saturday morning to see how my favorite daughter is doing?"

"I'm your only daughter." I peel one eye open. "Unless you have more kids out in the world I'm unaware of. Please don't light that cigarette."

Barbara rolls her eyes and tucks the cigarette into her leopard print bra strap. "Give me a little more credit, Summer."

"I wish I could," I mumble, watching my mom get up and help herself to some coffee in the kitchen.

"Someone have a little party last night? There's an empty bottle in the trash."

"Move over, Nancy Drew, Barbara Andrews is on the case." I sigh, staring up at the ceiling, wishing she would leave so I could figure out what to do about this trip to Italy.

She sits back down with her coffee. "So, Summer, I have a proposition for you."

And here it is…

"I thought maybe I could move in here for a bit. Before you say anything, let me give you some reasons why it's a good idea."

"I can't think of one."

"Don't be rude." She takes a sip of coffee. "Okay, one, I could help you with rent—"

"Barbara, you don't even have a job—"

"*Two*, I think it would be a good chance to bond—"

"I'm thirty-six. I think that ship has sailed."

"Exactly my point. You could really use my help." She

waves a hand at me and my surroundings.

"Help with..."

"Summerita, you're not getting any younger. Don't you want to have fun in your life?"

I gnash my teeth together, hating my childhood nickname she gave me. "Who says I'm not?"

Barbara arches a penciled-in eyebrow at me as she takes a sip from the coffee cup. "I may not have been around much when you were growing up, but I'm here now and I think this could be good for us."

I eye her suspiciously as she sets her coffee back down. I can smell her lie a mile away like a dead skunk. The smudged hot-pink lipstick on my coffee cup grates on my nerves. Everything about Barbara vexes me. She's always been the chaos to my calm. I drum my fingers on my knee, fighting the urge to call her out on her lies.

"I thought you had moved in with Rick?"

"Rick? He's old news. Brian and I got into a fight. It's over."

"Ahh, I see. So, you're homeless."

"I'm not *homeless*, Summer, geez. Just shopping around for something better. Getting ideas like that Pintry thing."

I scrunch my brows. "You mean Pinterest? Not really the same thing."

"Don't sound so superior. You know what I mean."

It's the same old song and dance she used to tell Grams growing up. *I want to spend more time with you. I just need a few weeks to get back on my feet. I lost my job again.* Grams would give her some money and always had a room ready for her in our small house. As soon as my mom met some new guy, she'd be off again without a thank-you or even a goodbye.

Barbara digs in her purse, retrieving a pocket mirror. She rubs her finger over her front teeth, an old habit of hers that brings me back to childhood. Pocketing her mirror, she stares at me, and I know if I don't give in, she'll never leave.

"So, if I gave you some cash—"

"I swear, I'll pay you back. It's just to tide me over until my job interview on Monday."

"Really? Where?"

"I don't want to tell you and jinx it. I'll let you know after the interview." She pats her short, freshly box-dyed hair.

"On Monday."

"Yep." She smiles and the lipstick on her nicotine-stained teeth sets me even more on edge, because I know she's lying. I tried to get my mom some help after Grams died, but you can't fix other people's problems if they aren't willing participants. She's been to rehab, she's been to therapists, but at the end of the day, it's always someone else's fault.

When I was ten, she told me I was the reason she was always broke. At fifteen, she gave me a box of condoms for my birthday and told me not to drop out of high school and become a teen mom like she did. On my graduation day, as I proudly wore the Summa Cum Laude stole, she was a no-show. At Grams' funeral, she didn't even cry. She flung her arm around my neck and said, *I guess it's just you and me, kid.*

It always ends up right back to me giving her cash to get her by. My bestie, Cara, thinks I'm enabling her, but I can't keep spending money on treatment she refuses to acknowledge. If I can help my mother stay afloat, she won't end up on the streets or in some seedy bar, or worse, dead. It's all I can manage. "I have sixty dollars…"

"That'll work." She snatches the money out of my fingers and grabs her purse. "Thanks, Summerita. You're the best."

"Wait, aren't you staying here?"

"Oh, hon…probably not. Janice and I are going to hit the town tonight. I'll just crash on her couch, or maybe I'll meet someone new." She waggles her fingers. "Mama needs to get her nails done."

"But I thought you wanted to spend time together." I hate that I sound needy when she was the one insisting on staying with me. I follow her out to my front door like a lost puppy.

"Summerita." She turns around and clucks her tongue. "You used to give me the same pitiful expression when you were little." She frowns, her smudged pink bottom lip pushing out as she plays with my hair. "Tell you what, I'll come by tomorrow to drop off some of my things if that will make you feel better. Maybe you can try on the purple dress I've been trying to get you to wear." She blows an air-kiss and breezes out the front door.

I collapse back down on the couch, feeling deflated. Dealing with my mom always messes with my head, which already hurts from this epic hangover. I check my email and see that I have a reply from Tuscan Bike Tours. Thank God for speedy responses.

*Dear Ms. Andrews,*

*I'm so sorry you believe there's been a mistake in booking your trip with Tuscan Bike Tours, LTD. However, according to our records, you signed up for the tour around twelve thirty Pacific Coast Time from Burlingame, California.*

*Your VISA credit card ending 5412 was processed. You initialed the introductory paperwork and filled out the questionnaire. According to our phone records, you called and spoke to Jolan about what kind of clothes to bring. If this was not you, or your credit card has been compromised, please let us know.*
*Buona giornata,*
*Sylvia Rococo, Sales*

No, no, no, no! This can't be happening. I grab my cellphone and check my recent call log. *Oh my God.* I close my eyes and vigorously rub them to make sure I'm correctly seeing the outgoing call placed at 12:40 a.m. to Rome, Italy. I hit redial and pray it's just a spam caller.

"Welcome to Tuscan Bike Tours! We are with a customer right now. Please wait on the line and someone will be with you momentarily."

Panicking, I hang up and look around my apartment. What the fuck did I do last night? *Dammit, Kevin, this is all your fault.* Could I say my credit card was compromised? I mean, technically it was used by a drunk madwoman hell-bent on going to Italy. I swipe to my credit card app on my phone and check my credit card statement. My eyes bug out when I see the amount charged to my Visa to Tuscan Bike Tours, LTD. Sober Summer can't afford that! I quickly type out a message back to Tuscan Bike Tours, then glance around again for any clues. Finding nothing, I turn on my TV and huff.

"Un-fucking-believable." Cued up is my favorite movie, *Under the Tuscan Sun*. I've always wanted to meet a man like Marcello and perhaps fall in love with a rundown villa and remodel it like Frances did.

*Oh.*

Putting two and two together, I must've got a wild hair in my ass and signed up for a bike tour in Italy. But why a bike tour? I drag my computer over to my lap and peer at my browsing history and scroll down a bit to the first website I visited after returning home. A website called *Tuscany on a Dime*, reveals beautiful pictures of sun-drenched hills dotted with tall Italian cypress, and water so rich and blue, it makes you want to dive right in. The next tab is *Tours of Tuscany*. I pull it up and notice I clicked on the link for *Tuscany on a Vespa*. I imagine my hair permanently knotted in a ball of frizz as I zip around the countryside, not to mention the potential of getting into an accident. I've heard Italians drive like maniacs over there. The final tab I had scrolled through last night was *Tuscan Bike Tours*.

My mailbox dings with a new email. I quickly open it up.

*Dear Ms. Andrews,*

*Thank you for emailing Tuscan Bike Tours, LTD. I am so sorry to hear you accidentally purchased the package while inebriated. Unfortunately, you did not purchase trip insurance as part of your package. I am afraid this trip cannot be refunded or transferred to another party. Please let me know if you have any other questions. We look forward to having you on Tuscan Bike Tours, LTD.*

*Buona giornata,*
*Salvator Pizzi, Tuscan Bike Tours LTD., Sales team*

Well, that's just fucking fantastic.

# Chapter 2

"ARE YOU TELLING me you booked a trip to Italy by yourself?" Cara pours me a glass of sparkling water and grabs a beer for her husband before closing the fridge with her hip. "Are you sure that's a smart move?"

"*Unintentionally* booked a reservation."

"How do you unintentionally book a trip to Italy?" she asks while I follow her out onto their back deck overlooking the bay and sink into a padded chair. She hands me my glass, which I gratefully take a sip from. "You sure you don't want wine?"

"No, thanks. I'm still hungover. After my horrible date, which, by the way, I will never use *The One* again, I took myself home and watched my favorite movie—"

"Not *Under the Tuscan Sun* again," Cara groans.

"Anyway, I might have drunk a little too much wine, ate a tub of Rocky Road...and apparently inspired by the movie, booked a trip to Italy. I guess drunk Summer was screaming for me to shake things up a little."

"Well, practical Summer needs to cancel the trip."

"It's nonrefundable. Drunk Summer didn't think I needed the trip insurance. They don't give refunds unless there's a death in the family or you're hospitalized. I've already paid for the trip in full. And..." I take a deep breath. "I know this sounds crazy, but the idea has kind of grown on me. You're the one always telling me to step out of my box and try new things, meet new people."

"I meant trying the speed-dating thing or joining a running group—not going to a foreign country! I think it's dangerous for you to go alone."

Damien smirks as he sits down next to Cara, slinging his arm around her shoulder. "Cara, she's a grown woman. Let her be."

Cara ignores Damien. "When is it again?"

"June fifth through the fourteenth."

"What about your job?"

"I'm using my vacation time. I have three weeks saved up."

Cara's brows scrunch. "The tour is what...ten days?"

"Yes, but I figured since I'm over there, I might as well travel around after. I've mapped out some places along the coast I'd like to see. Maybe even Venice."

She leans forward, her pointed red nails tapping on her glass. "So let me get this straight. You went on another disastrous date, took yourself home, drank two bottles of wine, ate a tub of ice cream while watching *Under the Tuscan Sun*, and accidentally booked a tour of Tuscany. And are *actually* going." She looks at me deadpan.

"I mean...it sounds way worse when *you* say it. And I only drank a bottle and a half." My smile wavers as Cara gives Damien a worried glance.

"Summer, I'm concerned," Cara says gently.

"Oh, here we go," Damien groans.

"Are you stressed? Did Barbara do something? Do we

need to go to the spa, take a few days to reevaluate? You realize how impulsive this sounds."

"Listen, I know this seems…irresponsible, but for the first time in a long time, I'm truly excited about something. What could be better than biking through Tuscany on a singles' tour and possibly meeting the love of my life?"

Beer sprays out of Damien's nose. He quickly wipes his face with his t-shirt. "Wait, hold up. This is a *singles'* bike tour? In Italy…as in pasta, olive oil, and Italian stallions?"

"Yeah. I didn't realize the tour I chose was for singles ready to bike and mingle." I sit up straighter and put a smile on my face. "But I've embraced it. Cara, you should be ecstatic, since you're the one always pushing me to date."

Cara's mouth goes slack and her eyes widen. "I didn't mean in Italy! Do you even own a bike? In the five years I've known you, I don't think I've ever seen you on a bike. Not even a Peloton."

Okay, she has a point. Cara and I met five years ago when I tried a free ninety-day membership at the gym she belongs to. She's a badass divorce attorney who enjoys intense cardio runs to help lower her stress levels. I was on the treadmill next to hers, jogging. My shoelace came undone, tripping me, and I flew off the machine, ending up with a scraped knee and a bloody nose. Feeling sorry for me, she invited me out for margaritas after and we have been inseparable since. She knows me better than my own mother.

"I'm not much of a biker, but so what? How hard can it be? It's going to be so much fun." I beam at them, convincing them to get on the fun-bus with me. They stare at me like I've lost my marbles.

Damien arches an eyebrow. "Do you even speak Italian?"

"I know *grazie* and *ciao*… Okay, so that's all I know, but everyone on the tour will be speaking English. I can take one of those audio courses if I have to. Oh, and Gucci!"

Cara blinks at me. "So, you know 'thank you,' 'hello,' and the name of a designer brand."

"You know gelato," Damien encourages me.

"Yes!" I point at him enthusiastically. "Good one, Dame."

Cara shakes her head and sets her white wine on the table. "What if some unwanted weirdo won't leave you alone on tour? What if you lose the group and get kidnapped—or raped?"

"Jesus, Care, calm down." Damien squeezes her shoulder. "You're scaring me, so I know you're scaring her."

"You guys, it's going to be *fine*. Just like in the movie. Frances went over on a tour and ended up buying a gorgeous villa to fix up. She fell in love, and her best friend moved in with her and had a baby."

"Who's Frances?"

"A character from her favorite movie," Cara tells Damien. "Summer, you know I love you, I do, but this is real life, *not* a movie. And I'm sure as hell not pregnant *or* moving to Italy with you."

"You better not be, woman." Damien gets up and chucks his beer in the trash can under the bar.

I stifle a giggle, unable to help the symphony of emotions humming in my veins. "You realize it's a true story, right? There's hope for me! I'm going to be fine. Great, actually." I smile tremulously at my best friend. "I know you're worried about me, but it's done. I'm not backing out now. I'm thirty-six and single, Cara. I've got nothing to show for my life except for a 401k from work. I *need* to do this. I feel like something is missing, and I won't know what it is until I find it. I've had *dreams* about it." I pause, then ask, "Haven't you ever felt so passionately about something, nothing can stop you?"

"Well, sure. I just don't understand why you need to go to Italy to find it."

"Because there's something romantic and mysterious about going abroad and falling in love with a handsome stranger," I say adamantly. "I've never done anything this adventurous before. I need it as much as I need to *breathe*."

"Not to be a Debbie Downer, but how are you going to afford this, and what about your mom?"

My bubble of excitement deflates faster than one of Damien's experimental souffles. "I put the trip on a credit card and have some savings I'm using toward it. As for Barbara, I'm going to tell her she can stay at my townhome."

Cara groans. "That's a bad idea with a capital B."

"B for Barbara!" Damien shouts from the kitchen.

"At least I'll know she's safe. I know it's asking a lot, but I was wondering if you and Damien could monitor things? You don't need to keep tabs on her, just make sure my house doesn't burn to the ground? I need this, Care. I need a break from always being the responsible one."

Cara sighs and pats the seat next to her. "Get over here, Summer." She pulls me into a hug, squeezing tight. "I hope you find whatever it is you're looking for in Italy."

"Me too."

"You better come back knowing how to make red sauce with a devastatingly handsome Italian man on your arm I can drool over."

"I can hear you," Damien gripes.

Cara smiles at me. "You're really going to do this?" I nod as the threat of tears smart my nose. "Then we better learn some Italian. *Gucci* will only get you so far. Are you scared?"

"Terrified." I laugh, the tears bubbling over.

I clink my glass with hers. *Italy, here I come.*

# Chapter 3

I KICK MY purse farther under the seat in front of me and settle back. I'm so excited to be going to Italy, I can hardly keep my knees from bouncing. I'm also incredibly nervous. Cara might have been right when she said it was stupid to go on this trip alone, but I've decided to live in the moment and make the best of it. Who knows, I might even find the love of my life on this tour.

I pull out my phone and text my mom. She readily agreed to staying in my townhouse when I asked. It's not exactly ideal, but at least Cara and Damien will be around to keep an eye on things.

**Me:** *Barbara, just checking in before my flight takes off.*

**Barbara:** *Summer, you need to relax and quit texting me every five minutes.*

**Me:** *I just want to make sure you don't have questions about the alarm system and remember no smoking inside and NO parties or random men over.*

**Barbara:** *Don't be such a buzz kill, Summer. What do you think I'm going to do, film a porno and burn your house down?*

That exact scenario did wake me up in a cold sweat last night. I don't trust my mom one bit. Luckily, I have nothing of value in the house. When my grandmother passed away, the only thing I kept of hers was a hand-knit blanket she made for me and a few knickknacks. I tuck my phone back in my purse.

A woman sits down in the aisle seat and sighs after she gets situated. I turn my head and smile.

"Hi."

"Hi," she says, her attention returning to the passengers taking their seats. She high-fives a couple of them as they pass by.

"Are those your friends? I can switch seats with someone if you'd like to be next to one of them."

"Oh, that's kind of you. It's okay. We're all here to go on a bike tour."

"Me too. Tuscan Bike Tours?"

"Yes." She eyes me curiously and holds out her hand to shake. "Ginny Pizaki from Grand Rapids, Michigan."

"Summer Andrews from San Francisco. It's so nice to meet someone in the group. I thought I was all by myself on this flight." I pull my hand out of her cold, vise-like grip.

"Oh no, there's a bunch of us. I think the tour tries to get most of us on the same flight out of New York, so it's easier to pick everyone up in Florence."

"That makes sense."

"I don't remember seeing you on the Facebook group page."

"I never got the chance. Not much of a Facebooker to start, but I was swamped finishing up some projects at work. Is that how you know everyone?"

"Yes, there are a bunch of us who talk regularly on

there."

I mentally kick myself for not taking the time to join the group page. I would have felt better going on this trip knowing someone. A young, gangly man dressed in a black hoodie and jeans with light brown hair and glasses stops in our row.

"I think that's my seat." He looks at his ticket and nods at the empty seat between Ginny and me. Ginny immediately gets up and lets the man into the row. He settles in and sticks his carry-on under the seat in front of him. He takes a small plastic container out of his hoodie pocket and shakes something into his hand.

"Tic Tac?" He holds his hand out to me.

"No, thank you." I turn my head toward the window while he offers one to Ginny. I discreetly cup my hand over my mouth and try to see if my breath smells funky. I did just get off a five-hour flight from California.

"Are you traveling to Italy for vacation?" he asks Ginny.

"No, I'm on the Tuscany Bike Tour. So is she."

"That makes three of us, then," the man says and turns his head toward me with an outstretched hand. "Harrison Gunner."

"Summer Andrews." I gingerly shake his hand. "You're on the bike tour as well?"

"Yep." He sighs and closes his eyes, stretching his long legs out. He looks like he's barely old enough to drive. Ginny digs something out of her carry-on while a guy in his early forties with a man-bun passes by. He pauses at our row and holds out a fist to bump. "Tuscan Bike Tour?"

Harrison cracks an eye open and side-eyes him. I clear

my throat and nod. Ginny pops up, holding a t-shirt to her chest. "Oh hey, Blake. Where's your seat?" She smiles goofily at him and bumps his fist.

"14A. Go A-team. Woo-hoo!" He pumps his fist into the air and continues down the aisle.

"That's Blake." Ginny turns to us, her cheeks rosy.

"I gathered," Harrison says flatly, resuming his nap position.

"What's the A-team?" I ask Ginny.

"Oh, well, if you were on the Facebook chat, you would know Blake dubbed some of us the A-team. We even had bike jerseys made." Giggling, she holds up the royal-blue shirt with her name and the A-team bedazzled on the back.

"Wow, that's—"

"Stupid if you ask me," Harrison grumbles. I nudge his arm with my elbow.

"I think it's fun. How do we get on the A-team?"

"Um, I guess you can ask Blake, but you won't have a shirt..." With a shrug, Ginny puts her prized shirt back in her carry-on. "We bonded in our group chat before the trip, so..."

We pause our conversation during the flight attendant's safety speech. Ginny turns toward us when she finishes.

"Are you guys skilled bike riders? Done any races? I love doing triathlons. Blake just finished an Ironman. Can you believe it? He reminds me of Lance Armstrong." She sighs and Harrison coughs into his fist.

"Uh...not exactly a bike rider. I practiced on my friend's Peloton, but I didn't get very far. Those classes were exhausting. But I enjoyed the music." I laugh, but it quickly dies when I notice Ginny's appalled expression.

"You mean to tell me you are going on a bike tour and aren't into *biking*?"

"That's exactly what she's telling you, Gin. Don't worry, Summer, we'll form our own team…the C-team."

"The C-team?" Ginny asks looking genuinely perplexed, like why would anyone want to be labeled a C?

"Yeah, the Cool team." Harrison holds out his fist for me to bump. I can't tell if he has a glint in his eye or if it's the sun reflecting off his glasses, but this moment feels like a turning point—a choice. And for some inexplicable reason, I like Harrison. I gingerly bump my knuckles to his and he grins. The plane hurtles down the runway and lifts off American soil.

"No turning back now." Harrison puts his earbuds in and cranks up his music loud enough for me to hear.

Ginny turns her back slightly on us as she takes a book out. Of course, it's *Wheelmen*, the story of Lance Armstrong's doping career.

Are Ginny and Blake a taste of what's to come on this trip? I worry my bottom lip. The tour is supposed to be for all biking levels, amateur to pro. Should I have brushed up on Lance Armstrong and done a few triathlons before committing to this tour? Not like I had much of a choice in the commitment department. But perhaps I should have tried harder on the Peloton or taken a spin class at the gym, maybe even rented a bike?

*What the hell was I thinking?*

Closing my eyes, I picture coasting down hills past sunlit fields of wheat, my legs outstretched like I used to do as a kid. I toss my head back, my face hitting the rush of wind that sweeps over me, and I'm finally, for once, feeling free. Harrison is biking beside me on my right, laughing at some witty remark I've made. Ginny and Blake, huffing and puffing behind us, struggle to keep up. I fist-bump Harrison and smile.

A chiming sound, alerting the flight attendant for help, jerks me awake. The cabin lights are dimmed and everyone else seems to be sleeping. I raise my window shade a fraction, but all I can see is inky blackness and the red flash of the light from the wing, as we cruise somewhere over the Atlantic. Ten hours to Florence and then a one-hour bus ride to San Gimignano, where we'll begin.

Harrison's right about one thing. There's no turning back now.

# Chapter 4

MY GEARS CLANK and groan, shifting as I push my leg down, forcing myself to look up at the line of riders in front of me on the slow incline. My legs are like Jell-O, wobbling in the wind, while my butt bone grinds against the unyielding seat. I hate biking with the intensity of a thousand suns. I also really dislike the pack of bike fanatics up front who came on this trip to meet people *and* bike. Their matching blue bicycle shirts with their bedazzled names on the back glint under the Tuscan sun.

Seriously, who enjoys this? It's grueling and sweaty and uses muscles not meant for everyday activity. My glutes feel like someone took a baseball bat to them. I thought we would ride for half an hour and take pictures of the beautiful rolling hills and wander around tiny villages, but I was wrong. So very wrong. We literally bike six hours a day with a half-hour lunch break. If we want to take a picture, there are scheduled stops, otherwise we must balance our cameras while pedaling away. I went through my photos on my phone last night and I either have pictures of my leg, the ground, or the landscape is so blurry it looks like Cara's great-aunt Nellie, who's in desperate need of cataract surgery, took the photos.

I'm in the back of the group with Harrison, the twenty-six-year-old Kohler sales agent from Houston, who looks barely old enough to shave. With our little group is Lynnette, a recently divorced fifty-year-old from Maryland, who is on this trip with her sister Janice. They thought it would be more fun than a singles' cruise, but Lynnette is definitely realizing her misstep as we start the slow burn uphill. She hates biking as much as I do. Her groaning and moaning can be heard for miles over the picturesque Tuscan hills.

I glance over my shoulder to make sure she's still with us. "You okay, Lynnette?"

"Doing great, sugar," she pants.

Her helmet is sliding off to the side, her white-blonde hair hanging limp with sweat, and her sunburnt pink skin glistens in the morning sun. Harrison rides in front of me, my eyes glued to his legs, which look like pale toothpicks. His bike wobbles from side to side, as if it might tip over and take us all down at any given moment.

I jump when another car passes, blaring its horn. The front of the pack all wave their hands in a friendly greeting. I should be basking in all of the glorious Italian vistas and having the time of my life, not griping about sore muscles. I know this—I do—I'm in Italy, for Pete's sake. But my tennis shoe keeps sliding out of the pedal clasp, and the automatic gear keeps shifting as soon as I find my rhythm.

The front riders begin to sing "Eye of the Tiger" and I make a noise of disgust in the back of my throat. That song has been on A-team's playlist since we started. I clench my teeth together, pushing forward, one leg and then the other. My shorts chafe against my thighs as my tennis shoe slips off the pedal, again. I now understand why the front riders came prepared with spandex bottoms and shoes that clip into your pedal. I thought they were being annoying overachievers, but I see the practicality now.

I reach down for my water bottle, squirting the last drops onto my parched tongue. Our lunch stop is hours away, and I haven't been sweating, which leads me to believe I'm severely dehydrated.

"Harrison, I've decided I hate biking," I gripe, putting my empty water bottle back in the holder.

"Ah, *cara*, it's a beautiful day! Enjoy!" Romeo, our overly enthusiastic Italian tour guide, yells from behind Lynnette. You could tell him his dog died, and his response would still be, *it's a beautiful day*. I thought perhaps it was the only English phrase he knew, but he disproved that theory a few minutes ago when he had a conversation with Lynnette about her life back in Maryland. Romeo is just a happy individual living his best life with a cute Italian accent. It's hard to get annoyed with him.

"Romeo, my butt hurts," I whine pathetically.

Okay, perhaps not his best life.

"Ah, the joys of biking!" Romeo shouts back. "Comes with the territory. You'll get used to it!"

Poor Romeo is stuck behind our sorry lot because 'No man gets left behind' is his mantra on this tour. I heard someone say he raced in the Tour de France. Now he's staring at Lynnette's backside, puttering along at ten miles an hour to keep us with the group.

Harrison weaves, and I almost crash my tire into the back of his bike.

"Harrison, are you drunk?" I squeak.

"I wish."

"God, me too."

*It's only day two.*

"SO, I HEARD you're from Cali. That's cool. I mean, that's great. I'm a cheese head. Wow, that came out all wrong." The sweaty guy with sandy-blond hair and a mustache plops down in the grass beside me without invitation, where I'm quietly trying to die alone during our afternoon break. "Hi, I'm Doug, from Wisconsin, thus the whole cheese-head thing."

"Oh, ha." I give him a wan smile. Even though this is a singles' tour, the last thing I want to do is flirt with Doug from Wisconsin.

"And your name is?"

"Summer." *Please go away, Doug.*

"Is this your first time in Italy?"

"Yes."

"Ah, me too. It's beautiful, isn't it? Are you liking it so far?" Doug has a pleasant smile, but he's wasting his time right now. I have zero interest in anything but a hot bath and a bottle of wine.

"Not really, Doug, no."

Doug chuckles and dangles his hands between his bent knees. "Well, hopefully, that will change for you."

Harrison dramatically sprawls out beside me and dumps a bottle of water in my lap. "I'm dying."

Doug smiles at Harrison. "Is this your son?"

I sit up and side-eye Doug. I may be exhausted and haggard-looking, but not enough to have a grown son. Sure, Harrison looks prepubescent, but still…why would I bring my son on a singles' bike tour? That's just weird.

I smile and say in my best Carrie Bradshaw voice, "No, Doug, he's my lover."

Harrison spits water all over himself.

"Oh, I…I didn't realize…" He glances from me to Harrison. "I'm sorry to bother you. I thought we were all single and ready to mingle here." He laughs nervously before he quickly stands and speed-walks away.

"Sorry, Doug from Wisconsin wouldn't leave me alone." I peel my sock off and poke the angry blister on my heel.

Harrison tucks his arms behind his head, watching Doug mingle with the others. "Yeah, he has desperate vibes written all over his face. Now he's hitting on that chick from Toronto. What's with the stache, anyway?"

"Don't be a hater just because you can't grow one. He'll probably be engaged by the end of the week."

"Mid-week."

"Bet you a bottle of wine on our last night here." I grin.

"Deal," he says. We limply fist-bump, too exhausted to put any energy into it. "What do you think of the A-team?"

I look over at the group of elite cyclists and peruse the potential knights in shining armor. There's the Lance Armstrong wannabe, Blake, whose skintight spandex shorts hug a disappointing bulge in front. Michael stands next to him, his dark skin glistening with a sheen of sweat. He is better endowed in the spandex department, but he laughs like a braying donkey. I could probably date him if he promised never to laugh. Don, the fifty-year-old who thinks he's Fabio with his wavy shoulder-length hair, chats in Italian with Ginny, while Garrett, the hipster New Yorker, stands off to the side with an air of superiority.

The women in A-team are just as bad. Toothy Naomi hangs on Blake's every word, while Jojo, who brought her medals from past triathlons, shows them off to anyone who will listen. Amy, from DC, laughs too loudly, drawing attention to herself, not to mention being so annoying when she and Michael laugh at the same time. And Ginny Pizaki from Michigan round out the group. The B-team is everyone else except us three—Harrison, Lynnette, and me—who didn't make it into the A-team, but I never comment on them because of Lynnette's sister. At least they don't wear matching cycle shirts.

Michael honks over something Don said, causing Harrison to clench his jaw. Lynnette, Harrison, and I make up the self-dubbed C-team. We're the group who got picked last in gym class. I've decided not to put much effort into finding the man of my dreams on this tour. I'm still hoping for a sign from the Universe I've made the right decision coming here.

Romeo and his co-guide Milo clap their hands to get our attention. "Listen up! We'll bike for another three hours and stay at a quaint hotel in Pienza, where we will have a wine tasting in the courtyard. Make sure you drink plenty of water."

I groan and pull my sock back up before gently shoving my tennis shoe on.

"I knew I should have booked the tour with an electric bike," Harrison grumbles.

"What do you mean, electric?"

"Didn't you see they offered a tour with motorized bikes that kick on if you struggle?"

"What? No! Is it too late to get one?"

Harrison smirks and stands, offering me a hand up. "Yeah."

I mutter an expletive under my breath and limp toward my ordinary road bike.

"Smile, Summer, it's a beautiful day, no?" Romeo yells as he pulls his bike up alongside us. I plaster on a smile for him.

"Romeo, can you drag me behind your bike?"

"Ah, Summer, you're a funny one. *Andiamo!*"

He starts to sing "That's Amore" while he waits for us to move. Harrison and Lynnette join in and I can't help but giggle as the A and B group look back at us curiously. I hum along, *When the world seems to shine like you've had too much wine…that's amore.*

I soak in the breathtaking landscape around me. Limestone castles on top of hills with terracotta roofs sit nestled between tall cypress trees, guarding their fortresses like soldiers. Vineyards, green as far as the eye can see, make grooves in the hillside as they slope down to the roads twisting across the landscape. Bright red poppies interspersed with white daisies dot a field to my left. Mountains that separate the sky from the earth sit majestically in the distance, like purple giants surveying their lands. Humming along with Romeo, I close my eyes, breathing in the fresh air and feeling the wind against my skin.

Maybe this trip isn't so bad after all.

Despite all my groaning thus far, I can't help but wonder if this is what heaven would look like. A quiet beauty that lets your soul relax. Turning my face to the afternoon sky, the wind whipping my hair, I smile. So, this is what it's like to feel carefree. For the first time since Grams died, I can taste freedom on my tongue, and it's decadent and sweet. Something magical is going to happen. I can feel it in my heart.

## Chapter 5

DAY FIVE, AND I'm still waiting for something magical to happen. Don't get me wrong, my butt has become accustomed to the hard seat, and my muscles are getting used to the daily grind. The landscape *is* beautiful, and the Italian people are incredibly kind and charming, but…

I don't know what I expected to happen on this tour. Scratch that—I was hoping to find a tall, dark, handsome stranger to sweep me off my feet as we biked through the beautiful countryside. I look over at my two companions sprawled out in the grass and snort. Lynnette is guzzling a split bottle of chianti which came with our picnic lunch. She's as red as a steamed lobster, even with her 70 SPF sunscreen slathered all over her. Her *Be Happy* blue visor glitters in the sun as she mops the back of her neck with a wet paper towel. Harrison hunches his bony shoulders over his picnic basket, searching for something dairy-free, which will be challenging since it's a bread and cheese basket. I hand him my grapes, and he smiles gratefully, quickly munching them.

"Slow down, Harrison. I'm not going to ask for them back."

I may not have found my Prince Charming on this tour, but at least I met these two. I wouldn't survive this without them.

Lynnette gathers our empty lunch boxes and chucks them in the trash for us. Harrison gulps the rest of his mini bottle of wine. Lynnette raises her eyebrows as she glances at me, and I shrug. He usually passes the lunch bottle to Lynnette or me because he's a lightweight and doesn't enjoy wine.

"Wow, Harrison, special occasion?" I ask.

"No." He brushes the back of his hand across his mouth. "My muscles ache. I figured this is better than ibuprofen." He chucks the bottle in the waste bin before we walk over to our bikes. My butt screams in protest as I saddle up. Okay, maybe it hasn't quite adapted to the seat yet.

"Oh, holy mother of God, I can't do this," Lynnette grumbles, straddling her bike. "Did y'all say we have a hilly route today? I swear Janice signed us up for the advanced tour. I told her I wanted the beginners' tour, but she never listens to me."

Smiling, I buckle my chin strap. "Only four more days, Lynnette. If I can do this, so can you."

"That's the spirit, *cara mia*!" Romeo passes by me and holds up his hand for a high-five, which I lamely slap. "It's a beautiful day!"

"I swear if I hear him say that one more time, I'm going to show him where he can stick that sunshine," Harrison grumbles.

I giggle and wait for him to get situated. "Wow, H, I didn't know you had it in you."

"I can be fierce when I need to be," he says smugly.

"Uh-huh." I watch his spindly legs try to push his bike in

a forward motion, but the lack of movement causes it to wobble. At the last possible second, he pushes off the ground with his toes and lurches ahead. It's like watching a kid learn how to ride a bike for the first time.

I follow suit and instantly feel relief from the cool breeze that glides over my back. That's probably the only redeeming part of biking—the constant current of cool air over your skin. The front pack starts an annoying cheer while Romeo points out a village in the distance. A car speeds by, honking its horn because some moron in the B-team enthusiastically waved. Harrison swerves and slams on his brakes. My shoe slips out of my pedal, and in the split-second I look down to fix it, I smash right into him, taking his bike down with me. We sprawl out on the side of the road in a tangle of limbs and bikes. I groan, trying to sit up.

"Summer, Harrison, are you okay? Don't sit up." Romeo blows three shrill whistles, alerting Milo leading the front of the group of our demise. "Harrison, you have a nasty gash on your leg. It might need sutures." He unzips his red fanny pack and takes out a bottle of antiseptic while Milo rushes toward us.

"My thumb feels funny." I gingerly lift my hand and almost pass out when I see it hanging at an odd angle.

"Oh Lordy, that ain't good." Lynnette gulps, crouching down next to Romeo.

"No, it isn't." Romeo's grim expression tells me everything I need to know. I cradle my hand against my chest and look over at Harrison.

"Are you okay?"

"Awesome," he groans.

"Why did you slam on your brakes?" Romeo asks.

"Sorry, the car horn made me jump, and I reflexively pulled the brake grip at the same time I hit gravel."

"We need to get you two to the closest hospital," Milo surmises after he has a silent conversation with Romeo. Romeo nods and turns, walking a few paces to make a phone call. Milo surveys the bikes with his hands on his waist and says something rapid in Italian. I'm guessing it's something close to this: *These fucking idiots. How do they not know how to ride a bike? Stupido C-team.*

The other cyclists hop off their bikes and form a claustrophobic circle around us. They murmur their condolences before walking away.

I turn to Romeo, who has ended his call. "What do we do now?"

"We wait."

# Chapter 6

WE WAITED AN hour for their company van to pick us up and take us into town to see the closest doctor. I probably could have walked there in the same amount of time. Not exactly how I wanted to spend my Italian holiday—bloodied, bruised, on the side of a road with a throbbing thumb. Lynnette wanted to stay with us, but Romeo persuaded her to move along with the group to the next destination. Romeo would meet up with them after the doctor checked us over. The bumpy ten-minute ride in the hot, stuffy van felt more like an hour of my life I'll never get back. The adrenalin has worn off and the pain in my thumb is excruciating.

We park on a narrow cobblestone street surrounded by golden sunlit limestone and hobble toward a sign hanging from a side door with a red cross on it. My muscles are stiff from the drive as I duck into the cool, dark office. Romeo rattles off Italian to the nurse while Harrison and I slowly lower ourselves into chairs. The nurse ushers Harrison to an exam room first to clean up the road rash on his left side. Then, another nurse leads me into a room down the hall, where I wait with Romeo.

The door opens, and my eyes drink in the tall glass of sparkling San Pellegrino wearing a white coat. My lips form an 'O' as my stomach flips. Holy Mother Italia of Tomatoes, *this* is the doctor? He looks like he just stepped off the set of a GQ photoshoot. His midnight-black hair is smoothed back from his tanned face while he looks over my chart. His white linen shirt under the doctor's coat is unbuttoned enough to reveal a tan chest, and his olive-green linen slacks are pressed perfectly. He's not wearing a ring, and my pulse flutters with an irrational sense of hope, which is ludicrous, given the circumstances.

He speaks rapidly in Italian, and my gaze pings between him and Romeo, who's gesturing at my hand. He turns his full attention on me, and it feels like the sun just warmed my soul.

"My name is Dr. Bianchi. I heard you were in a cycling accident. Can I see your hand?" His accented English makes my blood hum. I gingerly stretch out my dislocated thumb toward him. "Does it hurt?"

"Yes," I murmur, drowning in his twin pools of melted chocolate as he gazes at me.

His warm, smooth hand clasps my elbow while he examines my thumb. His cologne smells yummy and expensive, but not overpowering. I stare at his bent head and fantasize about running my fingers through his silky hair. He murmurs something in Italian to Romeo, who nods in reply.

"Is something wrong?"

"No, no. I'm going to put your thumb back in place. I'm afraid it will hurt, but it's better than the alternative, which is surgery."

I shake my head. "I don't want surgery."

He smiles tenderly at me and gently squeezes my hand.

"Do not worry, *signorina*, I will take care of you."

"Okay." You don't turn sexy, Italian-crooning men like him down. If Dr. Bianchi asked me to marry him in his next breath, I'd say yes. I don't care that I've spent less than ten minutes in his company and know absolutely nothing about him except his last name. I can call him Dr. Bianchi for the rest of my life if I have to.

"Take this medicine. It will help with the pain." He hands me a paper cup with two small aspirin-size pills in it. I should question what it is, but right now anything to dull the pain sounds delightful.

"Thank you, Dr. Bianchi."

He winks at me before turning to Romeo. "I'll be right back. I'm going to get my nurse to help."

"Summer, are you okay here?" Romeo stands up. "I'm going to check on Harrison."

"No problem."

After both men leave the room, I jump off the exam table to look at myself in the mirror.

My smile slides off my face as I take in my appearance. My frazzled brown hair tied up in a ponytail looks more like a dead squirrel hanging loosely off my head. A halo of frizz sticks out in every direction like I've survived a bike ride through a tornado. I have a scrape along my cheek, and mascara has clumped beneath my eyes. Awesome. Dr. Bianchi just professed his undying love to take care of me for the rest of my life, and I look like a truck dragged me for a mile down a dirt road.

I realize I'm being totally delusional about wanting to elope with the hot doc, but I can't help but think perhaps this is the sign I've been looking for since I arrived in Italy. Maybe the Universe made me wreck my bike and come to this little town because *this* is where I'm meant to be. I smooth back my flyaways, unable to fix my ponytail without using my thumb, just as Dr. Bianchi and his nurse open the door.

"Signorina Andrews, if you could have a seat, *per favore*."

"Oh, please, call me Summer."

Dr. Bianchi flashes a smile and gestures toward the exam table. He turns to his nurse and murmurs something in Italian. She moves next to me. "I hold your hand, yes?"

"Yes." I smile half-heartedly. She's exquisite, with the most flawless creamy skin and perfectly arched cheekbones I have ever seen. Her mahogany-brown hair shines in the fluorescent lighting while mine looks like I was buried alive. I feel dirty and insignificant next to this beautiful woodland creature as she gently clasps my non-injured hand. So much for catching Dr. Bianchi's attention when he works with this goddess every day. He rapidly rattles off something, and although I have no idea what he's saying, I squirm in my seat imagining him talking to me like that in bed.

"Summer, I need you to sit still. *Intorpidiró l'area.* I will inject some numbing solution around your thumb, yes? You might feel a little pinch…" Dr. Bianchi's voice pours over me like melted butter. He could inject me with a needle the size of my pinkie for all I care, as long as he keeps talking to me in that soothing timbre.

"Yes," I say. He injects the needle and I hiss, unprepared for the sting. "Motherfucker, that hurt!" Dr. Bianchi and his nurse stare at me wide-eyed. "Uh, sorry. *Scusi.*" I avert my gaze to the eye chart on the back wall. "Knee-jerk reaction. Apparently, I don't like needles," I mumble.

Dr. Bianchi says something to his doe-eyed nurse, and she holds me a little tighter while he injects again. The meaty part of my thumb instantly feels numb, the pain from my dislocation quickly dissipating. Dr. Bianchi hands the needle to Nurse Gorgeous and turns to me, smiling.

"Are you ready, Signorina Summer? This should be *velocissimo, sí?*"

"*Sí.*" *Uh-huh, whatever you say, Dr. Bianchi.*

He gently takes my injured hand in his. The injection has worked because I can't feel a thing. He moves my thumb around like a joystick for a few seconds before inserting it back into the joint. "Ah, there we go." He tosses me a wink. "Smooth, like a fine Italian wine."

I stare at my hand in wonderment. "Wow, that was so quick!"

"*Sí! Veloce.* I told you." He stands there, still holding my hand while we both stare at my thumb like it's a 14-carat diamond ring. I'm so dazzled by Dr. Bianchi's charming smile and killer cologne, I barely register Nurse Gorgeous slipping out of the room. I wonder how you say, *I want to lick you like gelato* in Italian. I'm sure Dr. Bianchi could teach me. I sway toward him, quickly moistening my lips with my tongue. His eyes meet mine, and his lips tilt up. Game on, Dr. Bianchi.

The door opens and Harrison and Romeo rush in, ruining whatever I thought was happening. Dr. Bianchi quickly bandages my thumb with a splint to prevent further trauma for the next few weeks.

"Summer, are you going to be okay?" Harrison nearly faints when he sees my bandaged hand.

I want to tell both of them to get lost because I was about to have a hot make-out session with the doc…but then I see the stitches on Harrison's forehead.

"I'm okay, are *you* okay? I don't remember you having that gash earlier."

Harrison touches his forehead gently. "Oh, yeah, when they were cleaning a wound on my leg, I fainted and apparently fell off the table and hit my head on the corner."

"Oh my God, Harrison! That's terrible!"

"Blood freaks me out. It's all good."

"Okay, Signorina Andrews, unfortunately, I'm afraid the bike tour is over for you," Dr. Bianchi interrupts, writing notes in my chart. "You'll need to keep that splint on for at least three weeks. After that, you can either schedule a recheck here or back with your doctor."

I just nod. Will I be here in three weeks? I'd be willing to stay if it meant I'd get to see Dr. Bianchi again.

"Summer, the company is going to set you and Harrison up at a hotel here in town tonight. A representative will call you to make arrangements to get you back to Florence."

"Oh, um, okay." My emotions seesaw as I go from a high at the prospect of seeing the handsome doctor again, to feeling crushed that I'm leaving Tuscany so soon. *It's now or never, Summer, take your chance. This is why you came here!* "Can I have a moment alone with Dr. Bianchi, please?"

"Of course. We'll be waiting for you outside." Romeo ushers Harrison out the door and gingerly closes it.

Dr. Bianchi finishes writing in my chart and looks up,

his breathtaking grin causing my knees to knock together.

"Dr. Bianchi."

"*Sí*, Summer?" He steps closer, and I boldly place my non-injured hand on his arm.

"Dr. Bianchi, I…I feel…" I lean in, my lips parting on their own accord, trying to recapture the moment we'd started to share earlier. I want to run my fingers through his glorious hair and skim my lips across his plump lower one. I want to tangle my tongue deliciously with his until I'm moaning his name. I raise my injured hand to feel the silky strands, so caught up in the moment, I don't realize I still don't have any sensation in it. It's more like a lead weight than a featherlight touch as I bang into his forehead. My lips land on his chin. Surprised, Dr. Bianchi steps back, rubbing his forehead, while gravity causes me to fall off the table. To my horror, he's laughing as he reaches down to help me up.

"Signorina Andrews, are you okay?"

"I…I—"

"Is okay, *sí*?" Dr. Bianchi smiles. "I think the drugs have gotten to you. Are you feeling…what's the word…woozy?"

"Drugs?"

"*Sí*, the cup I handed you when we started. Good drugs to numb the pain."

Ah, of course. That's why I'm acting like a lovesick fool. I'm not usually this bold or clumsy. I need to get out of here before I humiliate myself further. I give him a wobbly smile and open the door.

"*Grazie*, Dr. Bianchi, *grazie*."

Quickly backing out of the room, I slam the door shut. I lean against it, thudding my head against the hard wood. *Dr.*

*Bianchi was not hitting on you, moron.* He's just Italian and sexy and likes to wink and smile, a lot.

"Ready, Summer?" Romeo spies me from the waiting room. I nod 'yes' and we quickly leave and I'm sure the sexy Italian doctor is going to tell Nurse Gorgeous all about how the American with dead-squirrel hair tried to kiss him.

*Fantastico.*

# Chapter 7

HARRISON INSPECTS HIS fork while we wait for the server to return to take our dinner order. "Do you think they have dishwashers that sanitize utensils, or do they handwash everything?"

"No clue."

We're seated outside at a cute little place along a cobblestone street. Accordion music floats over us like a gentle breeze, the aroma of stewed tomatoes, garlic, and rosemary drifting out of the restaurant as the hum of diners speaking a foreign language embraces us like a warm hug.

Townsfolk stroll along the sidewalk, weighted down with shopping bags as they pop in and out of the shops and restaurants. Kids lick their dripping ice-cream cones down by the fountain of Saint Tuttoscano, throwing coins in and making wishes. The cobblestones bake in the late-evening sun, warming the air on this perfect summer night.

*This* is what I've been looking for since I arrived in Italy.

"It's charming here, don't you think?" I say to Harrison. "There's something about Italy that's magical. The people are so friendly, the views are spectacular. It's like real-world problems don't exist here." I pick up my red wine and take a sip. The tart zing coats my tongue, making me smile.

Harrison sets his fork down, pushing his glasses up on his

nose. "How strong were the drugs they gave you?"

"Harrison, I'm serious. I love small towns like this."

"I'm willing to bet real-world problems exist here, too. I don't know, Italy's been nice, but I'm ready to get back home."

"Really? I'm not sure I'm ready to leave. I feel like we just got here. There's so much to see and do still."

Harrison snorts and tears into a piece of fresh bread. "What? Are you going to live here?"

"I don't know..." *Could I live here?* It would be a pleasant escape from my dull life back home. An escape from Barbara. The idea sounds quite enticing the more it germinates in my head. "Maybe?"

"Summer, you can't be serious. That's ridiculous. You clearly didn't enjoy the bike tour."

"That's not true. I enjoyed meeting you and Lynnette. Romeo was fun, and the views were stunning. Is it ridiculous to wander Italy for the summer...maybe even stay?"

"Yes!" Still chewing his bread, he gives me a pointed look. "You're not a college student bumming around Europe. You're a grown adult with responsibilities like a job and bills to pay."

The server walks over, interrupting us. "*Desiderano?*"

Harrison whips out his phone and types into it. The server rolls his eyes. "Can I take your order?"

"Oh good, you speak English. I'll start with the salame Toscano and then the tagliata. There's no dairy in that, right? I have a dairy allergy."

The server nods as he scribbles. "*Signorina?*"

"I'll start with the pappa al pomodoro and the tortelli

with the wild boar ragù."

"*Sí*, very good." The server collects our menus and moves on to check on the other patrons.

"I have a bad feeling he ignored my no-dairy request." Harrison scratches something on the tablecloth with his fingernail. "So, what's your plan? You're just going to stay here?"

I shrug, watching the people walk by. "I don't know, maybe? I came on this trip hoping to find someone I could potentially fall in love with."

"And yet, here you are, sitting with me after having survived a bike accident and a dislocated thumb."

His words grab my attention. Is it possible Harrison has been the guy I've been looking for all along? I mean, he's eleven years younger than me, which makes me feel a bit dirty. I'm thirty-six, not exactly a cougar, but still... Cara would never let me hear the end of it. He's the complete opposite of my last date, Kevin. His arms are pencil-thin and he's as pale as the cream linen tablecloth on our table, but he's funny and he knows my name.

Am I attracted to him? Not really, but I can get past that, can't I?

"Tell me, H, why did you go on this trip?"

He tears another piece of bread apart. "We had a contest in my division. I won it for the most sales of the Kohler Veil one-piece. It's an expensive toilet." He pops the bread into his mouth.

"Seriously?"

"Yeah, I could have chosen between this trip or a fishing trip in Norway. Not much of an angler."

"Not much of a biker, either." I grin.

"Ha, true. But I wasn't about to pass up a free trip."

"So, you weren't looking to make a love connection on this trip?"

Harrison snorts. "Uh, no. The assistant who signed me up didn't realize this was a singles' tour. But whatever, I'm not looking to settle down anytime soon."

I pick up my wineglass and take a large gulp, not tasting anything. Am I so desperate to find my soulmate over here, I'm grasping at straws? Am I looking for a love connection or just a travel companion? I don't even know what I want anymore. Jesus, I can't believe I was even entertaining the idea Harrison might be the one. I must be feeling really down if I thought he and I could…

Harrison groans loudly, ending any foolish thoughts racing around my muddled brain as the server sets down our appetizers. We dig into the scrumptious food, the aromas tantalizing our senses.

"Oh God, this is so incredible. Another reason to stay." I savor the bite of heaven on my tongue. "You've got to try this, H." I fork some of the pomodoro on his plate.

"Summer, what are you going to do? Get a job? You don't even speak Italian."

"I'm picking it up…slowly. I haven't given much thought to the job part. I don't think I need to get one unless I move here permanently. I can work remotely."

He eyes me dubiously. "It's your funeral."

Irritation itches along my skin. What does Harrison know? He's only venturing to Italy because he sold some toilets. "H, haven't you ever wanted to be irresponsible and do something so frivolous it makes your heart beat wildly?"

"Nope."

"It's like I'm standing on the ledge and if I don't jump now, I won't know what's out there, like a stone skipping across smooth water. I need to be adventurous for once in my life!" I bang my fist on the table and immediately shrink back into my seat, Harrison's shocked expression giving me pause. I smooth out the tablecloth. "Sorry."

"*Mea culpa,* Summer." Harrison holds up his hands in surrender. "Look, if you want my honest opinion, it sounds like you're running away from something."

I frown, running my finger back and forth across the smooth linen. He's right, but I don't want to admit it.

"Nothing on this trip has gone the way I envisioned," I say, dejectedly.

"What did you envision?"

"Coming to Italy, being swept off my bike by a mysterious tall drink of water on the tour. Possibly staying longer and exploring the countryside together."

He peers at me over his water glass. "So, who would you have picked from the A-team if you had to?"

My mouth curls up, relieved he's dropped the 'what am I avoiding back home' line of questioning. "If I had to? Probably the New York guy—what?" I chuckle, noticing his pained expression. Harrison looks like I just told him Lynnette has a crush on him.

"Garrett? The guy who looks like he has a *Wall Street Journal* permanently shoved up his ass? I don't even know if he talks."

"He doesn't. That's why I find him attractive." I shrug.

"Who would you choose from the A-team if you had to?"

"Probably Jojo."

"Imagine all her trophies she couldn't bring to Italy with her. I bet she has a trophy room."

Harrison shudders. "You're right. I'd rather listen to Amy's awful laugh." The server brings our main courses out. "This looks so good. I wonder how Lynnette is faring?"

"I don't know, but I think she was pretty bummed she didn't get taken down in the accident as well."

"Yeah. How's your thumb feeling?" He stares at the splint and frowns.

"It's sore but doesn't hurt as bad as it did earlier today. How's your head wound?"

"Bandaged. I'm too nervous I'll faint again if I take it off." He shakes his head. "Tell you what, because I screwed up your vacation, the least I can do is pay for dinner tonight and help you find your way around this town tomorrow for...well, whatever it is you're looking for."

"Harrison, that would be amazing!" I reach around the table and hug his neck.

"Don't make me regret it," he says begrudgingly. "And you can't introduce me as your lover—*or* your son." He digs into his dinner, and I sit back down and do the same.

"Deal."

Harrison twirls his pasta around his fork and inspects it. "I wonder how far Doug got on the singles' tour. We'll never know if he got engaged."

"Maybe he hooked up with Lynnette." I waggle my eyebrows.

Harrison issues a queasy smile. "That's like telling me my

grandmother hooked up with one of my friends."

We finish our meals and Harrison yawns. "What do you want to do next?" he asks.

"Let's get some gelato and head back to the hotel. I promised I'd call my friend Cara tonight." I need to catch her up on the accident and *il dottore gnocco*.

"Sounds good." He slaps some euros onto the table to cover our dinner, then pats his stomach. "So, Garrett...?"

"He looked second best to Michael in spandex." I grin.

# Chapter 8

HARRISON MEETS ME the next morning down in the lobby. "Did the tour company call you last night?"

"Oh yes. Monica Morelli was most concerned I wouldn't be suing the company or leaving a bad review."

"Me too!" He holds the lobby door open for me.

"I told her I was going to stay a few more days, and she told me to call them to help book my flight back home."

"I'm leaving the day after tomorrow, but will head to Florence tomorrow morning, so you've got me for the day," Harrison says as we head outside.

"Well, we better make the best of it. I thought we could go in search of breakfast first?"

"Let's do it."

We set off down the cobblestone path until we find a small stand selling pastries and bitter espressos. Harrison buys a local paper before we sit down at a café table. He spreads it open and searches for the wanted ads.

"Let's see what Tuscany has to offer in case you need to get a job. There's an opening for a baker?"

"I'm only good at making slice and bake chocolate-chip cookies."

"Let's see…a *modella nuda.*"

"My Italian isn't quite up to par, but by the sound of it, I can tell you that's a hard no."

"*Coltivatore di olive in cerca di aiuto.*" Harrison quickly types the phrase into his phone. "Oh, this could be interesting. An olive grower looking for help, offering room and board. Kill two birds with one stone. Oh, I've heard about this. It's called workaway."

"Wouldn't it be fun to work at a vineyard?"

"I guess." He peruses the section. "No vineyards listed here. I think the olive farm is the next best choice."

"Hmm...olive oil does have a lot of health benefits. Is there an address?"

"No, but we can ask around. It's called the *Uliveto Rossi.*"

"Okay, maybe we can go tour over there and check it out. Look up how much houses cost here." I tap my leg against the table in a steady beat, not sure if it's the strong coffee making me jumpy or the fact I'm entertaining the idea of staying. Last night, I called Cara and told her all about the bike tour, about the accident, and about my future husband, Dr. Bianchi. She asked if I was coming home, but I told her I wanted to stay a few days and explore.

I know what she would say to me right now if she were sitting across from me. *Girl, you've lost your fucking mind.* I ignore her voice in my head while Harrison scans the listings, his eyebrows shooting up into his hairline. "What?"

"Well, there's a villa with a pool...seven hundred and fifty thousand euros. And there's another villa with its own vineyard, at a cool one million euros."

"There has to be something cheaper, possibly not a villa? I said it would be fun to work at a vineyard, not own one."

Harrison shakes his head. "Looks like they're all villas."

"Maybe I'll have to stay in town and rent an apartment. Work at a coffee shop!"

"Uh, apartments are eight thousand euros a month," Harrison says as he reads. "You'll have to learn how to be a baker, drive a Vespa, *and* speak Italian."

"Eight thousand euros? That's double what I pay in California! My future here isn't looking so bright," I say glumly.

"Let's go check this place out." Harrison peeks at his Apple watch. "They just opened."

"What's the point?" I ask hopelessly. "Why bother with a job if I can't afford to rent a place?"

"They said they offer room and board."

"On an olive farm? I'll probably be in a tent out in the groves or out in a shed with the donkeys."

"Sounds biblical…and cheap."

I look at him doubtfully as we gather our espressos and find a taxi.

THIRTY MINUTES LATER, we are standing outside a beautiful limestone home with fields sloping down into hills of olive trees as far as the eye can see. I shield my eyes against the warm Italian sun. "Casa Rossi. Are you sure this is the place, Harrison?"

"Yeah, I'm sure. Well, at least I think the cab driver said this was it." He brazenly walks up to the front door, and I follow suit because in the week I've gotten to know Harrison, I've never seen him act boldly. I note the beautiful terracotta pots glazed with turquoise on either side of the double front door, filled with red geraniums and lavender. He knocks loudly. Soft, melodic humming approaches us from the other side of the door before it swings open.

"*Sí?*" A plump older woman greets us. She's wearing a silk tunic top and matching palazzo pants in a pale shade of lavender. Her white hair is pulled back into a chignon, and deep lines etched into her tanned face crinkle as she smiles. "*Posso aiutarla?*"

"Are you Signora Rossi? Uh…*lei parla inglese*?" Harrison asks. I wring my hands nervously. Although she looks to be in her eighties, her blue eyes are vivid and shrewd as she looks us over.

"*Sí*, yes, a some. Can I help you?"

"Oh good, my friend here is looking to stay in Italy and we saw the ad for the job here. It includes room and board, *sí*?" Harrison asks, taking charge.

The woman eyes me from head to toe while Harrison babbles on about renting and becoming a baker.

"You want to uh…*cucinare e pulire*? *Sí*, yes, you stay and clean."

"Oh, no, I'm sorry you misunderstood. I want to pick olives," I say slowly and smile big.

Her smile dips into a frown. She shakes her head and points to my bandaged hand. "No, no olives. You stay here and you buy property, *sí*?"

"Wait, what? No, no buying property." The numbers Harrison had talked about earlier for villas flash before my eyes. There's no way I could afford a place like this. Not even with the money my grandmother left me or if I sold my townhome. My mind spins, afraid to let this opportunity slip through my fingers, not thinking through the logistics of it all. "Possibly rent? *Sí?*"

Gravel churns under tires, interrupting our conversation. A black Maserati turns into the small lot in front of the house. We turn to see a gorgeous man with tousled dark hair lending his hand to help a slim brunette, wearing a cream wrap dress, out of the passenger side. Dark sunglasses swallow up her face as she teeters on her skyscraper heels on the gravel. The man notices us lingering on the doorstep and says something to the woman while she grabs her satchel from the car. He strides toward us, his handsome face set into a mask of stone.

"*Nonna, chi è questo? Ho un incontro adesso con Daniella.*"

Harrison leans in and whispers as he looks at his phone. "I just typed it in my translator app. He said, 'Grandma, who is this? I have a meeting right now with smoking-hot Daniella'."

I stifle a giggle. "He did not say smoking-hot."

"How would you know? You admitted you know like one word."

"I said I'm picking it up. I can say hello and goodbye," I murmur, ignoring Harrison's snort. I'm too distracted by the beautiful Italian man marching up to us like a dark thundercloud. He makes Dr. Bianchi look like amateur hour at Nick and Ricks. His rich, artfully mussed, dark brown hair is effortlessly styled. His sharp jawline begs to be kissed until his plush lips curve into a smile. His olive complexion is dark against the linen button-down that matches the color of the sky behind him.

Nonna Rossi steps over the threshold and spits to the side. Harrison and I both jump, surprised by her reaction.

"This house is mine to decide, Lorenzo! I tell you already."

Lorenzo stills, looking perplexed. His shrewd gaze narrows on us. "American?"

"*Sí*," I say. "*Parli inglese?*"

"Yes. Excuse us, but we have a meeting. The store is up the road," he says curtly, brushing past us while glaring at his nonna. Daniella finally makes it to the flagstone path and exhales a sigh of relief. She smiles, nodding her head to us, and quickly steps around the old woman.

"Well, okay, we should probably get going, right, Harrison?"

"Right," Harrison murmurs, arching his neck to watch Daniella disappear down the front entry hall.

"Come, come." Nonna Rossi ushers us inside before we can escape. "You see it? You buy."

"Oh, this probably isn't the best time for you right now…meetings and such." I trail behind her, curiosity and Harrison's shove propelling me forward. "And I'm not interested in buying…" My voice peters off as I enter the old Tuscan home.

The wood floors, waxed to a beautiful honey brown, shine in the afternoon light. The ornate crystal chandeliers sparkle, and someone painted beautiful murals of the countryside on the limestone walls. I spin in a circle. It's otherworldly and beautiful. Large arched doors leading out to a veranda are open, letting a fragrant breeze blow through, whispering against the cornflower-blue silk curtains. Floor-to-ceiling windows on either side of the doors allow golden light to spill into the room.

This is it. This is my Frances moment. I can feel it with every fiber of my being. *This* is what I've been searching for...an old villa in Tuscany.

"I'll take it," I say breathlessly, ignoring my internal Cara voice, screaming for me to wait a damn second and think this through.

Nonna Rossi claps her hands together and smiles. "*Molto bene.*"

"It's not for sale." I whirl around and drink in Nonna's grandson leaning against the far wall. "The house is not for sale, despite what Nonna has told you."

His English is crisp and impeccable, even with his Italian accent giving it a silky texture. But there's no mistaking his tone. We are *non benvenuti*. His gaze lazily roams down my body and lands on my splinted thumb. Daniella perches on the velvet couch with her open satchel. She takes out a calculator, several pens, and a sheath of papers, spreading them across the low coffee table.

I arch an eyebrow at him, crossing my arms. "Your nonna says differently."

"*Ma, che sei densa.* Nonna is not well. She doesn't understand—"

Nonna Rossi screeches, making me jump and sending Harrison scurrying for cover. She waves her hands around, yelling in a rush of Italian. I back into Harrison, hiding next to a desk that looks to be a thousand years old.

"What is she saying?" I hiss.

"I have no clue. She's talking too fast for me to put it in my translator."

Lorenzo bows his head and has the decency to appear contrite while his grandmother rails on him. Daniella is blissfully ignorant to this entire exchange while she taps out something on her phone. Either she's hard of hearing, or this little screaming match is *normale*.

I step forward and hold my hands out for them to stop. "Please don't fight. If the house isn't available, I understand."

"*Cosa direbbe tuo nonno del tuo comportamento?*" Nonna Rossi stomps her foot, ending the argument with this sentence. The room falls silent.

Lorenzo looks up, his hazel eyes lasering right through me. He sets his jaw and grinds out, "Grandfather would say, 'do as your grandmother wishes'."

Nonna Rossi folds her arms over her chest, a sly smile spreading across her face. "You were always my favorite, Lorenzo." She pats his cheek and turns, barking an order at Daniella. The slim brunette hastily stuffs her papers into her satchel.

"Nonna Rossi is wicked scary," Harrison whispers in my ear. I just mutely nod, unable to tear my gaze away from Lorenzo. His eyes are unreadable before he turns toward the window. He folds his arms over his expansive chest, pulling his shirt tight against his muscular back, his body rigid. His jaw ticks as he peers over at his grandmother, contemplating. If he weren't so rude, I'd find him incredibly attractive.

Who am I kidding, he's gorgeous.

"*Un altra gatta randagia, Nonna?* Unbelievable." He

shakes his head. "Daniella, *andiamo ora*!" He pauses right before he exits and looks back, our gazes clashing. "We're not finished here." He swiftly leaves the house with Daniella scurrying after him, papers falling out of her satchel.

"What did he just say?" I whisper to Harrison.

"We're not finished here." His eyes linger on Daniella's backside while she exits the house as fast as her sky-high heels will take her. I snap my fingers in his line of sight.

"The other thing. The thing Lorenzo said in Italian."

"*Gatta randagia?* I think he called you a mangy cat."

Nonna makes a tut-tut sound. "Don't mind Renzo, he's unhappy with me." She collapses on the couch where Daniella was sitting.

I look over at Harrison and mouth, '*What should we do?*'

Harrison shrugs before motioning for me to sit in the chair across from Nonna. I wipe my hands on my shorts before I lower myself into the tufted chair. I can't believe I blurted out that I would take this house. I need to find out if she'd be willing to rent it for the summer.

"Signora Rossi, I'm sure I cannot afford to buy this place from you, but would you be willing to rent it out?"

She glances at me, her eyes clouding with worry. Her gnarled hands twist in her lap as she looks out the open window. I'm positive she's about to tell me 'no' when a dove flies into the closed window to the left of the French doors. Harrison screams like a little girl and crouches down behind the couch.

"It's just a bird, Harrison. It flew off."

"I hate birds," he whimpers.

"*Un segno*," Nonna says.

"*Un segno?*" I repeat. Chills zip down my spine. It's just like in the movie, except the bird poops on Frances' head. But I'll take a bird hitting the window over being pooped on.

"Nonno Rossi has sent a sign." Nonna raises her clasped hands to the ceiling.

"A good sign?" I scooch toward the edge of my chair.

"Birds in the house are bad luck. You being here protected this house. *Un segno.*"

"*Un segno,*" I repeat slowly.

She unclasps a necklace from around her neck and hands it to me. "For you."

I hold the gold horn-shaped trinket in my palm. It's warm and heavy. "Oh, I can't take this. It's beautiful, but it's yours." I try to give it back, but she ignores my outstretched hand.

"The golden horn wards off bad luck—*è una tradizione Italiana.* You stay—put on." She waves at me.

My eyes dart to Harrison, who shrugs.

"*Grazie,*" I whisper, clasping the necklace around my neck. "How much is it to stay here at the Villa Rossi?" I cross my arms over my chest and hug myself. The nervous energy humming through my veins is almost unbearable.

Signora Rossi shakes her head. "No, no…this is not the Villa Rossi. This is the guest house. The Casa Rossi. The villa is up the hill. I live there now since Nonno passed away, *dio benedica la sua anima.*" She crosses her chest.

I swallow. *This is the guest house?* "Signora Rossi, I appreciate the offer, but—"

"How many bedrooms is it?" Harrison jumps in. I gape at him. Shouldn't he be hiding from birds?

"Five bedrooms and baths."

I shake my head. I'll never be able to afford a place this big, despite it being the guest house. "No, too much. No, sorry, Signora Rossi." I stand up to leave.

"*Un momento, per favore.*" She holds up a hand. "Wait, please. We need help with reservations and to help at the store. *Amministrare.* You help with our *turisti, sí*?"

"Oh Signora Rossi, I don't speak—"

"*Sí, lo prenderà,*" Harrison speaks over me.

"What did you just say?" I hiss at him.

"I told her you'd take it."

"Harrison! *Mi scusi,* Signora Rossi." I grab his arm and steer him toward the hallway. "I don't know if you realize this, but I don't speak Italian!"

"You'll learn. Weren't you telling me last night you wanted to be adventurous? Well, here's your chance. Grab the bull by the horns, Summer, and take it!"

I bite my bottom lip. He's right. There's a reason I drunkenly booked a trip to Italy. I sensed something was missing from my life. But this is crazy.

I look around the room, my heart galloping in my chest. What other *segno* do I need?

Harrison grabs both of my arms and gently squeezes. "Don't get cold feet on me now, Summer Andrews."

"Ha, easy for you to say, you aren't upending your life on a whim."

"If it helps, I think it's really cool what you're doing. A little nutty, but cool." Harrison's smile is contagious.

"Can you help me barter a good rental price? And…" I bite my thumb, my brain whirling with panic. "Let's just say for the summer. I have two weeks of vacation time left and then hopefully I can convince my boss to work remotely. I don't know, I'll figure it out."

Harrison releases my arms and holds out his fist for a bump. "As long as I can come back and visit."

"Deal."

We walk back into the living room. Nonna Rossi hasn't moved from the couch. She wistfully looks out the open doors at the beautiful view.

Harrison clears his throat while I fidget behind him. I can't believe I'm doing this. I'm staying in Italy for the summer and perhaps…beyond that? I don't know, I can barely think past today. My knees shake. "Signora Rossi? We'd like to present our offer."

"*Sí, sí*, sit, *per favore*."

We both sit in the chairs opposite her. I run my palms along my thighs, thinking about the hell I'll catch from Cara. Oh God, I haven't even thought about Barbara. There's another phone call I'm dreading.

"Signora Rossi, Summer would like to stay in the house until August in exchange for upkeeping the house and yard."

My jaw drops open as I swivel toward him. "Are you nuts?"

Harrison ignores me. "She can work…*amministrare*. Help with your *turisti*. She will need a small salary to pay for expenses like food. Weekends off so she can…eat gelato."

"Oh my God, Harrison," I groan. "Nonna Rossi, excuse my friend, he means well. You see, I came to Italy kind of by accident. I was on a bike tour and injured my hand. I'm not ready to leave yet because…I'm looking for something."

"What are you looking for?" she asks.

"I'm...I'm not sure." My fingers tremble as I run them through my hair. "Have you seen the movie *Under the Tuscan Sun*, by chance?"

She scrunches her eyebrows together and shakes her head. "*Non capisco.*"

"She doesn't understand." Harrison sighs. "I'm a little lost as well, just FYI."

I grab the pillow from behind me and hug it to my chest, leaning forward. "I know this sounds crazy, but when I find it, I'll know. If you could please give me a chance. Pay me enough so that I can afford to live here and buy groceries. I understand I'll have to work weekends, but perhaps I could have a few days off once in a while to wander Tuscany."

Nonna Rossi studies her aged hands before she smooths back her chignon. "I do not know."

Harrison looks at me impatiently and huffs. "If you're not going to say it, then I will. She's looking for love. True love. The kind that happens once in a lifetime."

My cheeks heat and I want to smother him with the throw pillow. I give him the throat-slicing motion before I return my attention to the old woman.

Nonna's piercing blue eyes connect with mine. The lines in her skin etched so deep it's almost impossible to notice her eyes crinkle. "I too moved to Tuttoscano to find *il mio amore.*"

"She moved to Tuttoscano to find her one true love," Harrison whispers.

"Nonno Rossi almost ran me over with his *bicicletta* when I came out of the grocery one morning, *pazzo bello.*"

She smiles wistfully and wipes a tear from her eye. "That's what I would call him. *Pazzo bello*, my crazy handsome. He wasn't supposed to be in town that day. His *papà* sent him on an errand to fetch medicine for his donkey. If that *vecchio asino* hadn't gotten sick, I would have never met Luciano Rossi, the love of my life."

Smiling tenderly, I place my hand over the gold horn at my neck. I can feel the love and affection she has for Nonno as if he were standing right here. Sitting with her, reminiscing, reminds me of my Grams and how much I miss her.

"Signora Rossi, the house?" Harrison gently pushes.

"I do not know the pay, but we will make it work, *sì*? You find your *amore*." She taps the cushion with her finger and smiles. "*Un segno, sì? Benvenuti nella Casa Rossi.*"

Excitement fizzes in my veins. "Did she say welcome to the Rossi house?"

"Pick your jaw up off the floor, Summer." Harrison grins. "You just moved to Italy."

# Chapter 9

I DRAG MY one suitcase into the kitchen and sit down on the bench, looking around at the old house. Harrison and I went back to the hotel, packed up my things and immediately came back before Nonna's cranky grandson returned and locked us out. *I can't believe I'm really here and doing this.* "I'm living in Italy! Woo-hoo!" I yell at the top of my lungs.

"*Che cavolo?*"

I whirl around and see Nonna struggling with a large paper bag outside the kitchen screen door. I rush toward her, embarrassed she heard me shout. "Signora Rossi, here, let me help you." I take the paper bag from her and set it on the counter. "What does *che cavolo* mean?"

"What cabbage," Nonna grumbles. "It also means what the hell. You scared me, shouting like that."

"I'm so sorry, I was excited," I say, chagrined. I peek into the bag and almost melt to the floor as I inhale the aroma of freshly baked bread and tomato sauce. My stomach growls obnoxiously. I slap a hand over it and glance at Nonna. "Is this for me?"

"*Sí*, a little welcome dinner from the Rossi *famiglia.* My granddaughter, Fiore, is a chef."

"*Grazie*, Signora Rossi, this smells wonderful. I haven't eaten since this morning."

"Call me Nonna, *per favore*. Where is your friend? I packed enough for him, too."

"Oh, that's so kind. He went out to get a few things for me. He'll appreciate coming back to a home-cooked dinner."

"Is he, uh...staying here too?"

"Oh no, Harrison is heading back to the States tomorrow. He's just a friend helping me out."

"*Sí, sí.* It's nice to have good friends. *Molto bene.* I had fresh linens and towels put in the first bedroom at the top of the stairs."

"*Grazie*, Nonna."

Nonna sits down at the long trestle table. "I want to uh...*scusarsmi* for my grandson, Lorenzo. He was under the impression I was signing the house over to him today."

"Oh...*oh.*" Realization washes over me as I sit down across from her. "This is his house?"

"No...*sí. È complicato.*"

"So, I *am* living in Lorenzo's house? This isn't good." The memory of his fuming, smoky, hazel eyes flash in my mind. "Is he mad that I'm here?"

Nonna gets up and unpacks the bag, humming a jaunty little tune. I know she heard me.

"Nonna, is Lorenzo upset I'm living here?"

"*Chi se ne frega.*"

I arch an eyebrow. "I don't know what that means, but I don't want to make him upset and I certainly don't want—"

"I simply said, I don't care what Renzo thinks and you shouldn't either. This is still my house and I can do what I want with it and let *whoever* I want to stay in it. *Sí?*" She looks up and pins me with a no-nonsense glare.

My teeth grab my bottom lip and I drop my gaze. "Okay."

Nonna's expression softens. She walks over to me and gently pats my back. "Sh, sh, *figlia mia.* Do not worry yourself. I'll handle Lorenzo. You are here now and that is that."

She reminds me so much of Grams, the memories sting the corners of my eyes. "*Grazie*, Nonna, for taking a chance on me."

"You will find what it is you're looking for, Summer. *Sí? Ho fiducia in te.*" She slaps the table with her palm. "Now then, I must go. This old woman goes to bed early. You let me know if you need anything, *sí*?" She winks at me. "*Buona sera*, Summer."

"*Buona sera*, Nonna." I stand and kiss her soft, papery cheek and help her to the door. "Thank you for everything."

I pull out my phone and translate *Ho fiducia in te.* I swallow past the lump in my throat, reading the words. *I have faith in you.*

HARRISON STEPS INTO the kitchen after I leave another message for Barbara. I've left her four since I arrived in Italy, asking her to check in with me. It's so typical and frustrating of her not to text or call to acknowledge my messages while I'm thousands of miles away.

"Is there a cat who lives here?" Harrison asks.

"I don't think so…Nonna didn't mention a cat."

"Hmm, there's one on the front doorstep. Probably the neighbor's cat."

"I hope so. Cats and I are non-simpatico. My Grams had a cat growing up named Fancy. A big fluffy white cat that always swished her tail and flattened her ears. She used to attack my hair in my sleep and pee on my shoes. God, I hated Fancy."

Harrison smirks. "And that's why I'm 'allergic'." He air-quotes. "I picked up a few things to get you by until you can go. The grocery store isn't too far into town."

"Thanks H, that was really sweet of you. Nonna stopped by and dropped off some food not too long ago. I've been salivating over it, waiting for you to get back. She said her granddaughter is a chef."

"Sweet! I'm starving."

"How's your head wound?" I ask while I pull some plates from a cabinet.

Harrison touches the bandage on his forehead. "It's okay. I'll probably have a small scar from it."

"You could make up a good story, like you were driving a Ferrari through Italy and ran off a cliff or something."

"Then I'd be dead," Harrison chuffs, opening the bag Nonna brought. He takes out some plastic utensils and napkins. "Besides, I think it sounds kind of cool if I just nod my head and say, bike accident, and that's it. Leave them wondering."

I smother my laugh and nod my head. "Mysterious. I like it."

"How's your thumb?"

"It's not too bad. Tylenol helps with the pain."

"I'm sorry about the accident," Harrison says quietly.

"Hey, it wasn't your fault. Accidents happen. Besides, if we hadn't wrecked, we'd be listening to Blake quote Lance Armstrong while Ginny drools on herself right about now."

Harrison laughs. "Man, I will not miss those two. If I had to listen to one of Blake's Ironman stories one more time..."

"Or listen to Michael laugh at his own stupid jokes..." I cringe.

"Or watch Gary take selfies of his hair in the Tuscan sunlight."

"See? We dodged a bullet." I laugh.

We sit down at the table and dig into the spaghetti with marinara. We both groan in appreciation before settling into small talk about the tour.

"That was amazing." Harrison tosses his napkin onto his empty plate and sits back in his chair. He takes a sip of his Coke, looking around the kitchen. "Are you sure you don't want me to stay the night? This place looks old. Like a fire could start if you turn on a light switch, kind of old."

"Thanks for putting the image of the house burning down in my sleep tonight in my head," I deadpan, walking my plate over to the sink. I turn on the taps and the pipes make a horrible screeching sound followed by a few thumps and moans, like a gallon of water is trying to squeeze through a toothpick-size pipe. I twist around, my eyes widening. Harrison looks like he's about to be attacked by a dozen birds.

"What the hell is that noise?"

Before I can answer him, the water jets out of the faucet in spurts before trickling out.

"The pipes probably haven't been turned on in a while." Brown water flows and I hold my breath, hoping it turns clear, which it does after a few seconds.

"Summer, I strongly advise you not to drink the water."

"It will be fine." I wrinkle my nose. I hope they have bottled water at the store.

"Yeah, I've changed my mind on my offer. Are you sure you don't want to sleep at the hotel tonight?"

I rinse my plate with dish soap and set it on the drying rack. "I'll be fine. It's charming."

"Ooo-kay, if that's what we're calling it." He brings his plate over and washes it. "What are you going to do tomorrow? When do you start your job?"

"Tomorrow I'll go to the store to get the rest of the things I need and check out the town. I don't have to start work until Monday, so at least I have a couple days to get settled."

A horn blasts from outside. "Crap, that's my taxi. I told him to return after an hour. I can tell him to come back if you need me to stay longer, or if you want to come with me." He raises an eyebrow.

I shake my head, tears threatening to spill. I stand up on my tiptoes and wrap Harrison in a bone-crushing hug. "I'll be okay. Thanks for being my friend, H. I wouldn't have survived the bike tour without you."

"Actually, you probably would have. I'm the reason you dislocated your thumb, ending the tour early."

I laugh against his soft cotton hoodie. "Well, you know

what I mean."

"Summer?"

"Yeah?"

"Hugs make me uncomfortable."

"Of course they do." I chuckle and release him. "Keepin' it real, dude."

"Keepin' it real." He grins at Blake's stupid saying. He holds his fist out for a bump. I tap my knuckles to his and walk him to the door.

"Stay in touch, 'kay?"

"Ha, I'll be back. I now have a friend in Italy, and a free place to stay. Find out if smokin'-hot Daniella is single." He waggles his eyebrows.

I roll my eyes and laugh. "Bye, H. Keep in touch."

I close the door and the quiet suddenly crashes into me. I grab my cell and call Cara.

"Two calls back-to-back? To what do I owe the pleasure?"

"I need to tell you something, but first, have you been able to go over to my place to check on Barbara? She's not returning my calls."

"I stopped by yesterday after we got off the phone. I let myself in, but she wasn't there. Are you sure you two are related?"

"Regrettably, why?"

"She is not the neatest individual."

"I'm aware. Ugh, I hope she tries to clean up after herself. Thanks for checking." I pause, wondering how to bring this up. "Um, so I might stay here a little longer than expected."

"I thought you said last night you were coming home in a couple of days?"

"Well, last night, yes, that was the plan." I take a deep breath and pull off the proverbial Band-Aid. "I woke up this morning, found a rental place and a job at an olive farm, and now I'm living here for the summer."

"You *what*?" I hold the phone away from my ear while Cara lectures about responsibilities, jobs, Barbara, finding love, and cursing *Under the Tuscan Sun*.

"Are you done?"

"Look, you're a grown woman and can do what you want, but this is so not like you. What about your job?"

"I emailed my boss and asked if I could work remotely after my vacation time is up. I mean, it's all done on computers, anyway. Besides, I think I might want to try something different… I don't know, this has all happened so fast. I haven't wrapped my head around it yet."

"I just hope you know what you're doing." Cara clucks her tongue. "I'm not going to pretend I understand this Italian midlife crisis you're going through, but I'm here for you."

"I'm fine, Cara, I promise. By August I'll be ready to come back refreshed and ready to roll."

"What do you know about olives, anyway?" She chuckles.

I sit down at the kitchen table and sigh. "Not much."

"Does this have anything to do with the hunky doctor, by chance?"

Hazel eyes and dark, rich hair flash before my eyes. I haven't even told Cara about the dark thundercloud known as Lorenzo Rossi yet, but I'm too tired to explain it all right now. Meeting Dr. Bianchi yesterday afternoon seems like a lifetime ago.

"No, it has nothing to do with the doctor, I promise."

"Well, damn. I was kind of hoping you'd have some passionate love affair with a handsome Italian," she teases. "I miss you already. Send me pictures of the house."

"I will. It's old, but beautiful. How's Damien?"

"Damien is Damien. He's been watching Food Network obsessively since he's been working from home. I think he's following your lead. He wants to quit his job and become the next Bobby Flay. I tried to tell him he needs to take a cooking class before he makes any rash decisions. He accidentally lit our dinner on fire last night, so we had takeout for the third night in a row."

"Oh, man." I giggle. "How do you accidentally light dinner on fire?"

"He said he was trying a flambé technique. I walked into the kitchen, and the pan was fully engulfed. Maybe I can convince him to whisk me off to Italy this summer after I wrap up the Asher divorce, and he can take some cooking lessons there."

"That would be amazing. I miss you."

"I miss you, too. I've got a work call coming in. Be careful. I'll have Babs call you. *Ciao!*"

"It's actually *arriveder—*" I look down at my phone, the call disconnected. "*—ci,*" I mumble to myself.

I grab my suitcase and heft it up the stairs, turning into the first bedroom on the left, across from the bathroom. A soft breeze stirs the curtains from the window on the far side of the room. The walls are plaster and painted white. A vase of wildflowers sits on a small wooden bedside table. There's a pale green armoire in the corner painted with roses.

I sit down on the bed with the light pink quilt and bounce a little. It's small, but cozy. This is going to work out okay, I tell myself. It has to.

# Chapter 10

DUST AND DEBRIS salt my eye while I knock on the bathroom sink pipe with the wrench I found out in the shed behind the house. I'm not sure what I expect to happen, but after fifteen minutes trying to loosen the fitting, I've decided I'm not a plumber.

It's day three at Casa Rossi, and I've discovered I'm sharing the property with a brown tabby cat who slinks around the backyard. Pretty sure he's a stray. I tried to pet him when I saw him yesterday, even though every fiber of my being was yelling at me not to. He must have smelled my past-trauma-from-Fancy fear because he tried to take my face off, convincing me he's really a rabid racoon. Do they even have racoons over here? I don't know, but he's twice the size of Fancy the fluffball, as Grams lovingly used to call her.

The cat and I have come to a mutual understanding after two days of stare-downs. He won't attempt to enter the house, and I won't chase after him with the broom I left at the back door...mostly because I found the broom mangled this morning.

It was serendipity Harrison and I caught Signora Rossi here that day, according to Daniella, who stopped by yesterday to drop off some paperwork for me to sign. She and Lorenzo had arrived that morning with the papers to transfer the house from his grandmother to him. He wants to renovate it and turn it into a bed-and-breakfast for the farm. But Nonna changed her mind at the last minute. If Harrison and I had arrived ten minutes later, I might not be here looking at a rusty old pipe, but on a plane back to the States.

My phone buzzes on the countertop. I clank the pipe with the wrench again in frustration and wiggle out from beneath the vanity. I reach up and press the green button.

"Well, it's about time. I was wondering when you were going to call," I say irritably.

Barbara pulls on her cigarette before speaking. "Not everyone can jet off to Italy, Summer. The time difference isn't exactly convenient."

"I'm actually shocked you're up this early."

"Your friend Cara came over and woke me up," she gripes, taking another puff. "How is Italy, anyway?"

"It's been good, beautiful actually! The landscape is incredible, and the food is to-die—"

"I'd love to hear all about it, but I'm a little hung over. Stayed out late with Janice karaokeing. Can we catch up later?"

"Um, sure, but I need to talk to you about some ground rules while you're staying at my place."

I wait for her to respond, at least a groan of irritation, but I'm met with silence.

"Barbara, hello? Can you hear me?"

My home screen is black, the call disconnected. What the hell? I didn't even get a chance to tell her I'm staying longer, not that she'll care. I call her back, but it goes straight to voicemail. "Barbara, call me back, please. I'm staying in Italy a little longer, so I need to talk to you."

I turn on the bathroom taps again to see if water will miraculously come out, but it doesn't. I send a quick text to Nonna Rossi.

***Me:*** *Nonna, the water isn't working. Can you send a plumber over?*

***Nonna:*** *Sí, sí. I fix. Un idraulico.*

I stare at her response, hoping Nonna doesn't actually come try to fix this herself. I look up the Italian word and sigh in relief. *Idraulico* means plumber. Perhaps I was too impulsive in deciding to stay here. Maybe Cara was right for thinking I was crazy to do this alone. *Am I having an Italian midlife crisis?*

I was planning to get out of the house and explore this morning, but I have to get this water situation handled first. I bang on the pipe one more time and groan. This is hopeless. I sprawl out on the bathroom floor, wallowing. I stare at a brown stain on the ceiling and contemplate. How did I even get here? I should be biking and drinking wine right now, listening to the A-team gloat about how easy the ride was, not lying on someone else's bathroom floor, feeling sorry for myself.

What was I thinking when I said yes to Nonna? What was I thinking coming to Italy in the first place?

"Stop wallowing, Summer. You're in Italy, for fuck's sakes, make the most of it." I toss the wrench and it lands with a loud thud beside me. I throw my arm over my eyes, the glaze of tears threatening to erupt. I miss Cara and the comforts of home. I miss…

"Do you always talk to yourself, Summer?"

I yelp, scrambling to my feet. Lorenzo casually leans against the bathroom doorframe while my heart tries to leap out of my chest. "What are you doing here? How did you get in?"

He straightens. "The kitchen door was unlocked."

"You can't just barge in here," I say indignantly, swiping the tears from my cheeks.

"I didn't barge, I walked in. Besides, I was told to come over and help our *guest* with the water, but it's fine if you don't want my help, *ingrata*."

I fold my arms over my chest, my nostrils flaring at his *ingrata* comment. Even I can figure out what that means. I glare at him sidelong. "*You* are going to fix my plumbing?"

He raises an eyebrow, his mercurial eyes looking smoke gray as they burn into mine. His crisp white button-down tucked into jeans with a brown leather belt is snug enough that I can get a general idea of what he's packing. It's ten times better than Michael's in Lycra. I wonder what Lorenzo would look like in biker shorts. *No, concentrate on the task at hand, Summer. You need water, not sex with this hot Italian.*

"Eyes up here, *piccola randagia*. Can you show me the problem? I don't have much time." His lips twitch.

My cheeks burn, realizing I was zoning out on his crotch. Jesus, I need to have sex soon. It's been too long. *But not with Lorenzo Rossi.* Definitely not with him. Even though he's incredibly sexy and looks like he should be in a Ralph Lauren ad, he doesn't seem particularly fond of me, not that I can blame him.

I clear my throat. "I tried to turn on the faucet, but nothing is coming out."

Lorenzo walks over and turns on a tap. I huff in exasperation that he has to test my theory. Typical. "See?" Crossing my arms tighter, I lean against the wall. He ducks under the vanity and my eyes automatically rove over his butt in his tight jeans. Cara would approve. I quickly avert my gaze and stare at the stain on the ceiling when he glances over his shoulder.

"Have you tried the kitchen sink?"

"It worked this morning."

"Let's recheck it." With a nod, he stands back up, pointing to the wrench on the floor. "Were you using that?"

"I thought if I banged it on the pipe, it might dislodge whatever has it stopped up."

We both bend and reach for the wrench, but he beats me to it, swiftly scooping it up. I can't help but breathe in a combination of leather and mint and something distinctly Italian, transporting me to dappled sunlit woods. Dammit, why can't he smell like sweat or rotten olives? It would definitely diminish this zing of attraction I'm feeling toward him.

"After you." He gestures for me to leave the bathroom first. I walk out into the hall and peer at the open door of my bedroom. I hope he didn't poke his head inside on his way up here because it's a mess from unpacking. Clothes are flung haphazardly all over my unmade bed. I don't need his prying eyes or judgmental stares. I rush across the hall and quickly close the door with a bang, my chest rising with the burst of exertion. A cracking noise like wood splintering, echoes all around me. I scream as the door crashes down into my room, taking the frame and part of the surrounding wall with it.

"Summer!"

"Wha…what just happened?" I blink to clear my vision, a cloud of white dust floating around me. I turn in a circle to survey the damage, drywall dust coating every surface, including me.

Lorenzo grabs my arms and quickly scans my body. "Are you hurt?"

I shake my head, at a loss for words. He's so close, I can see the tiny flecks of gold in his greenish-gray eyes. He brushes drywall dust off my cheek, his thumb stilling. His brow furrows and he steps back, dropping his hand. He turns and surveys the wreckage, clearly not impressed with the state of the door and surrounding wall. "Are you okay?"

"I don't know what happened…all I did was close the door. Is it normal for a door, the frame, and part of the wall to come down?" I squeak, pointing to the door and crumbling plaster on the ground.

"I'm not worried about the door, *randagia*. Are you okay?"

"I'm fine. Uh, I'm not sure what to do about this." I wave a hand over the mess, avoiding the intensity of his hazel gaze. "Can you fix this too?"

He grumbles something in Italian, surveying the splintered doorframe. He runs his hand along the broken drywall. More debris and dust crumbles to the floor. At this rate, the entire wall will need to be repaired.

"I'm sorry. I don't understand what you're saying."

Lorenzo's shoulders rise and fall as he heaves a sigh. "This house is ancient. My Nonna and Nonno Rossi used to live in it before my grandfather passed away. Nonna is stubborn and has a hard time giving things up. You might want to find another place to stay."

"Ah-ah, I see what you're doing, trying to get me to move out. Well the answer is no. Not happening." I stubbornly return to arms-folded-over-my-chest position.

He shakes his head. "That's not what I'm doing, but if you insist on staying here, then you should move to another room. I'll send someone to clean this up." He waves at the mess before he starts down the staircase. I trail behind him, still dazed by the door *falling off its hinges*. "There's a lot that needs to be updated, but now that you're living here, plans have changed."

Point one for Lorenzo.

"Well, you can still make those changes if you need to," I hedge, following him into the kitchen. "I don't want to mess up your plans. You know what would be a great addition? A swimming pool."

Lorenzo crouches down in front of the kitchen sink and sends me a devastating smile over his shoulder.

"A swimming pool? Nice try. Nonna won't budge. No changes to the house while you're living here. Besides, you don't need to have a bunch of Italian men constantly hitting on you and going through your things."

"Oh, I doubt that would happen," I scoff.

He lifts an eyebrow. "Clearly you have not met many of my fellow countrymen."

"Speaking of the house, did you know there's a cat that

hangs out in the backyard?" I peek out the kitchen window and the cat in question is sitting on the back stone wall, staring at me like he knows I'm ratting him out.

"Who, Razzo?"

"*Razzo?*"

"*Sí*, it means Rocket. He showed up one day and Nonna Rossi took him in. Says he reminded her of Nonno. She named him Razzo because he used to run around the backyard like he had a rocket attached to his tail. He splits his time between here and the villa. He's an excellent mouser."

"Oh God, mice live here too?" I arch my neck, and Razzo flicks his tail.

"It's an old farmhouse, of course there are mice here." Lorenzo picks up a toolbox that was on the kitchen table and gets to work while I have a stare-down with Razzo.

My nose twitches. "I don't think he likes me very much. Does he have fleas?" I ask.

"Are you not a cat person, *piccola randagia*?"

"No, Fancy made sure of that." I turn from the window and lean against the counter. "Why do you keep calling me *randagia*? Is that like a type of cheese or something?"

"*Che cosa?*" he asks, his voice muffled.

"It sounds like cheese. Randagia…Mozzarella…Gouda…Parmesana."

He withdraws his head from underneath the sink. "What are you talking about?"

"*Randagia*, you keep calling me that."

With a shake of his head, he smirks. "*Piccola randagia* in Italian means little stray."

My mouth opens slightly. "You think I'm a stray? Like Razzo?"

"I think you and Razzo have more in common than you realize. And it's pronounced *parmigiano, not parmesana.*"

Heat crawls up my neck. I sink down onto the bench at the kitchen table, at a loss for words. *He thinks I'm a mangy stray cat that can't pronounce parmesan cheese correctly?*

"What happened to your hand?" he asks, ducking back under the sink. He flattens out on his back, his long legs stretched out.

"Biking accident." I turn my bandaged thumb over. "Your English is flawless, by the way."

"I went to study in the States at UC Berkeley, and then I worked on our olive farm in California for a year to learn all aspects of the business."

"Wow, small world, I'm from California too. Where's the olive farm?"

"Sacramento. We have one in Spain as well. My brother runs it with his wife's *famiglia*. Where are you from?"

"Burlingame, just outside the city. I'm a graphic designer for Granite Scholastics." I pull my dark hair up into a ponytail and secure it with a tie. "Actually, I don't know what the hell I'm doing anymore," I mumble to myself.

"You don't enjoy being a graphic designer?"

I watch his muscular forearms flex while he tightens the pipe. I imagine those arms, muscles straining, holding himself over me. I scrub my hands down my face, trying to eradicate the image from my brain. *Focus, Summer.*

"No, I do, I did. I just feel like something is missing. Textbooks aren't exactly...exciting to design."

His muscles ripple again, and I'm right back in my Lorenzo fantasy.

"So, why are you here?"

His abrupt question snaps me from my daydream like a splash of cold water to the face. "What do you mean, *why am I here*?"

"What brought you to Italy?" He cranks something on the pipe. "Is your family from here? You have that Italian look...olive skin coloring with your dark hair."

"No family here. I came for a bike tour."

"Alone?"

"Yes, alone. I'm quite capable of traveling by myself."

"Take it easy, *randagia*. You're like a *porcospino*...all prickly. How did you find yourself in Tuttoscano? They don't usually ride through our town."

"I was involved in a bike accident, and the closest hospital was here."

"Ah, I see. You were with a man the other day."

"Harrison?"

"Harrison," he grunts, tightening a nut. "Is he your boyfriend?"

I laugh. "God, no. Just a friend. I could never date a guy that screams like a girl when a bird flies by."

Lorenzo raises an eyebrow as he picks up another wrench. "Noted."

"So anyway, I ended up in a tangle of bikes with him when he suddenly stopped, thus the dislocated thumb. We had to leave the tour and ended up in Tuttoscano. I saw the ad in the local paper you were hiring with a place to stay at the farm. I wasn't ready to return to California, so here I am."

He sits up, wiping his hands on a cloth, his eyes solemn. "So here you are."

"I'm sorry I'm being prickly. It's been a strange turn of events for me and I haven't quite found my footing. I also hope there are no hard feelings between us. I had no idea you were trying to get Nonna Rossi to sign the house over to you. It's beautiful, and to be honest, I was just here out of curiosity, but everything kind of fell into place, and it seemed like fate..."

The words die on my tongue as his brows scrunch together and his lips flatten.

"Fate." He shakes his head and issues another soft grunt. "Look, Summer, it's not a secret I wanted the house to convert into a bed-and-breakfast. I'm not thrilled we now have a houseguest living here, but I have harvest coming up in the fall that I have to prepare for, so the house can wait. I don't have any ill feelings toward you, okay? When you leave, Nonna will be ready to hand it over, and I'll start working on it." He stands up, brushing off his jeans before collecting his tools.

"Can I ask how old you are, Lorenzo?"

"Why, are you interested in me, *cara*?" He folds his muscular arms over his chest and winks.

Heat blossoms on my cheeks. "What? No, most definitely not. Very much *un*-interested."

"Do you enjoy women, then?"

"What?" I splutter. "No. Just because I said I'm not interested in you doesn't mean I'm into women."

"Sorry," he says, ducking his head. "You were very adamant about how unattracted you were to me, I just assumed."

"I take it you're not used to women denying your advances?"

He grins, and it takes my breath away. "I'm thirty-two, *randagia*."

I nod. Four years apart is nothing. Ugh, why am I even entertaining this? Nothing will happen between me and Lorenzo. I have a better chance of going out with Dr. Bianchi.

"*Ride bene chi ride ultimo*, Summer." He waves as he exits the kitchen. "Your water should work now."

"Wait, you're not going to test it? Reedy ben-e…what the heck does that mean, anyway?" I yell at his retreating form.

"He who laughs last, laughs best. It's an old Italian proverb."

"But I'm not laughing!" I stomp my foot.

"*Arrivederci, randagia*!" he shouts from the foyer before the front door slams.

I get up and quickly turn on the taps. Water flows smoothly from the faucet. I rush upstairs and into my bathroom. I gasp as I look at my reflection in the mirror. I look like I had a fight to the death with Betty Crocker. Drywall is in my hair and all over my clothes. There's a smudge where he rubbed the dust away from my cheek. All the while I was drooling over Lorenzo, I looked like a powdered donut…*patetico*.

I reach out and turn on the taps. The water flows here as well. Damn it. Another point for Lorenzo Rossi.

I PAY THE cab driver and step out onto the cobblestone street. Soaking in the midday sun, I inhale the fresh air and release it. An older woman with a handkerchief tied over her head passes by, looking at me curiously.

"*Buongiorno*," I say enthusiastically. "Um, mi scusi, dove eel mer-cato?" I know I'm completely butchering, asking how to get to the market, but hopefully she doesn't mind. I tried practicing the phrase this morning before I left.

She points down the street and says something rapidly in Italian before bustling off.

Okay, not Google Maps, but at least I've got a general direction. I head down the street, excited to be out on my own. I eagerly greet every person I pass. For the most part, everyone is friendly in return. I round the corner and stop suddenly, thrilled by the open-air market in front of me. An older gentleman grumbles in Italian, stepping around me, as I let out a little squeal of delight.

The rainbow of colors overwhelms my senses in the most glorious way as I stop by flower, fruit, and veggie stands. Home-made goods under red umbrellas beg to be sampled as people bicker and barter for a better price. Everything looks so fresh and appetizing. I take a few pictures to send to Cara and Damien.

I buy fresh bread, cheese, fruit, and vegetables after trying all their samples. I marvel over blueberries the size of marbles, velvety green bib lettuce, and a stand with fifteen varieties of tomatoes. The merchants are patient while I count out the euros. I even splurge on some sunflowers, a candle, and a bottle of wine, because why not? I'm in Italy!

A dress at a corner vendor catches my eye. It's a simple linen sundress, but if I'm staying in Italy and working at the olive shop, I'll need something more than athleticwear and my two dresses I brought. The old Italian woman selling them measures my waist and speaks to me in Italian, even though I tell her I can't understand her. I just nod and smile as she hands me a dress in my size. I pick out two more and she beams, quickly wrapping them up in tissue.

I pay for the dresses and wander past an art gallery, a *pasticceria*, and another dress shop called Carmella's. The colorful, designer dresses in the window are fun, but a little too pricey and fancy for everyday wear. Two young Italian men whistle at me across the street.

"*Bella!* Over here! *O, signorina!*"

I giggle and duck my head, ignoring their catcalls. I hastily turn the corner and drop my bags at a little table outside a pizzeria, suddenly starved after the day of shopping. I order a glass of wine and a small pizza while watching the locals and tourists stroll by loaded down with their own goods. I decide Italians aren't so different from Americans, they're just better dressed and have magnificent bone structure.

I smile at a woman sitting with her two small children at a nearby table. Pizza sauce is smeared on their cheeks while they chitchat and giggle. The hum of the romantic Italian language buzzes all around me while I sip my red wine. I wish Cara were here to experience this with me.

The server places the pizza in front of me. It's not like American pizza. I look over at the other diners and note they eat their pizza with a fork and knife, so I do the same. My eyes roll back in my head as I taste the gooey cheese and the spicy red sauce. I hum with delight while I sit in the afternoon shade, sipping my red wine, and soaking in my surroundings. They say the state of Virginia is for lovers, New York is the city that never sleeps, and Paris is the city of love. But Italy—gorgeous, breezy, lazy afternoons sipping wine, Italia—is the country of pure pleasure. If only every day could be this perfect.

# Chapter 11

THE MORNING SUNSHINE warms my skin under the cloudless sky. It's my first day working at Rossi Olive Farms, and the butterflies in my stomach are a good indication of how I'm feeling. I grab the rusty old red bike with the brown basket hooked on the front and wheel it out of the garden shed, checking the tires. They are in surprisingly good shape. Nonna Rossi said she'd make sure the bike was in working condition for me to get to the farm. I'm not exactly thrilled to be back on a bike so soon, but it will be much quicker than walking. Careful not to injure my thumb, I swing a leg over and push forward, the bike groaning in protest as I coax the pedal around. A little elbow grease, and I could have this baby looking good as new.

I stuff the paper with directions inside the basket, along with my bag that holds my lunch, wallet, phone, and passport. I pedal across the gravel drive and out onto the dirt road, taking my time and soaking in my surroundings. I begrudgingly admit to myself I *kind of* miss Romeo from the tour and his 'It's a beautiful day' comments when I roll past the serene green hills dotted with olive trees. I turn my face up to the bright blue sky laced with white wisps of clouds floating leisurely by.

I woke up this morning feeling excited and renewed, like

I had a purpose. On my way home from the farmers' market yesterday, I stopped at the local *supermercato* for groceries. Everyone was helpful, even though I could only speak a few phrases in Italian. It felt like another accomplishment, being able to successfully buy groceries in a foreign country. They called me *la donna che vive nella Casa Rossi*, 'the woman living in the Rossi house'. I kept trying to tell them my name was Summer, but they just smiled and nodded their heads and said, '*Sí, sí, estate*'. *Yes, you idiot, it is summer here. Why does this woman keep mentioning it?*

I glance down at the map Nonna Rossi drew with a shaky hand and turn onto a road marked with a large boulder. I pump my legs as the dirt road inclines. Despite my darndest to block it out, I swear I can hear the dreaded song, "Eye of the Tiger" echoing in my head. Leaning down, I surge forward. *Take that, A-team.* The dirt turns to pea gravel when I reach a plateau and I take a quick sip of water. The road evens out and I sail past lush gardens filled with purples, blues, and pinks. Butterflies dance from one frothy flower to the next while the bees hum happily, collecting their pollen.

I turn the bend, and my breath catches at the magnificent house ahead of me. The cream limestone estate makes my little villa seem like the rear garden shed. Wooden shutters hug large windows encased by wrought-iron balconies. Bright red geraniums and lavender spill over the sides. Terracotta tiles bake in the morning sun, beckoning travelers to come out of the heat. I lean my bike against the low stone wall of the gravel parking area. There are several buildings off in the distance behind the main house, next to the olive groves. It's like I just arrived at my dream home in Italy. I take in the view of the hills below and the town off in the distance.

I head toward the detached building a little ways from the main house, with fuchsia bougainvillea climbing up the right side. An 'Aperto/Open' sign hangs on the door and a little bell jingles when I walk inside, announcing my presence. The room is dark and cool, smelling of polished wood and olive oil.

"Hello? Uh, *ciao*?" I finger the golden horn necklace Nonna Rossi gave me while I peruse the walls of olive oil bottles. "Is anyone here?"

"I be right with you!" an accented female calls out from another room. I exhale, my nerves sizzling in the pit of my stomach. I walk around the room, taking in the terracotta floors and mahogany bar with glass dishes spaced a foot apart from each other. A fresh loaf of crispy white bread sits wrapped in a white hand towel on a wooden cutting board. I wonder if this is the tasting room. My mouth waters just thinking about fresh bread dipped in pure olive oil.

I wander to the shelves stacked with beautiful green bottles of Rossi Organic Olive Oil, Rossi Extra Virgin Olive Oil, bottles of oil infused with herbs, and bottles of olives and olive tapenade. Rossi cookbooks and other knickknacks for sale fill up the additional shelves. I pick up a cookbook and scan the beautiful cover.

"*Buongiorno!* You must be Summer!"

My heart lurches out of my chest as I whirl around, nearly dropping the book. "Oh, you scared me! Hi, yes, *buongiorno*," I fumble. "I'm Summer Andrews. Do you happen to speak English?"

"*Sí*...yes!"

"Oh, thank God," I murmur. "I'm here for the job? Signora Rossi said she'd meet me here at ten."

"Ah, welcome, my name is Fiore Rossi. I'm the chef here at the farm." Her wide smile is warm and inviting, like we're sharing a fun secret. Her light brown hair is tied back in a French braid, and her hazel eyes remind me of another Rossi I know. She's petite, but commanding, dressed in a white chef's coat and black pants. "Nonna wasn't able to get here in time, so I told her I'd show you around."

I snap my fingers at the mention of her name, and smile. "Oh Fiore, you made me spaghetti the other night. It was incredible! Thank you so much."

"It was no trouble. I'm glad you enjoyed it. Is your hand hurt?"

"It's fine. I was in a bike accident last week and dislocated my thumb. The splint is just cautionary."

"Ouch. Bikers are everywhere in these parts. Be careful because Italian drivers will unintentionally run you off the road."

"So I've seen. Are you related to Lorenzo?"

She smiles easily. "*Sí*, Renzo is my older brother. Have you met him?"

"I'm surprised the whole town hasn't heard the story of the American who stole the Rossi house right out from under him," I grumble to myself, but she snickers.

"Oh, I've heard. He came storming up here that day madder than the devil with a bee sting. Renzo is a sweetheart, but Nonna pushes his buttons. And when he doesn't get his way, he acts like *un bambino*. He's all about *l' azienda*. The Business."

"The business?"

"*Sí*, Lorenzo runs Rossi Olive Oil. My father semi-retired a couple years ago and now Lorenzo runs the empire."

"Oh wow…empire. Naturally, when you own something this beautiful, you would be protective of it." I take a minute rolling the word 'empire' around in my brain. This is not a mom-and-pop shop, that's for sure. And the King of the Rossi empire helped me with my plumbing…*oh God*. "Is this your cookbook?"

She beams and steps up next to me. "I released it last year. I have it in Italian and English." She slips a cookbook off the shelf and lovingly runs a hand over the cover. "My greatest accomplishment."

"Congratulations, that's amazing. I'm not much of a cook, but I'd love to learn." I flip through the glossy pages of colorful, mouthwatering dishes. "What's your favorite?"

"The Osso Bucco, but my brother's favorite is ragù Bolognese." She winks at me. "Here, take one. On me." She hands me a book in English and takes the Italian version I'm holding.

"Wow, thank you. Maybe you can teach me how to make the Osso Bucco sometime?"

"Of course. You can always come back in the kitchen with me if there aren't any guests."

"Is there a restaurant here?"

"I own a small café right behind this little building. I serve lunch and dinner for guests out on the patio. I can make you some lunch today unless you brought something."

I think of the apple and packet of crushed chips I quickly packed. "Lunch would be amazing, thank you." I place the cookbook with my things on the front bar. "So, do you know what my job will entail? Will I be helping you? Out in the fields picking olives?"

"No, no, I have Fredo helping me. You'll meet him soon. You will work here with Nina. Greeting guests, setting up the tours, olive oil tastings—"

"Tours? What do you mean by tours?"

"Oh, you don't have to give the tour. That's Nina's job. We have three tours a day—ten thirty, noon, and two p.m. She should be here in a bit."

I blow out the breath I was holding. "Oh, okay. Do you think it will be a problem that I don't speak Italian very well?" *As in, at all.*

"You'll be fine. Most of our tourists are from other countries and speak English."

"Do you live near here?" I lean against the counter.

"*Sí*, I live with my parents and Nonna in the main house. Renzo has an apartment in town."

"The main house is beautiful."

"Oh, yes, I'll give you a tour at some point, and if you like to swim, you are more than welcome to come up and use the pool."

"You have a pool? I will take you up on that generous offer." I smile. I'm really enjoying talking to Fiore. She's so easygoing and sweet, I feel like I've known her forever.

Her eyes zero in on my necklace. "Your necklace is just like mine! Did someone special give it to you?" She holds up her necklace for me to see.

"Oh..." I slap my hand over it.

"Nonna Rossi gave it to her, along with the house." That deep baritone rumbles through me, causing goosebumps to break out along my skin. Turning, I bite down on my tongue to keep it from lolling out across the floor. Lorenzo's leaning against the door jamb leading into a hallway, presumably where the café is located. His muscular arms are crossed over his chest, causing his white dress shirt to stretch tight. He's wearing gray dress slacks, a black belt, and black dress shoes. His dress shirt is casually unbuttoned at the collar, showing a v of tanned skin, and his sable-brown hair is artfully tousled. I quietly groan, trying like hell to return my attention to Fiore, who is speaking rapidly in Italian.

"My sister says I'm being rude," he says, looking like he's not in the least bit sorry for it.

"Seems to be a trend with you," I mutter. The door jingles, saving me from his intense stare. A pretty raven-haired girl in her twenties swings in.

"*Buongiorno! Che bella giornata.*"

"*Sí*, it is beautiful today," Lorenzo translates for me, his hazel eyes pinning me to the spot. Nina eyes me curiously.

"*Chi è? È un turista? Sembra Americana.*"

Fiore frowns and steps forward. "Nina, this is Summer Andrews. She *is* American and will be working here for the summer until Cristina comes back. Her Italian isn't great, so we will help her out, *sí*?"

Nina gives me a dismissive once-over before she pours a little olive oil into a dish and rubs it along her lips. She turns her attention to Lorenzo. "*Lorenzo sei proprio da mangiare stamattina. Vieni con me a fare il tour insieme?*" she purrs, her voice low and smoky.

Fiore rolls her eyes while Lorenzo straightens from the wall and clears his throat. "No, I will not be joining you on tour today. I have business meetings all day, but Carlo will be available if you need help."

Nina's lips twist into a frown. "*Carlo puzza come un maiale.*"

Lorenzo scowls in return. "Carlo does not stink like a pig, Nina. Please speak English around Summer and help her with Italian when she needs it. Fiore, I'll be back at lunchtime with Mamma and Nonna." His liquid gaze settles on me, and I immediately feel heat pooling in my nether regions. Jesus, just a glance from this man has me simpering like a wet noodle. "Summer, let Fiore or Nina know if you have questions. Try not to break any pipes at the farm this morning." A hint of a smile ghosts across his lips.

"Hilarious. I'll try not to," I say. Nina's eyes dart between us, a sour expression marring her pretty face.

"Okay, Summer, let me show you the computer and where we keep the appointments for tours and tastings. You can keep your things back here." Fiore ushers me to an office.

"I don't think Nina is happy I'm here," I admit, setting my things down on a chair.

"Don't worry about her. She can be a bit...*drammatica*. She'll warm up to you. She doesn't like surprises, and you are most definitely a surprise."

"Does it upset you that your nonna gave me this necklace?"

Fiore peers over at me, her eyes twinkling. "Not at all.

Nonna is an excellent judge of character. She seems to sense things about people others can't see. She probably knew you would need protection while here…especially from Renzo. He can be intense." Fiore laughs and waves her hand. "But don't worry about him either. He's a tender ravioli under all that sauce."

I swallow past the knot in my throat. "I think he resents me being in the house down the hill."

"Probably, but oh well. It was Nonna's decision to make. Renzo can be like a child sometimes, but he'll get over it. Besides, you're here just for the summer, *sì*?"

"I—"

"I think Nonna just needed an excuse not to give the house to Renzo, and you showed up like *un segno*…a sign. She's not ready to say goodbye to her memories with Nonno quite yet. Renzo has all these grand plans to turn the house into a bed-and-breakfast—thinks it will bring more tourists in, but between you and me, the house is a dump. It's so old, it's falling apart. We need to bulldoze it to rubble." She cringes slightly. "Sorry, I mean, it's a lovely place to live. It's just old. Renzo did a couple of updates for Nonna before she moved up here. Anyway, let's get you logged in, and I'll show you the reservations and how to do the tastings."

She logs into the computer while my brain tries to catch up with her bubbly disposition. She goes over the reservations for the week. Luckily, there's an option to view them in English, and she shows me how to make the bookings and enter them into the computer. Next, she shows me where her reservation list is for the restaurant and how to print it out. Sometimes I will have to take calls for the café if the call gets bumped. She also gives me her and Lorenzo's cell numbers in case I need to reach either of them.

"Try some of the oil with the bread for the tastings today."

We walk back into the tasting room and find Nina checking her makeup in a mirror.

"Nina, I have to get started on today's lunch menu," Fiore tells her. "Can you show Summer how we do tastings? *Ciao!*"

Nina shrugs and puts her makeup away. I walk over to the sink and wash my hands.

"First, we set out the dishes. All the olive oil bottles are kept under here," Nina explains. She leans down and pulls the bottles from the cabinet under the bar. "They are all marked with which one you're pouring. We start with our refined olive oil. *È un po' insipido*, uh, it tastes bland, but it allows the customer to taste the difference. We only pour a little in the dish because people don't enjoy it as much."

I nod as she pulls another bottle out.

"This is virgin olive oil. It's what we use for cooking. It has a stronger flavor. Then we have our line of extra virgin oils. This is what customers love. We have a rosemary and garlic-infused one they can try. If customers press their own olives, then we have them taste it if they choose to."

"Oh wow, you can press your own olives here?"

"*Sí*, we're one of the few farms that have their own olive press. That's pretty much it. Serve each tasting with a piece of bread for them to dip into the oil. You can also have them try some olive tapenade, which we keep in the fridge, but that's just another dish to clean, so I don't offer it. You'll have to talk to Fiore about trying them." She shrugs and picks up her phone. "That's it."

"Seems simple enough. Were you doing the tastings before?"

"No, we had Cristina here, but she had a baby and is taking the summer off." She gives me another once-over before returning to her phone. "I told them I could handle it, but I guess they hired you."

"How long have you worked here?" I pour the oils in the dishes and slice off a piece of bread. I dip it in the first golden-green oil. It's good, but like she said, not much flavor.

"Two years," she says, typing on her phone. "But I've known the Rossi family forever."

The second oil is a bit more robust. I dip my bread in the green oil of the extra virgin oil. The bread melts on my tongue, flavor bursting in my mouth. I close my eyes and hum in appreciation. It is fruity and earthy and so incredibly fresh compared to anything I've tasted back home. "This is divine."

Nina looks over at me and frowns. "I don't think Fiore would appreciate you eating the customers' bread."

I take another bite of the bread, sopping in oil, and shrug. "Fiore said it was okay. She wants me to try the product before I have my first tasting, so I know what I'm talking about. And according to the calendar, there's a group coming in this morning."

Nina wrinkles her nose and turns from me. I collect the cups and bring them to the sink to wash. She may be upset I've taken Cristina's place, but it was Nonna's decision. I look over my shoulder at her and chew my bottom lip. Having to befriend a hostile coworker was definitely not on my bingo card for this trip.

"Nina?"

"*Sì?*" She doesn't look up as she picks at one of her nails.

"Thanks for helping me learn the ropes. I think you and I are going to work great together." I smile and try not to laugh at the confused look on her face. As my Grams used to say, kill them with kindness.

# Chapter 12

THE BELL JINGLES, announcing a visitor. I'm elbows-deep in suds cleaning up after our last tasting.

"*Ciao*, Lorenzo," Nina says silkily. I glance over my shoulder. Nina leans over the tasting bar, her cleavage not leaving much to the imagination. She straightens up when a petite woman follows Lorenzo into the store.

"*Ciao*, Nina. *Buongiorno*, Summer." Lorenzo's smooth voice rolls over my body like a fine Italian wine. He walks over to where I'm washing. His clean, masculine scent invades my senses in the most delicious way as he leans against the counter next to me. "How was your morning?"

I smile and turn off the water. "It was good. I was really nervous, and I fumbled a little talking about the olive oil, but Nina jumped in and helped. We had two couples from Germany, and they were very friendly. They bought a case of olive oil."

"Mmm, *bene*. You'll get the hang of it." He pushes away from the counter. "Summer, I'd like you to meet my mom, Stella."

I quickly dry my hands and turn around. Stella Rossi looks like an older version of Fiore. She pats Nina's hand and turns to me with a wide smile. "*Buongiorno*, Summer, it's lovely to meet you. I've heard a lot about you from Lorenzo and Mamma Rossi."

I smile nervously, my eyes darting to Lorenzo.

"Fiore said you'll be joining us for lunch today? I'd love to hear more about the adorable American woman my Renzo won't stop talking about."

Lorenzo snorts and shakes his head. "Mamma, *per favore smettila.*" He stuffs his hands into his pockets, looking chagrined. Stella waves her hand at him.

"Oh, well I—"

"*Sí! Mi piacerebbe...*I'd love to. We all go to lunch." Nina claps her hands, ignoring Lorenzo's steely gaze. She flips the front door sign to 'closed'.

"Lunch is the most important meal of the day in Italy." Smiling, Stella gently takes my arm, steering me down the hall. "Wait until you have Fiore's Bolognese. It's to-die-for."

The café is more like a beautiful fairy garden, with flowing fountains and blooms in every color, butterflies flitting from one bud to the next. It has a stunning view of the olive orchard below and distant rolling hills. Six tables with red umbrellas sit in the garden, four of them already occupied. Where did these people come from?

As if reading my mind, Stella leans in to me. "The café entrance is on the other side. There's a gift shop I help run that sells dishes, knickknacks, and kitchen utensils. People are encouraged to shop or wander around the gardens. If it's slow on your side, then you'll come help over at my shop."

Nonna Rossi is already seated at the table in a silk cream top and palazzo pants, which seems to be her signature outfit. Lorenzo dips down, kissing her cheek. "Renzo, I was hoping you'd invite Summer to lunch." Nonna smiles affectionately at me and pats the seat next to her. "You sit here by me."

"*Ciao*, Signora Rossi."

"*Ciao*, Nina," Nonna Rossi says, pursing her lips.

A man with black hair dressed in a black apron approaches the table. "*Buongiorno, famiglia!* Ah, you must be Summer." He bows, his vivid blue eyes sparkling. "I'm Fredo, your humble servant. What can I get you to drink?"

"Two bottles of red, Fredo, and sparkling water, *per favore*," Lorenzo answers for the table.

"*Sí, sí.* The special today is Bolognese. I will bring out some antipasti."

My stomach rumbles as the delicious aromas drift out into the garden.

"Fiore doesn't have a menu here. It's pretty much what she makes is what you get," Stella explains.

"But no one ever complains. Fiore is a genius in the kitchen," Lorenzo adds.

"Unless you're *vegetarian*," Nina jokes, but it falls flat. Nonna Rossi glares at her.

"Summer, have you toured the farm yet?" Stella asks.

"No, not yet."

"I'm sure Renzo can take you this afternoon." Stella smiles.

I choke on the sparkling water Fredo poured me. "Oh, I'm sure he has plenty to do without having to give me a tour," I say, feeling Lorenzo's gaze wash over me.

"She can jump on the two p.m. tour with me." Nina examines her reflection in the spoon, making a pouty face.

"No. Lorenzo takes her," Nonna Rossi demands.

"I have a meeting at two, but we can go right after lunch, *sì*?" Lorenzo says, checking something on his phone.

"Uh, sure, if it's not too much trouble."

"Lorenzo is *always* busy," Nina gripes. "Giving a tour to a store girl is the last thing he needs to do. You're putting him out, Summer."

My eyes widen, and my cheeks are on fire as I look around the table. *Hello awkward, my old friend.*

"Honestly, I don't need—"

"Nina, *fatti i fatti tuoi*," Nonna Rossi says sharply.

"Nonna." Lorenzo gives his grandmother a warning glance. "It will be fine, Nina. Summer is not putting me out."

Everyone at the table stares at Nina, except me, because I'm gulping my wine. I'd like to hide under the table until closing time.

"What did I say? I must have used the wrong English words." Nina types away on her phone, oblivious to the tension she caused.

"*Ci scusiamo.* Nina, vieni qui," Nonna says, scooting her chair back. Lorenzo helps her up from the table.

"Nonna Rossi *è molto drammatica*," Nina grumbles before excusing herself from the table to follow Nonna.

Fredo and Fiore bring out plates heaped with pasta. "This here is pappardelle all'anatra. This one is penne alba fiesolana, and this one is tortelli Mugellani with olives and sausage. *Mangiare, bere e godere!* Eat, drink, and enjoy." Fiore kisses her mom and brother's cheeks before moving on to check on another table.

I groan after tasting the first bite. The food is orgasmic.

The flavors roll over my tongue, tasting of sunlit hills and warm breezes, of shady tree-lined roads, open pastures, and calm seas. I open my eyes to find Lorenzo staring intently at me. His eyes darken into stormy gray pools. His gaze drifts to my lips.

"Did I moan out loud? Sorry, I can't help myself. This food is incredible."

"It's always a pleasure to watch someone enjoy Fiore's cooking for the first time." Stella laughs. "Have you always lived in California?"

"Born and raised." I smile. "I love it, but it's getting expensive to live there. The weather is perfect, but the taxes are very high and the traffic is awful."

"Sounds like Rome," she says. "Do you have a boyfriend?"

"Oh, um…" I pick up my wineglass and gulp.

"She's single," Nonna Rossi says loud enough for the next town over to hear, as she returns to the table.

"Such a pretty girl not to have a boyfriend, don't you think, Renzo?"

"Mamma, *smettila di molestarla.*" Lorenzo glares at his mom.

Stella waves him off. "And what do you do in California?"

"I'm a graphic designer."

"Oh, how wonderful! I can't find my way around a computer to save my life. That's why I stick to the shop."

"Don't let her fool you, Summer. Stella Rossi is one of the sharpest women I know. She could run Rossi Olive Oil blindfolded." Lorenzo leans back and grins.

"Ah Renzo, *basta.*" Stella blushes.

"Her friend says that Summer loves to cook and clean. She's a baker," Nonna pipes up.

*Wait, what? Is she talking about me?* I groan remembering when Harrison told her I could be a baker.

"Wonderful, Summer! Perhaps you and Fiore can cook together," Stella says.

"Oh, wait. No, you misunderstood, Nonna. I'm not a baker or a cleaner. I mean, I'm not awful, like burning-toast horrible, but nothing like this…and I don't clean." *Backpedal, Summer.* "I'm *clean*…tidy, but I don't clean people's houses for a living. Of course, I can vacuum with the best of them, but…" My voice trails off as Nonna and Stella stare at me with quizzical amusement. I press my lips together.

Lorenzo chuckles and pours more wine.

Thankfully, Nina returns to the table and the conversation is dropped.

"Ready, Summer?" Lorenzo asks after Fredo clears our plates.

"I'm so full. Are we walking?" I stand, holding a hand over my stomach, the wine and afternoon sunshine making me groggy.

"You'll get used to eating Italian food after a while." Lorenzo pushes his chair back in. "The key is small bites and portions. We'll take a golf cart."

I stop him by placing my hand on his arm. "You don't have to give me a tour. I can go with Nina later." Although I'm a hundred percent positive she'd *accidentally* run me over with the golf cart.

He looks at my hand and then up at me. "*Lo voglio*

*far*...I want to."

I drop my hand and turn to Nonna Rossi and Stella. "*Grazie*...er, for lunch."

"*Grazie per il pranzo.*" Lorenzo grins.

"*Grazie per il pranzo*," I repeat, earning a big smile from him. Nonna Rossi wraps me in a hug before roughly pushing me toward Lorenzo. For such a delicate-looking woman, I'm amazed by her arm strength. Nina excuses herself and heads toward Fredo.

"Have fun." Stella winks at me before helping Nonna Rossi toward the French doors.

LORENZO AND I walk through the café out to another parking lot out back by the Rossi buildings. We approach what looks to be a mini Rolls Royce. "Wow, is that a golf cart?"

Lorenzo chuffs, sliding into it. "It's a Garia design out of Denmark. They are modeled after a Mercedes Benz."

"Fancy," I muse, running a hand over the custom leather seats that are nicer than my car.

"Ready?"

"Ready." I brace myself for a bumpy ride, but the golf cart takes off smoothly.

Lorenzo points toward the olive groves. "My great-grandfather bought the farm with twenty trees at the turn of the century. We now have two hundred acres." I hear the note of pride in his voice, and it makes me smile. "The busiest time of year at the farm is during harvest season in November. We store the olive oil in the cellars underneath the farmhouse here."

We pull up next to a large warehouse.

"I'm confused. Where is the farmhouse?"

Lorenzo chuckles. "Sorry, we call this building the farmhouse because it's where the original structure was. We needed a large space for storage when the temperatures drop to freezing."

"What happens during the summer?"

"During the summer, we take care of the trees, get ready for harvest, and promote the tourism of the farm. This isn't just an old olive farm, it's a multibillion-dollar business. The corporate offices are in that building over there." He points to a one-story building with large windows, designed to match the villa.

"It's really impressive," I say, nodding my head in appreciation, which earns me a devastating smile.

We stop at an overlook next to a stone wall and get out. I sit down and take pictures of the beautiful rolling hills and the town tucked down into a valley. I breathe in the clean air and soak in the sunshine. I feel on top of the world up here.

"It's beautiful, Lorenzo...*bello*."

He sits down next to me. "Please, call me Renzo or Ren. All my friends do."

My heart does a jumping jack. *Are we friends now?* "How do you know which trees produce black olives and which produce green?"

"They are one and the same. Green olives are normally

picked in September or October. Black olives are ripened green olives we pick in November. Green olives have more antioxidants, while black olives, as they mature, contain more water and oil. We mainly grow Frantoio and Leccino varieties, which are best for olive oil production. We handpick all of our olives to preserve nature and to make our lives more difficult." He throws me a grin. "But that's the way my great-grandfather did it, so we carry on the tradition."

"Wow, how long does it take to pick a tree?" There are rows and rows of olive trees sloping down the hillside. I can't imagine the amount of people they have working here.

"Traditional way is three to four pickers per tree, taking them about an hour to rake off the olives, or we use a *scuittatore* to shake the olives from the branches. Then we wrap up the nets and dump the olives into large crates. We harvest in the morning and crush in the afternoon. The olives then go into a conveyor belt where all the leaves are blown off. We compost the leaves, and the olives go into the mill where they are washed. The oil and water are separated from the skins to make Olio Nuovo. The first oil from the olive. Oil is stored in large tanks and bottled on demand. Bottles are green to prevent light from getting to the oil, and then a machine labels them with Rossi Olive Oil. It's a lot more complicated than my brief description, but you get the idea. If I really got into production, your eyes would glaze over."

"I think it's fascinating to see how it all gets made. I love learning new things." I glance over at his profile.

"Maybe on a day I'm not so swamped with meetings, I

can show you the bottling facility."

"Thank you, I'd love to see it." I marvel at the trees in the orchard below us. "That's a lot of trees to handpick. Nina kind of explained the difference between extra virgin and regular olive oil, but you can definitely tell by the taste."

"Extra virgin, the highest-quality oil, is produced without any chemicals in a cold press and has the lowest acidity levels. Virgin, the next best, also unrefined but has a slightly higher acidic level than extra virgin. Then there's refined, a cheaper, commonplace oil with higher acidity, and lastly pure, a blend of extra virgin and refined olive oil with the highest acidity."

"I feel like I should be taking notes."

He looks over at me and his lips curve, making my heart thrum unevenly. He's so attractive, and he doesn't even try. "*Sí*, there will be a quiz at the end of the tour."

"I'd ace it." I crack my knuckles.

He gives me a dubious look and I laugh. "Okay, probably not."

"I'm happy you're showing interest. I'm kind of a nerd when it comes to olives. It's my passion." His eyes sparkle and my blood hums in response to his enthusiasm. "On another day, I'll take you to the press and let you taste fresh-pressed olives. It's otherworldly."

"I'd really enjoy that."

"I'm happy you want to learn." He bumps his shoulder with mine.

I swallow past the rumbling nerves his touch alighted. I clear my throat and take in the picturesque landscape. "Is it true you're not supposed to eat an olive right off the tree?"

"*Sí*, they are very bitter. You have to cure them first." He smiles lazily at me.

"You were hoping I'd have bitten into one, weren't you?"

"Perhaps when I first met you." He chuckles.

"Hey," I cry in mock protest, elbowing his side.

"Just teasing you. I save those moments of pleasure for my sworn enemies."

"I'm not a sworn enemy?"

"No, Summer," he says, tucking a lock of wayward hair behind my ear. I freeze, my lunch doing flip-flops in my stomach. "*Non potrei mai odiarti.*"

I swallow past the nervous ball of energy and lose myself in his grayish-green eyes flecked with gold. "I don't know what that means."

Lorenzo leans in, sucking the breath right from my lungs. He's so close that if I lifted my chin, my mouth would meet his. His words whisper over my lips like soft fluttering butterfly wings, our breaths mingling. "*Non potrei mai odiarti…*I could never hate you."

His cellphone rings, halting the magical spell he's put me under. He groans and sits back, pulling his phone from his pocket. "*Sí…*"

Was Lorenzo going to kiss me? Did I want him to? I take in his profile while he talks on the phone. He has the classic straight Roman nose and a strong jawline. There's a faint scar on his upper lip, and his silky dark hair needs a fresh cut. The wind lifts his hair and I practically have to sit on my hands so I don't twine my fingers through it. The beautiful cadence of his accent soothes my nerves. Hell yes, I want Lorenzo Rossi to kiss me. He puts his phone away and stands up, offering me his hand.

"*Mi dispiace*, Summer. I'm sorry, I have to take you back. A supplier showed up for an impromptu meeting and she's waiting for me. Sometime this week, I'll clear some time in my schedule and give you a tour of the mill where we press the olives."

"Of course, no problem." I place my hand in his, and he helps me up off the wall. He pauses and I think maybe he'll pull me into his chest and kiss me senseless. *Yes, please.* But instead, he smiles and walks me to the cart. We drive the short distance back to the café. "*Arrivederci*, Ren."

"*A presto*, Summer." He waves and pulls away, heading in the direction of the corporate offices.

The wind whips around my sundress while I finger the gold horn around my neck. Indeed, Fiore was right about Nonna Rossi giving me the necklace. My heart might need protection from Lorenzo Rossi.

# Chapter 13

I GRAB MY clothes off the line in the backyard, noting the dark clouds rolling in. A big fat raindrop bounces off my cheek, announcing the impending storm. The violent wind whips up, practically knocking me over. I grab my basket and run into the house before I get blown across the yard. Ominous thunder rumbles in the distance while I run around the house closing all the open windows. A gust of wind blows the kitchen door open, causing it to crack against the wall. A scream rips from my throat as a brown streak darts into the house before I can bolt the door. I hope that was Razzo and not some other wild animal.

Lightning flashes, thunder answering a heartbeat later, causing the house to shake. Please, God, don't let this old place crumble to the ground. The rain rushes in on the wind, pouring down in sheets. I light a candle in case the power goes out and place it on the coffee table, snuggling into the couch. I try to distract myself from the thunderstorm raging outside by checking my email on my phone. My finger scrolls through junk emails, looking for one in particular from my boss, Allen Krantz. It's weird that he hasn't responded to my request to work remotely this summer.

A sizzling sound has me glancing over at the candle. It flickers and then snuffs out. I get up and head into the kitchen to grab the lighter. A loud clap of thunder rumbles the house, making me jump. I love a good summer storm, but being alone in this big house is making me a touch nervous. Snatching the lighter, I race back into the family room, relighting the candle. It fizzles out as soon as I sit back down. Dammit. I lean over the candle and wince when a drop of water plops on my head. A leak in the roof? Great. Another thing to add to the list for Nonna.

I'm heading back into the kitchen to grab a pot when a loud whip-like crack hits the windows and the lights go out. Screaming, I run for the kitchen stairs so I can hide in my bedroom under my covers. I may be thirty-six, but the dark still scares the shit out of me. Lightning flashes and illuminates the stairwell. My pulse kicks up a notch while I picture an ax murderer meeting me on the stairs. I stumble in the pitch black until I realize I have the flashlight feature on my phone. Lighting up my bedroom, I quickly scoot under the covers. Raindrops plop around me through the Swiss-cheese roof. Another flash of lightning lights up the room.

"One one-thousand, tw—"

Thunder booms, making the house shake again. Razzo meows pitifully next to the bed. I peek out from under the covers, and he's looking at me with sad, scared eyes. I lift the quilt.

"Come on, Razzo."

He leaps under the covers and settles behind my knees. A million fleas are probably jumping off into my bed right now, but I don't care. Razzo and I are riding out this storm together. A text message flashes across my phone.

***Lorenzo Rossi:*** *Summer, are you okay? The lights went out at the villa but have turned back on. Are yours on?*

***Me:*** *Lights are out here. The roof is leaking.*

I wait a few minutes, but give up when he doesn't respond. He's probably just worried about the house and wants to make sure a lightning strike doesn't burn it down. Oh God, now *that* scenario is running through my brain. I'm going over all the closest exits when a banging sound downstairs has me tossing the covers off. Did a window fly open, or is someone at my door? Maybe I imagined the noise because I don't hear it again. Probably a tree branch slamming against a window. No sane person would be out in this storm. A raindrop hits me right on the eyebrow and drips down into my eye. "Gah!"

Footsteps pound up the stairs, a beam of light slicing the darkness. Screaming, I look around for something to clock the intruder in the head with. I grab Razzo, who howls in protest.

"Don't kill me!"

"Summer, calm down. It's me, Ren." He sets his lantern on my bedside table. I shine my phone light in his face, holding onto the cranky, squirmy cat with the other hand.

"*Dio Santo!* Can you get that light out of my eyes?"

I put my phone down. "Sorry, I thought you were an ax murderer. What are you doing here?"

"Is that Razzo?" His handsome features splitting into a grin. I let go of the cat, who proceeds to hightail it out of the room. "I never would have predicted you two would become friends."

"We're not."

"A pair of grouchy companions snuggling together like two peas in a pod." Lorenzo chuckles. "Who would have thought?"

"No one, because we're not." I pull the sheet up to my chin. Raindrops cling to his wet, dark hair and bead against his black raincoat. "Look, I'm glad you came over to talk about how I have the same demeanor as the grumpy stray house cat, but you can run along now. I'm fine." I shoo him away with my hand.

"Do thunderstorms always make you this cranky? I came to check on you. I did a quick search downstairs, and it appears the living room has several leaks. I'm not sure it's a good idea for you to stay here." He removes his raincoat, and I can't help but appreciate how good he looks in a black t-shirt that looks tailored just for him.

"Oh ho, no you don't, mister. I'm not leaving this house so you can call it dilapidated or unfit to live in and take it back. I'm staying right here." I cross my arms and two raindrops bounce off my cheek and forehead. "I might drown in the process, but I'm not leaving."

Sighing, Lorenzo runs his hands through his wet hair. I zero in on the sliver of hard muscle exposed underneath his shirt when it lifts with the movement. "You're acting ridiculous."

"Really? Are you telling me you no longer wish to turn this house into a bed-and-breakfast?"

"I'm telling you to quit being stubborn and come stay at the villa tonight to stay warm and dry. We have a generator and our roof isn't leaking. You can return to this dump in the morning."

I rear my head back in indignation. "This house is not a dump!" Two more raindrops drip on my head. Lorenzo's eyebrow lifts. "I can't leave Razzo."

"You don't even like the cat," he huffs.

"Well, we've bonded tonight. He's scared, and I refuse to leave him alone during this hellacious storm."

"*Mannaggia*," he grumbles under his breath. Thunder claps loudly, causing me to jump. "Move over, *randagia*."

"What?"

"Pretty sure I spoke English. *Spostati*, move over." He grabs the blanket off the end of the bed. Hesitating, my eyes rove over him, head to toe, before I scooch over. My self-defense instructor, Marcos, is screaming in my head this is all kinds of wrong, and that I'm putting myself in a compromising situation. *What are you thinking, Summer? I'm not thinking, Marcos, so zip it. You'd understand if you saw how gorgeous Lorenzo is.*

He toes off his boots and stretches out on the bed next to me.

"You smell like summer rain and your shirt is damp," I say, nervous by his proximity. Marcos is screaming in my head for me to knee him in the balls and run, but I don't want to.

Without warning, he sits up and pulls his t-shirt off. My mouth drops open while I take in all his tanned, glorious muscles.

"I didn't mean…shirt…take off…" My brain can't keep up with what my eyes are drinking in.

He pauses and quirks an eyebrow. "Razzo got your

tongue, *randagia*?"

"Hm, huh?" My eyes flash to his before quickly resuming their perusal of the ridges in his abdomen. It's like I've never seen a man with muscles before. I'm itching to run my finger over his pecs and follow the dusting of hair that leads down into his pants. On top of the mouth-watering physique, I'm mesmerized by his heady smell, rain mixed with his own signature scent.

"Should I take off my pants too?"

"Yes, you most definitely should," I say, biting down on my lower lip. A brief clip of him doing a striptease plays in my head. Marcos is rolling his eyes and throwing his hands in the air. *I know, Marcos, I know. I'm an idiot.*

Lorenzo chuckles. "Are you sure? I'm not wearing any *calzoncini*."

I shake my head to clear the porn video broadcasting in my brain. "Wait. Did you just ask me for a calzone? Right now?"

He snorts and shakes his head. "Summer, you asked me to take off my pants. I'm not wearing boxer briefs...*calzoncini*."

I have the hottest guy in Italy in bed with me, shirtless, with his fingers on the buttons of his jeans. It's been verified he's not wearing underwear, and I ask him if he wants a calzone? *What the fuck, Summer?*

"Wait, wait, I can't think with you all shirtless and muscly and smelling like rain. I meant, *please do* keep your pants on and your shirt." I pick up his t-shirt and throw it on his chest. I currently hate responsible me.

I roll over, turning my back on Lorenzo, and sandwich

my hands under my head, so I don't do anything stupid with them, like skim my fingertips along his silky skin.

"You can go. I'll be fine here."

"Did you know you have several leaks in here?"

"I'm aware. Thanks."

He adjusts his pillow. "How can you sleep in this bed? It's too soft."

"I *can't* sleep if you keep yapping."

He chuckles next to me, and it makes my insides gooey. Is it weird Lorenzo is lying in bed next to me? Yes, one thousand percent it is. But it's also kind of nice having him here. He's much warmer than Razzo, he doesn't carry fleas, and he smells better too. He's also incredibly sexy and wet from the rain, and he *did* come to check on me, so it would be mean to send him back out into the storm.

Thunder shakes the house, and I jump again.

"Do thunderstorms scare you?" he asks quietly. His fingers softly drift through my hair. I freeze at first, but then relax because it feels amazing and I don't want him to stop.

"A little. Why are you being so nice to me?"

He sighs. "Tell me about your favorite thing so far in Italy."

"My favorite thing?" I ask drowsily, sedated by his magical fingers. "That's a toss-up between the pizza and gelato."

"We do have the best. I know of a secret place for pizza. I will have to take you there. I should warn you about the gelato, though. They are a tourist trap."

"A tourist trap?" I turn over and face him, frowning. "Please don't ruin gelato for me."

"I wouldn't dream of it." He takes his index finger and

presses it to the corner of my mouth and pushes up. "You're pretty when you smile."

I huff out a laugh and swipe his hand away, the butterflies beating wildly in my stomach. "Tell me about the gelato traps."

"Italy is trying to make it illegal to sell bad gelato. So here are the rules." He repositions the pillow under his head, bringing his serious face closer to mine. "Rule number one. Never go for the bright-colored gelato that looks like a *puffo*…um, a Smurf. *Non va bene.* Gelato should be earth tones. For example, pistachio gelato is brown, not green.

"Rule number two, never get the gelato that is swirled in mounds like a puffy cloud where you can see a pound of it sitting in the case. Gelato should be stored in flat metal containers with lids. And last, gelato should not have vegetable oil or unnatural flavors in its ingredients."

"So not only are you an olive aficionado, but a gelato one as well? I'm impressed." *And incredibly turned on by his husky voice.*

"Well, just looking out for you." He smiles and I want to bring his lips to mine.

"What else should I look out for?"

"Italian men."

I giggle. "Does that include you?"

"Most definitely me." His brows pinch. "But seriously, Summer. Italian men are very forward. Obnoxious even."

"You don't say?" I tease, arching an eyebrow. "Does that happen to include men who come over during a rainstorm and try to take off their clothes?"

"Yes, they are the worst. Stay far away from those guys."

His teeth grab his bottom lip and he blows out a breath before giving me a lopsided smirk. "You make me do idiotic things."

"*I* make you? I'm pretty sure that was all you, buddy."

His eyes drift to my lips and back to my eyes. "You have the most beautiful eyes, Summer. Like liquid copper. And the cutest dusting of freckles."

"That's very forward of you, Mr. Rossi," I murmur.

"*Sí, mi dispiace.*" He averts his gaze. "See? I told you. Stay clear of Italian men."

"You realize that's going to be quite challenging, living in Italy and all."

"Hmm." He brushes a lock of hair off my cheek. "Tell me what you like to do back home."

"I like to read, go to the movies, go for walks. Hang out and drink wine with my best friend Cara and her husband Damien. What about you?"

"Not much free time for me, I'm afraid. But I like to work out and read as well."

I imagine Lorenzo, shirtless, with a hot pair of reading glasses on, lifting a barbell in one hand, and reading a book in the other. *Heaven have mercy, Marcos, my willpower isn't that strong.* I snuggle in closer to the amazing heat his body is giving off. "What do you like to read?"

"Thrillers. You?"

"Romance." I smile lazily. "I especially love romances with hot Italian men."

"Hmm. Turn over." He shifts and I turn my back to him. He pulls me into him, and it feels so perfect being spooned by him, like he's my shelter in the storm. It's taking all my strength to keep my eyes open. I don't want to miss one minute of this.

"What's your favorite thing?" I mumble.

"Thunderstorms on a summer night next to a gorgeous woman."

"Smooth-talker...Someone warned me about guys like you."

He makes a deep humming noise and pulls the blanket over us.

"Summer, I think the storm is finally leaving." His voice sounds like a purr in my ear as sleep tries to pull me under. "I should go."

"Don't go, Razzo. Stay."

"*Buona notte, il mia piccola gatta randagia.*" That rumbling timbre goes through me like the departing thunder and makes me want to slide my thighs apart.

It feels so nice to have him wrapped around me while I fall asleep.

When I wake in the morning, alone, I wonder if I dreamed the whole thing.

# Chapter 14

I HAVEN'T SEEN Lorenzo since the storm two days ago. I've looked for him around the farm, but decided it's foolish of me to indulge in a one-sided obsession with my boss. But every time the bell above the door rings, I can't help but hope it's him. It's been ages since I've had a crush like this. I haven't even kissed the man, but I'm obsessed with his scent, his smile, and the sound of his voice. I'm a lovesick fool and it's pathetic.

I'm finishing up with a group of American tourists who keep raving about the fresh-pressed olive oil and how they'll have to make a trip back next year to pick and press their own.

"Have you done it yet, Summer?" Kira, the bubbly brunette from Georgia, asks me. "We didn't get to press olives, but we got to try some right out of the stainless-steel vats. It was incredible."

"No, I haven't had a chance to see the mill yet. We've been so busy with tastings and tours." I smile and slice more fresh-baked bread for them. It's nice to talk to people from the States. I didn't realize how much I missed the connection of familiarity. Everyone in Italy has been incredibly kind, but hearing an American accent is oddly comforting.

"Well, make a point of getting over there. It's so much

fun."

I smile, dishing out some olive tapenade for them. "I will."

"Chuck, we need to buy a vat of this stuff!" Kira shouts to her husband, who holds up two fingers to me. I giggle and write down their order.

After chatting with them a bit longer, I walk their group over to the gift shop and convince them to stay for a late lunch, because Fiore's cooking is out of this world. I decide to head over to the mill on my break, and Stella happily gives me directions. I choose to walk instead of taking a golf cart, enjoying the late-afternoon breeze.

The air is cool and earthy as I enter an old stone building flagged with terracotta floors and bricked archways. There's a large stone fireplace and an ancient-looking round contraption of wood and stone that looks like a firepit with a crank handle and press. This equipment looks antique. I can't imagine this old stone wheel cranking out thousands of bottles of olive oil. I bend down and pick up an old woven basket.

"Looking for something, *randagia*?"

I pop up at the sound of his voice, my heart pounding at being caught snooping. "Jesus, you're like a ninja."

He shakes his head and grins. "I'll be sure to announce myself next time. Do you need something?"

"I was looking for the mill, but I have a feeling this isn't it."

He rubs his hand along his jaw, his eyes dancing. "Well, this used to be the mill. The donkey would walk in a circle, turning the stone that would grind the olives to a pulp. But when he died, we upgraded."

I look back at the mill. "Poor donkey," I whisper.

"Don't worry, that donkey was spoiled rotten by Nonno Rossi and did not die tragically walking in circles here. He was retired out to the pastures where he lived out many years under the blue Tuscan skies. We still have his descendants out in the back paddock." He winks at me, causing my heart to do double-time. "I can show you the new and improved mill."

"Oh, I know you're busy. You can just point the way."

"No offense, Summer, but I can't have you wandering around the mill aimlessly. One of my guys will call me and tell me there's a *bella ragazza Americana* lost in the mill. I have some time."

My stomach does a quick flip over him calling me beautiful. "Thank you, that's very generous of you."

We walk outside of the old mill to a large contemporary warehouse behind the ancient stone building I saw on my first day here. He hasn't mentioned the storm and I'm beginning to wonder if the other night really was just a dream. A figment of my overzealous imagination. He's all business talking to me as if I were a stranger touring the facility. We step inside and he hands me a paper hairnet, jacket, and gloves. He puts on his own gear, and the jerk still looks hot as sin.

"Okay, so this is where we send the olives after they've been washed." He guides me over to a conveyor belt. "Once they're done here, they go into this machine called the melaxer, which crushes them and mixes the paste. Then it goes into a centrifuge where the oil is separated from the paste."

"Why aren't the machines running now?"

"Olives have to be pressed right after they're picked. We can't store the olives and press them whenever we want. They lose their flavor and antioxidants. This place is a hive of activity in the fall."

"But I thought you stored olives underneath?"

"*Sí*, we store those underneath the farmhouse for the tapenade and lower-grade oil. You were paying attention." Smiling, he places his hand on my lower back, guiding me over to a row of floor-to-ceiling stainless-steel drums. "This is where we store the olive oil." He grabs a glass and draws fresh olive oil, handing it to me. "*Olio nuovo.*"

I take a sip of the golden-green liquid, and my eyes roll back in my head. "Wow, this is incredible. It's fruity, earthy, spicy, and…indescribable!"

Lorenzo laughs and takes the glass from me, taking a small sip. "Mmm, *molto buono.*" He hands the glass back to me, his eyes sparkling. "I wish you could be here for harvest season. The farm is alive with excitement. *Vieni*, I want to show you what we use for tourists."

His fingers brush against mine as we pass by where they bottle and label the oil. A thrilling jolt makes my insides tingle. I stop and take a video to send to Cara, enthralled with how fast the bottles are labeled and capped. We enter another building which looks similar to the old stone building I first came upon. Following Lorenzo's lead, I rip off my paper hat, jacket, and gloves and stuff them in a trash can.

"This is where the tourists who have picked some olives

come and press with a stone press machine."

"So, the whole donkey thing was just for show?"

"No, no, we used the donkey, but this replaced him, and then as we grew, the machinery in the main building replaced this. Fiore and I had the idea of olive-picking tours where you press and drink the oil you harvested. That's usually in late August to September before it gets busy here."

I run my hand along the cold stone wheel and marvel over the history of this place. "*Grazie*, Lorenzo, for showing me all of this."

"*Grazie*, Summer, for wanting to learn about it." He lifts my hand, threading his fingers with mine. My breath catches at the intimate gesture, but I don't pull away. Relief floods through me. The other night *was* real. I try to quickly conjure up a pros and cons list in my head for having an Italian summer fling with Lorenzo Rossi, but I'm struggling to piece anything together.

All reasoning goes right out the window when he steps closer, his hand sliding to my waist. I'm positive he can hear my heartbeat thudding against my ribcage. He places the hand he was holding on to his shoulder and my fingers automatically slide into the silky hair at his nape. His hazel eyes turn to smoke, his lip curling into a sexy grin. I can barely breathe, my head spinning from our proximity.

"Summer, *voglio baciarti*."

"I…I don't know what that means," I stutter, desire racing through my blood. My tongue darts out to wet my lips.

"*Voglio baciarti*…I want to kiss you."

Hell yes, I *want* him to kiss me. It takes all my self-control not to rip his shirt off and pull him to me. My eyes close and my breath hitches in anticipation. His warm breath skates over my lips before his nose glides along my jaw. It's deliciously torturous. I arch into him, tilting my head, granting him better access. But the kiss doesn't happen. His lips never touch my skin. I open my eyes, my toes curled in anticipation.

His jaw clenches and his hands squeeze my waist as if he's fighting some internal battle to contain himself from ripping off my dress. Permission granted, Ren. Rip this sucker off.

"*Il tuo profumo mi fa impazzire*," he whispers next to my ear. His lips skim my neck and I shiver. I'm in serious trouble if this man is driving me wild with just a puff of breath along my skin and some Italian words. Hell, he's barely touched me, and I'm calculating how fast he can sit me up on the ledge of this stone press and have his wicked way with me.

Lorenzo's phone buzzes, and he growls in response. He drops his hands from my waist and takes a step back, pulling it from his pocket. My body screams in protest and my chest heaves, like I just sprinted for the last gelato cone at the stand. His molten stare burns a hole right through my panties while he says something rapidly in Italian to the person on the line.

He shakes his head, driving his fingers through his hair before hanging up. He takes a deep breath and turns from me. "I'm sorry, Summer, that shouldn't have happened. *Mi dispiace*, I don't know what came over me."

"Oh…" It's all I can manage as disappointment strangles

any last vestiges of simmering desire.

"I'll walk you back." He smiles, but it's perfunctory. Something's off. The hunger I saw in his eyes a few minutes ago is replaced with cold disinterest.

I hang back, my fist rubbing over my chest. "Um, Ren? What was that…I mean, what the hell just—?" I point between us.

His cheeks flush adorably, and he hangs his head sheepishly, stuffing his hands in his trousers. "*Mi hai stregato.*"

"English please."

His eyes meet mine, and they are liquid smoke. "You bewitch me, Summer Andrews, but I shouldn't have done that. I got carried away at the one place I'm supposed to be in total control. Being CEO of Rossi Olive Oil is my priority, and I lost focus for a moment. I'm sorry."

"I…bewitch you?" I want to kick myself for sounding so breathless. *I bewitch him?* He was right to stop whatever was about to happen between us. He's my boss and we're out in public where anyone could have walked in on us. But I can't help the looney smile from spreading across my face.

I, Summer Andrews, have put the oh-so-hot Lorenzo Rossi under a spell. *I am a bewitching badass.*

He takes my hand and leads me out of the mill. "Come on. Nina will be pacing, wondering where you are."

"I doubt that. She's probably hoping I'll get lost in the olive grove and can't find my way out."

"She'll soften, *randagia.* She's just trying to throw her weight around since you're new."

"Hmm, maybe." We walk in silence for a moment. "Can I ask a favor?"

"Of course, anything."

"Can you find another name for me besides *randagia*? It just doesn't seem very...um, friendly."

"Are we friends now?"

I glance over and the glint in his eye is teasing. He squeezes my hand.

"Well, we've spooned during a thunderstorm..." *And you mauled me with your sexy eyes a minute ago.* I shrug as heat crawls up my neck, feeling vulnerable under his stare.

"*Siamo amici.*"

"*Siamo amici.*" I test the words out as they roll over my tongue. *We're friends.* I should be happy he said them, but the little butterfly fluttering around in my stomach back in the old mill breaks a wing and takes a sudden nosedive. I'm so confused. Does he want to be friends or more? What do I want? I think I want more, but I want him to be all-in with me.

"What should I call you, then?" he asks, pulling me out of my funk.

"Huh?"

"You said you don't want me to call you *randagia*. You need an Italian nickname. What should I call you?"

"Hmm...how about something feminine and pretty, like rainbow or moonbeam?"

"I'll think of something." He chuckles. "Let's go this way. I want to show you one more thing." We veer to the left down into a grove of olive trees.

"I was kidding about getting lost in the trees, you know."

He lets go of my hand, and I immediately miss the connection. He steps up to a gnarled tree, the trunk twisted and aged. "See this tree? It was the first tree planted on Rossi Farms. It's over four hundred years old."

"Really? That's incredible it's survived so long." I run my hand along the gnarled wooden trunk. "Imagine what it has seen in those four hundred years."

"*Sí*. I come and sit under this tree when I need to think, or I'm having a bad day. Its ancient wisdom brings me solace." He peers up into the leaves, lost in his thoughts.

"It's beautiful, Ren. I hope it lives for four hundred more."

"Under my care, it will," he says wistfully, taking my hand and threading my fingers with his as we stand under the canopy of the tree. Late-afternoon sun dapples through the silver-green leaves, kissing our skin with sun and shadow. He tucks a lock of hair behind my ear, a tender expression in his eyes. I want him to kiss me, but he just smiles and leads me out of the grove. I kick myself for letting my heart go there. *Siamo amici* after all.

# Chapter 15

I AWAKEN TO the early morning chatter of birds through my open bedroom window and a soft morning breeze kissing my skin. I open my eyes and smile. I could wake up like this every day for the rest of my life. Checking my phone, I yawn and rub my eyes. It's seven thirty. I was hoping to sleep in a little on my first day off, but I'm too excited to go back to sleep. Throwing off the covers, I quickly do my morning skincare routine and get dressed. The sky is the limit on what I might do and where I might travel. I pull up the train schedule and head into the kitchen. A note on my kitchen table under a wooden bowl has me stopping in my tracks. That wasn't there last night.

*Amica mia, come outside when you wake up. —Ren*

I grab my purse and run to the front door, throwing it open. Ren is leaning against his car reading something on his phone, looking hotter than ever in a t-shirt, shorts, a baseball hat turned backwards, and a pair of black Wayfarers. He looks adorably American.

"What are you doing here?" I ask, sounding breathless.

"*Buongiorno*, Summer. It's Friday. You have the day off, *sì*?"

"Yes...but shouldn't you be at work?"

"I want to show you something." He shrugs, like it's no big deal he's playing hooky.

"Oh, um, okay. Actually, I was going to head to the train station and go somewhere." I look wistfully over my shoulder at the road that leads into town.

"Where?"

I toe the gravel with my shoe. "I haven't decided."

"Nah, this will be better. Come on." He opens the passenger door. I hesitantly walk over to him and climb in, leaning back against the buttery leather. He slides in next to me and I inhale the scent of woods mixed with mint and leather. It's heavenly. I could bottle it and sniff it obsessively.

"Where are we going?"

"Fiore asked me to run to San Miniato for some truffles and then I thought perhaps you'd like to come along and we can drive to Pisa and then up to a little hideaway called Isola Santa. It's a day trip though. Is that okay?"

"Yes, that would be amazing!"

"*Va Bene.*" He smiles before revving the engine, his tires spinning on the gravel as we speed away from the house. "I brought you a coffee." He points to the paper cup in the holder and I groan gratefully, making him smile. "So tell me, how are you able to take off so much time from work for the summer?"

"Um, I'm not." I take a sip of the espresso and stare out the window. "I'm waiting to hear from my employer to see if I can work remotely after my vacation days are up. But don't worry, it won't interfere with working at the farm. I can do it at night, which actually works better with the time difference."

"Ah, I see. What will you do if they say no?"

"Well..." I take a deep breath, remembering I'm sitting next to my other employer, who probably is wondering if I'm going to leave them high and dry.

He glances over at me before returning his eyes to the road. "Surely you've thought about what might happen if they say you can't work remotely."

"To be honest, I've been stuck in that job for years. It's a means to an end for me, not a passion. If they say no, then I've thought about freelancing."

"Hmm, that can't be easy...freelancing, especially while living in Italy."

"I have some contacts I could call on." I bite my lip, hoping like hell this will all work out. "Working in a job you no longer love isn't easy either."

"True. What are you *appassionato* about?"

"Passionate? Oh gosh, I don't think anyone has ever asked me that before."

"Would you still be a graphic designer if you could change your job?"

"Yes, but I love print-ad design. I kind of fell into the job at Granite right out of college and stayed with it because it was a steady paycheck and I knew what to expect. At the time, my grandmother was sick, and I needed something practical. There was never the excitement of having to think out of the box." I scrunch my brows together. Perhaps that's why I've outgrown it there. "I've always wanted to be a creative director in advertising."

"Hm..." Lorenzo scrubs his jaw. "Would you like to run some ideas by me for Rossi Olive Oil?"

"What...are you serious?"

He flashes me a sexy grin. "I never joke about business, *bella*. I'll pay you for your time."

I can barely keep myself from throwing my arms around him. "But don't you have an advertising team already on payroll?"

"Yes, but I'm the boss." He shrugs like it's no big deal running a multi-million-dollar business. "If I want to see some new creative work from someone else, I can."

"I bet you always get what you want, Lorenzo Rossi." Watching the countryside zoom by, excitement zips through my veins.

"Not always, *tesoro*." He shifts in his seat, tapping the steering wheel with his thumb, and glances at me as I glance at him.

"I'll come up with some ideas as soon as we get home."

"Good. I look forward to it. Ah, I'm sorry, never a day off I'm afraid." He picks up a call coming through and speaks rapidly in Italian. I sink into the leather and my thoughts get lost in the passing scenery.

An hour and fifty minutes later, he maneuvers the Maserati on to a long dirt road surrounded by woods. A small, weathered cabin with smoke curling out of the stone chimney stack stands at the end of the lane like a dreamy Thomas Kinkade painting. An older gentleman with a white beard, dressed in linen pants and a matching vest, waves at us from the front step. A King Charles spaniel bounces around him, barking.

"Where are we?"

"You'll see." Ren releases my seatbelt and quickly hops

out, waving to the man. "*Ciao, Zio Gino!*"

I gingerly open my door as the dog bounds toward the car. Gino shouts a command, which stops the dog in its tracks. Lorenzo walks around and helps me out of the car. "Summer, this is my great Uncle Gino Ferraro. He is Nonna Rossi's brother. He lives out here in the beautiful countryside of San Miniato and runs truffle tours with his sweet pup, Biscotti."

I shake hands with Uncle Gino. "*Buongiorno*, Gino." Biscotti circles around me and sits on her haunches, her tongue lolling to the side. "*Buongiorno*, Biscotti, *sei bellissima*." I run my fingers over her silky ears.

Uncle Gino gives a gap-tooth grin. "*Pronti a scovare qualche tartufo?*"

"Oh, um…" I turn to Ren for help.

"He asked if you're ready to hunt for some truffles."

"What exactly do you mean by hunt?" I survey our surroundings. "We're going into the woods to find them?"

"*Sí*, only the best for Fiore." Ren rolls his eyes and smiles. "Come on, *tesoro*, it will be fun. No guns or hurting animals involved. Tourists pay lots of money to have Uncle Gino help them find their treasured truffles."

I nod and smile at Uncle Gino. He claps Ren on the back and we start off into the woods, Biscotti zipping ahead. "If you're here in November, there's a huge truffle festival and a hunt for the rare white truffle only grown in these parts. It's a lot of fun and the food is out of this world—all made with truffles, of course."

"*Ho sempre i tartufo bianchi*," Uncle Gino mutters. "It was my father who had the largest truffle in nineteen fifty-four, not that *stronzo*, Rizzotti." He spits on to the ground.

I stumble over a small log and Ren quickly grabs my hand to steady me. "Uncle Gino said he always has white truffles in his woods. The largest truffle in the world was found back in nineteen fifty-four. Nonno Ferraro claimed it was found in these woods, but word got back to his competitor and neighbor, Fabrizio Rizzotti. Fabrizio stole it from him in the middle of the night and presented it to the Truffle Society as his the next day. Nonno Ferrari couldn't prove it, but both families knew the truth. Our families have been feuding since."

"Very Capulets and Montagues…without the star-crossed lovers." I laugh.

"*Rizzotti può mangiare le sue stesse palle*," Uncle Gino shouts, lifting his fist in the air.

"Uncle Gino wishes fervently for the Rizzottis to die a painful death."

"Wait, doesn't *mangiare* mean to eat? What does he want him to eat?"

Ren sighs, removing his hat, and runs his fingers through his hair. "*Mamma mia, tesoro*, don't make me say it."

I grin as his cheeks flush adorably. "What does Uncle Gino want Rizzotti to eat, Ren? I can always ask Nonna—"

"His own balls, Summer. Uncle Gino said Rizzotti can eat his own balls."

I laugh and swing our clasped hands back and forth while we walk. "That's a filthy mouth you've got there, Signor Rossi."

He side-eyes me and grunts.

"But I promise, lips sealed. I won't ever mention the

name Rizzotti or the great white truffle controversy."

"*Sí*, especially don't mention it around Nonna." Lorenzo squeezes my hand and chuckles. "It makes her…lose her mind."

"This is so fun. I never dreamed I'd be going truffle hunting." I smile up at him. "So, what are we looking for exactly?"

"*Cacca fossilizzata*," Uncle Gino says, trudging ahead of us.

"*Cacca*…uh, is that what I think it is?" I look over at Ren's profile. The sun filtering through the leaves dapples his rich brown hair. He looks like he's in a photoshoot titled, *truffle hunting by Ralph Lauren.*

He shakes his head and grins. "*Sí*, he said fossilized poop. It will look more like a light brown ginger root or a rock. We are looking for a black truffle called *Tartufo Nero Scorzone.* Biscotti will help find them. Uncle Gino used to use pigs to hunt for the truffles, but they kept eating them when they'd find them, so he switched to training dogs like Biscotti."

"Biscotti, good girl." Uncle Gino pats her side.

Sure enough, five minutes later, Biscotti barks at a spot in the woods. Leaning down, Uncle Gino picks up a black rock and sniffs it, his wrinkly face breaking into a smile. "*Tartufo Nero Scorzone.*"

He hands it to Ren, who also sniffs it then holds it out to me. I arch an eyebrow.

"Smell it, *tesoro.*" His eyes twinkle.

"It matches Uncle Gino's description accurately." I wrinkle my nose, causing him to laugh.

"*Credimi.*" His long black eyelashes frame the most beautiful greenish-gray irises, his soulful gaze holding mine. "Trust me."

I nod and clasp his wrist, leaning forward to smell the truffle. It's earthy scent transports me back to when I was little and helped my Grams in her garden, picking out the wild onion. "It reminds me of summer evenings."

"*Sí.* Black summer truffles are more mild than the winter ones. Black truffles have to be cooked, but white truffles can be eaten raw. Fiore will be thrilled."

Uncle Gino unearths a few more and Ren puts the truffles into a bag before we head back down the trail. We thank Uncle Gino and Biscotti and head back to the car.

"Can I ask you something?"

"Anything."

"I know how busy you are. Why are you out in the middle of the woods on a Friday morning gathering truffles for your sister? Your uncle could have brought them to her or she could have asked Fredo to do it."

"True, I could have sent someone to bring them to us, but then you would have missed out on a century-old tradition of truffle hunting…and I wouldn't have had the chance to spend the day with you."

I wonder if he can hear how loud my heart is pounding against my rib cage. "I—"

"Besides, everyone who comes to this region needs a Leaning Tower of Pisa picture." He opens the car door for me.

I settle back into my seat. "You mean a picture of me holding it in my hand?" I smirk.

"*Sì, esatto.* Friends don't let friends leave Italy without visiting the famous tower."

"Okay, friend." I shake my head, my feelings for him growing more confused than ever. Or maybe just…growing.

HE LOOKS OVER at the position of my hands, and nods. "Push the throttle gently. Your right hand." He shows me what to do on his Vespa.

"Oh God, I'm so nervous." I take a deep breath. "Just move my hand forward?"

"It's just like riding a bike."

"Look how well that turned out for me," I gripe, moving my hands over the black handlebars.

"Concentrate, *tesoro*. You can do this. Your grip should be relaxed, but firm."

"Relaxed, but firm. I can do this. Just like riding a bike," I repeat under my breath, pushing forward, but the handle doesn't turn. "Nothing's happening!"

"Your *other* right hand." Ren's lips twitch, while he patiently waits for me to figure out my left and right.

"This is insane." I wipe my sweaty palms on my shorts.

We rented the scooters to zip around Pisa. Ren said I needed the whole Italian experience. I think his plan is to try to kill me by Vespa so he can take back the house. Sweat breaks out on my brow as I push the right throttle forward. The Vespa lurches and I scream, my feet dragging across the pavement. The Vespa swerves back and forth. People on the sidewalk blur past me as I increase the speed. A horn blares from a man on a scooter charging right for me at full throttle.

"Summer, turn!" Ren shouts from behind me.

"Watch out," I shriek at the man. He honks his horn, gesturing wildly at me, yelling not-so-nice words in Italian while swerving around me.

"Oh God, I don't want to die today. Not on a Vespa." That was close…too close. I make a sharp right turn and head straight for a parked car.

"Brakes! Pull the brakes!" Lorenzo yells. My fingers wrap around the left handlebar brake and I jerk it back. The Vespa jolts and shakes. "Use both at the same time!"

My right hand moves to the brake lever instead of the throttle and I pull both brakes back. The Vespa comes to a stop, but not before bumping into a parked car. Lorenzo pulls up beside me and turns off his scooter.

"Oh God, oh my God, I hit someone's car. Did you see that guy screaming at me? We have to leave a note. We have to wait for them to get back and tell them what happened. Will my insurance pay for this? That jerk literally almost ran me over!"

"Summer, calm down." Lorenzo's voice soothes my frazzled nerves. He reaches around and turns off my Vespa. "The car is fine, not even a scratch. If you own a car in Italy, you expect someone to dent it. Don't worry about it." He helps me down and removes my helmet. "You're shaking. Are you okay?"

"I'm…" Tears threaten to spill over. Without asking, he wraps me in a hug, my face pressing into his chest. He murmurs something calming in Italian and I melt against him. My arms wrap around his waist and I cling to him, waiting for my pulse to resume to its normal beat.

"I almost died. I should come with a warning label. I'm terrible at driving Vespas. I shouldn't try to experience Italy," I say against his chest.

"I noticed." I can hear the smile in his voice. "Perhaps we'll just park this one and you can ride with me. Are you okay?" He moves me away from his t-shirt and rubs his thumb across my cheek. I'm already missing the warmth of being wrapped in his arms.

"I'm okay."

"Let me just roll this off the bumper," he teases, releasing me. He pulls the Vespa back and parks it against the curb. He climbs on his scooter and holds out my helmet, motioning for me to get on behind him. I slide onto the seat and gingerly place my hands on his waist. He takes my hands and wraps them around his middle so my chest is pressed flush to him.

"Hang on, *tesoro*."

I drop my forehead to his back and tighten my grip as he pulls out into traffic.

"I'll show you Tower of Pisa and the best pizza in the city and then we'll have gelato in Isola Santa, *sì*? But first you're going to have to loosen your grip. You're about to rip my shirt off." He pats my hand.

"Sorry." I loosen my hold on him a fraction. His body heat blocks the chill of the mid-morning breeze as we zip in and out of traffic. "Which city do you like better? Pisa or Florence?" I ask him.

"Definitely Florence, but it's opposite of where we were going today. If you'd like to go, I can take you and show you around another day."

I smile into his shirt. "I'd like that."

"*Perfetto.* Me too."

WE SPENT AN amazing afternoon in Pisa and Isola Santa, a tiny medieval town next to the most brilliant emerald-green lake tucked between two mountains reflecting the surrounding hills and blue sky. We walked across the dam and up the mountainside to an old, deserted town. The views were worth the hike that left me out of breath. Ren looked like he could have walked it in his sleep.

We sat at a little restaurant in the nearly deserted village looking out over the lake and chatted over cappuccinos about everything and nothing under the fading afternoon light, savoring our time together. It was *magnifico.*

He pulls into the crushed gravel courtyard in front of Casa Rossi and turns off the car, dusk clinging to the night sky.

"Would you like to come in?" I ask.

"Another time." He smiles. "I need to swing by the office to check on some things and give Fiore her truffles."

"Ah, yes. Truffle hunting seems like a lifetime ago." I unhook my seatbelt and turn toward him. "Thank you for today, Ren. I had an amazing day."

"Except for the Vespa."

"Except for that. I'm glad the company didn't charge you for the scuff mark." Heat blossoms on my cheeks as I give him a wobbly grin. "Well, I should go inside."

His beautiful, smoky hazel eyes lock on to mine. He brushes his thumb across my cheek, and the air between us stills. My lips part, unspoken words bouncing between us. He cups my jaw like he's going to pull me forward to his lips, but just as quickly, he drops his hand.

"Summer..."

"Yeah, Ren?"

"I had fun today, too. *Buona sera, tesoro.*"

"*Buona sera*, Ren."

I scramble out of the car and practically run inside the house before I do something ridiculous and beg him to kiss me. *Keep your head on straight. He just wants to be friends.*

I lean back against the front door and sigh, hearing his tires crunch over the gravel. There's definitely an attraction there. I know he feels it too, but he's holding back. I pull out my phone and look up the word *tesoro*; it means 'treasure' in Italian.

*O Dio mio*, I'm in trouble.

# Chapter 16

I OPEN THE kitchen door to gather the laundry drying on the line when I almost step on a dead mouse.

"Gah! Dammit, Razzo, stop leaving me these disgusting presents! We're even!" Razzo sits across the yard on the stone wall, ignoring me while he slowly licks his fur.

Ever since the storm, I've come home to find disembodied mice left on my back doorstep as if he were saying, *Ciao, annoying human lady. Here is a nice present for giving me shelter during the rain. Be grateful I bring you such wonderful gifts.* Gagging, I grab a biodegradable grocery bag and scoop up the mouse.

"*Niente più regali!*" I yell at him in Italian in case he doesn't understand English.

I dispose of the mouse in the trash. If Razzo's expression could be interpreted right now, he'd be giving me the middle finger. "Yeah, well, right back at you, buddy."

I pull the clothes off the line and fold them at the large kitchen trestle table.

"*Buongiorno*, Summer. Do you have company?" Nonna Rossi knocks on the open door leading to the side garden.

"*Buongiorno*, Nonna, come in." I smile when I see her holding fresh flowers and some cookies.

Sometimes I'll come home from work, and there will be

pasta or fresh bread waiting for me on the counter or the amazing fruit-centered cookies she's holding now. She reminds me so much of my Grams. I love when she pops by for a visit.

She looks around the tidy kitchen. "Everything here okay, *sí*?"

"*Molto bene*," I say around a mouthful of buttery cookie. "Oh, except I think you need a new roof, the door to my room is no longer attached to the wall, and your cat enjoys leaving me sacrificial offerings…but I love it here."

Nonna Rossi smiles quizzically. "*Sí, sí, va bene.*" She puts the flowers in a vase she procures from a cabinet. "I'm here to invite you to *cena*…dinner. We are having a party for *la famiglia*. I want you to be there."

"Oh, thank you, but I don't want to intrude on a family get-together."

"*Certo che no, che sciocchezza*—nonsense. You come, *sí*? Six. Dress nice, fancy…*sí*?" She smiles at me encouragingly, pointing at my messy bun and sweats.

"Oh, tonight? Um…"

She slaps her hands down on the table. "*Molto bene.*" She gets up to leave before I can tell her I planned on soaking in the tub with a glass of wine and a book. My muscles are aching after the hike in Isola yesterday. "*Fiore verra a prederti*…she'll come pick you up, so you no ride *bicicletta. Arrivederci!*"

"*Molto bene.*" I sigh after she leaves.

My thoughts wander to Lorenzo, who I can't stop thinking about. He wants to be friends. We *are* friends…but I can't help feeling there's more between us. I'm definitely attracted to him. A blind woman would be, for Pete's sake, but I want more. I want Frances' Marcello in *Under the Tuscan Sun.* The Italian man who reignited her passion for love and life. I feel like I had that connection with Lorenzo yesterday, but it's as if he's holding me at arm's length, deciding if I'm worth the risk.

I glance down at my gray sweats and frown. Nonna said to dress fancy, but all I have is simple. Remembering that cute little store I saw in town, I throw my underwear and socks on top of the folded clothes and dash up the narrow stairs from the kitchen to my bedroom. Realizing I won't have time to bike into town, I fish my cellphone out of my bag and call a taxi. I quickly text Cara an SOS message explaining my evening plans and to be on standby to help me choose something. I'll pick out something quick enough to give me time to get ready.

THE PUSHY BUT chic store owner, Carmella, shoves another dress into my changing room while I'm slipping one off. I shriek, covering my bare breasts with my arm. The front of the store is all glass windows. The inside walls are blush colored with gold accents. Carmella prefers a minimalist approach to her store, only showcasing a few items. I'm hoping she'll pull something out of the back off a rack, but my chances aren't looking good.

"*Come se non l'avessi mai visto prima...*I've seen it all."

She sashays away and I yank the curtain closed and step into the dress she brought. It's a white and red polka dot with a sweetheart neckline, a poofy skirt, and the biggest shoulder pads I've ever seen. It looks like an eighties prom dress. I grimace and stare at myself in the mirror, not even wanting to zip it up. I snap a quick picture and text it to Cara.

**Me:** *I look like a clown.*

**Cara:** *Yeah, that's a hell no.*

I quickly let it drop to the floor and kick it to the side. I want a beautiful white dress that makes me feel sexy, like the one Frances wore when she went to meet Marcello. I want to feel confident and *Italian*, like Sophia Loren. I try on a red one Carmella insists is all the rage in Rome. Now we're talking. I slip it on over my head because it only has a side zipper. I tug it down and keep tugging. It's a little tight, but not too bad. I turn toward the mirror, and my eyeballs almost roll out of my head.

**Me:** *This one is a little tight…*

**Cara:** *Vava-voom! Are you planning on seducing everyone at the dinner party tonight? Because that dress is H.O.T. Do I see nip?*

I look closer in the mirror and sure enough the material is completely sheer. This is more like a going-out-to-a-nightclub type of dress for a twenty-something, not for meeting Lorenzo's *la famiglia* for the first time.

**Me:** *Yes. Nothing says family dinner like a see-through dress. I'm doomed.*

I try to peel the weird nylon material away from my skin so I can breathe a little easier, but it sucks itself back into place. The curtain whips open and I yelp in surprise.

"Ah, *bellissima*. You like?"

"No, too tight." I show Carmella by pulling away at the material. I try to walk out of the dressing room, but the dress restricts my movements to small steps. "No like. Do you have anything with a full skirt?" I show her by fluttering my hands around my knees. She frowns and turns, hopefully to find something a little less skintight.

I walk back into the dressing room and slowly try to peel the finger trap off my body. I undo the side zipper, but it doesn't make a difference. In the five minutes I've had this dress on, it has suction-cupped itself to my body. Sweat glistens on my skin while I try to peel from the bottom, the hot lights overhead making me feel dizzy. I'm out of breath by the time I get it to my hips, my arms aching from the struggle.

Carmella appears and pulls open the curtain while I stand there and pant. At this point, I'm too winded to care if the whole town sees me in my underwear. She purses her lips and says something in Italian before helping me tug the dress off. I bend forward as she yanks it over my head, stumbling backward.

"*Mannaggia la miseria*," she mutters, regaining her composure, patting a stray hair that fell out of her French twist.

"Oh, thank God, I thought I'd have to cut that thing off." I gasp for air, hanging on to the dressing-room curtain for dear life. Carmella disappears for a moment and walks back over with a flowy dress, just like I was envisioning.

"This color looks good with your hair and eyes." She hands me an emerald-green silk dress. "You slip over your head." She motions for me to do it as I stand there braless in my panties, staring at the dress, petrified to get stuck in another. Maybe the polka-dot one wasn't so bad—shoulder pads *do* make the waist appear slimmer.

She huffs and rips the dress out of my hands, roughly pulling it down over my head. I think Carmella wants me out of the shop as much as I want to be done with this nightmare.

"*Bellissima. Sì!* This one."

I turn toward the mirror and gape. The rich, vibrant green contrasts beautifully against my sun-kissed skin. My greasy brown hair looks miraculously glossy and lush next to the satin. The capped sleeves and deep V neckline that twist into the waist shout elegant yet sexy. Carmella adds a gold belt and gold heels, and I can't say no. It's *perfetto.*

***Me:*** *I think this is it.*

***Cara:*** *YES!!! Gorgeous.*

"You like?"

"I love," I breathe.

"*Molto bene.*"

I gather my purchases and head out into the golden afternoon sunlight.

I TAKE OFF my splint, deciding my thumb is healed enough, before plugging the curling iron into the power converter and sticking it into the socket. Tapping my finger on the ceramic wand, I test the heat and part a section of hair, wrapping it around the barrel. My cellphone rings on the counter, startling me. *Barbara.*

I put her on speakerphone. "Are you alive? I've left you a message every day. What is going on?"

"Don't be so dramatic, Summer." She sucks in a lungful of cigarette smoke. "I've been busy."

"Busy with your new job?" I ask hopefully, unwinding my hair. I wrap another section around the barrel.

"What job?"

"The one you said you got before I left for Italy?"

"Oh that. It didn't work out. The guy wanted me to be there by eight a.m. Can you believe that?"

I grind my teeth. "It's called a job, *Mom.* You need one to pay bills and rent. To put gas in your car and pay insurance. To be…I don't know, a responsible adult!"

"What's the fun in that?" She blows out. "I can see Italy hasn't loosened you up at all. Speaking of cars, where are your keys?"

I testily wrap a new section around the barrel. "Why?"

"I need to borrow your car tonight."

"What's wrong with your car?"

"Ugh, it got a boot put on it. I swear I parked it in a yellow zone for twenty minutes!"

"So, pay the fine and take *your* car."

"I don't have time to pay the fine right now. Mark needs to pick his kids up."

"Wait…who is Mark?"

"The new guy I'm dating." I can practically hear her eyes roll.

"Well, why the hell doesn't he have a car?"

"Because his license is suspended." She clucks her tongue. "Summer, I need the keys. I promised I would help him out."

"Why is his license suspended?"

"Because he's had a couple DUIs." She sighs, like my questions are completely irrelevant and out of line.

"A couple? How old are his kids?"

"I don't know. I didn't ask." She huffs. "What's with the interrogation? Can I borrow it or not?"

"Let me get this straight. You want me to loan you my car to pick up your new boyfriend and his kids who you have never met, because he has a drinking-and-driving problem and got his license suspended? Yeah, no."

"Don't be such a judgmental pill, Summer. I don't ask you for much."

I make a strangled noise and stare at my phone incredulously.

"Forget it, I'll just borrow Janice's." She hangs up before I can formulate a response.

"Ugh! She's infuriating!" I shout to my image in the mirror, which is when I notice my hair is still wrapped around the barrel and it's smoking. "Shit, shit, shit!"

Attempting to unravel it, the hair breaks off where the curling iron is clasped around it. "Noooo!" Dropping the curling iron, I yank on the cord, dislodging it from the wall. "No, no, no!" I pick up the clump of hair and hold it to my head as if it would miraculously grow back together. The hair floats down to the counter.

Whimpering, I pick up my compact mirror and turn around, eyeballing the hair fried to a crisp. I try to blend it in with the rest of my hair, but it refuses to cooperate, sticking out at a weird angle.

Flipping my hair over to tousle it, I notice the front of my wrap dress gaping open, revealing more than just cleavage. I straighten up and smooth the silky fabric down against my chest. As I lean forward, it does it again. What the hell? How did I not notice this in the shop? Perhaps I'm missing a snap or button. I peer down the front of my blouse in search of a hook or button, but can't find one.

A man clears his throat behind me. Yelping, I pick up the curling iron and hold it out in front of me. *What are you going to do with it, Summer, burn the intruder's hair off too?* My heart is in my throat, but I quickly recognize the tousled dark hair and smoky eyes.

"Jesus, Mary, and Joseph." I drop the iron and place my hand over my chest, willing it to a regular heartbeat. "I think we need to work on your door-knocking skills. I almost clocked you on the head with my curling iron."

"I did knock, but you didn't answer. I thought you were taking a *pisolino*." He gives me a charming smile.

"You thought I was taking *a piss*?" I hiss, heat splashing across my cheeks.

Lorenzo rubs a hand over his jaw, chuckling. "*Pisolino* means taking an afternoon nap. It's common here in Italy to take a *pisolino*."

"Oh...right. A nap." I nod, wishing someone would try

to knock *me* out with the curling iron. "Don't you have a dinner party to attend?" I grumble.

"*Sí.* Nonna asked me to pick you up. Is something burning in here?"

"Uh, nope. Everything is *perfetto.*" I laugh nervously. "I thought Fiore was picking me up."

His brows knit in confusion. "No, she's making dinner. She's up to her elbows in pasta. Are you almost ready?"

"Uh sure, okay. I'll be downstairs in a second. Let me just grab my bag."

He leaves the bathroom, thankfully not noticing the clump of hair on the counter. I try to pin my hair back in a last-ditch effort to conceal the frizzled mess, but it looks odd. Stuffing some gloss and my phone into a purse, I spritz myself with perfume and head downstairs.

Lorenzo's eyes quickly peruse over me while he waits by the front door. He looks so incredibly handsome in a dark gray suit, obviously Italian and tailored to him perfectly. His dark hair is gelled to finger-tousled perfection. Eyes more smoky gray than green are framed by thick black lashes, and I can't get over how gorgeous they are when he smiles.

"*Sei bellissima stasera.*"

"I'm not sure what you said, but I'm going to respond with thank you."

He chuckles, and the sexy sound causes my skin to pebble. He opens the door of his Maserati and helps me in. "I said you look beautiful tonight, *tesoro.*"

"*Grazie,* Ren." I adjust my dress and pull the seatbelt across my chest, reminding me I forgot to grab something to pin the top.

The smell of rich Italian leather, his masculine scent, and his close proximity wrap around me like a warm hug I don't want to let go of. The engine roars to life as The Police croon "Every Breath You Take." I inhale deeply through my nose and exhale, sinking into the designer seats. He maneuvers the car out of my little gravel lot and up the hill to the main house.

"Fiore said you live in town. Did you grow up in the main house?"

"*Sí*, I moved out when I returned from the States."

"I think I would have stayed at the big house. It's beautiful."

"It would have been hard to bring a girlfriend back to my place if my mom and grandmother were peppering her with questions and my sister was shoving pasta in her face."

My stomach churns at the thought of him having a girlfriend. I mean, it's none of my business, but it never crossed my mind he might have a significant other by the way he flirts with me. For all I know, he could be casually dating Nina or Daniella, the woman I saw on my first day here. He did warn me about Italian men.

This unfamiliar agitation swimming in the pit of my stomach feels a lot like jealousy, and I'm not sure I care for it. Perhaps Lorenzo keeping me at arm's length is the right thing to do. As much as I'm attracted to him, he and I shouldn't date. Nonna Rossi generously let me stay in her house and work at her business. Getting romantically involved with her grandson was not part of the deal.

I glance over at his handsome profile. I bought this dress so I could feel sexy and beautiful tonight. Perhaps Lorenzo is my Marcello from *Under the Tuscan Sun.* Someone I find incredibly attractive, but the stars aren't aligned in our favor. That thought makes me depressed.

"You're quiet. Are you okay?" He flashes me a brief smile before turning on the road to his parents' house. I crush down my jealousy and confused feelings for him and give him a bright smile.

"Just wondering how big the Rossi clan will be. Truth be told, I'm a little out of my element. I can only pick up a little Italian."

"You'll be fine. My aunt, uncle, and cousins will be here, so fairly small. The only one who doesn't speak much English is my great-uncle Giovanni, my grandfather's brother, but you won't have to talk to him." He parks the Maserati next to a yellow Ferrari. The gravel parking lot is full of cars.

"Seems like a big party." I swallow past the ball of nerves lodged in my throat. I'm not sure if I prefer small and intimate or getting lost in a crowd tonight. He quickly reaches me before I step out, offering his hand. "*Grazie*, Ren."

I immediately zero in on our clasped hands as he steers me toward the front door. Are we walking into the party holding hands? Is Lorenzo my date? I need clarification on what's going on here. I'm working up the nerve to ask him when he gives my hand a light squeeze before dropping it.

"I noticed you're not wearing your splint tonight."

"Oh, yeah, my thumb feels good. Besides, it clashed with my dress."

He chuckles and opens the front door, ushering me in

front of him. Chatter and music filter down the entryway hall. Lorenzo's mom, Stella, beams when she sees us and greets us with outstretched arms. She reaches me first and pulls me into a hug, her perfume cloying.

"*Buona sera*, Summer! So glad you could join us." She kisses my cheeks. "You look beautiful in this dress."

"*Buona sera*, Signora Rossi, and thank you for having me."

"Of course, and please, call me Stella." She lets me go and hugs Lorenzo, speaking rapidly to him in Italian. "*Raffaelo, vieni qui*," she shouts over her shoulder. Lorenzo looks over at me and winks. I fan myself with my clutch before I catch myself. *Jesus, get a grip Summer, he just winked.*

A handsome, older man with silver hair and Lorenzo's eyes joins us and extends his hand. "*Benvenuta a casa nostra.*"

"Raffaelo, this is Summer Andrews. The one Lorenzo has been talking about *incessantemente*." Stella clasps her hands together. "Summer, this is my husband, Raffaelo."

Lorenzo glares at his mom and says something in Italian, causing her to press her lips together. Signor Rossi smiles graciously, shaking my hand.

"I'm going to introduce Summer to everyone." Ren grabs my hand and pulls me away from his parents. "Let's go into the living room."

"Oh, okay." I tuck my clutch under my arm and follow him into a beautiful house where there are at least thirty people. Small gathering? I'd hate to see a big family get-together. I plaster an anxious smile on my face while Lorenzo introduces me to some of his cousins, aunts, and uncles. Little kids run throughout the room, squealing.

"I thought you said this would be a small gathering?" I whisper.

He chuckles, placing a hand on my lower back. "It is."

We turn the corner, and my jaw drops. Pouring a glass of wine at the bar talking to another man is none other than Dr. Bianchi.

# Chapter 17

I SHAKE HANDS with Lorenzo's cousin, Giovanni, Gio, for short. My skin prickles with anticipation and my stomach does somersaults. I turn just as Dr. Bianchi's eyes trail down my dress.

"Dr. Bianchi, what a small world. It's so good to see you, again."

Dr. Bianchi tilts his head and gives me a charming smile. "Ah yes, the beautiful American who hurt her thumb in a bicycling accident." He reaches for my hand and runs a thumb over my palm. "How is my most favorite patient?"

It's the wrong hand, but who the hell cares? Goosebumps break out over my skin, and I simper while he massages my thumb. "I'm good, I mean, it's good. All better."

"I see you took off the splint."

"Yes, it was making me clumsy." I giggle like an idiotic teenager with a crush. Dr. Bianchi's gaze drops to my lips and then my chest, and I flush. Lorenzo clears his throat, breaking the trance Dr. Bianchi has me under.

"You've met my cousin, Angelo?"

"*Sí*, he fixed my thumb when I got into the accident with Harrison."

Angelo's eyes roam over my body, stopping at my breasts. "The beautiful American damsel in distress."

Lorenzo clenches his jaw, pinning Angelo with an icy glare. Stepping in front of me, he partially blocks my view of Angelo and Gio. He says something rapidly in Italian, to which Angelo responds with a scoff. Lorenzo quickly takes my elbow and leads me down a hall.

"Hey, I was talking to Dr. Bianchi."

"I think your dress has come undone," he says. I peer down and gasp, as the top of the dress is indeed gaping. I quickly close the stupid thing. Lorenzo politely shows me to the powder room while I curse Carmella's name under my breath. Shutting myself in, I look in the mirror.

My cheeks are ruddy, and my eyes are bright like I've had one too many glasses of wine. The front of the dress has come loose, gaping enough to show plenty of cleavage *and* my lacy bra. No wonder Lorenzo looked piqued. I tuck the top part into the wrap belt until it's taut. I need a safety pin to keep it closed. I open all the drawers next to the sink, but they are empty. I shut the last drawer when someone knocks. "Hold on," I say, trying to fix my hair and adjust the skirt of my dress before opening the door. This night is *not* how I pictured dinner with the Rossi's would go.

I expect Lorenzo, but it's Nina leaning against the wall, waiting for the bathroom.

"Oh, hello, Nina."

She eyes my dress. "*Ciao.* Cute dress, Summer."

"Thanks, yours too."

"What are you doing here?"

I look behind me, confused by her question. "Using the bathroom?"

She rolls her eyes. "What are you doing at the party?"

"Oh, Nonna Rossi invited me."

She shoulders her way into the bathroom and grabs my wrist as she passes me, her eyes widening. "*Dio mio*, what happened to your hair?"

I pat my hair self-consciously. "Curling-iron accident. Is it bad?"

"Hmm," is all she says before shutting the door in my face. I reluctantly head back to the party. Would anyone miss me if I hid in the kitchen with Fiore? She'll know where I can get a safety pin and a bag for my head. Angelo stops me from slinking off to find the kitchen as soon as I enter the living room.

"*Bellissima*, come, let me check your thumb." Charm oozes out of him and I struggle to say no. He places his hand under my elbow and guides me to a couch. I scan the room for a familiar pair of smoky eyes, but I don't see him.

"Uh, okay, but then I need to find Fiore."

He takes my hand and sits close to me on the couch. Dr. Bianchi is acting a lot more forward than that day in his office. He picks up my hand and strokes it, setting my fight or flight on alert.

"Your hands are so soft and smooth. I was told you are working for *la famiglia* Rossi. It would be a shame to ruin these beautiful hands."

Marcos, my self-defense instructor, is back, waving red flags in my head.

"Oh no, I'm just helping with the tastings. Uh, that's the wrong hand, though."

He chuckles. "*Mi scusi*, I don't have my report in front of me."

"It's no problem. I've had no issues with it, so I think it's healing well. You did a great job." I try to tug my hand back, but he holds on and looks into my eyes. I nervously wet my lips because, holy hell, the Italians have a special knack for making you feel like you're the only person in the room with just a look.

He glides his thumb up and down my hand. "How long are you in Italy for? I thought you were leaving the next day. Imagine my surprise when the beautiful American woman I couldn't stop thinking about shows up on the arm of my cousin."

"Small world, huh?" I choke out, craning my neck, looking for Lorenzo in the crowd. Although Dr. Bianchi is incredibly handsome and makes me lose a few brain cells with just a smile, he's not Lorenzo. Not even close, and the longer he holds my hand, the more uneasy I feel. He's too much as he sits practically on top of me, his cologne overpowering my senses, his touch too…touchy. I discreetly try to slide my hand out of his because his eyes have taken on a wolfish gleam. I lower my gaze to my top to make sure it's still in place. Angelo's grin widens.

"That's a beautiful dress on you, *bella*."

"Summer, here." Lorenzo appears at my side and shoves a wineglass toward me. I accept it, grateful for his interruption.

"*Grazie*, Ren." I stand up, embarrassed to be caught getting a hand massage from his cousin. I feel dirty and ashamed because I don't want Lorenzo to get the wrong idea.

"Renzo, how did you meet this beautiful woman?"

"She's living in Nonna Rossi's old house at the bottom of

the hill."

Angelo laughs. "Weren't you supposed to be renovating it for a little bed-and-breakfast?"

I grind my teeth, my attraction to Dr. Bianchi dimming quite rapidly as he sneers the words *bed-and-breakfast.*

"Summer, dinner is ready." Ren ignores Angelo, quietly offering his hand like an olive branch. I slip my hand into his. He squeezes it gently, and it's comforting. "I tried to find some safety pins for you, but I couldn't locate any."

"Thank you for trying."

Angelo stands, flanking my other side, while we make our way to the dining room. "You should come to the clinic this week, so I can properly check out your thumb, *sì*?"

"Oh, I think it's fine." I give him a tight smile before Lorenzo steers me to a seat between Nonna Rossi and Gio. If I weren't mistaken, I'd think Ren was trying to keep me away from Angelo, but the resourceful doctor snags a chair across from me, winking as he sits down. Nina huffs, sitting down in a chair to his left while Fiore and Lorenzo sit with their parents at the opposite end of the long trestle table. I fiddle with my dress and make sure it's pulled extra tight across my chest.

Mr. Rossi stands, holding his glass up. "*La condivisione del cibo è un momento sacro. Grazie di essere venuti stasera. Mangiare, bere ed essere felici!*"

"*Mangiare, bere ed essere felici,*" the table jovially echoes. Gio leans into me and whispers, "He thanked everyone for coming together tonight. He said the sharing of food is sacred, and to eat, drink, and be happy."

"Thank you for translating." I smile gratefully.

"You'll have to learn to speak our language if you stay here permanently, no?" Nonna pipes up on my right.

"Oh, um...I'm picking up some phrases, but I don't plan on staying past the summer." I bite my bottom lip. Will I stay on at the end of summer? My head tells me no, but my heart says it's possible.

Laughter and the beautiful Italian language buzz around me. Incredible aromas waft from the platters of food, making me feel drunk with happiness. The garnet red of the wine in the crystal glasses twinkles in the light as I seek the handsome Italian among the strangers at the table. He laughs at something his dad says, and I itch to be closer to his end of the table.

I take a bite of the tender beef Fiore has prepared. My eyes roll back in pure pleasure. "Oh my God, this is so good."

"Fiore is the best cook in Tuttoscano. Better than all the chefs in Florence," Gio says proudly.

"She has definitely earned that title," I say.

"I love a woman who appreciates good food," Angelo says smoothly, which does not sit well with Nina. She stabs the meat with her fork. A few weeks ago, those words coming from his lips would have made me melt to the floor in a pool of desire. But tonight, Angelo Bianchi is not the Italian who makes my sauce simmer.

I spoon some risotto and contemplate. The whole reason I'm here, staying on in Italy for the summer, is to have a little adventure, and if I'm lucky, have a wild affair with a sexy Italian. It's hard to do that when the one you're interested in has friend-zoned you. I furtively glance down the table. Lorenzo's gaze skirts to mine, and his lip curls up like we're sharing a funny secret. His attention is pulled back to the conversation with Fiore.

The truth is, I want to spend my summer with Lorenzo. My devastatingly handsome friend and boss, who leaves me feeling confused and hot. *But I can't have him.* He's not even an option. His signals range from yellow to green to *Do Not Pass.*

"So, Gio, what do you do?"

"Ah, I'm Lorenzo's right-hand man at Rossi Farms."

"Oh really? I haven't seen you walking around."

"I'm usually holed up in the office with Lorenzo, but he has been sneaking off, wandering the property lately. Now I know why." He chuckles, then shoves pasta in his mouth. Fiore wraps her arms around me before I can respond.

"Summer! I'm so glad you could make it. I'm sorry this is the first chance to say hello. I have been slaving away in the kitchen all evening. Did you do something different with your hair?"

I immediately place my hand over my hair as Fiore bends down to kiss my cheek. "Curling-iron accident. Everything is amazing! There's something in the risotto I've never tasted before. What is it?"

Fiore glances over at Nonna, who is deep in conversation with Stella's sister, and then says in a low voice, "Truffles from the ones you and Renzo picked."

"Wow, it's incredible! Ren was telling me I should go to the truffle festival."

"Truffles? Where did you get truffles from?" Nonna shouts. "*Non da quel cane Rizzotti, spero! Ma vaffanculo tutta quella famiglia Rizzotti!*" For whatever reason, the whole table falls into a stunned silence.

Everyone looks at me and I squirm in my seat. Next to me, Gio snickers.

"*Cazzo*," Fiore mutters. "*Nonna, calmati.* No one mentioned the Rizzottis. I was telling Summer that I used truffles in the dish."

Nonna raises her fist in the air and yells, "*Preferirei morire piuttosto che mangiare un tartufo da quel bastardo, Rizzotti!*"

I catch Lorenzo's eye, and he just smirks and shakes his head. The family resumes eating and talking like Nonna Rossi didn't just totally lose her shit at the dinner table. Lorenzo wasn't kidding when he said not to bring up truffles around Nonna.

Fiore rolls her eyes. "Anyway, I love your dress. What are you doing tomorrow?"

"Oh, I don't kno—"

"Great, you must come over and spend the day with me by the pool. I haven't had a day off in forever, and I need some vitamin D! Meet me at eleven, *sì*?"

Before I can answer, she's moved on to kiss Nonna Rossi's cheek and murmurs to her in Italian. Nonna pats her hand and nods.

"I think that's the first time I've ever heard a non-family member make Nonna curse, besides those who cannot be named." Gio snickers beside me.

"Oh no, what did she say?"

"That the Riz—the family that can't be mentioned—can go fuck themselves, and she'd rather die than eat a truffle from them."

I choke on a piece of meat. Gio gently taps my back, then turns his attention to Angelo. "Swimming sounds like the perfect day. We'll all come over tomorrow as well. What do you say, Angelo?"

"I have to run to the clinic in the morning, but I wouldn't mind lounging by the pool in the afternoon." He runs his tongue over his bottom lip while he looks at me like I'm a piece of Fiore's tender beef. I shift my eyes down to my plate and concentrate on twirling my fork in the pasta.

"I want to come!" Nina claps her hands giddily. I grit my teeth. So much for time alone with Fiore.

"*Sí*, we'll all come over." Angelo winks at me before Nina wraps him up in conversation, stealing his attention away.

*Va bene.*

I WANDER DOWN the hall toward the bathroom. I've had at least three women ask me if I'm aware my hair has a chunk missing. Yes, cousin Giada, I'm aware. Not to mention having to continuously fix this damn dress all night and stand there with my hand on my chest like I'm saying the pledge of allegiance to keep it from gaping open. Lorenzo's great-uncle Giovanni *did* want to talk to me and was being a total perv as he tried to get a glimpse of my breasts.

I stifle a yawn and look for Ren to tell him I'm ready to call it a night. I've had so much food and wine that I might just walk home, although knowing him, he'll insist on driving me. I wander down the hall when I pass a small study with a blazing fire. It looks warm and cozy, a perfect place to hide from the crowd and sip some wine.

I'm about to slip into the room to see if he wandered in here when I hear my name. I stop, melting into the shadows. Lorenzo is leaning against a bookshelf across from the hearth, his arms crossed while Nina stands in his personal space. She's clutching a glass of wine, smiling up at him, then flirtatiously touches his arm.

"*Cos'è Summer per te?*" she asks.

"*Siamo amici, perché?*" He takes a sip of wine and Nina giggles, moving closer, which I can't believe is even physically possible. She stands up on her toes and whispers in his ear. His hand slips to her waist, steadying her. I can't watch this. I dart away from the room, using the shadows to keep concealed.

Nina is very beautiful, and Lorenzo is a total catch. The thought of them together makes the ugly green monster squeeze my heart...my dreams and hopes quickly flushed down the toilet. *Dreams and hopes? Get a grip, Summer.* So what if the devilishly handsome Lorenzo Rossi made my heart jump with excitement every time he was near? Who cares if the color of his eyes, a swirl of smoke and olives, made me want to melt on the spot?

I deflate against the wall outside the living room, my hands clenched. *You don't even know him. He could be the biggest Lothario in the Tuscan province.* I blow out a breath and try to calm down, but the phrase, *he's not into you*, pummels continuously like a drumbeat against my heart. *Mi amici.*

I look for Fiore or Nonna Rossi to tell them goodnight and thank you. I find Nonna first and give her a gentle hug. "*Grazie*, Nonna, for inviting me tonight."

"Renzo taking you home, *sì*?"

"Oh, um…he's preoccupied. I'll be alright."

"No, you find him. *Immediatamente.*"

I untangle myself from her embrace and nod. "*Sí*, Nonna Rossi. *Immediatamente.*"

"*Brava ragazza*, good girl." She lovingly pats my cheek before turning toward a cousin. I make my escape and practically run to the front door before anyone else can try to stop me. I fling open the door and am greeted by pouring rain. *Ugh, no!* Oh well, this dress is crap anyway. I take my heels off and dash out into the storm. I've made this trip several times on my bike, so at least I know where to turn onto the main road. I slow down to a walk as rain pours on me. The house is probably flooded by now.

What at first felt like warm rivulets of water running down my cheeks has turned into cold needles pricking my skin. I shiver and wrap my arms around myself, slowly making my way down the pebbled lane. High beams flash over me. I step to the side of the road to let them pass, but the black Maserati pulls up right next to me. The automatic window glides down, and Lorenzo looks furious.

"*Tesoro*, get in."

"No!" I continue to walk, ignoring him, but he rolls his car alongside me.

"Summer, don't be a fool, get in! You'll catch pneumonia."

"No, *grazie*!"

"*Porca puttana!*" He puts the car in park and slams his door. He comes around the front of the car to block my escape. "Get in the car!"

"Leave me alone, Ren!" I shout, tears of frustration mixing with the rain. My fists clench tight at my side when he steps into my personal space.

"I can't," he yells back. I shove him to get him to step aside, but it's like shoving a brick wall. Why won't he get back into his pretty car and leave me alone?

"*Stronzo!*" I shout.

His head rears back at the one curse word I learned from Harrison. "Did you just call me an asshole?"

I note the shock and disbelief on his face and can't help but feel a bit of satisfaction as he runs his hands through his wet hair.

"You're getting soaked. Go home, Lorenzo." I deflate. "Besides, Nina will wonder where you are."

"Why would I care about Nina?"

I snort and hug myself tighter. "Of course, you wouldn't care."

"I do not understand."

I fling my arms out. "What do you want from me?"

"I want you to get in the goddamn car!"

"No! I don't want to go anywhere with you."

"Why the hell not?"

"Because I saw you with Nina tonight in the study," I scream back. "I saw her clinging to you. It looked like a pretty cozy scene to me."

He shakes his head slowly, his face a mask of regret. "*Tesoro*, no. Nothing happened. Yes, she was in the study with me, but I was looking for pins for your dress when she came in."

I snort. "Looking for pins while drinking wine by the fire? Do you think I'm *stupido*?"

"No!" He slices his hand through the air. "I'm not into Nina. You're the only one I see."

Before I can react, he pulls me to him. His hands drive into my wet hair as his lips capture mine in a sizzling kiss that makes me forget about the needles of rain on my skin, of Nina, and the fact that I'm upset. His lips move over mine and wipe my mind blank. There's only me and Ren. My fingers wrap around his neck and thread into his hair. He slants his lips for better access, and I acquiesce, trembling with need while his tongue tangles with mine. He tastes like wine and spice and I'm drowning, never wanting to come up for air.

I moan, and he squeezes me closer to him, our wet bodies molding to each other. A pulsing heat unfurls in my core, and becomes so intense, I need to be closer to him. He groans when I wrap a leg around him, feeling his hardness against my core. His hands run down my back to cup my ass, pulling me up into him. I gasp, feeling like I'm about to unravel. He deepens the kiss and picks me up, shoving me against the car for better leverage. This kiss in the rain, this man...he was wrong about me bewitching him, because he's the one who is casting the most delicious spell over me.

Car lights flash coming down the hill. He pulls away, both our chest heaving for air. He swipes a thumb across my lower lip, looking at me tenderly, rivulets of rain running down our cheeks. "Get in the car, *tesoro*. You're shivering."

I nod, my ire toward him dissolved by the rain and the best kiss of my life. He opens the door and I slip into the heated passenger seat. He says something in Italian to the car that stops next to us and quickly jumps into the driver's seat. A million thoughts swirl around in my head like a blender, but I can't focus on one. I need to say something. I should say something, but my brain refuses to work with my tongue. Will he kiss me again? Will he take me upstairs to my bedroom and bang me against the door so hard it will cave in too? I'd risk it.

I quickly glance at his profile, my stomach doing somersaults as I mentally retract what I said about not dating the boss. Could Lorenzo and I have a fling for the summer, perhaps even something beyond that? Could I stay here in Italy and see where this goes? I turn in my seat to face him.

"That kiss shouldn't have happened," he says quietly, his jaw clenching.

*And…that was not anything close to what I was hoping he'd say.*

Brutally disappointed, I sit back and stare out the window while trying to salvage my pride. "Do you not like me, Ren? Because I'm getting some pretty fucked-up signals from you."

"I do, *tesoro*. I *really* do, but…" His hands flex on the steering wheel. "It's not a good idea."

*Gah! Why does he keep saying that?* "I don't understand."

"It's not a good time for me to get involved with someone right now. Work is crazy, and you're only here for the summer," he says, and I die a little inside. I've just had the most incredible make-out session of my life and he's not just pushing me through the friend-zone door, he's slamming it in my face and locking it.

He pulls into the gravel lot in front of the house and turns off the car. Without a word, he gets out, the door shutting with a quiet click. He comes around to my side and opens the door, offering me a hand. We run to the front door, the rain still pelting down on us. We stop under the overhang. Rain drips down Lorenzo's beautiful bone structure, his wet eyelashes black and beautiful against the olive green of his eyes. Reaching up, he brushes the tears that have mixed with the rain from my cheek.

"Summer, I'm so sorry I'm giving you mixed signals. If this were another time, and I was…" He drives his fingers through his hair. "*Cazzo*, this is so fucked up. I want to get to know you better. That kiss was—"

"Ren." I swallow and close my eyes. That kiss…the intensity, the pull it had over me…his indecision, it all makes my stomach twist into knots. It scares me a little. "I think you should leave me alone."

"That's the problem, *tesoro*." He runs a thumb over my bruised lips. "I don't think I can."

# Chapter 18

I UNCAP THE red polish and start painting my toes while I talk to Cara on speakerphone.

"And then what happened?" she asks.

"He said, *I don't think I can*, and then got in his car and drove away."

"What? That's it? He left you standing in the rain with that?"

"Oh, Cara, I'm so fucked. I'm a total headcase with this guy. It scares me."

"You've said that like five times already," Damien shouts in the background.

"Damien, shush! Go light something on fire," Cara says.

"One time, woman. One small fire, and you won't let me forget it. I can cook!"

"Oh geez, he's gyrating his hips and swinging a kitchen towel around in the air."

I giggle, but then sober with Cara's next question.

"Why are you scared?"

"I don't know…he's got me all mixed up inside."

"You really like this guy?"

"I do. I did. I don't know. There's only so many times you get rejected before you throw in the towel. He says he can't have a relationship right now."

"Hmm. Maybe he's afraid to get invested because you'll have to end it when you come back home."

"Maybe." I rest my chin on my knee.

"Why does it have to be this big declaration of love between you two? Have fun! Sow your wild oats with the hot Italian olive grower. Keep your heart out of it."

"Keep my heart out of it. Solid plan." I cap the nail polish and don't tell Cara my heart is already compromised. "And now I have to go to a pool party with Dr. Bianchi, Nina, and Gio."

"Aw, look at you making friends. Hey did you ever hear from Granite? You only have a couple days left of vacation."

"I know. It's weird I haven't heard from Allen yet, but it's the weekend. I'll call on Monday." I groan, flopping back on my bed. "What do you think I should do about Lorenzo?"

"I think you should go hunt him down and tell him the truth. That you understand his reluctance, but you want to see where this might lead…hopefully to a horizontal position."

"You want me to put myself out there for him to shoot me down again? Sounds like an awesome plan."

"He's obviously into you if that kiss was life changing. You don't let someone like that walk away. Put your big-girl panties on and find out what's holding him back."

"But he's my boss, Cara."

"Boss, shmoss, it's not like it's a permanent position or you're his personal assistant. Quit making excuses. At least get some good sex out of it!" She snickers. "Seriously though, you haven't shown this much interest in a guy since Chris."

"And look how that ended. Not well."

"I think Barbara's co-dependency on you sunk that ship."

"And his blonde spunky coworker," I grumble.

"Well, it's just you and Lorenzo in Italy. Make the best of it."

"Cara, I *need* you," I whine pathetically.

"No, you don't," Damien shouts again.

"She wasn't talking to you," Cara shouts back. I can picture Cara rolling her eyes and swatting him with the dishtowel. My heart sinks, missing them like crazy.

"Maybe I should just come home."

"I'll admit, I thought this idea of yours was insane at first, but I think it's been good for you. You sound…happy."

I snort. "This is happy?"

"Okay, well, not right now. Go have your Italian love affair. Be wild for once, Summer. You owe it to yourself."

"But—"

"What did Frances do in the movie? She went out and bought a pretty dress and said she was going to find her bees, or butterflies, or whatever the hell kind of bug she was looking for."

I giggle. "Ladybugs."

"Whatever. My point is, she went for it."

"Yeah, and when she got there, he was with another woman." I stand up and pull my two swimsuits out of a drawer. I eye the sexy two-piece dolefully. I'm almost forty, I should wear the one-piece. I pick it up and frown because it's not as cute as the bikini and the butt has pilling.

"Okay, well shit, I forgot about that part, but she put

herself out there, yeah?"

"I guess."

"Put yourself out there, Summer."

"You make it sound so easy."

"Take pics of the pool party. I need to see some tight Italian asses in swimsuits."

"I heard that," Damien calls out, making me smile.

"Will do, love you," I say.

"Love you, too. Goodbye, beautiful! *Ciao, bella!* See? I'm learning."

"*Ciao, bella.*" I smile and hang up with Cara, releasing a big sigh. She's right. I came here with a purpose to have some fun, and dammit, I'm going to make it worth my while. I throw the one-piece back in the drawer.

She's also right about Lorenzo. I need to find him and tell him how I really feel. The point of me coming to Italy was to channel my inner Frances. I owe myself that much.

THE POOL IS long and rectangular, with crystal-blue water reflecting the cloudless sky above. I sit back against my cushioned lounge chair. Fiore hands me her sunscreen.

"I'm so glad you could come and hang out today. I'm sorry I didn't get to talk to you much last night. Parties like that are always so crazy for me."

"Oh, no worries," I tell her. "Thank you for having me. And I'm sorry Gio, Angelo, and Nina are coming by later."

Fiore waves her hand. "I don't mind, but I should warn you, it will get crazy. Gio is always loud. He probably invited a bunch of people, too."

I chew my bottom lip, wondering how to ask Fiore about Lorenzo. "Will your brother be over?"

"Ah, who knows with Renzo. He was pissed you left the party last night in the rain." She turns her head in my direction and arches an eyebrow. "Did he catch up with you?"

"Uh, yes. He was mad."

She giggles. "I hope you gave it right back to him. I tried to tell him a woman can leave whenever she pleases."

"I did." *More than you know, Fiore.*

"Ah, good. It's about time his big head is put in its place."

Even though her English isn't perfect, I get her meaning. "Is he…dating anyone?"

"No one serious, at least not since Gabriella."

"Who's Gabriella?"

"His ex-fiancée." She purses her lips.

"Oh." A thousand questions are on the tip of my tongue, but I don't want to seem too eager or nosy.

"Renzo met Gabriella at a party in Florence. She was young, beautiful, and full of life. He was completely smitten by her. It was love at first sight for both, and they got serious fast. But they were ill-fated from the start. Renzo was immersed in the business, and Gabriella wanted to run around with her elite rich friends. She was too much for Renzo, like a wild horse he tried to tame. And with any wild horse that's been captured, she became difficult to control.

Renzo wanted her to live here in Tuttoscano, and she wanted to be in Rome where the action was. He wanted a family, and she wanted champagne toasts with her friends on yachts."

"He didn't see they weren't right for each other?"

"I think he didn't want to see it, you know? She was very charming and fun. I believe my brother loved her, but not for the right reasons. She hurt him deeply when they called it quits, and he's never quite recovered. It's been five years, and I keep hoping he'll meet someone new. Don't get me wrong, he's not a monk. He goes on dates, but it never turns serious. He works too hard."

My stomach clenches at her mention of him going out with other women. "How did Gabriella hurt him?"

"That's something Renzo will have to share with you." She frowns, sliding her glasses up. She turns on her side and smiles at me. "Are you interested in my brother?"

"Oh, no…I was just curious." I replay the scene from last night in my head. It's all starting to make sense. Is he afraid I'll hurt him like Gabriella? Fiore's lip juts out in a pout, so I quickly change the subject before she can dig deeper. "So, Fiore, are you dating anyone?"

"No, not really."

"Fredo's pretty cute."

"*Sí*, he is…but I prefer the shape of butternut squash to a meatball," she says, her cheeks turning rosy.

"I don't even know what that means…squash to meatballs? *Non capsico.*"

She laughs. "I like the boobies, Summer."

"Oh…oh!" My brain catches up a few seconds later.

"You don't have a girlfriend?"

Fiore's smile falls. "I did, but she did not like being kept a secret."

"Why did you keep her a secret?"

"Because it would upset my mother and grandmother too much if they knew. I don't share that world with them."

"Oh, I'm sure they would be happy for you—"

"No, Summer, they would not understand. My family is *tradizionale*. They don't accept a woman can love another woman. It goes against the Catholic church." She sighs. "Sometimes I go out with Fredo just to get Mamma off my back. Fredo is one of my best friends, so he's happy to help me out."

"Do your brothers know?"

"*Sí*, they know and accept me as I am, but no one else in my family knows. Not even Gio or Nina."

"But, times have changed, I think you'd be surprised—"

"No, not here in Tuttoscano. You can't tell anyone, Summer. Promise me."

"I would never betray your confidence, Fiore. But I'm here for you if you ever need to talk about it."

"*Grazie*, Summer, that means a lot." She sighs, shielding her eyes against the sun. "Mamma drives Lorenzo and me *pazzi*, asking when we're going to get married and produce lots of grandbabies. We should have five kids a piece by now."

I swallow. "Does Lorenzo want lots of children?"

"I don't think so. He's thirty-two and so busy with the farm he doesn't have time for a family. We always say he's married to the olives." She laughs. "But if he met the right woman, that could all change." She smiles lazily at me, her eyes dancing with mischief. My cheeks heat as I study the smudge on my painted toenails.

"Thank you for sharing with me, Fiore. It means a lot."

"Thank you for listening, *sorella.*"

We sit in companionable silence for a few minutes while the blistering sun beats down on us.

"I think I'm going to test the water." I get up and dip my toe in before sitting down and dangling my legs in the cool water.

"*Salta nell' acqua,*" a male voice shouts. Gio, Nina, Angelo, and Fredo saunter through the gate.

"*Ciao,* Fredo!" Fiore jumps up and runs over, flinging herself into her best friend's arms. My heart breaks a little for Fiore at that moment. How awful it would be to have to hide a part of yourself. I anxiously wait for one more to arrive, but he doesn't show.

Nina dumps her bag on a chair next to mine before walking down the length of the pool with her perfectly toned and tanned butt cheeks on full display. Everyone is chatting in Italian, and I've never wished I had learned the language more than in this moment. I feel isolated, and it suddenly dawns on me that every time Lorenzo is around, everyone speaks English. My heartstrings tug.

Gio grabs Nina and pulls her into the pool, and she lets out a loud squeal. A body sits down next to me. I glance over and thank God I'm wearing my sunglasses because Angelo is wearing the tightest, brightest yellow bikini briefs I have ever seen. His dark skin is slick with tanning oil, and a gold cross lays against his chest.

"*Ciao, bella.*"

"*Ciao*, Angelo."

"*Sembri un buon bocconcino*," he says silkily.

"I'm not sure what you said."

He smiles wickedly. "Ah, how do you Americans say it? You look good enough to eat. Are you going to get in? We could join the fun."

Heat crawls up my neck. I watch the others playing chicken in the pool. "Ah, not exactly my style."

"Shame." He runs a finger down my thigh. I take his hand and place it on the sliver of concrete between us. I can't help but notice the bulge in the shockingly yellow briefs.

"Your suit is like a flag to a charging bull," he says.

"I'm sorry?" I check my bikini top to make sure everything is in its place.

"Your red swimsuit. It drives me crazy, like a bull. It's like the ties on the side are teasing me and the color red has always made me...*insaziabile.*" He licks his lips, and I lean away from him. Lorenzo warned me Italian men are forward, but Dr. Bianchi's bedroom eyes are intense. Perhaps I had a mild concussion after the accident for thinking this guy was appealing before.

"Well, you know what they say...mess with the bull and you get the horns." I laugh lightly, edging away from him.

"Eh? You Americans and your funny sayings. I like my women spicy...*piccanti*. Are you spicy, Summer?"

"Angelo! *Vieni nell' acqua!*" Nina shouts before I can respond, and for once, I'm thankful for her interruption because I'm utterly tongue-tied.

He raises his hand. "*Un minuto!* They want me to get in

the water. Are you sure you don't want to join?"

I smile briefly. "Go on, enjoy. I'll get in soon."

He flashes me his pearly whites before he dives in. Water splashes on my skin, making me shiver. Another group of people stroll into the pool area, and Gio shouts to them in greeting. My quiet afternoon with Fiore has quickly turned into a spring break pool-fest. I search the party, but no sign of Lorenzo.

"*Meglio solo che male accompagnato.*"

His deep, familiar voice startles me from my ruminating. I turn around, a quiet groan escaping my lips. Lorenzo is lounging in a chair next to Fiore's. His bare, bronzed, muscular torso soaking up the sun with his arm stretched above, cradling his head like he doesn't have a care in the world. His eyes are hidden behind a pair of dark Wayfarers, but I know he's looking at me. His washboard abs sparkle with a sheen of sweat. He leisurely gets up and saunters over to me, my fingers itching to touch the smooth expanse of his tanned chest. I tuck them under my thighs to squelch the temptation.

Cara was right. I need to speak up for what I want and sow my wild Italian oats with this man. His fitted black and blue swim trunks are much more appealing than Dr. Bianchi's loud yellow briefs. He eases down next to me, putting his legs in the water.

"What did you say?" I ask.

"Better to be alone than in bad company, *tesoro*."

"You think your cousin is bad company?"

"I think…you should be careful."

"How long have you been sitting there? I didn't even see

you come in."

"Long enough, *bullfighter.*" He playfully bumps his shoulder with mine. "I came up the back way." He splashes some water on his arms. "The red suits you. Are you going to get in?"

"Yeah, maybe. You?"

"Sure." He smiles, and it makes my heart beat out of control. The suntan lotion and the sweet smell of sweat on his skin make my hormones kick into overdrive. Flashbacks from last night in the rain, his lips on my skin, nearly pull me under.

He eases into the water, careful not to splash me. He turns around and places his muscular arms on the ledge. It takes all my self-control not to lick the drops of water sliding off his shoulder.

"Come on. It feels good."

"Okay," I agree, sliding into the cool water. He's right. It feels refreshing to my fevered skin. Butterflies thump wildly in my stomach as I prepare to lay it on the line. "I'm glad you're here because I wanted to talk to you about last night—"

"I can't, *tesoro,*" he says, interrupting what I planned to say. He turns and watches Gio throw Nina into the water, her squeals starting to get on my last nerve. "We should stick to just being friends. That's all I can offer you."

The butterflies in my stomach freeze and crumble into dust.

"It's no secret I'm a busy man. My work consumes me and it's my priority. I don't have time to get involved with someone." He waves a hand between us.

"I'm not Gabriella, Ren." My words hang in the air like a gunshot in the dark. He arches an eyebrow.

"How do you know about Gabriella?"

"Fiore told me."

"Ah, of course she did." He huffs, shaking his head. "All the same, *tesoro*. I'm sorry I kissed you last night. I shouldn't have done that. *Ho perso la testa ieri sera.*"

I quirk an eyebrow.

He smiles guiltily. "I lost control of myself last night."

"I'm not sorry," I whisper, but Nina's shrill screams drown me out. I gather my courage and try again. "Lorenzo, you can't deny there's an attraction between us. You even said so last night. Why can't we just have a casual affair?" Even as the words tumble off my lips, I know I'm fooling myself. Nothing about Lorenzo Rossi screams casual.

"Friends, Summer. That's all I can give you," he says again, with finality.

"Yeah, sure." I slowly sink into the water, wanting to drown myself in humiliation for putting myself out there. Not only did I have the best kiss of my life with this man, but now I've managed to keep myself friend-zoned until I leave. I can't *make* him want to be with me.

His hand wraps around my bicep, pulling me up. "*Tesoro*, don't drown on me now. I'm going to play volleyball with the guys. Want to join?"

Across the pool, Gio and Angelo set up a net. "Uh, I'll sit this one out."

"Okay…" He looks like he wants to say something more. Something important. Perhaps I should kiss him and show him that being friends is *way* overrated. I snort and shake my head. *If I had a dime for every time one of his lovers thought that...*Lorenzo Rossi probably breaks hearts all over Tuttoscano like it's his second job.

"Are you okay, Summer?"

*I'm completely devastated and embarrassed, Ren. How do you think I'm doing?*

"I'm fine," I lie.

"Join us in a bit, *sí*?"

"*Sí.*" I lift myself out of the pool and Gio and some other guy whistle.

"*Basta*, Gio," Lorenzo growls, sending his cousin a scathing glare.

I'm so grumpy right now I don't even care. I plunk down onto my chair. Fiore and Nina join me a few moments later.

"Ah, I see my brother came. He must have snuck in under Gio's radar."

"Mmm, look at all those fine men," Nina purrs next to me. Only one tanned Italian god stands out to me as he jumps up to spike the ball, his muscles rippling with the effort.

Fiore leans forward. "So Nina, a little birdie told me you and Angelo might have *baciato*...kissed."

"*E non solo...*" she says, smiling wickedly while checking out her nails.

Fiore laughs and slaps my leg as she waggles her eyebrows. "She said they did more than that."

He was flirting with me and trailing his fingers up my thigh not even fifteen minutes ago and he was with Nina? What a slimeball.

"Summer, you look like you just swallowed a lemon. Are

you okay?" Fiore asks.

"*È solo gelosa.*"

I grimace. "I am definitely not jealous, Nina."

"Tell me, Summer, if you could have your pick of one of those men, who would you choose?" Fiore asks.

*Lorenzo. Hands down Lorenzo Rossi.*

"None strike my fancy."

Nina snorts. "*Bugiarda.*"

"She's not lying, Nina." Fiore sighs. "I was hoping you would say my brother."

I rub sunscreen on my arms. "Your brother and I are just friends."

"Well, that's no fun. Renzo needs to let loose with someone."

"I'm available," Nina purrs. I want to squirt sunscreen in her eye.

"I doubt Renzo would be interested now that you've hooked up with Angelo." Fiore frowns. "I'm going to get some Pellegrino. Would you like some?"

"*Sí, grazie.*"

"*Limone, per favore.*" Nina glances over at me once Fiore is out of earshot. "Summer, what's your arrangement with the Rossis, anyway? How did you snag that house for yourself and get the easiest job up at the farm? Does your family know them?"

I shift uneasily, uncomfortable with this line of questioning from Nina. "No, I stopped in the house one day looking for a place to stay."

She snorts. "Signora Rossi just *gave* it to you? No wonder Lorenzo was so angry."

"She didn't just give it to me, and I keep it clean and the garden tidy—"

"So, what's your angle, Summer?"

I look at her sidelong. "I'm not sure I know what you mean."

She sprays oil on her legs as she formulates her answer. "*La famiglia Rossi é ricca sfondata*, or as you Americanos like to say, rolling in the dough. Everyone in town would like a piece of the Rossi fortune. It's no secret how wealthy they are and how much their estate is worth."

"What? No, no. That's not—"

"And you just show up, out of nowhere, dazzling the whole family like *un truffatore*—"

"Nina, that's not how it happened."

Fiore comes back over with our drinks. I force a smile as she hands me a tall glass of bubbling water with a lemon wedge, but I want to throw up.

"Summer, you're from California? Do you know anyone famous?" Nina plasters on a fake smile like she hadn't just accused me of being a gold digger.

"Ooh yes, Summer! I'd love to meet Brad Pitt," Fiore gushes.

"No Fiore, he's *so* old. *Ma bacerei volentieri* Harry Styles."

"Sorry." I shrug. "I don't know any celebrities. I'm in the northern part of California. Not a lot of celebrity sightings up there."

"Disappointing." Nina gets up and walks the length of the pool to the shallow end. Anything I'd say at this point would disappoint her. Gio gets hit in the head with the volleyball as he watches her.

"Fiore, how long has Nina been working for you?"

"Uh, about two years now."

"Have Lorenzo and her ever dated?"

Fiore and I watch while she playfully dips her toe into the water and splashes Lorenzo.

"No, not that I'm aware. She's too uh…*immatura* for Lorenzo. She's twenty-six, but acts younger."

I blow out a breath I didn't even realize I was holding. "Ah…I see."

"Are you *gelosa*, Summer?"

"Relieved is more like it."

She grins at me and playfully slaps my leg. "*Molto bene.*"

"Fiore, what does the word *truffatore* mean?"

"Uh, a scammer or a con artist. Why?"

I swallow thickly. "Nina said something, and I just need you to know I'm not here to take advantage of your family. I…just wanted you to know."

Fiore smiles. "Don't worry, Summer. Lorenzo had a background check done on you when Nonna hired you."

"Oh." *Well, that's news to me.* This information might have been upsetting, but I'm relieved the Rossis don't think I'm a con artist like Nina does.

I pray this family never has to meet my mom, Barbara. All my credibility will go right out the window.

LATER THAT NIGHT, after showering, I open up my email. I hold my breath and click open the one I've been waiting for from my boss, Allen.

*Summer,*

*We hope you're having a wonderful time over in Italy. I apologize for the delay in my response, I didn't want to bother you during your vacation time. I have received your request to work remotely for the summer. Because of your dedication and loyalty to the company, your request has been approved.*

I whoop and jump on my bed. Yes! I still have a job. I settle back down and continue reading.

*We just won the bid for the Chemistry for College textbook series and I will need you to work on this project at the end of August. It's a very important client of ours. Let me know your progress on the Algebra Series for Phoenix International after your vacation. I've set up a Zoom link for you.*

*Sincerely,*
*Allen Krantz*

*VP of Product Development, Granite Scholastics*

I fall back against my pillows and blow out a breath. I quickly text Cara and Barbara, updating them about my plans to stay in Italy until the end of summer.

# Chapter 19

I GET HOME from a morning run the following week and see a note on my kitchen table in Nonna Rossi's shaky handwriting:

*Summer, please meet me in the garden up at the house, subito—Nonna*

Worried she might be in trouble, I quickly grab a bottle of water and my bike. I turn the bend in the road, and spy Nonna Rossi bent over in the lavender. I lean my bike against the stone wall and shout, "I'm here, Nonna Rossi! Are you okay?"

She's pulling weeds and putting them into a basket. She looks up and waves. "*Tutto bene. Sto parlando con le api e le farfalle*...uh...talking to the bees and the butterflies."

"Oh, you said to meet you immediately. I thought something was wrong."

"*No, mi godo il sole.* Enjoy the sunshine, Summer. *Vieni qui.*" She waves me over. I step over the stone wall, relaxing a fraction now that I know she's okay. She's tucked in between rows of lavender and geranium, wearing a wide straw hat and a linen button-down with linen pants.

"Sorry, I'm a little sweaty. I went for a run."

"No matter." She hands me a basket. "Weed over there."

She points to some rosemary next to a section of wall where Razzo is lounging. Nonna Rossi smiles and pats my cheek. "*Brava ragazza*, good girl."

"Uh, okay…sure."

Razzo eyes me like he'd like to scratch his claws down my face. I guess our time of friendship has ended. I approach with hesitant steps, giving him the signal I'm watching him. He yawns in response and flicks his tail. A light breeze sings through the trees, cooling the sweat on my skin.

"Nonna Rossi, do you take care of these gardens all by yourself?" I set my basket down and Razzo immediately jumps in it. "Beat it, *gatto*." I reach in to remove him, but he tries to bite me.

She chuckles, bending back down. "No, too much for me, but I love to get out here every day that I can. Brings joy to me and keeps my strength up. *Sí?*"

"*Sí.*" I smile and squat down, breathing in the clean air and the smell of lavender, rosemary, and basil. I toss a weed on Razzo and he flattens his ears. We work in companionable silence for a few moments before Nonna speaks up.

"The house okay for you, Summer, *sí*?"

"*Sí, è bellissima e grazie.*"

"Ah, *perfetto*. And how are you and Renzo?" She looks at me shrewdly.

"Lorenzo?" I pull out a weed, considering what to say. "Um, good, *va bene*. We're fine. Just fine."

"That *Americano* word—fine. You say it a lot. What does fine even mean? In Italy, you say it is wonderful or *è terribile*. Not this in-between word of fine."

I chew my lip, wondering how much I should share with

Nonna Rossi. "He wants to be friends, so that's…*va bene*."

Nonna throws down her trowel. "*Non va bene! Lorenzo ha bisogno di svegliarsi e annusare le olive! Lo amo, quell'asino.*"

"Uh…Nonna Rossi, I don't understand what you're saying."

She picks up her trowel and digs vigorously. "Lorenzo needs to stop burying his head in the olives. I love him, but he's a horse's ass. *La mia opinione* is that a woman who knows what she wants will make an effort to get it."

"With all due respect, Nonna, I'm not sure *he* wants…" My voice trails off when she stabs a plant with her trowel. Between Razzo and Nonna, I'm feeling like a trapped rabbit.

"If you want to be more than *fine* with Lorenzo, then you need to learn Italian. Become a part of his world."

"But, I'm leaving—"

"*Sí, sí, stai partendo.* You're always leaving. You've been leaving since the day you arrived. *Mamma mia!* How do you expect to have any kind of relationship if you're not truly present?"

I'm stunned into silence, mulling over her words.

"Sometimes in life, *piccolina*, you have to tell yourself, is okay to stay, *sí*? You spread your roots in the soil and grow into un *bellissimo albero*…a beautiful unbending tree. You stay put. The adventure you seek is in your heart, not in the distance of where you go to next."

Raw pain from my past tries to bulldoze rational thought. Nonna doesn't know that all I've ever wanted is to stay rooted.

"My entire childhood was centered around my mom leaving. She moved out and left me to live with my grandmother when I was three. She said she was going on an adventure, and that she'd be back, but she didn't come back for a long time."

Nonna stays silent while we busily pull weeds. It's nice to have something to do with my hands.

She probably can't understand half of what I'm saying anyway, so I ramble on because it's therapeutic talking to her. The memories of those tumultuous times crash into me, wave after wave, taking me under.

"My mom would get bored with whatever guy she was dating and eventually come back. My grandmother would be furious with her, calling her irresponsible and immature, encouraging her to give up her parental rights. They were constantly screaming at each other. It was a confusing time for me because I wanted my mom to be a part of my life, but I was also relieved when she'd up and leave, restoring peace to the house. Grams gave me love and stability, something my mother could never do. As an adult, I clung to that stability and predictability because I never wanted to be like Barbara.

"I'm thirty-six years old, Nonna, and I've never done something as spontaneous as this trip. Italy was calling to me. In some ways, I feel guilty, acting like my mother who only thinks about herself. In other ways, I feel like I'm standing on the ledge needing to jump, or I'll never learn to fly."

"And when you land, then what? Better to be a tree with roots than a bird with wings."

"Maybe so, Nonna, but I need to be a bird first to find a safe place to land."

I thought I needed to find love and be adventurous, but perhaps Nonna Rossi is right. What I'm looking for has been in my heart the whole time. Grams was constantly reminding me happiness comes from within, not from who you surround yourself with.

"You're right, Nonna. I haven't given Italy or the wonderful people here a chance. I've been afraid of what might happen if I allow myself to feel like I belong."

Nonna looks at me with something akin to sympathy. "You belong, *picolla stella.*"

"Would you teach me some Italian?"

"*Sí, pensavo che tu non chiedessi mai…*I thought you'd never ask." She grins and motions to me. "*Ripeti: Sono innamorata di tuo figlio.*"

"*Sono innamorata di tuo figlio.*"

"*Voglio sposarlo,*" she prompts.

"*Sono innamorata di tuo figlio. Voglio sposarlo.* What does that mean?"

"It means Nonna is being meddlesome. Don't repeat anything she says," Lorenzo's deep baritone grumbles, sending chills racing down my spine. He steps over the stone wall into the garden.

"Ah, Lorenzo, Summer is learning Italian. Isn't that wonderful?"

He glances at Nonna with a raised eyebrow. "*Sí.* I see you've also roped her into helping you weed the garden." He leans down and scratches Razzo's head. The little traitor immediately purrs.

"Oh, I don't mind." I smile up at him and yank out another weed. "What are you up to on this beautiful

Sunday?"

"I stopped by your house to see if you wanted to have lunch with us."

"*Sí*, Renzo, why do you think she's here?" Nonna says impatiently. "Your parents just got home from Mass."

"Why didn't you go this morning?" he asks.

"*È maleducato fare a tua nonna questa domanda.*"

Lorenzo snorts and looks at me. "She said it's rude of me to ask her that."

I smile and stand up, brushing off my hands. "I'd love to have lunch, but as you can see, I need a shower and a change of clothes, so I'll take a raincheck."

"No, you come." Nonna stands and stretches her back before heading toward the house. "Be a tree, Summer! *Vieni, ora!*"

"*Vieni, ora?*" I ask.

"It means come now. I'm not sure what be a tree means."

"Oh, crazy Nonna." I chuckle nervously and turn to face him. The light breeze ruffles his tousled hair, making me want to glide my fingers through the silky strands. Friends can do that, can't they? *No, Summer, they cannot.*

Lorenzo throws an arm around my shoulders and guides me out of the garden. I shrink away from him, worried I smell disgusting. Damn Nonna Rossi for making me rush up here after a run for a Sunday lunch she failed to mention.

"I really should go shower first."

"No time, *tesoro*. If my parents are home from Mass, then Fiore already has food on the table. Don't worry, it's just us today. We'll seat you on the end away from everyone." He smirks and I jab him with my elbow. He grabs my bike, and we walk up the drive to the main house behind Nonna. "I've been so busy at work this week, in meetings, and I had to go to Rome. How have you been?"

"I was wondering why I hadn't seen you much. I looked for you by your tree." I clear my throat, heat splashing my cheeks. "Anyway, we had a couple of groups come in each day, so it was busy. I worked on some ad campaign stuff for you to see."

"Ah, *fantastico*! That was quick."

"Well, they're just some ideas I've come up with." I wring my hands together. "If you approve, I can mock them up. But if you don't like them, that's okay. It won't hurt my feelings. I mean, I want you to be honest with me. Don't like them just because we're friends."

"Summer, I'm sure they're wonderful. I look forward to seeing them. Send them to me tonight." He smiles down at me and leans my bike against the stone wall by his car before we walk into the house.

Stella welcomes me with a hug, and Signor Rossi shakes my hand before sitting down at the head of the table with the Sunday paper. He and Lorenzo talk about *La Nazionale di calcio dell'Italia* and the latest *competizione*, so I quietly excuse myself to go freshen up in the bathroom.

Has it only been a week since I kissed Lorenzo? Seven days since he formally friend-zoned me? My heart sinks while I stare at my reflection in the mirror. I'd friend-zone me too if I looked like this. My limp ponytail hangs off-kilter, and a halo of frizz frames my face. I pull my ponytail out and wet my fingers with some water, smoothing out my hair. I pull it up again and grimace. Now I look like I'm sweating again. I open a drawer to find a clean towel and burst out laughing. The drawer must have at least a hundred safety pins in it. *Dammit, Lorenzo, how can I not fall in love with you?*

Running a washcloth under the faucet, I quickly wash my face and armpits, giving myself a mini bath. Well, it's somewhat better than before. Everyone is waiting for me at the table when I return.

"Oh, I'm so sorry for making you wait."

Fiore beams at me. "Summer, I'm so glad you're here!"

I smile back and fold my napkin in my lap. Signor Rossi says a quick prayer over the food. Stella pours wine into everyone's glass before sitting back down.

"Summer, Nonna says she's teaching you Italian," Stella says.

"*Sí*, I'm very excited."

"That's wonderful. What have you learned?"

"Oh, well, we just started today." I take a small drink of my wine, trying to remember the phrase from twenty minutes ago.

"Summer...," Lorenzo rumbles, slightly shaking his head in warning.

I glance at him curiously, brushing him off because Nonna beams and nods, encouraging me to repeat it. "*Sono innamorata di tuo figlio!* Uh... *Voglio sposarlo!*"

Fiore bursts out laughing as Signor Rossi raises his eyebrows at Stella. Lorenzo runs a hand over his face and glares at Nonna.

Panic washes over me. "Oh God, what did I say?"

"You said I'm in love with your son and I want to marry him." Fiore laughs.

Heat flashes up my neck. Reaching for my wineglass, I gulp it, wishing I had ignored Nonna's invitation to lunch. Stella claps her hands and giggles. "Wonderful first-day lesson, Summer."

*Yep, fucking wonderful, Stella.* Nonna looks like the cat who ate the canary while she helps herself to a dish. Lorenzo glances over at me and raises an eyebrow, his expression saying, *I tried to tell you, dumbass.* He turns to his dad, thankfully spinning the conversation in a different direction, bringing up something about the upcoming harvest.

Fiore leans over to me. "Stop by the café kitchen tomorrow after work. Nonna and I are making sauce. You said you wanted to learn, *sí*? We can also practice your Italian." She winks.

I nod my head as I dig into her pasta. "*Sì, per favore.*"

"*Benissimo*," Fiore says.

# Chapter 20

AFTER WORK, I arrive in Fiore's kitchen and cross to the sink to wash my hands. Fredo nods hello to me while he kneads dough on the counter. Nonna and Fiore stand on the opposite side of the kitchen, conversing in Italian while they chop fresh herbs from Nonna's garden.

"*Ciao.*"

"*Ciao*, Summer. Sono *così felice che tu sia venuta*. So glad you're here." Fiore wraps me in a hug. I kiss Nonna's cheek and settle in next to her at the counter.

"Today, we are making Bolognese sauce. Ragù Bolognese. It's Renzo's favorite." Fiore winks at me.

"Uh yes, I remember you told me that."

"I've already made the pasta. That will be a lesson for another day. We use tagliatelle, flat broad noodles with our ragù here." Fiore passes me an onion, celery, and carrots. "First, we start with these three vegetables that make up the *battuto*. We sauté them in butter, and that's what makes up the *soffritto, sì*?"

My head is spinning with all the different names Fiore is throwing out. She hands me a cutting board. "You can chop them up. The *soffritto* is the base for most pasta sauces. It's a very important step."

I nod and grab a sharp knife out of the woodblock. I

watch Nonna expertly chop herbs. "I don't think I'll be as fast as you two."

"*Non c'è problema.*"

I repeat the phrase meaning, *no problem*, and Nonna nods approvingly.

"What have you decided about your time here? Are you still planning on leaving at the end of summer?" Fiore asks, opening a can of tomato paste.

"I—"

"You must stay at least past *Ferragosto*! We all go on holiday to the seaside together."

"That sounds lovely, but I'm not sure of my plans yet. My boss is letting me work remotely until we start a new project in September." I frown, chopping the carrots. I can't imagine Lorenzo would want me going on his family vacation.

"*La vita è come una fotografia. Se sorridi, viene meglio,*" Nonna says.

Fiore chuckles. "Nonna said, life is like a photograph. If you smile, it comes out better."

"*Goditi la tua vita.*" Nonna motions to me.

I repeat the phrase and Fiore smiles warmly before translating. "Enjoy your life, Summer. *Vivi il momento presente!* Live in the moment."

"Nonna is right." I smile and slice the onion in half. "*Goditi la tua vita.*"

"*Bene.*" Nonna tilts her head. "*Ferragosto, sí?*"

I chuckle, knowing I'm being railroaded once again by Nonna Rossi. "*Sí.*"

"You're nothing like Gabriella, Summer. I think you

should know that," Fiore says softly. "She hated cooking, hated the farm, and would never go with us to *Ferragosto.*"

"Oh, Ren and I are just friends—"

"*Sí*, Gabriella was weak." Nonna whacks a tomato while she talks over me. "You are *sole e sorrisi*, sunshine and smiles. She was never happy here. She wanted the finer life, and being an olive farmer's wife was beneath her."

"*Sí.*" Fiore nods. "She couldn't accept Lorenzo for what he was destined to be."

"That's a shame," I say, sad for Lorenzo, but also feeling slightly uncomfortable that we're talking about him and his ex-fiancée. By the pool with Fiore, I was curious, but I feel like a gossip with Nonna here.

"She would never have come in here to cook and chat with us." Fiore frowns.

"Really? I think this is the highlight of my week." I smile, and Fiore wraps me in a side-hug.

"*Sole e sorrisi.*" Nonna smiles. "*Ferragosto, sí?*"

I chuckle and chop the garlic. "*Sí*, Nonna."

"*Bene, piccolina.*"

Fiore and Nonna speak in Italian, translating words for me, and I repeat them while we spend the next hour making the Bolognese sauce. At one point, Stella comes in, tastes the sauce and kisses her fingertips, just like I've always pictured Italians doing after they try something delectable.

It's nice laughing and talking with the three generations of Rossi women. Something I never had growing up. I think back to my grandmother, who worked until she was seventy-five at the diner down the road from our small house. She had to take care of me and her wayward daughter, who couldn't or wouldn't hold down a job.

I'm so grateful Grams took us in and provided me with stability. It wasn't an easy life for her. I've played it safe for so long, afraid to go against the grain and turn into Barbara, but I don't want to end up working until the day I die like Grams. She would want me to smile for the photograph and be happy.

Fiore's laugh brings me back to the present moment. "Ah Renzo, glad you came down from your stuffy office! Taste what Summer made."

He lifts an eyebrow and removes his suit jacket, rolling up the sleeves of his dress shirt. How can a man's forearms be so sexy? He tastes the spoonful of sauce shoved in his face by his sister. "*Molto buono*, Summer."

My stomach twists with pleasure over his compliment. "I have excellent teachers."

"Perhaps you'll want to stay and learn more about our Italian culture." Nonna winks before she pushes past us. "You should take her to Rome and Florence, Renzo."

"I did promise to take you to Florence." He leans against the island and folds his arms over his chest, his lips curving into a smile.

I mimic his pose and stand in the cramped galley across from him, holding a bottle of Rossi Olive Oil.

His eyes flicker to the bottle and then back to me. We stare at each other, the chatter and banging pots in the crowded kitchen falling away. I get lost in the gold flecks in his eyes. I imagine him picking me up and setting me on the counter, slowly peeling off my clothes, dropping kisses to my fevered skin, tasting me like I'm one of Fiore's desserts.

His tongue would start at my navel, torturously licking his way…

A clattering of pans breaks the spell Ren has me under. I clench my thighs together. He leans forward and takes the bottle out of my hand, putting it safely down on the counter.

"It's bad luck to spill olive oil." His husky voice zips over my skin like wildfire burning out of control. Desire drips between us like a hot, humid night.

"Woo! *Qualcosa ha preso fuoco qui!* Something is on fire in here! I'm getting hot and bothered just looking at you two." Fiore raises her eyebrows and fans her face. "I wish someone would look at me like that. Scorching!"

Lorenzo rubs a hand across his jaw and shoots his sister a scathing glare as heat spreads across my already-flushed cheeks.

"*Non mettermi in imbarazzo*, Fiore. I've got to head back to the offices. Save me some of this for dinner, *per favore*. I'll be working late." He kisses Nonna and Stella's cheeks before he strides out of the kitchen without a backward glance.

"I embarrassed him." Fiore chuckles and turns to me, waggling her eyebrows. "Would you like to deliver his dinner later, Summer?"

"Uh, no, I'm good." I bite my cheek while Stella, Nonna, and Fiore stare at me with big stupid grins on their faces.

I wonder how to say, I'm screwed, in Italian.

# Chapter 21

MY PHONE BUZZES with an incoming call from Cara.

"Nina, are you okay if I take my break?"

She waves at me without looking up from her phone. I exit the door of the shop and walk toward the farmhouse and answer the call. "Hey girl, perfect timing. I'm on my break. Everything okay?"

"Summer, I went to check on your place yesterday."

Dread fills my belly. "Did something happen?"

"It's a mess. There are beer bottles littering every surface. It looks like she's been having parties every night. I cleaned it up, but wanted you to know. I think she's been driving your car too, because it wasn't in your driveway."

"Crap, I can't believe her. She must have found where I hid the keys." I breathe in through my nose and out through my mouth. "Thank you so much, Cara. I'm so sorry you're having to deal with this. I'll handle it."

"Okay, hon. I'm here for you if you need me."

"I appreciate you more than you know. I'll talk to you later, okay?"

"Okay. Luvs you, Summer."

"Luvs you." I hang up with Cara, furious with Barbara. I dial her number, ready to leave her a scathing voicemail because I know she won't answer at seven a.m.

"You realize it's the crack of dawn here, don't you?" she croaks into the phone. A man in the background mumbles something. "It's just my kid. Go back to sleep, babe."

Shocked she actually answered, I'm momentarily tongue-tied. "Where are you?"

"In bed, Summer, where else would I be?"

"Barbara, we need to talk. Cara told me you took the keys to my car when I explicitly told you not to."

"I had an emergency. My car is still in the city lot."

"She also said you've trashed my house like you've been having parties there every night."

"Are you having her check on me?" she slurs. *Is she still drunk?*

"I asked her to keep an eye on everything while I'm gone. Friends do that for each other, Barbara." Anger bubbles in my veins. "I think it's time you looked for your own apartment."

"You're so selfish, Summer. It's always been like this since you were little because Grams spoiled you rotten. Poor Summer needs her mom, poor Summer doesn't get the attention she needs, everything has always been about *you*. Well, what about me? When is it *my* turn? Not everyone can afford the luxury of gallivanting all over Italy. Don't concern yourself over me. I'll be out of here tomorrow." The call disconnects.

I can barely see straight, I'm so angry. I immediately call her back, but it goes straight to voicemail.

"Barbara, you are not allowed to drive my car, do you hear me? I will have the police pull you over if you get behind the wheel. I'm letting you live in my home and this is the thanks I get?" I swipe tears from my eyes, sounding just like my Grams used to when dealing with her. "Call me back. You at least owe me that much."

Fuming, I hang up, not sure what my options are. I stare at my phone, wondering what the hell I should do while walking aimlessly toward the mill.

"Oof." Hands circle my arms as I walk right into a human wall. My phone clatters to the ground next to a pair of expensive Italian dress shoes.

"Whoa, steady there. I was just coming to find you. I looked over some of your branding ideas and they're great! I really like the emphasis on family and taking it back to the beginning when we first started. Trust the Rossi family, trust the brand. I love it!"

I gaze into Lorenzo's smoky eyes framed by long black lashes, but I'm not really listening.

"I'm sorry, Lorenzo, but can we talk about this later?" I try to bend down to pick up my phone, but he holds on to me.

"Summer, are you okay?"

"No, I'm not okay."

*I'm incredibly attracted to you and can't act on it. My mother is an alcoholic who refuses to get help and I don't know how to handle it. My time in Italy has an expiration date I'm not sure I want to end, and all I really want to do is bury myself in your arms and cry, but I can't.*

His brows scrunch as he tries to read the emotions skittering across my face. "Is there anything I can do?"

"No."

*Hold me.*

He looks over at the building I exited and his nostrils flare. He drops his hands and folds them over his chest. "Is Nina bothering you?"

"No, Lorenzo, it's not Nina." I turn from his intense gaze. "What are you doing down here, anyway? Don't you have meetings or phone calls or something in your office?"

His jaw clenches. "I told you I was looking for you to tell you—"

"Sorry." I hold up my hands as I back up a few steps. "I'm having some personal issues."

"Let me help."

I laugh humorlessly. No way in hell will I dump my issues with my wayward mom on Lorenzo. "No. I can handle it. I always have."

He slides his hands in his pockets and nods. "I know you can. Why don't you take the rest of the afternoon off?"

"I don't need you to coddle me, Ren."

His eyes narrow. I can't help but take my frustration of Barbara out on him.

"I'm not coddling." He clenches his jaw. "We don't need you acting like this around the customers."

"Acting like what?" I feel like a boxer jumping around my opponent, waiting for the perfect jab, but Ren doesn't want to get in the ring with me. His lips part like he wants to say something more, but he shakes his head instead.

"Go home, Summer. That's an order, not a request." He turns on his heel and walks away without a backward glance.

# Chapter 22

SINCE REN ORDERED me to leave the farm, I decide to head into town. I need a distraction and sitting at the house having a staring contest with Razzo won't cut it. I haven't seen Ren that pissed since the day I took the house from him. I feel bad I took my anger out on him, knowing he was only trying to help.

I figure I can burn off this negative energy by walking around and thinking about how best to handle the Barbara situation. Dinner at a cute little café might ease the tension. I wish Harrison or Lynnette were here so I could wander around with a companion. I've kept in touch with them since they left Italy, but life has moved on for both and neither will be returning to Italy this summer.

It's probably best I'm alone. I'm not exactly the greatest company. Thinking of Harrison, I send him a text.

**Me:** *Ciao H. How's the toilet business?*

**Harrison:** *Summer! How's my favorite ex-pat doing?*

**Me:** *Italy is incredible. I'm currently licking hazelnut gelato.*

**Harrison:** *How is the scary old Italian lady?*

**Me:** *Nonna is pushy but lovable. She's trying to set me up with her grandson, but he's friend-zoned me.*

***Harrison:*** *The one who wanted to murder you when we came to the house? Lol.*

***Me:*** *Nah, we're good now. Sadly, my heart is still single.*

***Harrison:*** *Any news on smoking hot Daniella?*

***Me:*** *Haven't seen her, but I'll ask Lorenzo about her for you.*

***Harrison:*** *Yes! Tell her I can remodel her whole bathroom with Kohler. Women love that shit.*

***Me:*** *Erm…okay.*

***Harrison:*** *I've got an important meeting to get on. Keep me posted! Arrivederci!*

***Me:*** *Arrivederci, H! Sell some more toilets so you can come back!*

I tuck my phone in my purse and find myself standing in front of an art gallery. I woefully throw my half-eaten gelato in the trash before wandering into the minimalist room with glossy dark wooden floors and white walls. I immediately fall in love with the bright colors splashed across the canvases.

"*Buongiorno.*" A blonde woman smiles at me behind a desk.

"*Buongiorno.*" I return her smile, walking around the room, studying the paintings. "*Parli inglese?*"

"*Sí,*" she says.

"Are you the artist?" I ask her over my shoulder while I stand in front of an impressionistic painting of olive trees on a hillside. I love how the artist mixes dabs of blues and greens with terracotta browns and burnt sienna.

"Ah, no, but he is local. Are you interested in this piece?"

"How much…" I stop and remember my lessons with

Nonna. "*Quanto per questo?*"

"That one is ten thousand seven hundred euros."

My eyes widen as I stare at the painting. "Ten thousand?" I squeak out. "That's like twelve thousand US…"

"*Sí*, we can ship to the US if you need us to. Would you like to see the artist's studio? He hasn't used it in a while, but there might be something in there to pique your interest?"

The thought of peeking into an artist's private sanctuary makes me uncomfortable, especially when I don't intend to buy.

"Oh, no, that's okay. Do you have any prints?"

The woman looks disappointed as she points to a bin. "The artist has some prints over there."

I thumb through the bin and find the olive one. "*Cuanto questo?*"

"Forty-two euros. I have a framed one for sixty-two."

I gaze at the picture, drawn to the landscape. It looks like the old tree Lorenzo showed me on the farm. I haven't bought much since I've been here except for the dresses, and looking at this picture makes me happy. "Okay, *sí*, I'll take this one, with the frame."

She rings it up and I tuck the picture wrapped in paper inside my messenger bag. I wander back out to the street, and stand on the corner deciding on a place to eat while tourists and locals mill about, returning home from work.

"Summer? What are you doing here?" Dr. Angelo Bianchi walks toward me. I didn't even realize I was close to the clinic.

"Oh, hi, Dr. Bianchi. I was off work early, so I thought I'd head into town and do some shopping."

"Please, call me Angelo. I think we're past formalities, no?" He looks up at the apartments above the art gallery. "I thought you were waiting for Lorenzo. He lives here."

"Really?" I look up, surprised by his revelation. God, that would have been embarrassing if he had caught me wandering aimlessly outside his apartment. "Ha, no, I was trying to decide where to go grab something to eat."

"Have you tried the pizza? *Troppo buono.* We go and eat, *sì?*"

"Okay…sure, why not."

"Why not." He nods his head and places his hand on my lower back. "This way."

I don't really want to go to dinner with Angelo Bianchi, the bikini bull fighter, but I also don't want to eat alone, and pizza does sound *perfetto*. The good news is, I'm no longer dazzled by his good looks or his charm, especially when I'm attracted to another man who kissed me in the rain like it was his last dying wish.

We sit outside a quaint little restaurant with twinkling lights, around the corner from Lorenzo's apartment. A violin player softly strums in the back corner.

"This place is always busy, so it's good we got here early."

"It's amazing! Do you live near here?"

"About a five-minute walk from here. *Cittadina…*small town." He smiles and picks up the menu.

A server bustles over and plunks down a bottle of Chianti and two glasses, before lighting the candle on the table. "Wow, they don't waste time, do they?"

Angelo chuckles. "It's standard here to have their house-made wine with the pizza. So, how do you like our quaint little village of Tuttoscano so far?"

"It's absolutely lovely. Exactly what I imagined when I booked my trip."

"Are they working you too hard up at the *azienda olivicola*?"

"Oh, no, the Rossis have been so kind."

"Have you been to the bigger cities like Florence? I studied and practiced there before I came back home."

"Not yet, but I will. I'd like to visit the seaside, too."

"Ah, yes…Viareggio is very nice. I could take you there on your next weekend off?" He smiles, perfect white teeth flashing. An image of him in his banana-yellow bikini briefs standing in the surf immediately plays like a movie in my head. Nina comes running into the water like she's on *Baywatch.* A big wave crashes into her and takes her down. Dr. Bianchi laughs and helps her back up and they kiss passionately.

"*Ciao…*Summer? Where did you just go?" He waves a hand in front of my face.

"Sorry, I was thinking about something." I tune back into the present, and give him a lopsided smile. "Wouldn't you want to take Nina there instead of me?"

"Nina? Uh…" His brow furrows like he's trying to remember who Nina might be. The server interrupts before he can answer, and writes down our pizza order.

"So, tell me about—"

"*Che stai facendo?*" Lorenzo approaches our table, looking murderous.

"*Ceno con il tuo amante Americano, cosa ne pensi?*" Dr.

Bianchi smirks.

Did he really just say he was having dinner with Lorenzo's American lover? Oh god. My eyes bounce between the two men. Lorenzo is practically snarling at Angelo. He turns away from his cousin, his steely gaze falling on me. Even though we parted ways a couple of hours ago, it feels like days have passed. I feel terrible for snapping at him earlier.

"I've been trying to find you. You're not answering your cell."

"Oh…" I dig my phone out of my purse, seeing two missed calls from him. "I'm sorry, I didn't realize it was on silent."

"Do you mind if I borrow your dinner *companion* for a minute?"

"Um, of course." I furrow my brow. Why is he so upset? I try to convey with my eyes this is not what it looks like. It's dinner between two people who bumped into each other on the street and happened to be hungry, but he's not catching my drift. Angelo rolls his eyes and excuses himself from the table. The two men exit the courtyard of the restaurant and cross the street.

The server drops off our pizzas and refills my glass. The two men gesture and argue while people walk around them on the sidewalk, casting curious glances. The pizza smells so damn good, and the violinist seems aware of the thick tension in the air because his notes turn into a more staccato rhythm. I pick up a slice and bite into it, not even realizing I'm doing it, absorbed by Angelo and Lorenzo's rapid-fire Italian argument across the way. Lorenzo clenches his fist and looks as if he wants to punch Angelo in the face. I wonder why they dislike each other so much. They are *famiglia* after all.

Lorenzo ends the quarrel by abruptly turning away from Angelo. He quickly walks down the street until he disappears from view. He doesn't glance in my direction once or wish me a *buona notte*. I'm not surprised, though. I was such a jerk to him earlier. I want to throw some euros down on the table and run after him and apologize, but something tells me now is not the time.

By the time Angelo returns, I've demolished my pizza. He looks surprised when he stares at the empty plate.

"Sorry, I was hungry. Is everything okay?"

"No need to apologize *bella*, it is me who is sorry. My cousin certainly has a flair for the dramatic." He testily cuts his pizza with a fork and knife. "So…when would you like to go to Viareggio?"

"Oh, uh…" I gulp my Chianti, stalling. Shit, what would Cara do at this moment? She would tell him to go to hell. "I'm not sure—"

He smiles. "Next weekend, then. *Molto bene.*"

I want to go to Viareggio, just not with him.

WE FINISH DINNER and Angelo offers to have me come over to his apartment, which I promptly decline. I pull out my phone to call a cab, but he insists on driving me home. He revs his yellow Ferrari, which matches his swimsuit, and take the road out of town like we're on the Autobahn. I grab the door handle like a lifeline and triple-check my seatbelt. Angelo looks over at me, grinning.

"Uh, could you please keep your eyes on the road?"

"Do you not like fast cars, Summer?"

"I do…I just like my body parts attached better. So, is yellow your favorite color?"

"Actually, it's red. Why do you ask?"

"Never mind," I mumble, closing my eyes, scared I might puke on the plush leather interior.

He pulls into my parking area, gravel spraying. I take a moment to gain my equilibrium before unfastening my seatbelt and scrambling out of the death trap. Angelo follows me to my door. I turn, holding out my hand, not wanting him to think this is an invitation to come in. His chest bumps into my palm and his lips quirk.

"I had an enjoyable evening with you, Summer."

"Yeah, it was great. You're a nice friend, Angelo. Thanks for dinner."

"Summer…" He takes my hand and presses it to his chest. I wiggle it out of his grasp.

"Okay, well, thanks for the ride home," I say, backing up until my back hits the wall.

He puts a hand against the door, caging me in. "Aren't we more than friends, Summer?"

He licks his lips and leans in, making his move. Instincts kick in and I grab his arm and twist it back, shoving him into the side of the entryway, and stomp on his foot. He curses and stumbles while I reach for the door handle.

Marcos, my self-defense trainer, would be so proud.

"Okay, thanks for dinner! See you later, Angelo!" I unlock the door in record speed and quickly shut it in his face. My chest heaves while I take a moment to catch my breath, adrenalin sprinting through my veins. I can hear him curse in Italian on the other side of the door and wait for the sound of his tires to crunch over gravel. I exhale a deep breath. Jesus, that was close.

I lock the front door and run up the stairs to my bedroom and call Cara, telling her about my night.

"Okay, let me get this straight. You told Lorenzo you want to be more than friends, but he's not ready for that step even though he admits he's attracted to you, and now hot Dr. Angel wants to sweep you away for a weekend to an Italian seaside town? I don't feel sorry for you."

"Dr. *Devil* had sex with my coworker after flirting with me all night!"

"He's Italian, what do you expect? They're hot-blooded and virile."

"You really need to stop reading Damien's *GQ* magazines."

She laughs. "I'm just trying to get you to relax about this whole situation. Yeah, the doc is a total slimeball, but he's offering to take you away for the weekend. Go have fun. Insist on staying in a separate hotel room and be a nun."

I picture myself trying to use self-defense moves on Angelo all weekend. No, thank you.

"But I don't want to weekend with Angelo. I want to go with Lorenzo." I put the phone on speaker so that I can talk to her while I hang my new framed picture. I pick up a hammer and nail.

"But Lorenzo hasn't asked to go away with you. He's also made it clear he just wants to be friends."

"Semi-clear. He's been sending me some strong I-want-you vibes."

Cara snorts. "If I remember correctly, the whole point of this trip was to find something you're missing in your life."

"Yes, but…" I eyeball where I want to hang my print and place the nail on the wall.

"Be adventurous, Summer. Go screw your brains out with the hot doctor who wants you and forget about the brooding olive farmer."

"But that's the problem. I can't forget about the brooding olive farmer."

I hit the hammer on the nail hard. It goes in smoothly, but a sizeable chunk of plaster around the nail crumbles. "Oh, shit," I mutter, staring at the hole in the wall I created.

"Are you okay?"

"I just took a chunk of plaster out of the wall. How the hell am I going to cover this up? My picture isn't that big."

"Hang something light over it, like a towel or something."

I survey my room, grab a t-shirt off the end of my bed, and drop it over the nail.

"What do you think I should I do about Barbara? Call the police?"

"I don't know. Technically, she's done nothing illegal," she says.

"Unless I report my car as stolen."

"You don't need Barbara getting arrested," Cara reasons.

"I know. God, what a mess."

"I can ask my friend Tony. He specializes in that kind of stuff." She sighs. "Listen, I've got an appointment I have to run to. Hang in there, Summer. I'll try to stop by your place after work today and sort it out with Babs. Remember, *you're* in control. If you don't want to be friend-zoned by the grouchy olive farmer, then go over there and say something. Call me tomorrow. *Ciao*, babe."

"*Arrivederci*, not *ciao*."

"Whatever. Miss you, love you."

I hang up with Cara and try another area on the wall to hang my picture. I gently hammer the nail into the plaster, and it sticks. I mentally give myself a high-five and hang the painting. I step back, admiring the brushstrokes of color, when a chunk of the wall comes loose. The plaster and picture crash to the floor.

"No!" I shout and rush to the print, picking it up out of the debris. Miraculously, the glass didn't break. I gape at the wall. How the hell am I going to fix this? It's not like there's a Home Depot down the street with all my DIY needs. I groan and fall back on my bed. "Can't anything go fucking right today?" I rub the gold necklace at my throat between my two fingers and say a prayer to the Italian gods, whoever they are.

Cara's right, this trip *was* supposed to be an adventure. I need to put my big-girl panties on and take life by the horns. Nonna's words reverberate in my head. *You're always ready to leave.* I sit up and grab my phone and text Fiore.

***Me:*** *Fiore, it's Summer. Sorry to bother you and I know it's late, but can you tell me your brother's apartment number?*

I hit send before I chicken out, immediately regretting asking her. What if she's with Lorenzo? What if she screenshots the text and sends it to him? What if—

***Fiore:*** *3E* ☺

I grab my purse and call a cab, hoping it's not too late in the evening to show up on his doorstep. I need to tell Lorenzo that I want, *no, I need* to be more than friends, and it can't wait until morning.

# Chapter 23

MY FINGER REACHES out, but I hesitate. *Just do it, chicken.* I take a deep breath and press the doorbell. The loud buzz makes me want to hightail it back downstairs. Footsteps come closer before a lock releases and the door opens to the most gorgeous…*woman*? I back up a few steps and glance at the door number—3E. No, no, this can't be happening. What if Fiore meant 3B and accidentally typed 3E? Smoking-hot Daniella eyes me curiously, trying to figure out where she knows me from.

"*Sí?*"

"*Daniella, chi è?*" Lorenzo's voice floats down the hall while I stand frozen, unsure of what to do.

Daniella…God, I'm such an idiot. I mentally slap myself on the forehead. Of course, he's seeing her. Now I know exactly how Frances felt when she arrived at Marcello's apartment and found him with another woman in *Under the Tuscan Sun*. Sucker punched. Luckily, Daniella's clothes are all on, and he's not necking with her in the window, but still…devastating. I should never have come here.

Daniella's brows furrow. "*Posso aiutarLa?*"

"Uh, no, no, I don't need help. Wrong um…*appartamento*." I back away from the door and pivot to run to the elevator when Lorenzo's voice halts me.

"Summer? What are you doing here?"

"Oh, hi! *Ciao.*" Slowly I turn around and lamely wave my hand. "I, um…I thought you might want to grab a cappuccino, but I can see you're busy, so perhaps another time. *Arrivederci!*"

"Wait." Lorenzo reaches out and grabs my wrist before I can dart away. I gaze at the elevator longingly. He says something in Italian to Daniella over his shoulder. She looks at me curiously before closing the door, leaving us standing in the hallway.

"You came into town at ten o'clock at night for a cappuccino?"

"I've heard Luigi's makes the best." My smile falters. I focus on his hand clasped around my wrist. "You're right, I should have called first. I was worried when you didn't say goodbye at dinner. You seemed upset, so I thought you might want to talk about it, because that's what friends do, right? They check on each other, but clearly, you have Daniella here, so…"

"Inside," he grunts, tugging on my wrist before he opens the door.

"I don't want to interrupt—"

"It's a little too late for that, don't you think?"

He pulls me into his apartment, and my lips part in awe as I take in the beautiful interior—glossy dark hardwoods with navy walls and accents of white. The colorful paintings from downstairs are hanging on the walls.

"Make yourself comfortable. I'll be right back." He gestures down the hall before he walks into his kitchen and busies himself. Instrumental music that sounds a lot like U2 plays from hidden speakers. Curiosity propels me into his family room. There's a large flat-screen TV across from a brown leather sectional. Above the couch is a massive painting similar to the one I bought earlier. I stand for a moment, absorbed by the dabs of color, the strokes blending into each other. The family room opens to a formal dining room, a den, and a hallway leading to the bedrooms, which is where I'm assuming Daniella is hanging out, waiting for me to leave. *Mamma Mia*, I need to go.

Lorenzo meets me in the hallway with two cappuccinos.

"It's not Luigi's." He shrugs.

"I should get going."

"But you just got here. You said you wanted a cappuccino, *sí*?"

"Oh, uh…right…sure." Crap, I didn't think this through. Now I'll be up all night. I take the cappuccino and he leads me over to the couch and sits down. I take the chair opposite him.

"Won't Daniella want a coffee?"

Lorenzo takes a sip and looks over at me. "She left."

"She left? I didn't see her scoot past us in the hall." I take a small sip of the bitter coffee, my eyes darting nervously around the room.

Lorenzo gives me a tight smile, setting his drink down on the coffee table. "She left through the back entrance."

I follow his lead and place my drink down, my nerves humming. I'm now alone with him in his apartment. "I'm sorry if I ruined your date."

His jaw clenches. He leans back into the couch, stretching his arm along the back, turning his complete focus on me. “What are you doing here, Summer?”

*Gah, I don’t know, Lorenzo. What the hell am I doing here?*

“I told you. I wanted to check on you after your argument with Angelo.”

“That was hours ago. Why are you just coming by now?” He drums his fingers.

“I…I was doing a little redecorating at home first.” I pick up my coffee and take a large gulp, the bitterness making my nose wrinkle.

Lorenzo’s cool gaze slides over me, chilling my skin. “So, let me get this straight. You are concerned about the fight I had with Angelo and my hurt feelings, but you finish dinner with him and then go home for a couple of hours to…*redecorate*?”

“Okay, I sound like a shitty friend, I realize that, but I swear that’s how it happened.”

He arches an eyebrow, his smoky eyes pinning me to the spot. His jaw clenches again.

“Are you angry?”

“Angry? No.” His nostrils flare. “I’m *incazzato*.”

“Why are you…*incazzato*?” My coffee cup trembles as I set it back down. “And what exactly does that mean?”

“Beyond pissed,” he grumbles.

“Oh.”

“Why are you having dinner with Angelo, anyway? I told you he’s bad news and you should stay away from him. Do you *like* him?”

“I—”

“And you’re going away with him next weekend?”

“No…yes. I—”

"And you come over here after *redecorating* with Angelo, pretending to be my friend? Yes, I'm *incazzato*!"

"Wait! Hold on just a minute. I did not *redecorate* with Angelo. He took me home and dropped me off."

Lorenzo snorts, which makes my temper spark.

"Nothing happened with Angelo, not even a friendly kiss on the cheek. Oh, he tried, but I'm not interested in him."

"Could have fooled me. People don't agree to go on romantic seaside trips together if they aren't interested."

"I never said yes! He bulldozed right over me. What was I supposed to do?"

"He bulldozed right over you…" He gets up from the couch and paces.

"Why are you so angry? Are you *jealous*?"

"*Sì!* I'm fucking *geloso*, Summer!" He throws his hands in the air, and I'm stunned. "It makes my skin crawl that you're going away with him next weekend."

"How do you think I feel when I show up here and gorgeous, long-legged Daniella opens the door?" I stand up, exasperated.

Lorenzo looks at me, anger marring his beautiful face. He shakes his head. "We were working. We're just friends."

I choke out a laugh. "Ah, I see. You like to do that, don't you? *Just friends.*" I air-quote obnoxiously and step into his space. "You can't be jealous of Angelo, just like I have no right to be jealous of Daniella, because you and I are *just* friends!"

"I don't want you going away with Angelo next weekend!" he explodes.

"Oh, well, that's nice, as if I need your permission. Let

me write that down on my calendar. Weekend away with Angelo. Oh wait, I can't, because Lorenzo said no." *Jerk.* I turn to leave.

"*Non voglio che tu vada con lui, ma con me!*"

"I don't know what you're saying," I cry out, waving my arms in frustration. This entire conversation is not going the way I planned. He runs his hands through his hair and takes a deep breath as we glare at each other.

"I don't want you going away with him because I want it to be me. Don't you get it? You're all I think about, all I see. All I want is *you.*"

I stand there with my mouth open. He walks toward me and cups my face in his hands.

"I lied," he says quietly. "I lied when I said I only wanted to be friends. I was protecting my heart."

"Protecting your heart from what?"

"From you."

His lips crush against mine in a sizzling kiss that has mine parting for more. I moan as his tongue dances with mine. He tastes of something sweet mixed with the bitter coffee, and I can't get enough. My fingers curl up into his silky hair, tugging him closer. He lifts me, wrapping my legs around his waist. He groans and squeezes my ass. I fit perfectly against the rock-hard bulge in his jeans. All the pent-up tension heating up between us for the past month roars to life like a raging wildfire.

"*Tesoro*, I can't hold back anymore," he whispers against my lips.

"Then don't," I murmur, seeking his mouth again.

The reasons he thought we shouldn't be together disintegrate, like ash in the air. His kisses slowly pull me apart as he walks me down the hallway while I hastily unbutton his shirt. I rip it off and a little moan escapes from my lips as I dance my fingers over silky-smooth muscle. It's even better than in my fantasies.

We enter his bedroom, and he sets me down on his bed. I kneel in front of him, worshiping his body with my fingertips, and flick my tongue against his nipple. His sharp inhale makes me smile, my fingers trailing down the hard ridges of his abdominal muscles as I work his belt buckle. He runs his hands up my thighs, then higher, lifting my sundress over my head. Tossing the dress to the side, his lips seek mine while his fingers trail down my navel to my panties, dipping into me. He pumps his finger in and out of me, just like I daydreamed. He groans into my mouth as my hands wrap around his hard length. I squeeze and pump, luxuriating in the feel of him.

"*Tesoro*, you're going to make me come, and I don't want to yet. I want to taste you first."

I gasp as the pad of his thumb swirls over the tight bundle of nerves, his teeth grazing over my neck. He trails kisses down to my breast.

"*Bellissima*," he growls. His eyes swirl to smoke as he takes my nipple into his mouth. He groans as I arch into him, the swirling of his tongue over my sensitive bud making me ache in the most delicious way. It's all I can do not to slide to the floor. I'm so wet and throbbing with need, it's ridiculous.

"Lorenzo, I need you," I pant. He answers by sliding my panties down before taking off his pants and boxer briefs. He stands gloriously naked in front of me like a Roman god, muscles rippling while my eyes glaze over with lust as I scoot back on his bed. He climbs over me, his smile taking my breath away.

"*Tesoro*, you are the most beautiful woman I've ever laid eyes on."

"Oh God, say it in Italian," I whimper as he places my leg over his shoulder.

"*Sei la piu bella donna che abbia mai visto in vita mia.*"

"Oh God, yes. Permission granted to speak Italian all night long."

He chuckles before his tongue flicks against my wet heat. I arch off the bed. *Jesus, it's been a long time.* His tongue delves into me like a spear, and I moan as he licks me like I'm the best fucking hazelnut chocolate gelato he's ever tasted. I drive my fingers into his hair and tug him closer to me. He groans, his tongue working me into a state of liquid pleasure as I move against him. The symphony building inside me comes to a crescendo. I arch into him, screaming his name, my body bursting into a thousand points of light.

He lifts his head as I come down off my high, giving me a devilish grin. "*Dolce come una pesca*, Summer. You taste so good. Creamy and sweet like a juicy peach. I've dreamed about what it would be like to taste you, and it's better than I imagined."

Sweet Jesus, I could come again just from his words.

He leans over and opens his nightstand drawer, taking a condom out. Liquid heat hums in my veins in anticipation. He sits back and rolls the condom on. I lick my lips, taking in his perfection. He's flawlessly built, in *that* department.

It's as if Michaelangelo himself carved him out of marble.

"Are you sure about this, *tesoro*?" Ren murmurs, his hooded eyes perusing my flushed skin.

"Yes, I'm sure. Are you?"

"Considering I've wanted to do this the moment I laid eyes on you, *sì, sono sicuro*." He smiles slowly, entering me, stretching my walls. I'm slick with need as he pulls out a little and pumps back in, careful not to hurt me.

I grab his perfectly sculpted ass and pull him hard into me. The surprise in his eyes makes me laugh. "More, faster."

His grin is so wide my heart does a little dip. "*Ancora, più veloce*."

"*Ancora, più veloce*," I repeat.

He pulls back and pumps harder back into me and grabs my thigh, going deeper. "*Quanto mi piaci*...you feel so good. So fucking good."

"*Quanto mi piaci*," I pant as he picks up his pace. He sits back and places my leg on his shoulder, going deeper. It feels incredible. I cry out when his thumb finds the tight bundle of nerves. He draws little circles, making me climb higher. I want this moment to last, but I can't hold on.

"Oh God, I'm going to come, Ren," I whimper as he slams into me harder. I splinter apart, arching off the bed. He pushes in and out of me, fast and erratic, his eyes flickering down to where we're joined as the aftershocks of my orgasm leave me languid. He closes his eyes, sweat glistening on his skin as he chases down his orgasm. I could watch this man forever. He growls unintelligible Italian as he comes undone. Gently lowering my leg, he supports himself over me and kisses my lips.

"*Tesoro*...that was..."

"*Incredibile*."

"*Sì, incredibile*." His lips curve. He kisses my nose before he stands up and disposes of the condom. He lies back down beside me and my mind whirls with what this means. He pulls me to him and brushes a strand of hair off my cheek.

"You will not get much sleep tonight, *tesoro*." He nuzzles my neck.

"You want me to stay the night?"

"*Sí*, of course I do." He kisses right under my jaw. "I haven't had my fill of you yet. I've wanted you since I saw you talking to yourself on your bathroom floor."

"Not one of my finer moments."

He runs a finger over my lips. "You had me at mozzarella."

"What are you talking about?" I giggle, tracing his jawline.

"When I called you *randagia*, and you thought I was calling you a type of cheese. It was cute."

"You have issues." I grin.

"I warned you to stay away from Italian men." He props himself up on an elbow and gazes down at me with a tender expression.

"Ah, so you did. No regrets." I run my fingers through his hair. It's a strange feeling, because I've daydreamed of doing it more times than I can count.

"Will you tell me why you were so upset today? I want to help."

I quickly sober, turning in his arms, and stare at the ceiling. The last thing I want to do is bring my issues with

Barbara into bed with us. "Not tonight, Ren. Tonight, it's just you and me."

He trails kisses along my collarbone, his fingers grazing over my nipple. "Okay, for now, but I want you to know you can trust me."

"Okay." I luxuriate in the feel of his skin against mine. I never thought we'd ever get here. "What are we going to do about work?"

"What about it?" He smiles, shifting for better access. "*Questo non cambia nulla.*"

"But....I think we need to keep this casual, right? I'm leaving at the end of summer..."

"*Sí, informale.*" He nuzzles my neck and then places a kiss on my shoulder. "This changes nothing, *tesoro*, don't worry."

I give him a weak smile, closing my eyes. He's wrong though. This changes everything.

# Chapter 24

I SMILE AT the Swedish couple raving about the olive oil, but my mind keeps wandering to Lorenzo. I haven't seen him since I left his bed this morning, after the best sex of my life. Not that I expect him to blow off work and hang out in bed with me all day, but I was hoping he'd at least pop into the shop and give me one of his panty-dropping grins. *Get a grip, Summer. He runs an extremely busy olive farm. You're keeping it casual. He warned you his work would take priority, which is why he wanted to be friends.*

But I can't help smiling as I think about him. I like him, *a lot.* I have another month left here, and then what? I glance at Nina, who is busy applying lip liner in the mirror. She would shit a brick if she knew Lorenzo and I had slept together.

The Swedish couple gives me their address to ship them some olive oil. They are our last appointment for the day, and it's my turn to stay until six, helping in Stella's gift shop after they leave. I clean up the dishes and fill the sink with warm, soapy water.

"Do you have plans tonight, Nina?"

"*Sí*, I'm going to dinner with Angelo."

I cringe, wondering if she has any idea he invited me on a getaway next weekend. Dr. Bianchi definitely likes to keep a couple of women in his pocket, and I'm relieved I dodged that bullet.

"Why do you keep staring off into space, smiling? It's weird." A sour expression mars her pretty face.

"Can't a girl just be happy?"

"*Dà fastidio*—it's annoying."

I wipe down the counter, ignoring her. I refuse to let her cloud roll over my sunshine. She and Angelo deserve each other. "Have fun on your date, Nina."

"*Grazie*, I will." She collects her things, waving her hand in the air on the way out. "*Arrivederci.*"

I dry the dishes before heading over to Stella's shop. For the thousandth time today, I wonder what Lorenzo is doing and if he's been thinking about me as much as I've been thinking about him.

Waking up in his arms, his tongue and lips on my skin, was better than any fantasy I'd conjured up in my sex-deprived brain. We didn't make plans this morning to reconnect today when he dropped me off at my house, and now I'm wondering if I should text him again. *Jesus, it's only been eight hours. Don't seem so needy.*

"*Bongiorno*, Summer." Stella smiles at me.

"*Bongiorno*, Stella. What can I help with this afternoon?"

"If you can unload the box over there." She points to a box by the Italian dishware.

"*Certo.*"

"*Splendido.* And can you go tell Fiore her eight-o'clock reservation canceled? *Grazie.*" The keys on her wrist jingle as she walks away to help a customer looking at Fiore's cookbooks. I head back to the kitchen and wave hello to

Fredo, who is covered in flour. He points to the galley where Fiore is stirring something in a bowl.

"*Ciao*, Fiore!" I call out. She looks up and smiles.

"*Ciao*, Summer! Have you come to help me cook?" Her eyes twinkle with mischief.

I laugh and sidle up next to her. "Oh, no, that would probably make your customers never come back. Mmm, that smells wonderful. What is it?"

"I'm making strawberry shortcake. It's my brother's favorite."

"Oh, that's nice. Is he around?" I glance over my shoulder, hoping he's standing there.

"He's been tied up in meetings all day."

I lean against the counter and cross my arms. "Your mom wanted me to tell you your eight p.m. canceled."

"That's a relief. We're overbooked tonight as it is." She pours the batter into a pan, her lip curling into a smile. "Are you looking for someone?"

My ears burn at being caught staring out into the courtyard. "Just waiting for someone."

"That someone wouldn't happen to be my brother, would it? Did you find his apartment okay?"

"Yes, I mean, no. I didn't...go out." I chew my thumbnail, uncertain whether I should tell Fiore about last night.

"Ah, I see. That's a shame." She grins knowingly while she mixes batter in a bowl.

"Can I ask you something?"

"*Certo*. What is it?"

"When you go out with an Italian man, is it normal for them not to call you or come see you the next day?"

She chuckles. "I wouldn't know, Summer…"

"Oh crap, I'm sorry."

She swats my side. "I'm teasing you. *Sí, questo è normale.*"

"What do you think the protocol for dating an Italian man is? You know, if you were interested in them." Oof, I sound like the biggest *idiota.* I scrub my hands down my face. "American men contact you the next day…well, the polite ones do and ask if you can go out again."

Fiore thinks for a moment before shoving the batter into the oven. She turns to me and folds her arms over her chest, checking her hip into the counter. "If he doesn't have the *testicoli* to call you the next day, then he isn't worth two tortellini."

I nod at her sage advice. "You're right. *Grazie.*"

"And if we're talking about *il mio stupido fratello* Renzo, then I'll make sure he has food poisoning for the next decade. *Sí?*" Fiore smiles brightly and I can't help but giggle.

"Uh, let's hold off on that plan for now."

"If you're sure…"

I wave and hurry back to Stella's shop before Fiore can pry into Lorenzo and me or prematurely give him food poisoning.

*'SUMMERITA! IT'S YOUR mother. I haven't heard from you in a while and I wanted to check in. Weren't you supposed to be back*

*by now? I know Italy is keeping you busy. You're probably knee-deep in grapes at a vineyard somewhere. Anyway, I had to borrow your car, but don't worry, I put gas in it. Oh and I got a note from your HOA, but nothing I can't handle. Talk to you soon.'*

I stare at the phone after listening to Barbara's message. Did she not remember our conversation yesterday? I replay it and listen to her voice. She's upbeat and sober as far as I can tell.

"Ugh!" I fall face-first down on my bed, groaning. Cara warned me it was a bad idea to let her live at my place, but I didn't listen. I keep waiting for her to change, to grow up and be a responsible adult. It's a hard pill to swallow, knowing she might never be. I made a promise to Grams when she was sick that I would always keep an eye out for Mom, but when do I put my needs first? When will I ever be free from feeling responsible for her?

I should leave Italy and go take care of stuff back home, but that's the last thing I want to do. I've *just* found Lorenzo and I'm happy.

There's a light tap on the doorframe. I quickly pull myself together and sit up.

"Do you always moan face-down on your bed?" Lorenzo asks, leaning against the open door, looking fucking spectacular in a navy suit with his white-collared shirt open, revealing his tan chest.

"What are you doing here?"

His smile slips a little, a show of hurt flashing in his eyes before they shutter. "I wanted to see you today, *tesoro*. I can leave if you don't want company."

"Sorry, I do." I take a deep breath and blow it out. "I'm just frustrated. I'm glad you're here."

He takes off his jacket, folds up the sleeves of his shirt, and sits down next to me. He smells woodsy and clean. I want to crawl into his lap and beg him to make me forget about my problems back home. Instead, I straddle his lap and lightly kiss his lips. The freedom to be able to is an adrenalin rush.

"I'm sorry I didn't get a chance to see you today. We had some issues in Spain, so I was in meetings all day."

"What kinds of issues?"

"Worker strikes, that kind of thing. Hopefully it's resolved now. My brother will let me know in the morning." He leans in, returning my kiss. He looks as tired as I feel. "I've missed you so damn much today." He cups my cheek. "Want to tell me why you were wallowing?"

I'm embarrassed to tell him what a disaster my mom is, and how much heartbreak and anger she causes me, so I swallow it down. "Worker strikes back home." I smile ruefully and bump his shoulder. "Nothing I can't handle."

His brow furrows as he skates his hands up my thighs. "Do you need to go home?"

"No," I say too quickly. "No, it will be fine. I'm not leaving Italy. You have no idea how happy I am to see you."

His grin is infectious as he tucks a lock of hair behind my ear. "*Bene.* I have something to show you." He nudges my side and I slide off him. He stands up and reaches his hand out to help me up. He pulls me into his arms and gives me a gentle hug.

My heart stutters in my chest, the hug being just what I

needed. Tears threaten to spill as my nose burns. I stare at his throat, wondering if he'd mind if I unbuttoned his shirt a little more so I could run my fingers over his silky skin. He's the perfect distraction to take my mind off Barbara.

He grazes his lips against mine. "Summer?"

"Hmm?"

"Why do you have clothes hanging on the wall?"

*Shit.* "Oh, that. Um…remember when I said I was re-decorating? It's no big deal. Let's go."

He steps out of our embrace and walks over to the t-shirt and lifts it off the nail and blinks. "*Tesoro*, why is there a hole in the wall as big as my hand?" He quickly surveys the three other shirts I hung to cover up more damage. "Please tell me these aren't all holes."

"They aren't *all* holes."

He drops my favorite tee and walks over to another and lifts it off.

"Uh…so about that. I mean, who knew this plaster wouldn't hold a picture? I guess I should have known, considering it couldn't hold a door…I was going to fix it, but I don't know how to patch drywall."

"What picture?" he growls, walking over to look under another shirt.

"I was in the art gallery under your apartment, and I bought a print because, holy cow, those paintings are pricey. And I wanted to hang it in here because I love it so much, but every time I'd put a nail in the wall, it would crumble."

His eyes crinkle. "So, after the second time with little success, you decided to keep trying?"

"Well, by that point, I was frustrated."

"Where's the picture?"

I point to the picture leaning against the wall by the window. He walks over to it and stares at it for a moment. "This one is your favorite?"

"Yes. I love how the artist uses the colors, and his brushstrokes are so powerful. It reminds me of the farm. It's kind of like the one in your apartment."

"*Sí.* That's the old tree on the property." He looks up and smiles.

"I knew it!"

"Hmm, it's interesting that's the one you chose." He looks at the picture for a moment and turns abruptly. "Ready to go?"

"You're not mad about the walls?"

"I'm not happy about the walls, but they can be fixed like everything else in this house." He kisses my temple before guiding me downstairs. "No more redecorating, okay?"

"*Sí*, okay."

LORENZO PULLS THE Maserati into his designated parking space at the farm.

"Why are we here?" I ask.

He glances over at me and winks. "You'll see." We walk hand in hand toward the olive grove. "I asked Fredo for a little help," Ren says.

"What kind of help?" I carefully pick my way in my sandals as we walk through the rows, nightfall coming on fast as the dusky skies sink into the horizon.

"Remember the oldest tree on the property where I like to come and think? The one in the painting?"

All I can do is nod. I'm awestruck by the scenery in front of me. The old tree is lit with what has to be a thousand fairy lights. It's dazzling and spectacular, and I'm humbled he planned this all just for me. I grab his hand and squeeze it. A blanket is spread underneath the canopy with a picnic basket.

"Lorenzo, this is so beautiful."

"I thought we could have a picnic dinner under the stars tonight."

"How did you get the lights out here?"

"Magic." He beams. "And a generator."

I chuckle and sit down on the blanket. He follows suit, removing his socks and shoes. He opens the picnic basket and takes out two boxes. "Are you hungry?"

"Starving," I admit. He uncorks a bottle of red and pours me a glass. "I can't believe you did all this. I've never been on a picnic before."

"How is that even possible? You never went on one when you were little?"

"No, I didn't have the most conventional childhood."

"Tell me about it." He passes me cutlery and a box. Fiore's cooking smells mouthwatering as I lift the cardboard flap and my stomach clenches in anticipation. I don't really want to think about my mom at this moment, so I give Lorenzo the quick version. Like ripping off a Band-Aid.

"I've never met my dad. My mom had me when she was a teenager. We lived with my Grams." He looks up when I pause and the warmth shining in his eyes makes me feel safe. "My mom left when I was three and was in and out of the picture. Grams is the one who raised me, and when she died a couple years ago, I lost my entire world."

"I'm so sorry, *tesoro*. I was very close to my Nonno Rossi, so I understand the loss."

I shrug. "So yeah, that's my story in a nutshell."

"Where's your mom now?"

"In California. She wasn't around much growing up, but I see her more now that Grams passed away." I furrow my eyebrows. *I see her when she needs something from me.* I fold the hurt and tuck it away in that deep, dark place no one can get to. "Grams was too busy working at the diner to help make ends meet, so no, we never had picnics, but I have lots of other fond memories of her." I twist my fork in my pasta. "Family is so important here. I didn't grow up with cousins or siblings, aunts or uncles. I was a latchkey kid that had to become independent at an early age. It was pretty much just me and Grams…and now it's just me." I shrug. "My best friends Cara and Damien are more family to me than my own mother."

Lorenzo glances at me. "*Famiglia* is important, but not in the way you are thinking. It's not about how many cousins you have, or aunts or uncles. *Famiglia* are those you can count on no matter what. Through thick and thin, through quarrels and times of peace, *famiglia* will always be that rock you can cling to. *La mia famiglia è la tua famiglia.* My family is yours." He reaches over and gently brushes his thumb down my cheek.

"*Grazie*, Ren. That means so much to me." I take a deep breath. "You asked me when we first met, why am I here…I don't really know, to be honest. I came to Italy to find adventure, possibly fall in love." I blush at my admission and glance over at him. He gives me a small smile.

"I felt like something was missing in my life, like I was stuck in the same old monotonous routine," I continue. "I was scared life was drifting by and I hadn't truly lived. Grams was always living paycheck to paycheck. I didn't want to be like that. I chose a safe, honestly boring life for myself. Coming to Italy was the one wild thing I allowed myself. And…"

"And?"

"And…I think being here has taught me to appreciate the beauty surrounding me. Not just the landscape, but the people, the language, the food." I smile, setting my fork down in the box. "I was lost when I came here, but Italy has shown me what happiness could look like."

Lorenzo moves the picnic basket and our boxes and pats the blanket. He lies on his side and I mirror him, resting my head on my hand.

"Sorry," I say, "I didn't mean for this night to be about deep discussions."

"I don't mind. I'm getting to know you. I *want* to know more about you."

"What was your childhood like here?" I ask.

"It was moments of pure joy interspersed with hard work and school. My family is lucky we never struggled, and we had the best education. We had support from my grandparents and never felt unloved. But with privilege comes responsibility. From a young age, my brother and I were groomed to take over the family business. It was our destiny. My father oversees a lot still, but he wants to fully retire in the next year. So, I've been selected to take over the Italian Rossi business while my brother controls Spain, and my father's younger brother, Lucian, runs California, but he wants to retire soon, so Gio is in line to take it over. Although, he needs to mature a little before that happens."

I laugh. "Yes, Gio likes to party."

Lorenzo chuckles and nods in agreement. "Growing up here was wonderful, but there was always that heavy weight of responsibility. 'People are watching you, Lorenzo, make a good example. Don't disappoint us, don't screw up'." He sighs. I comb my fingers through his hair, his dark lashes framing smoky green eyes. "It's in my blood to grow olives. I made a promise to my nonno to carry on the Rossi name and I intend to keep it. It's tradition…one I take seriously. It's one reason my ex, Gabriella and I, broke off our engagement."

"Ah, Gabriella."

"You're not anything like her." He looks at me with a tenderness that makes my heart do funny things. He lies on his back and closes his eyes. "Fiore and Gabby were like oil and water. Fiore thought she was all wrong for me. Turns out she was right. Gabby didn't understand the responsibility I held for the company, the promise I made to Nonno. She wanted me to drop everything and cruise the Med or go with her friends to Cannes for a week. She didn't know the meaning of hard work because her father gave her everything. That wasn't my reality. Truthfully, I was hoping she'd want to settle here and start a family, but that wasn't in the cards for her."

"Do you want a family with loads of children?" I smile, but my stomach clenches. Something akin to jealousy fires up inside of me as I think of the unknown woman he'll marry and produce a minivan of children with.

He turns his head and squints. "Do *you* want a family with loads of children?"

I pause a beat, thinking of my relationship with Barbara and how I would be such a different mom if given the chance. "I want a family. I don't think I'm able to have *loads* of children. I'm thirty-six, so…"

"Hmm, there's still time. You could have *un bambino* every nine months and have five by the time you're forty, possibly forty-one, if you need a quick break." He chuckles as my eyes widen in horror.

"That sounds awful." I laugh and lie on my back to stare up at the night sky.

His fingertips brush against mine. "Tell me what makes you happy, *tesoro.*"

"Hazelnut gelato always makes me happy."

"Mmm, noted. Fiore's strawberry shortcake makes me happy."

"I know. Your sister likes to point out your favorites to me."

His fingers slide against mine and he pulls my hand to his chest, his heartbeat thumping steadily. "Really, and what else did she say I like?"

"Bolognese, Italian red wine, olives…maybe, me?"

He props himself up on his elbow and runs his hand over the curve of my hip, his eyes dropping to my lips. "Definitely you. *Ti voglio bene.*"

He captures my lips in a tender kiss that makes my toes curl.

"*Le vere storie d'amore non finiscono mai.* You've bewitched me, body and soul." He pulls away, but I grab his shirt and guide him back to me, wanting more than just a sweet kiss.

He slides his tongue leisurely over mine, his hand gliding up my thigh under my dress, leaving a trail of goosebumps. He squeezes my thigh, groaning against my lips. Sitting up, he gently peels down the top of my sundress. He cups my breasts and leans down, slowly sucking on the tender bud, making me ache. He lavishes the other as my skin flushes with desire.

"You drive me crazy...*pazzo.*" His lips trail up my neck as I arch into him. "Wild, Summer."

"In a good way, I hope."

"In a *I will die a sudden death if I can't be inside you right now*, kind of way. *Ho bisogno di te.* I need you."

"I don't want you to die," I murmur, his hands sliding up my thighs under my dress. He pushes my panties aside, and I moan as his finger dips into my wet heat.

"So ready for me, *cara mia. Così caldo e bagnato.* So hot and wet," he says, pumping his finger. He adds another. His fingers move expertly, bringing me close to the edge.

"Oh God, I'm so close, Ren."

I whimper when he drags them out of me and tugs off my panties. He sits back on his heels and gazes at me splayed out underneath the twinkling lights. "*Bellissima.*"

He spreads my thighs before I can blink, and his mouth is on me in one swift move, his tongue swirling against my soft folds. My fingers drive into his hair and I unabashedly yank him closer. I want to break apart into a million pieces and have him put me back together again.

I'm jumping from one plateau to the next, building upward until I hurdle off the cliff and burst like a firework. My orgasm comes swift and hard as I cry out his name. He sucks on me until I come all the way down off my high. Unzipping his pants, he grabs a condom from his pocket and rolls it on. He lifts me up in his lap so I'm straddling him. I slowly lower myself onto him, my dress floating around us once I'm completely seated.

"*Tesoro...*" he growls, grabbing my hips and pumping in and out of me, my breasts bouncing with the movement as he loses control. I meet each of his thrusts, feeling like a queen on her throne as I stare down into his glazed eyes. My legs shake as I get close once again, and I gasp when his lips close over my nipple. His thumb circles the tight bundle of nerves, and it's too much as I fall apart once more, the twinkling lights above me glazing into nothingness.

He follows suit, quickly coming after me.

"Jesus, Summer. I lose all control when I'm around you," he pants, kissing my bare shoulder.

I graze my fingers over his stubble. "I like that I make you lose control."

He pulls the top of my sundress up, kissing the swells of each breast, and then disposes of the condom while I pull my panties back on and smooth out my dress.

I look around at the grove of olive trees and the twinkling lights as music floats down from Fiore's café. "I can't believe we just did that out in the open. What if someone had come walking by? What if the diners from Fiore's restaurant could see us? What if—"

Lorenzo chuckles, pulling the strawberry shortcake out of the basket. "No one was coming down to the grove tonight, I promise you."

"Yeah, but they could have seen the lights…they could have heard us."

"*Cara mia…*" He passes me the shortcake and a fork. "…don't worry. Fiore's diners can't see down here. As for the others, well, when the boss sends everyone home, no one is sticking around, I promise."

"You sent everyone home tonight…for me?"

"*Sí.*" He takes a bite of shortcake and groans in pleasure. My nipples tighten in response. "I wanted to surprise you."

"Thank you, that was incredibly sweet. Especially after the day you've had."

"Well, I also had Fiore threatening bodily harm if I didn't do something nice for you after not being able to talk to you all day." He throws me a smirk.

"Gotta love sisters."

"*Lei é una ficcanaso.*"

"Hmm." I stare at his beautiful mouth and want to kiss him again. Thank goodness for nosy sisters. "How did you get the scar on your lip?"

"Ahh, I wish I had a good story, but I don't. Angelo gave it to me."

"Your cousin?"

"*Sí*, when we were teenagers. We were fishing with friends, and there was a girl."

"Ha, there's always a girl."

"Yes, it seems that way with Angelo and me. Anyway, we ended up getting in a fistfight over her because she couldn't choose between us, and he shoved a fishhook in my lip, ripping it. He got the girl."

I cringe just thinking about it. "Well, he didn't get this one."

"I think I would have had to move out of the country if I had to see you two together all the time."

"You two have never seen eye to eye, have you?" I ask.

"No."

I watch him devour his shortcake and my heart does a somersault in my chest. Hooks remind me of pins, and I suddenly remember all the safety pins in the drawer. "By the way, thank you."

"For what?"

"I saw all the safety pins in your parents' powder room. There must be a hundred."

Lorenzo rubs his jaw, his cheeks flushing. "Well now I won't have to spend *hours* looking for one."

"Haha, okay. I appreciate the gesture."

"Anything for you, *tesoro*."

My heart pounds wildly as I lean in for a kiss.

"*Cara mia*…" He pauses, his stormy eyes piercing into mine. "I hope you find whatever it is you're looking for while you're here."

"Me too." I peer back up at all the stars in the sky. *Me too, Ren.*

# Chapter 25

IT'S BEEN A week since the picnic under the old olive tree, and I've stayed over at Ren's apartment almost every night since. At night, I work on my Granite projects or come up with more marketing ideas for Rossi Farms while he sits with his laptop and watches Italian football. One of us usually gets bored and teases the other until we end up with our clothes off in bed. One incredible week and I've let my heart go to places it's never been before.

I call Cara while I walk out back to the tasting room on my break. "Did I wake you?"

"No, Damien was up making breakfast in bed this morning."

"Aw, that's so sweet! What did he make?"

"Burnt eggs on soggy toast with some kind of weird cream sauce that tasted like metal."

"I didn't know it was even possible to burn eggs..."

"Me neither. It was a struggle to get down, but he was so proud, I didn't have the heart to tell him it was awful."

"Poor Damien. I think I've gained fifteen pounds since I've been here."

"You're such a jerk." She laughs. "Here you are in *Italy* complaining about the all-you-can-eat pasta and I'm over here wondering if I should go on a carrot stick diet just so my husband will stop cooking for me."

I laugh and sit down on the stone wall that separates the buildings from the grove. The view of the hills overlooking the town never gets old. "Maybe he should try a cooking class?"

"That's actually a really good idea."

"Make it a surprise so it doesn't hurt his feelings."

"Brilliant." She pauses. "Have you talked to your mom lately?"

My mood plummets. "Not since she left me that weird, happy voicemail. I don't even know how to get her out of my condo at this point. Barbara does what Barbara wants to do, no matter who it might affect or hurt."

"Maybe you should come back sooner?"

"I'm hoping she'll move in with her latest flavor of the month and this will all just go away," I say brusquely. The last thing I want to discuss is going back home to deal with Barbara.

"I wouldn't hold your breath. How's the hot and sexy olive farmer?"

"Hot and sexy."

"Have *you* moved in with him yet?"

"Cara, it's been a week."

She hums. "You're on borrowed time, sister."

I swallow past the knot in my throat at her mention of having to leave soon. "I think I'm in trouble."

"Oh my God, you're pregnant!" Cara screams into the phone.

"What? No, I think…I think I'm falling in love with him kind of trouble," I say softly, twisting around to make sure no one is nearby.

"Oh, Summer..."

"I know."

"Do you know if he feels the same? Have you told him?"

"God, no." I snort. "But he looks at me sometimes like I'm the most perfect olive."

Cara cracks up. "The most perfect olive? Oh geez. I think you've consumed too much olive oil."

"I agree."

"You only have a couple weeks left there."

"I know, Cara," I say irritably.

"Hey, don't shoot the messenger. You knew the deal."

"Sorry, I'm just so tired of feeling like my time here has an expiration date."

Cara stays silent a beat. "I just don't want to see your heart get broken. Whatever happened to the philandering doctor?"

"Lorenzo told him I was no longer available for any future arrangements, including dinners, lunches, coffee dates, or weekenders. I'm pretty sure he went all caveman on him, beat his chest, and said, *questa è la mia donna*. My woman."

"Look at you speaking Italian like a pro! I'm glad he took care of it for you."

"Yes, although it was super awkward when Angelo came to pick up Nina for a date and he could barely look at me."

"Lorenzo probably said something more colorful than *my woman*." She giggles.

"You better be learning how to make a red sauce!" Damien shouts in the background.

"Please, baby Jesus, I hope you can teach Damien a thing

or two," Cara whispers.

"You didn't eat your eggs. Did you not like them?" I hear Damien ask Cara.

"Sounds like you need to go." I smother a laugh and say goodbye, preparing myself for the dreaded phone call with my mom. I pull out the leftover pasta Lorenzo made for me last night. He's almost as good of a cook as his sister. I pull up my mom's number and call her.

"I was wondering when you were going to call your poor mother, who suffered through sixteen hours of labor for you. When are you returning? I feel like you've been in Italy forever. Don't you have a job here?"

"Barbara, I told you I would be here for the summer," I say flatly, stabbing a mushroom with my fork. I'm surprised she's awake this early and sounding sober. Perhaps her new boyfriend is a good influence on her.

"The entire summer? But…I miss you. Your place is so lonely without you around."

She wants something, but I'm too annoyed to play this game.

"You never told me what the HOA letter was about," I say.

"Oh, I don't remember. Your neighbor, what's her name, Gleason?"

"Mrs. Gladstone?"

"She's so nosy, asking me all kinds of questions, wondering where you are. Such a nuisance."

"Please don't upset my neighbors. I like living there, which is why I wish you would stop having people over and trashing it. If I hear of any complaints from neighbors or the management company, I'll have to ask you to leave."

"Is that any way to speak to your mother?"

"Actually, I have a lot more to say, but I think we should do it in front of a counselor."

"I'm not going to therapy with you," she scoffs. "I will not listen to some quack tell me all the things I've done wrong. That's on you."

She hangs up on me before I can utter another word.

I sit in silence and eat my lunch, not tasting the food, wondering what to do about Barbara. I startle when a hand gently brushes my shoulder. I look up and see Nonna easing herself down onto the stone wall. She's wearing black silk palazzo pants with a black button-down silk shirt and a wide brim straw hat.

"Oh, Nonna, you scared me."

"I was calling out to you, but you were lost in your own thoughts." She smiles, smelling like roses and morning dew. "Is everything alright?"

"Yes…" I sigh and put my lunch to the side. "Actually, no. You're right, Nonna, I am lost."

"Ah, I see." She folds her delicate hands in her lap. "My body is old, and my mind is not as sharp as it used to be, but my eyes? My eyes have seen many beautiful things in my eighty-five years. These eyes, *stellina*, watched a caterpillar build a *crisalide*, a cocoon around itself.

"For weeks, I waited patiently, making sure nothing harmed it. I would shoo away birds if they got too close, protecting the vulnerable creature inside to the outside world. And then one day, I was lucky enough to catch the beauty emerging. The most brilliant butterfly appeared with wings blue as the sky above, and a body black as the night. It fluttered and flew away to live a new life. I clapped and cheered, which is silly, I know. But what a miracle to witness! A plain caterpillar morphing into something free and beautiful."

"But Nonna—"

"*Non ho finito,*" she grumps, patting my leg. "Trust these eyes, *caramellina.* They see great things within you. They see a caterpillar waiting to bloom into a beautiful butterfly. These eyes have seen you written in the stars. You were meant to be here." She squeezes my hand. "You are not lost, child. You are just beginning. Trust what's inside here. *Ho fiducia in te.*" She gently taps my heart. Tears prick my eyes as the familiar Italian words soothe my heart. *I have faith in you.*

"Thank you, Nonna."

"I don't know what troubles you, but give it time."

"I'm not so sure time can help this one. My mother is an alcoholic. She is constantly blaming me for all her failures…it's been thirty-six years, and she can't move forward." I swipe the tears falling from my eyes. "I don't know how to fix it."

Nonna hums, handing me a tissue from her bag.

"Sometimes, people don't like to see when another is growing into something better. They can't move forward with you and it stirs up jealousy and anger inside themselves. Your light is too bright, *stella,* your colors too beautiful, *farfallina,* to be dimmed by someone else. *Ha perso la strada…*she has lost her way. Sometimes we can help them find it and sometimes we have to move on and let them find it for themselves. It is not your job to fix it." She pats my knee and stands. "Dry your tears, *sì*? This old woman needs a nap."

"*Grazie*, Nonna." I stand and wrap her in a fierce hug.

She gently pats my back. "*Basta*, you're wrinkling my shirt."

"Oh, sorry." I laugh and release her. I clean up my lunch, gather myself together, and head back into the shop.

I'm surprised to walk in and find Lorenzo and Nina together, laughing. Nina says something in Italian, and a streak of jealousy courses through me. I'm back in the study on the night of our first kiss all over again. In all honesty, Nina is a much better match for Lorenzo. She's young and pretty and still has time to produce loads of children for him. She's Italian, doesn't have family baggage, and she's not leaving at the end of the summer. My heart dips.

"*Ciao*, Summer." Lorenzo winks at me as I put my purse down.

"*Ciao*, Lorenzo."

"Nina was just telling me about the Greek couple this morning who argued that Kalamata olives are better."

"Ah, yes. They were charming," I deadpan. "Hands down, the most difficult group I've encountered this summer, demanding a refund and threatening to write bad reviews on Tripadvisor."

Lorenzo walks over and takes my hand, squeezing it. "I'm sure you handled them with kid gloves, *cara mia*."

"I gave them two free bottles of olive oil." I shrug. Nina's eyes laser in on our hands. I drop mine and take a step back.

"Did they walk away happy?" he asks.

"*Sí*," Nina says grumpily, inspecting her nail.

"Then all is right in the world." Lorenzo winks at me. "Summer, can I speak with you for a moment in the back office?"

"Sure." I follow Lorenzo into our office and put my purse on the desk. He closes the door and clicks the lock. "Nonna Rossi is so amazing. She just—"

He sweeps me into his arms and nibbles my neck. "*Tesoro*, I don't want to think about my grandmother right now." He captures my lips in a dizzying kiss. He smells so good, like expensive Italian leather and woods.

His tongue parts my lips and tangles with mine as my fingers thread through his silky hair. All my misguided thoughts about Nina being a better match fly right out the window as I feel his thick, hard length through his trousers. He lifts me onto the desk, spreading my legs.

"Wait, Lorenzo! We can't do this. We're at work and Nina is right outside."

"I don't care," he growls into my neck.

"No." I giggle, pushing him away. I stand, putting space between us. "We need to be professional."

He turns and perches on the edge of the desk, folding his arms over his chest. "You're right. Sorry, *perdo la testa quando sono vicino a te*. I can't help myself when I'm around you."

"You can't lock me into an office every time you can't control yourself." I smirk.

He sends me a devastating smile that makes me want to retract my last statement. "You're right, *tesoro*. I'll just make love to you in public from here on out."

The thought of Lorenzo pushing me up against the old stone mill and having his wicked way with me has my core throbbing.

"Hello, Summer? Where did you just go?"

"Huh?" I'm ripped from my fantasy, back to the cramped office. Maybe I *should* let him play seven minutes in heaven.

"So, the reason I asked you in here, apart from wanting to kiss you senseless, is to ask you something. In Italy, we celebrate what's called *Ferragosto* in August."

"Oh yes, your sister and Nonna mentioned it. What exactly is it?"

"We shut down the farm and go to the coast for a week with the whole *famiglia.*"

"You shut down?"

"*Sí,* it's a tradition in Italy for shops to close during the week of the Assumption and enjoy a little rest and relaxation. Most of the town will be away, and I don't want you to be here by yourself. It would mean a lot if you would spend it with me. Will you say yes?"

"*Sí,*" I answer without hesitation. I would pretty much say yes to whatever Lorenzo asked me to do. *Mamma mia*, I'm in trouble.

"*Bene.* And *this* weekend our town is holding the Feast of San Lorenzo. Would you like to go with me?"

"Are you named after a saint? Tell me more." I step in between his legs and run my hands through his hair, kissing his luscious lips. His hands run down my backside and squeeze. He growls, sending shivers of anticipation up my spine.

"It's a tradition...that started in Florence when Saint Lorenzo gave out blessed bread to the people, and they feasted on watermelon at night. Everyone in Tuttoscano comes together to celebrate. We eat, listen to music, and watch the stars." He groans. "*Cara mia*, I can't think when you nibble my jaw."

"Sounds fun," I purr, biting his earlobe before I lean back. "Are you sure about going with me? People will wonder about us..."

"*Tesoro*, you're not a dirty little secret." His brow furrows. "I'll shout it from the rooftops if I need to. I was just keeping it low-key because of you."

I smile as warmth envelops my heart. "I just...you know, because we're keeping it simple. I didn't know—"

He takes my face in his hands and looks into my eyes, his smoky gray-green flecked with gold. "Summer, I want—" The door jiggles. Fiore curses on the other side in Italian. Lorenzo sighs, letting go of me, and turns to unlock the door.

"Oh, *ciao*, Renzo, *non sapevo che eri qui dentro*...oh, Summer, I didn't see you." Fiore's eyes dart between us, her smile widening. "Sorry, I didn't know anyone was in here. I was coming to grab the reservation list, but the door was locked."

I look down at the desk I'm perched on and quickly grab the list. Heat burns my cheeks as I pass it to her. Lorenzo leans against the wall, crossing his arms, his eyes twinkling. "I was asking Summer to join me for the Feast of San Lorenzo and to come away with me for *Ferragosto*."

Fiore squeals and jumps up and down, crushing me into

a claustrophobic hug.

"Did we just get engaged?" I laugh as I glance at Lorenzo over Fiore's shoulder, struggling not to fall off the desk.

"No, but I just made you and me official. *Mettersi insieme.* We are seeing each other exclusively." He smiles ruefully as he looks at his watch. "I've got to run. Fiore, get off her." He pulls me to him and lightly kisses my lips. "I hope you're okay with that, *tesoro*. Exclusive, *sì*?" All I can do is nod as he strides out of the room, leaving me a bit shell-shocked. So much for promises of a casual fling.

"*Non vedo l'ora che vi arrivino dei bei bambini!*" Fiore shouts after him before turning to me with a wide grin.

"What did you just yell? I heard *bambini*."

"I can't wait for you two to have beautiful babies."

I choke as I stand. "Fiore!"

"What? It's true."

"Too soon for the baby talk," I grumble. We walk out of the office to return to the tasting room.

"I'm excited for you and Lorenzo, though. He's been so happy lately."

"It was your strawberry shortcake." I grin.

Fiore bumps my hip. "I think it was *your* strawberry shortcake." She laughs. "*Ciao, sorella.*" She leaves me blushing outside the tasting room. I walk in, my head whirling with everything that just happened in the last fifteen minutes.

"Why did she just call you sister?" Nina challenges the second I walk through the door.

"I'm sorry?"

"*Sorella*...sister."

"Oh, I don't know. Perhaps she meant to say Summer?" I hedge, uneasy with the intensity in Nina's gaze. "So, tell me about the Feast of San Lorenzo. Are you going?"

"*Sí*, everyone goes." Nina slowly flips through a magazine while she sips her cappuccino. "The whole town comes together with food and music." She eyes me over her cup. "If you need to go with someone, I'm sure I can ask Gio."

"*Non è necessario, grazie.*"

"You're going by yourself?"

"No, I'm going with Lorenzo."

Her mouth drops open. Thankfully, a small group walks in for their two p.m. tour before she can question me further. "*Buongiorno!*" I smile brightly.

# Chapter 26

LORENZO SQUEEZES MY hand as we walk toward the large gathering of people in the center of town. Guitar music floats down the narrow cobblestoned streets, while throngs of people chat and visit with one another. Old women gather around the long trestle tables loaded with pans of lasagna and watermelon. The name, *San Lorenzo*, seems to echo off the ancient limestone walls.

People keep stopping Lorenzo and chatting amicably while they stare at me curiously. He's a celebrity among the locals, and it's heartwarming to see him in his element, giving them a charming smile and kissing their cheeks. I try to keep up with what they're saying, but they speak too fast for me to understand, so I just nod and smile. Lorenzo gently guides me through the crowds, murmuring into my ear who they are and what they are saying.

"Should I have brought some lasagna?" I smile at another couple eating from paper plates while they walk.

"Don't worry, you're with me, and we donated plenty." He kisses my temple and nods to another passerby. "Prepare yourself, *tesoro*. There's Nonna. Fiore spilled the sauce about us."

Nonna looks up as if she heard him whisper it into her ear. Her eyes zero in on our hands, and for a split-second, I can see a hint of a smile before her mask of indifference slides into place.

"Renzo, it's about time you arrived. Help Signora Picorna pass out the plates," Nonna says brusquely. Lorenzo looks down at me, concern etched across his face. "*Calmati*, I'll take care of Summer."

"You can stay here with me. You don't have to go with Nonna," he says in my ear.

"I'll be fine," I assure him before he reluctantly releases my hand and moves around the table to help Signora Picorna.

Nonna Rossi takes my arm and tucks it to her side. She's wearing her signature silk outfit in a shade of midnight blue tonight, her hair pulled back. "Help an old woman make her rounds, Summer."

"Of course, Nonna Rossi."

We walk a little way, nodding to different people. Nonna is clearly on the hunt for a particular person when she suddenly pulls me to the side.

"*Ciao*, Mirabella!" Nonna shouts to a plump older woman with grizzled black hair, wearing a purple scarf and garish makeup. "*Vorrei presentare la fidanzata di Lorenzo*, Summer Andrews. She's from California." Nonna smiles triumphantly, so I do the same. I hold out my hand to the other woman.

My smile slips as Mirabella's lips flatten before she spits to the side. She lifts her fist to yell something rapidly in Italian. Nonna giggles gleefully before she takes my arm and quickly guides me away from her.

"Why was that woman so angry? What did you say?"

"That old witch is a Rizzotti."

I groan. "Oh no, not the Rizzottis."

"She has said for years Lorenzo would never marry, ever since he refused her granddaughter, but who could blame him? She's a complete cow, not to mention she has Rizzotti blood running through her veins. Mirabella tried to put an old Italian curse on him and said his balls would turn black and shrivel up, but look who's laughing now! She can stuff that truffle in her catoosh."

I'm shocked Nonna knows the English word for 'balls' and that I can still hear Mirabella screaming what I can only assume is Italian profanity as we walk away.

"What did you *say* to her?"

She shrugs. "I said you were Renzo's new friend."

I eye her surreptitiously. Her reaction was a little harsh for being introduced as just a friend. "Nonna, please don't walk around telling everyone I'm Lorenzo's girlfriend. We haven't even defined—"

Nonna claps her hands in my face, cutting me off. "*Sciocchezza!* Nonsense! You and Renzo *siete scritti nelle stelle*," she says as she waves her hand toward the night sky. I look around, confused, as she huffs. "You were written in the stars. We need to work on your Italian more. Ah, Elena! *Ti presento la fidanzata di* Lorenzo..."

"Nonna," I warn, knowing she's calling me something other than a friend, but before I can take a breath, a busty short woman with cropped salt-and-pepper hair pulls me into a hug and squeezes me tight as Nonna proudly looks on.

"Summer, this is my best friend, Elena."

The woman speaks rapidly to Nonna as she pets my hair and pinches my cheek. I'm pretty sure they're discussing my good birthing hips when Nonna cackles. A hand reaches around Elena and grasps mine, pulling me away. At this point, I wouldn't care if it were Dr. Bianchi or Great-Uncle Giovanni, anyone besides Nonna and her handsy bestie, Elena. Luckily, it's my handsome Italian knight in shining armor.

"Nonna," Lorenzo chastises as she and Elena chuckle.

"*Rilassati*, Lorenzo! Relax, she's fine."

"I'm sorry, *tesoro*, I got stuck being pinched by all of Nonna's friends over by the food. Are you okay?"

"I think Nonna has already married us off, telling everyone I'm pregnant with twins." I'm expecting a horrified expression to wash over his features, but his eyes warm as the edges crinkle with an affectionate smile.

"Come, we'll find a good place to eat and watch the stars without meddling grandmothers."

"Watch the stars?" I ask. Nonna's declaration that Lorenzo and I were written in the stars resonates in my head.

"*Sí*, the Feast of San Lorenzo is also known as the night of the shooting stars because the Perseid meteor shower falls annually on this night, August tenth. This meteor shower is interpreted as the tears of Saint Lorenzo."

I gaze up at him and shiver. "Not only are you incredibly romantic, but also very knowledgeable."

He bashfully ducks his head, grabbing two plates of lasagna off the table. "Glad to be of service, *cara mia*. Can you grab some watermelon?"

I pick up two paper bowls before he leads me through the throng of people.

The music, lively chatter, and aromas warm my soul. I'm

falling deeper in love with this charming little village and possibly with the man walking beside me. We climb a steep cobblestone hill until we reach a small courtyard with a stone wall overlooking Tuttoscano. Lorenzo hands me a plate and pulls two small bottles of water out of his pocket as we sit on the wall, our legs dangling over the edge.

"I figured Nonna wasn't looking to feed you. *Mangia.*" He gestures to his own plate with his lasagna. I dig in, not realizing I was starving.

"Oh my God, this is so much better than Stouffer's."

"Who's Stouffer?"

"A crappy frozen lasagna that shouldn't even be talked about in this lasagna's company. I'm sorry I even brought it up," I murmur to my pasta.

Lorenzo shakes his head and laughs. "Did you just whisper to your lasagna?"

"Maybe." I smile goofily back at him and take a big bite, groaning. "So good."

"I've never met anyone like you, *tesoro*," he says tenderly. "*Ti adoro.*"

"I—"

"*Sta iniziando!*" a little boy shouts, pointing toward the darkening sky.

"It's starting," Lorenzo murmurs.

I put down my plate as he shifts behind me and pulls me against him. I watch in wonder as the stars look like they're falling from the sky.

"Wow..." I whisper in awe.

"Tradition declares those are San Lorenzo's tears and in honor of his suffering, one must make a wish of your heart's desire on the stars, and your wish will come true. *Stella, mia bella Stella, desidero che...* Star, my pretty Star, I wish. Make a wish, *amore mia.*"

I watch the glowing stars fall from the inky sky like burnt embers and silently wish Lorenzo would be mine forever. His lips graze over my temple as we sit in the dark, and my heart feels like it might burst with love. If I could make a second wish, I'd ask to stay in this moment forever.

I turn my head. "Did you make a wish?"

"Of course."

"Do you think it will come true?"

"The stars never lie, *tesoro.*"

He leans in and kisses me, sealing our fates.

# Chapter 27

THROWING SOME CLOTHES into my suitcase, I'm excited for some time away with Lorenzo for the week. I toss in my red bikini and some sexy lingerie I splurged on from Carmella's shop last week. He told me it's a tradition for the whole family to go but that we're staying in a small cottage separate from his parents, sister, and grandmother. I throw in my makeup and hairdryer when my phone rings. I don't recognize the number. I'm about to ignore it, but something makes me pick it up.

"Hello?"

"This is the Burlingame County Jail with a collect call from *Barbara*. Do you accept the charges?"

"Yes…Hello? Barbara?"

"Summer, I need you to come home," she chokes up.

"Barbara, I can't understand you. What's going on? It's three-thirty in the morning there."

"Summer, listen to me." She breathes heavily into the phone. "I need you to come home now, please."

"Are you in jail?" I clench the t-shirt I'm holding, lowering myself to the edge of my bed. Dread fills my belly.

"I had an accident. I wrecked your car. I need you to come home and bail me out of jail."

"An accident? Are you hurt? Why are you in jail?"

"I'm not hurt, just a few bruises. The nurse said I was lucky. The other person has some bruises but is okay, from what I'm told. I…I was drinking and driving."

*Fuuuuck.* White-hot rage explodes through my veins as tears streak down my cheek. I didn't even realize I was crying. I scrunch the shirt and wipe my face.

"How did this even happen?"

"Mark and I left a bar, and he was too drunk to drive. I had a couple. I didn't think I was that bad. We got in a fight on the way to your place and I ran a red light. My memory is a little fuzzy, but evidently I sideswiped a car. Mark is fine, but he's in jail, too."

"You could have killed someone, Barbara." I'm shaking.

"I know."

"Jesus." I close my eyes and think. What the hell am I supposed to do from Italy? "Okay, I'll handle it. I'll call Cara and we'll take care of this."

"What about Mark?"

"Honestly, I don't give a flying fuck about Mark. He can get his own lawyer."

"Okay…I'm at the Burlingame precinct on Trousdale. And Summer? Thank you," she says before the line goes dead.

I stare down at my phone and immediately call Cara, even though it's the middle of the night.

"Summer? What's wrong," Cara's sleepy voice rasps into the phone.

"Cara? I…I need your help. My mom just called me from the Burlingame precinct. She's been arrested for drunk driving."

"Shit. Hold on." Sheets rustle as she murmurs something to Damien. "Sorry, I'm here. Just had to go into my office. Okay, Burlingame precinct. Did they set bail?"

"Um...she said I needed to bail her out, but I forgot to ask how much."

"It'll be okay. Did she kill anyone?"

"No." I swallow thickly as the implications of what could have happened crash down around me. "She said the other person has some bruises. She had a passenger who was also drunk. He's in jail as well, unharmed."

"Okay, okay, at least she's got that going for her," Cara says. "I'll call my friend Tony in the morning. He's the best with DUI cases."

"You can't take the case on?"

"Summer, I'm a divorce attorney, not DUI. Don't worry, Tony knows what he's doing. I think it's time for you to come home."

I burst into tears. "I know, Cara, but...*non sono pronta*."

"Whoa, English, please."

"I'm not ready," I blubber.

"I know it's hard to say goodbye, especially under these circumstances, but you need to come home and deal with this. I can bail her out in the morning, but I can't babysit her until her hearing. You'll need to meet with Tony and deal with your car and insurance."

"I know, I do. It's just...I was supposed to go away this weekend. This is so..."

"I know, love, but the end of your trip was coming. It sucks it has to be cut short because of this, but it's time. Barbara has been a wheel spinning out of control all summer."

"Why do I have to be responsible for this woman?" I shout to my ceiling. "Cara, I'm not sure I want to come back. I know that's incredibly selfish of me, but I'm happy here. For once, I'm happy!"

She's silent for a moment. "I love you. You know I do, but we're going to have some real talk happening right now. I know you're upset. Lord knows, I would be too, but sometimes we don't get to choose. Sometimes, we have to put our needs to the side and do what's right."

"But I love Italy. I love the Rossis and I'm in love with Lorenzo. I'm not ready to throw that all away. Besides you and Dame, the Rossis are the first family I've had since Grams died."

"Oh Summer…shit. You're in love with him?" She pauses for a moment. "Have you guys talked about what you are to each other?"

Fresh tears soak my pillow. "We've agreed to be exclusive, but we've been avoiding the talk about what happens when I have to return. I was going to bring it up this week."

"Summer, I was all on board for you to find yourself in Italy with a hot Italian man, but I'm sorry, babe, you have to deal with Barbara."

"What if I come home, deal with Barbara, and come back—"

"You know it's not going to be a quick fix. Barbara's situation is going to take months to resolve, maybe longer."

"We can do long distance." But even as the words leave my lips, I know it won't happen. We're too far apart on crazy time zones. Life will get in the way. It always does.

"Okay, let's say you return to Italy. Have you considered what will happen if things don't work out between you two? What if he decides he doesn't want a girlfriend, and you find yourself kicked out of that fancy villa? Where will you go? You won't be able to work there anymore."

"It's not like that…I can get my own place," I say with little conviction. I'm grasping at straws and she and I both know it. "My adventure was just beginning, Cara. You don't understand, Frances stayed—"

"Dammit, Summer, this is not a movie! This is reality, and your mom is in jail. Your life is here. I'm sorry, I'm so sorry…I wish it could have been different for you." Her voice cracks while I sob into the phone. "Come home, Summer. You've had an amazing time in Italy, but your old life awaits."

Like a bird tethered to its cage, I know I don't have a choice. I hang up with Cara, my heart heavy as I call the airlines to book my flight back home.

# Chapter 28

FOOTSTEPS POUND UP the stairs while I lay in bed, bereft, unmoving.

"*Tesoro?* Are you up here?" The sound of my nickname makes my heart rip in two. I can't answer him, though. He pauses in the doorway and surveys the room. "Summer, we're going for a week, not a lifetime. I'm not sure I have room in the trunk for all of these bags."

"I can't go," I croak, burying my face in my pillow.

The bed dips as he sits down and strokes the wet strands of hair away from my cheek. "What's wrong? Why are you crying?"

"I can't go with you on holiday. I…can't go." Fresh tears spring free. I try to push him away.

"*Cara mia*, I don't understand. Why can't you go?"

"I have to go back home. My mom…" I'm too embarrassed to admit my mom was arrested for drunk driving. "I have a family emergency."

Lorenzo sits back and sighs, running his hand over my back. "What happened?"

He helps me sit up and I clasp my arms around my knees, burying my head. He stands and walks out of the room, returning a minute later with a tissue.

"*Grazie.*" I blow my nose, searching for the right words

to explain. "It's my mom. She's…been irresponsible my whole life. She was in a car accident, and I need to get back home to help straighten everything out."

"*Dio mio.* Is she okay?"

"She's okay, but she totaled my car. I have to take care of insurance…it's a mess."

He nods and looks away. Standing, he rakes his hands through his hair while he paces the room. I want him to shout for me to stay. To tell me he loves me, and we can make this work, but he doesn't.

"Say something, Ren."

"I'm not sure what to say, *cara.* I didn't expect you to be leaving. I feel sucker punched."

I get up from the bed and wrap my arms around his waist, burying my head against his chest. I want to tell him I love him, to hear the words in return. That I'm wanted here and I belong here with him, but doubt rolls in like an early morning fog. I can't seem to navigate my way through it without a beacon of light from him to guide me.

We always said this would just be a summer fling. If I tell him I love him and I want to stay, will he make excuses as to why I need to return, or worse, tell me he doesn't feel the same? I need to nip this in the bud and make it final for both of us, as much as it will kill my heart. I drop my arms in defeat. He cradles my face in his hands before I can step away.

"Summer…I …" His eyes reflect the sorrow that's clawing my heart apart. "When do you leave?"

"Tonight," I whisper.

His jaw clenches. "Tonight?"

"I know." The tiny flecks of gold stand out against the greenish-gray in his eyes. I try to take a picture in my head and hold on to the memory so it will bring me comfort when I'm feeling sad. I'm hoping all of this will not be forgotten. *You idiot, how will you ever forget him?*

"I'll come with you."

"You can't. You're going on holiday."

"*Tesoro, non me ne frega un cazzo* about going on holiday."

"You can't leave your business. Busy season is coming up." I can't have Lorenzo stop his life for me because my mother is a train wreck. "I need to do this by myself, Ren. I have to."

"Well, at least let me take you to the airport." I can hear the frustration in his voice.

"No, it will be too hard to say goodbye there. We'd just be prolonging the inevitable. Besides, you have your trip. You said your brother and his family will be there tonight. Go, I'll be alright." I breathe in his woodsy, masculine scent and run my hands up his chest to his shoulders. "Is Nonna Rossi home? I'd like to say goodbye to her."

"No, she and my parents have already left."

I nod, my heart breaking a little more at not being able to say goodbye and thank her for everything she's done for me. For the chance she gave me. "Please tell her how sorry I am that I didn't get to say goodbye. Say goodbye to your whole family for me. I'm going to miss you, more than you'll ever know."

He bends and kisses my lips, his nose grazing against mine. "I don't want you to go."

His phone buzzes in his pocket. I give him a watery smile as I pull back. "You should probably get that."

"Summer, I don't give a fuck who is trying to call me right now. I always knew you had to go, but I thought I had more time with you. I thought…" He caresses my cheek, his voice trailing off as his eyes beg for mercy. His phone buzzes again.

"*Cazzo*," he yells, making me jump as he checks his phone. "*Cosa vuoi? Sí. Sto arrivando, dammi solo un minuto!*" He hangs up and sighs. "Fiore and Fredo are waiting for me in town, but I don't want to leave you." He kisses me, his lips gently parting mine.

I want to say fuck it and run away with him, but I can't. Cara's right. I need to take responsibility for my mother's actions, and he has an olive oil empire to run. I gently push away from Lorenzo and smooth his shirt where my fingers scrunched it.

"Come visit me when you're in California?"

He groans, crushing me to him. "*Rimani qui con me. Non andare. Ho bisogno di te. Tu appartieni a me, piccola gatta randagia.*"

Tears track down my cheeks. "I don't know what you're saying…"

He kisses my temple, holding me to him. "It means…take care of yourself, my little stray cat." I know there's more he's not telling me, but I can't think straight. My heart is splintering in half. He gently kisses my lips. His phone rings again. "I am going to murder my sister."

"Go, Lorenzo. Please. I can't do this."

He nods and takes a step back. "Call me when you get

there. I'll need to know you are safe." He runs his thumb tenderly over my bottom lip before he strides out the door without a backward glance.

My throat tightens, my heart begging my brain to tell him the truth. This was always more than just a summer fling. More than anything I ever anticipated. I run to the stairs to scream that I love him, but the front door slams, and my soul unravels. There's no point to any of it.

# Chapter 29

I CURL INTO the seat as much as possible, sobbing. Next to me, the poor American man hands me two mini bottles of alcohol he's dug out of his carry-on at his feet. "Here, take them. I think you need them more than I do."

"Thanks." I sniffle and down the bottle. I shake my head and down the second, hoping it will ease the pain. Usually, I wouldn't take drinks from strangers, but desperate times call for desperate measures. I hand him back the empty bottles and turn away from him as I blow my nose.

"Uh, okay, I'll just throw these away." He stuffs the bottles into the seat pocket in front of him. "I'm going to put my noise-canceling headphones on. Tap me if you need something." He pats my shoulder and opens his laptop.

I'd be really embarrassed if I weren't so fucking sad. That word doesn't even come close to describe what I'm feeling. I'm devastated. I miss Ren so much my heart feels like someone ripped it from my chest, balled it up like a piece of paper, and shoved it back in, crumpled and barely beating.

I didn't want to get on this plane. Walking through the airport, I could only hear the beat of my heart, people a blur as I passed by them. I moved on autopilot, handing my passport and ticket over to the agent. She barely looked at me as she directed me down the gangway to the airplane. I wanted her to stop me and say this is all a big mistake. That I *must* stay in Italy and I wasn't needed back in California. But she didn't. No one stopped me.

I kept looking for a tall, handsome Italian man with greenish-gray eyes and chocolate-brown hair to yell out my name and tell me he loves me, rescuing me from this black abyss of sadness, but he never showed.

So here I am, curled in a ball like a little hedgehog, sobbing my eyes out next to this poor man, who has a wife and two kids three rows up, and I'm drinking the last of his alcohol. I want to rock myself and scream into a pillow, but I don't want to scare the other passengers. If I do that, it will get me kicked off this plane, and then I'll have to stay in Italy...probably in a holding cell. Cara would strangle me.

I ruminate over my conversation with her. She's always been my voice of reason—I don't fault her for that. She was right to tell me to return. It was the appropriate decision. I can't run away from my responsibilities back home. I have my job there, my townhome, and, of course, Barbara. She's the one who taught me when life gets rough, you run. I'm not Barbara, though. Not even close.

Family. *Famiglia.* That's what the Rossis are...were to me. Even though I only knew them for three short months, they had become my family. So much more than Barbara ever was. They welcomed a complete stranger into their lives with open arms, and I willingly walked into their fold and let myself think I could be a Rossi.

Perhaps Nina was right...I am a con artist looking for my next fix, but it wasn't the Rossi fortune I was after. I craved their love and acceptance and stability.

I didn't get to say goodbye to Nonna. I wonder what she thinks about me now? The bird who flew away onto her next adventure. If only she knew the truth…that this bird is tethered to an unforgiving cage. I didn't get to thank her for everything she did for me. I didn't squeeze Fiore or Stella into a fierce hug and thank them for making me feel like I was a part of the family from day one. I won't get to listen to Raffaelo talk sports with Lorenzo or talk shop about the farm during Sunday lunch ever again. I even miss Razzo and his mouse offerings, Angelo's affinity for all things yellow, and Nina's snarky observations.

I left, just like Nonna Rossi reprimanded me for doing. I didn't listen to my heart. I look at the translation I looked up on my phone for the hundredth time. The words that Ren told me before he left. I run the pad of my finger over them.

*Rimani qui con me. Non andare. Ho bisogno di te. Tu appartieni a me, piccola gatta randagia.* Stay here with me. Don't go. I need you. You belong with me, my little stray cat. Tears drop on my screen, blurring the type.

The flight attendant approaches our aisle with her cart, smiling. "Hi, would you like something to drink? I have water, soft drinks, juice, or cocktails."

The man next to me takes off his headphones and orders a mini bottle of Chianti. He hesitantly glances in my direction, and I shake my head. He whispers to bring a bottle of water and some tissues. The flight attendant takes one look at my puffy eyes and gives me a pitiful smile. A few minutes later, she returns with our drinks, two mini green bottles, and a basket.

"I thought you could use a little sustenance. Don't tell

anyone, but I snagged these from first class for you." She smiles warmly, setting down a basket of French bread with the bottles. "Our movie tonight is an oldie, but we love playing it on the way home, so it might make you feel better. It's *Under the Tuscan Sun.*" She winks like she's doing me a huge fucking favor before she moves down the aisle.

I peek at the Rossi Olive Oil bottles tucked in next to the bread and hysterically wail as I bury myself into the blanket and pillow I have wedged against the window. Of course, they have mini bottles of Rossi Olive Oil on the plane ride home. Nonna would have called it *un segno.* I call it a cruel fucking twist of fate.

My seatmate quickly gets up to talk to his wife, giving me some space to compose myself. I'm sure he thinks I'm a complete lunatic, but I don't care. I don't care about anything anymore. It's a dangerous place to be.

Throwing the Rossi bottles out of my sight, I snag his bottle of Chianti and chug it, hoping the alcohol will do its job and numb the pain. When I wake up a couple hours later, the bottles and bread are long gone, and the movie credits are rolling.

# Chapter 30

IT'S BEEN TWO weeks back home, and I can't seem to lift myself out of my funk. At first, I thought it was jet lag, but that would have worn off by now. It doesn't help every time I walk down the hallway of Granite Scholastics someone cheerfully asks me about my trip. I'm depressed, is what I am.

Cara bailed Barbara out of jail during my flight back home and immediately transported her to a local rehab center her friend Tony recommended, where she will stay for the next month. I am allowed to see her at the end of this week for our first family therapy session. I'm honestly surprised she hasn't checked herself out yet. Perhaps she's finally seen the light…but I'm not holding my breath. We've been through this before.

Lorenzo and I have texted back and forth a few times. Each text like a lifeline to my heart, but it's getting to be busy season at the farm, and his messages lately have been quick and distracted sounding. I get it. It's impossible to keep a relationship going when you live in two different countries, and he's nine hours ahead. Cara doesn't think it's healthy for me to continue this charade, and she's probably right, but I can't seem to let him go.

"Knock-knock, Summer. Mr. Krantz would like to see

you." Betsy, Allen's assistant, sticks her head in my cubicle.

"Okay, thanks, Betsy." I smile briefly before I get up from my desk. *Please don't walk with me. I'm not in the mood to chitchat.*

"Right this way," she singsongs, like I've got amnesia and can't remember where my boss's office is after fourteen years of working here.

I tuck my laptop under my arm while Betsy zings me with a dozen questions.

"How was Italy? What was your favorite thing to do there? Did you meet any handsome Italians?" She waggles her eyebrows. "I bet you have like a million pictures. Didn't you do a bike tour? That sounds like so much fun, but I think I would die on a bike, but you have great legs so I'm sure it was easy-breezy for you. I've always wanted to go there, but Mike complains the flight is too long. Was it bad?"

*Jesus, does anyone talk to this poor woman during the day?*

"Uh, no, I slept through most of it."

"Oh, I'd be way too excited to sleep. What was the most amazing food you tried over there?"

Memories of Fiore's cooking burn the back of my throat as tears threaten to spill. I reach out to knock on Allen's door, praying he isn't on a phone call. "The pizza was great. Thanks for coming to get me."

"Oh, I loooove pizza—"

I enter without waiting for Allen to call me in and close the door on Betsy. I can still hear her talking on the other side of the door.

Allen looks up. "Summer, thanks for coming in. Please

sit, I'll be just a second."

I take the chair across from him while he finishes writing something. I can't stop staring at the florescent light glaring off his bald head. He puts his pen down and laces his fingers together, smiling blandly.

"Summer, I wanted to check in and see how you're doing. Are you feeling okay?"

"Yes, I'm good. Excited to start the new project." I try to push some cheer into my voice, but it falls flat.

"Are you, though? Because I get the sense that you're unhappy. A colleague reported you were crying in the women's bathroom the other day."

Crap, I thought I was alone in there. "I, um, received a phone call from my mother. It was upsetting."

"I'm sorry to hear that." He leans back in his chair and steeples his fingers. "Jeremy mentioned you snapped at him when he asked you if you had the New World Algebra chapter ready."

I want to roll my eyes but keep them focused on Allen. "With all due respect, Allen, Jeremy was asking me about the copy an hour after I received it. I'm fast, but not that fast."

Allen waves a hand, chuckling. "He is a little intense at times, but I've noticed you've been wearing black every day, like you're in mourning." He leans forward and smiles again, like he's offering a kid a lollipop if they'll be good. "Granite Scholastics wants a positive experience in a fun environment. Bright colors and cheerful attitudes. Can you do that for me, Summer?"

"Yes, of course." I glance down at my black t-shirt and leggings. I hadn't even realized I was wearing black every day.

"Also, I'm assigning Jeremy as project manager on the Chemistry for College project."

I bite back the groan wanting to escape and sit back, but I must have not covered my disappointment well. Allen waves his hand.

"I know, I know, but I think if you all work together and communicate, it will go smoothly."

Jeremy Wells has a reputation among the design team as being a demanding tyrant, sending text messages on Saturday evenings at eleven p.m. asking when he can view the layouts. It's a college textbook, Jeremy, you're not Anna Wintour editing *Vogue* magazine.

"Can you be a team player, Summer?" Allen asks.

I nod my head.

"Great." He clasps his hands together. "How about we call him in now?"

"Oh, okay, great," I mumble.

Allen picks up his phone. "Betsy, can you send Jeremy in? Thanks."

He makes small talk while we wait. "So how was Italy? My wife and I went about…oh, five years ago. We stayed in Rome. It was very hot and crowded."

The last thing I want to do is reminisce with Allen about my time in Italy. "It was great. I didn't make it to Rome, though."

"Ah, well, next time, right?"

*There won't be a next time, Allen, but thanks for the stab in the heart.*

The office door opens and Jeremy strides in like a used-car salesman on the brink of closing the deal on the new Cadillac. He rubs his hands together before pulling out the chair next to me and winks. "Allen, Summer."

"Jeremy, thanks for joining us. I was discussing with Summer that you will be point man on the Chemistry for College textbook series project—"

"Yes. I'm really excited about this. I think we can dazzle them, don't you, Summer?" His knee bounces like he's hopped up on Red Bull, and it takes all my self-control not to put my hand on him to still it. I try to match his enthusiasm, but let's be honest, how much can you really dazzle when it comes to a chemistry textbook?

"Sure…" I paste on a smile.

"Excellent, glad you're being a team player on *this* one."

Wait, what? I'm always a team player, consistent with making my deadlines. Allen nods enthusiastically, missing the passive-aggressive barb. As Jeremy drones on, my mind wanders to golden sunlit hills and Lorenzo standing in front of me, bending to kiss my bare shoulder.

"Don't you think, Summer?"

"I'm sorry, what?"

"I said, we can have this done within two weeks, right?"

"As long as the graphics are JPEGs at three-hundred DPI resolution and the copy has been proofed, we should be set."

"I'll have them send you the files immediately," Allen says, leaning back in his chair. "Great to have you two working on this together."

"It's going to be the bomb." Jeremy holds out his hand for me to high-five. I slap his hand because I *am* a team player.

"Thanks, Allen." I scoot my chair back. "Anything else?"

"I think we're good. Jeremy?"

"I'll check in with you later, Summer," he says.

"Sounds good." I exit the office and return to my cubicle to pack up for the day. I have a missed call from my mother's attorney and one from Cara. I'm supposed to go over to her place for dinner tonight, but all I want to do is crawl under my covers. I can't even watch *Under the Tuscan Sun* anymore without crying hysterically and throwing cookies at the television screen while Frances turns on the water. Happy endings don't exist in real life.

I call Cara on my way home.

"What's going on, Italy?"

"Damien, why are you answering Cara's phone?"

"She's on a call in the office. You coming over for my fabulous attempt at shrimp scampi?"

"Yeah, about that…"

"Nah, you're coming over. I've been slaving over this for an hour."

"But I'm tired."

"You can put that whine next to my beer—you're *not* backing out. See you in an hour." He hangs up before I can say anything else.

I pull into my driveway and stop short as my headlights flash over a large rectangular package leaning against the garage door. I park the car and get out. I can't believe someone didn't steal this. It's addressed to me, and the return address is from Italy.

I drag the package up to my tiny front porch and tear the paper off. I gasp when I tear back the bubble wrap from the canvas. It's the painting of the olive grove. The exact one I wanted to purchase in the gallery but couldn't afford.

"Oh my God," I mutter, running my fingertips over the oils swirled on the canvas. "I can't believe he did this." I check the time, but it's two in the morning in Italy. I unlock my door and haul the painting inside and carefully cut off the rest of the packaging. A little notecard is attached to the back of the frame.

*Tesoro, a little piece of me for you. Come una stella cadente nel cielo, ti cercherò sempre. Con amore, Ren*

I quickly translate the Italian and sigh. *Treasure, a little piece of me for you. Like a falling star in the sky, I will always look for you.*

Memories from the night of San Lorenzo crash into me, and I crumple to the couch and sob, holding the notecard to my chest. After a while, I sit up and blow my nose. I wander over to the painting as memories of us beneath the old olive tree make my heart clench. I read the card again. A little piece of me for you.

"Goddamn it, Ren, how do you expect me to ever get over you?" I squint at the tiny signature on the painting and gasp. *L Rossi.* No way…

I back away from the picture and slowly sink back down on the couch. It all makes sense. The gallery and art studio beneath his apartment. All the paintings he has around his house. The beautiful mural in Nonna's old house.

Why didn't he ever say anything? He could have easily said, yeah, I painted that, but he didn't. I check the time and jump to my feet. I'm late for dinner, and I still need to shower. I rush out of the room, contemplating what the painting means and why Lorenzo never said he was the artist.

# Chapter 31

I WALK INTO the kitchen just in time to see Damien douse the pasta in fake lemon juice.

"Uh, Dame, aren't you supposed to use real lemon juice?"

"What are you talking about? This is real." He holds the bottle up and examines it. "Right here, one hundred percent real juice."

Cara arches an eyebrow and shakes her head, leading me into the living room. I fill her in on the painting from Ren.

"So, he's not only running a million-dollar company, but he's an artist too?"

"Yes, but I don't understand why he didn't tell me."

"It was sweet of him to send it to you. So, what does this mean?"

"I don't know."

"Are you two going to try to make this work?" Cara asks, looking at me doubtfully.

"Between our two schedules, we can't even find time to call each other. He's so busy with harvest season."

Cara places her hand over mine and squeezes. "I'm so sorry, Summer. I know you were hoping for something more. Someday, these memories won't feel so fresh in your mind, and you can look back on them fondly as the time you let yourself be adventurous in Italy and met a dashing Italian. The pain will soften into happy memories."

I nod my head, trying to keep the tears at bay. Not only am I sick of crying, but I don't want to show Cara how her words affect me. I'm terrified of time edging the memories, blurring the lines until they're just colors in my mind. I don't want to forget one second of my time with him.

"Allen pulled me into his office today and told me to stop wearing black and then put me on a new project with Jeremy Wells as the project manager."

Cara makes a pinched face. She's heard the Jeremy stories. Her eyes flick to my all-black clothes.

"I did it again, didn't I?"

She nods, pursing her lips.

"I don't even consciously do it."

"What's the latest with Barbara?"

"I have to go visit her tomorrow for our first therapy session, which I'm sure will be her blaming me for everything."

"Oh, girl…" Cara looks at me with pity. "Things will be much better once this whole DUI is cleared up. Tony is an excellent attorney."

"Dinner is ready!" Damien shouts from the kitchen.

"Oh lord, here we go. Whatever you do, just smile and say it's good. He's been so sensitive lately about his cooking."

We sit down at the table, and Damien shreds parmesan over the pasta. "Now, I know this isn't fresh pasta like you had over in Italy…"

"I'm sure it's going to be amazing." I smile up at him.

He sits down, and we dig in. I twirl a small amount onto

my fork and stab a piece of shrimp. I put it into my mouth, waiting for the explosion of flavor, but it doesn't come. What I taste is acid from the fake lemon juice, and heat. I quickly chew and swallow, but my tongue is on fire. I grab my water, dousing the hotness.

"Huh, should have used less red pepper flakes." Damien chews thoughtfully. Cara reaches for her water, her eyes watering.

"How much lemon juice did you put in?" she asks.

I laugh, unable to keep it in. Damien looks insulted at first, and then his face splits into a grin. "It's pretty bad, isn't it?"

"It's awful." Cara coughs into her napkin.

"Guess I should have used real lemon."

"I have a great cookbook you can borrow," I offer.

"I followed the recipe…kind of." His brows scrunch together as he stirs his pasta. "I don't get it."

"Yes, but you have to follow the exact measurements and use the ingredients they list, not substitute," Cara says.

"Let's order pizza." He gathers our plates.

"It was a good effort, Dame," I call out to his retreating form.

"I seriously need to enroll him in a class. I know I've been talking about it, but I keep hoping he'll get better. He's not getting better."

"I think that's a good idea." I laugh. For the first time in weeks, I feel like my old self. "Thanks, Cara."

"For what?"

"For being here for me."

She gets up and wraps her arms around me. "Always. I'm

glad you're home. I know it's been hard, and you're sad, but you did the right thing."

I nod and squeeze her back. I wish I believed her.

# Chapter 32

AS PROMISED, ALLEN sent me the files for the new project. And as expected, everything is a complete mess. Text documents are out of order and pictures aren't numbered with the pages they are supposed to be grouped with. I have a headache thrumming at the base of my skull, and I have to leave in twenty minutes to drive an hour to meet Barbara at the rehab facility.

A shadow falls across my desk and the smell of cheap cologne invades my space. Jeremy leans against my cubicle.

"Summer, do you have the first five chapters done yet?"

"Allen just sent the files this morning and they are a disaster. I'm not a miracle worker," I grumble.

"That's not the response I was hoping for. How about a more positive attitude? A *yes I can do* kind of attitude. I'd like to have it by four." He wraps his knuckles on the top ledge of my cubicle before he walks away, whistling a jaunty tune. I hate him.

I open up a file and import the text, wrapping it around a picture of molecules. I used to find pleasure in the steady rhythm of formatting. Placing the text where it needed to go, making sure the margins were correct, that the words flowed correctly, spacing it as needed. But I no longer find joy in it. The creative juices that flowed in Italy are fighting against the monotonous rhythm I once found easy and comforting.

I glance at the clock. It's three thirty p.m. here, which means it's twelve thirty in the morning in Italy. Lorenzo is probably asleep.

I find myself glancing at the clock a lot these days, wondering how he's doing and what everyone at the farm would be doing at that hour. I haven't talked to him in weeks. He's been so busy with harvest. I called to thank him for the painting, but got sent to his voicemail. Is this what my life has turned into? Looking at the clock and wishing I was somewhere else with someone else?

Wishing I didn't feel stuck.

I WALK TOWARD the palatial building in front of me surrounded by beautifully manicured lawns and tropical flowers. This looks more like a resort than a rehab facility. I check in at the front desk and show my ID before I'm asked to take a seat in the light, airy lobby.

I'm checking my messages when a woman approaches me with a warm smile. "Summer Andrews?"

"Yes, I'm Summer." I stand and shake her hand, immediately at ease by her warm smile.

"Hi, I'm Dr. Naomi Rice. I've been assigned to your mother's case. It's a pleasure to meet you, and thank you for driving all this way to visit with us this evening. Why don't you follow me. Barbara is waiting in my office."

"Thank you so much, Dr. Rice. I haven't been allowed to talk to Barbara since she arrived and was detoxing. Is she doing alright?"

"She's doing beautifully." The doctor smiles as we reach her door.

"That's great to hear."

Relief washes over me. I try not to get my hopes up, but perhaps this time treatment will work. She pauses, her hand on the handle, and turns to me.

"Summer, I want to warn you, this won't be easy today. Sometimes in therapy, people say things that aren't always kind, because they are in a safe space. For Barbara to move forward, I will need you to come back again for more sessions, as painful as they might be."

"I understand, Dr. Rice. We've been through this before."

Her eyes tilt down. "Yes, I know. I'm not giving up on Barbara without a fight. Are we in this together?"

I nod my head, tears threatening to spill down my cheeks, too choked up to agree with words. It's the first time I've ever had a therapist want to fight for her.

"Very good," she says, turning the handle. We step into a spacious room decorated in calming cream tones. "Barbara, Summer is here."

Barbara is sitting on a suede couch, her bare feet tucked under her. She looks small and frail. She pulls out a pack of cigarettes, sliding one out, but doesn't light it. She holds it between her fingers. "Trying to quit." She smiles ruefully at me.

"That's good." I give her a small smile in return, taking a

seat in a comfortable-looking chair perpendicular to her, as Dr. Rice sits opposite me.

"Thank you for coming today, Summer." Dr. Rice opens her leatherbound notebook and jots something down. "I want open communication during this session. This is a safe place for you both and I am here merely as a buffer. I'm not here to take sides or to help settle a dispute. This session is to help you both understand each other better. Does that sound good?"

We both nod.

"Great, let's get started. Barbara, why don't you go first."

Barbara takes a deep breath. "Summer, I am sorry for the accident, for stealing your car, for being negligent. I want to be a better person, a better parent."

Barbara doesn't meet my eyes and I'm wondering if she's being sincere. Is she just saying what Dr. Rice wants to hear so she can get out of here faster? Guilt floods my chest for thinking it, but old habits are hard to break.

"Summer?" Dr. Rice prompts.

"Well...I accept her apology, but to be honest, I've heard it all before. It's the same song and dance with Barbara. Every time she screws up, she apologizes and then the pattern starts all over again. I *hope* she wants to be a better person, but I think we're past her being a better parent."

"Barbara, do you see yourself repeating the pattern?"

"No, I'm being truthful, Summer," Barbara huffs.

"Barbara, why don't we start from the beginning. Perhaps it might shed some light for Summer."

"I got pregnant with you when I was fifteen. It's no secret I never wanted to have a baby, but my mother made me keep you until term, hoping it would teach me to be responsible. Your father was long gone at that point. He was a dish-washer at the café my mom worked at. As soon as I told him I was pregnant, he left town, so I was all on my own. The first few years were the hardest.

"Sure, I had my mom, but she was always working, being a single mother herself. She was constantly breathing down my neck. I couldn't see my friends anymore, or go to parties, homecoming, graduation. Everyone's life was going on without me while I was stuck at home changing diapers. I was severely depressed and angry. I was so angry at the world, so angry at her. You idolized my mom. Grams this and Grams that…I felt like I wasn't needed or wanted."

Dr. Rice passes me a tissue. I hadn't realized I was crying. This is the first time I've ever heard Barbara express raw, honest truth.

"Summer?" Dr. Rice says.

"As a kid, all I wanted was to be loved by you."

"I couldn't give you that…I wasn't capable of that. I'm sorry."

"Barbara, do you think you resented Summer?"

"Damn straight, I resented her. Her Grams gave her all the attention. Her entire world became Summer. I tried to bond with her, but I was too depressed. Here I was doing my best, incapable of loving my own child. I thought I was a monster, that I was defective. I didn't want to be a mother. *My* mother constantly shamed me, calling me unfit, so I started drinking for comfort. In my mom's eyes, I was her biggest failure, so why not live up to her assumption? When she threatened to take my parental rights away, I gave up on everything."

"Summer, how does it make you feel to hear that?"

I take a deep, shaky breath. I never knew Grams treated her that way.

"It makes me sad…for everyone involved. It's hurtful to hear you were never wanted or loved. I always knew Barbara resented me, I just didn't understand why."

"Barbara, do you still resent Summer?"

Barbara looks down at the carpet and then up at Dr. Rice. "Sometimes. I resent how successful she is. I resent that Grams treated her differently."

"But can you understand that's not Summer's fault? She chose her path just as you chose yours." Dr. Rice turns to me. "Can you sympathize with Barbara?"

I pause, chewing my lip, mulling over the doctor's question. I've heard of women experiencing postpartum depression before. I can't understand not loving a child, but then again, I've never walked in her shoes. I imagine myself at fifteen and there's no way I could have cared for a baby by myself. Barbara's entire world changed, and not for the better. It's as if Barbara stayed stuck in the mentality of a fifteen-year-old all these years, but the world moved on and grew up without her.

"I can sympathize," I say slowly, and I mean it. "I wish she had told me this years ago, instead of waiting for her to step up to the plate every time I needed a parent."

Dr. Rice leans forward. "Do you think we can rebuild this relationship, or do you think it's too far gone?"

Barbara flips the cigarette between her fingers, her shoulders hunched, eyes cast down. Nonna's voice whispers in my head like wind rustling through leaves. *Famiglia.* She's family.

"Barbara and I will never have a traditional mother-daughter relationship. That ship sailed long ago. But if she can start taking responsibility for her life, continue with therapy and do the hard work, then I'm willing to meet her halfway."

"Barbara, can you meet Summer halfway?"

My mom looks up, tears shining in her eyes. "I want to be a better person, Summer."

"Barbara, that's not what I asked," Dr. Rice says.

"Yes. I'm willing to do the hard work and meet her halfway."

I nod and give her a small smile. For once, I'm willing to believe her.

# Chapter 33

I SIT DOWN on my bed in a huff. "I don't want to go, Cara."

She throws a shirt at my head. "I know, but you have to get back out there. You need to get over Lorenzo. Living in this limbo state like you have for the past few months is not good for your mental health."

"What if I don't want to get over him?"

"Summer, you haven't heard from him in two and a half months," she says gently, sitting next to me on the bed.

She's right, I know she's right, but going to this holiday party tonight feels like I'm betraying him somehow. I wonder if he's met someone, and that's why I haven't heard from him. That thought is like being stabbed by a dull knife.

The painting hangs center on the wall across from my bed where the TV used to be. It's painful to have the constant reminder of Italy and him, but it's too beautiful to tuck away in a closet. I fall asleep each night, reliving our night together under the tree. The red silk tank sits on my bed like a beacon, calling to me to move on with my life. I slip it on over my head.

"Cara?"

"Yes, love?"

"Do you think the pain will ever go away?"

She draws me into a side-hug. "It will. You'll meet someone new, and life will take over. It just takes time. Things will get better, I promise. I honestly think it's good you haven't heard from Lorenzo in a while. Maybe he needed to let go, too." She picks her wrap up off my bed. "I'll meet you outside."

I pick up my phone and stare at the blank screen. My finger hovers over the text button, but I don't press it. Perhaps Lorenzo is doing us both a favor. Pressing the button, I read the last text message I sent him.

**Me:** *How are you? I miss you.*

That was from a month ago, and I never received a response. I need to move on and forget Lorenzo Rossi. Well, maybe not forget, but remember him fondly from the time I got lost in Tuscany.

THE CROWDED BAR is hopping with singles and couples ready to mingle. It's a meet-and-greet holiday mixer hosted by the dating site, *The One*. I can't believe I let Cara and Damien drag me out to this. The only reason I agreed was to get Cara off my back. She's been hounding me for weeks since she received the email about this event. I told her she could have one hour of my time, and then I'm out.

Cara meanders off to find Damien, who is meeting us here, while I melt into the crowd. I step up to the bar and squeeze myself in between two people while I try to signal the bartender. If I'm going to survive the next hour, I'm going to need something stronger than wine or beer. The guy next to me glances over and smiles. He holds up a finger, and the bartender nods his head. "What would you like?" he asks me.

"A vodka and Sprite, please."

"A vodka and Sprite for the beautiful woman in red. Hi, I'm Carter."

"Hi Carter, Summer." I shake his hand. He has a cute smile.

"Have you been to one of these events before?"

"No, my friend Cara dragged me out tonight." I roll my eyes, making him chuckle.

"My first one, too. It's crowded. You from around here?"

"Yeah, Burlingame."

"I live in the city. I'm in real estate," he says.

"Oh wow, that must be interesting. I'm a graphic designer."

"Really? I'm actually looking for someone to help with my logo and website design."

"Oh yeah? I can help you with the logo." I fish my card out of my purse. Before Italy, I would never have had the confidence to offer my design skills, but Lorenzo gave that gift to me, encouraging me to step out of my box.

"Granite Scholastics," he reads the card.

"Yes, it's my day job, but I freelance in design."

The bartender drops off my drink, and I fish a twenty out of my purse. Carter puts his hand on my arm. "It's on me. Just put it on my tab," he says to the bartender.

"Oh, thank you, that's really sweet." I take a sip of my

drink and smile. Maybe Cara was right about getting back out into the dating pool.

"You're cute. How is a beautiful woman like you still single?"

Someone bumps into me from behind, and my drink splashes onto Carter's pants. "Oh no, I'm so sorry." I pick up my thin little cocktail napkin from the bar and try to soak it up, but it doesn't help.

Carter grabs some more napkins and dabs his pants. "It's not a big deal—"

"Sorry, didn't mean to bump…hey, don't I know you?"

I tear my attention from Carter to the drink-bumper behind me. I close my eyes. This can't be happening right now.

He snaps his fingers. "Cindy, right? Cin-Dee!"

"Uh, no." I try to turn back around, but he's not giving up.

"No, I know we've met. I never forget a face."

"Lucky me," I mumble.

"Lucky's bar, yeah! So, how have you been, Cindy?" Kevin, the orange-toned bodybuilder who caused me to go home, drink two bottles of wine, and sign up for a bike trip through Italy, grins. The worst date in the history of ever.

I'm packed between people at the bar with Kevin looming in front of me. "It's Summer, and I'm actually in the middle of a conversation with someone." I turn back around, but Carter has vanished. *Crap.*

"Oh, I remember you now. You were the one who got all huffy on our date when I asked if you were a feminist."

I grit my teeth, looking around the room. Where the

fuck are Cara and Damien? "I didn't get huffy. I decided I had had enough."

"You were cute in a grumpy librarian kind of way. Are you here with someone?" He steps closer. *This guy is smoking something if he thinks I'm interested.*

"I'm—"

"So, what do you say, Cindy? Wanna get a drink?" His eyes flicker down to my breasts.

"Honestly? That's the last thing I want to do." I turn to leave.

"Come on, don't be like that."

His fingers brush my backside, and I snap. I twist back around and throw what's left of my drink in his face, but he's a lot taller than I am, so it ends up all over his shirt. He looks down at his shirt. We both stand there, stunned. Time seems to freeze while everyone around us is staring. Someone hands Kevin a napkin.

I set my glass down and push my way out of the bar into the cold December night.

# Chapter 34

PULLING INTO MY driveway, I put the car in park and thud my head against the steering wheel. I scream in frustration. I don't want this life anymore. Cara has been blowing up my phone, but I don't want to talk to her. I don't want to talk to anyone right now. After a few minutes, I get out and lock my car and slowly trudge up the front steps of my porch.

"Do you always scream in your car, *tesoro*?"

I freeze. Am I imagining his voice now? Did I hit my head too hard against the steering wheel? Have I finally hit rock bottom and am conjuring up his voice in my head?

The porch swing creaks as he stands, and he walks into the light. He's wearing a black wool overcoat, a white button-down, and jeans. He looks so damn good, but his expression is cautious. I fling myself into his arms, and he catches me easily. I breathe in his woodsy, familiar scent and silently cry in his arms. I'm home, right where I belong.

"Are you real?"

He gently puts me down and holds my face in his hands, his thumbs wiping away the tears tracking down my cheeks. "Yes, I'm real." He smiles. "I've missed you so much."

"What are you doing here?"

"I had some business to take care of at our farm here."

"Oh." My heart drops. He didn't come for me. He's here

on business. I gather myself together and take a step back, the initial shock of seeing him wearing off. "How did you find out where I lived?"

"It was on your paperwork." He grins sheepishly. "I hope you don't mind me showing up on your doorstep."

"How long have you been sitting out here? It's cold."

"About an hour."

"Why didn't you call me? When did you get here?" I unlock the front door.

"Tonight. I came straight here from the airport. I wanted to surprise you."

I shake my head. "I'm so sorry, you must be freezing. Come in."

I forgot how tall he is as he enters my small foyer carrying his luggage. I turn and shut the door, soaking in the sight of him. He runs a hand through his hair and the familiar movement makes my heart pump harder. I wonder if he's as nervous as I feel. He looks around my townhome, tucking his hands in his coat pocket. Thank goodness Barbara is on a weekend retreat with her AA sponsor.

"I can't believe you're really here. Can I get you something to drink?" I wipe my hands on my pants and do a quick survey of my small living room to make sure Barbara doesn't have a bra hanging out somewhere. "I have water and some diet coke."

"Water, please. *Grazie.*"

He sits down on my sofa while I dash into the kitchen. I grab a bottle of water when my phone buzzes with an incoming call from Cara.

"Girl, what the hell happened tonight? My friend Jill said

you dumped a drink on some guy. I lost you in the crowd—" she shouts over the noise at the bar.

"He's here," I hiss.

"Who's there? The guy from the bar?"

"No! Lorenzo. He's in my living room."

"What?" Cara screeches.

"I'll call you tomorrow."

"Call me first thing in the morning."

I hang up with her and walk back in, handing him the bottle. I sit down in the chair perpendicular to him. He uncaps the water and takes a sip.

"How long are you here for?" I ask.

"A couple of days."

"Oh."

"Summer—"

"How have you been?" I ask, feigning cheer while I try like hell to override the hurt in my heart. In the light, I can see dark shadows under his eyes.

"I'm miserable," he says.

"Why?"

He snorts and looks over at me as he leans forward and puts his elbows on his knees. He scrubs his face with his hands. "*Mi chiedi perché?* Because I can't stop thinking about you. It's been six agonizing months. I've been consumed with work, and yet you interrupt my thoughts every minute of every day. You're the first thing I think about when I wake up and the last thing before I fall asleep, if I even fall asleep. *Sto impazzendo e non riesco farci niente.* I'm going crazy and I can't fix it."

"You haven't called or texted in months."

"I know, and I'm sorry, *tesoro*. I had to forget about you for my own sanity. I forbade anyone to mention you, but everywhere I turned, there were pieces of you left behind. I couldn't even go to the old tree to think without memories of you wrapping around me. Even damn Razzo has been following me around, meowing at me like he's cussing me out for letting you go. Fiore is furious with me, and Nonna hasn't talked to me in months.

"I swore to myself after Gabriella I would never let another woman get under my skin and make me lose control of my heart. When she and I parted ways, it broke something inside of me I thought I'd never be able to repair, so I threw myself into work. It worked until you showed up, out of the blue…a stray cat like Razzo."

He shovels his hands through his hair. "I wanted to be mad at you for moving into the house, but Nonna Rossi is always right when taking in her lost little strays. She had a plan the minute she laid eyes on you. Her anger toward me about buying the house was all just an act. Nonno had left it to me in his will, but not until Nonna was ready to sign it over to me. She agreed the house needed a major overhaul. But one glimpse of you, and she knew we were *scritti nelle stelle*."

"Written in the stars," I whisper.

He nods. "From the very first day, I couldn't keep my eyes off you or stop thinking about you. When Angelo started sniffing around, I went nuts. He liked the challenge you presented. Nina was too easy and willing for him. Did Fiore tell you he slept with Gabriella?"

I shake my head, a sick feeling churning in my stomach.

"Right before we broke up, she and I had a terrible fight. She ran right to him, knowing it would hurt me. I've never forgiven either of them for that."

"I never should have had dinner with him," I mutter.

"You didn't know, *tesoro*." He looks at me with sad eyes. "I am angry with myself. I should never have let you go. You made it clear you were always leaving, so I tried my damnedest to not get attached. I thought I was doing the right thing for you. I should have come here with you. Selfishly, I wanted to lock you in the house and throw away your passport so you could never return to the States, but I knew I had to let you go. It was the hardest thing I've ever had to do that day when I walked away from you. I should have told you I wanted you to stay, and I was in love with you. *Ti amo*, Summer. I'm so desperately in love with you, I can't see straight."

The anguish on his face breaks my heart apart. "*Ti amo*, Lorenzo. I wish you had told me all of this that day. I wanted to stay, but I thought making a clean cut was for the best."

He nods. "I was *un codardo*...a coward. I thought I had more time. During *Ferragasto* I was going to ask you to stay, to move to Italy and be with me, that I was in love with you and couldn't let you go."

"I wanted to stay."

"You needed to go. Family comes first."

A tear slips down my cheek. "You weren't the only coward. I should have told you how I felt, but I was scared to lay my heart on the line."

He looks down at his hands. "Are you happy, Summer?"

The truth bursts from me like a dam breaking. "No. God

no, I'm fucking slowly dying inside. Like I'm walking around, going through the motions, but not feeling anything. I don't fit into my old life anymore. You've ruined that for me. Italy has ruined that for me."

"I'm so sorry, *tesoro*. I know the feeling well."

I get up from the couch and slide onto his lap. He sits back, his hands squeezing my thighs as his breath shudders.

"I've missed you, Ren. More than I care to admit. I've been walking around here for months, a shadow of my former self. I love you, but I can't do this all over again."

"I was hoping you would say that." His fingers flex against my waist. "Because I can't walk away and leave you behind again."

My lips brush against his, and my heart sighs in contentment. Like a key fitting a lock, it opens the door to home. He sucks my bottom lip, gently biting it. "I've missed you so much, *amore mio*."

Our kisses start slowly, our lips remembering the tastes and texture of each other, savoring the feel of us being together again, but that only lasts a minute before our desire takes over. Our tongues tangle greedily as I rock against him, my fingers driving into his hair. He lifts my silk blouse over my head, and his hands immediately circle my rib cage as his thumbs glide over my satin bra. He kisses the swell of my breasts, unhooking my bra. His mouth closes over my tight bud, and I arch into him. He lavishes it with his tongue as I rock into him, creating a delicious friction between our bodies.

"Ren, take me to my room," I pant. He caresses the other breast and I'm about to explode. I can't take this slow torture. He stands, still holding me, and I guide him down the hall to my bedroom. He turns to close the door, and that's when he spots the painting hanging on the wall across from the bed.

"I was wondering if you kept it or trashed it."

"I could never have trashed something so beautiful. Something you created from your soul."

"I wouldn't have blamed you if you had." He brushes a tender kiss across my lips before lowering me to the bed. He yanks off my pants and sheds his clothes. He pauses a moment, his gaze igniting my blood as he holds himself over me. "*Sei squisita.*"

"*Non sei male neanche tu.*" I smile up at him, telling him I find him exquisite as well.

"*Tesoro*, have you been learning Italian?"

"Mmm, I might have downloaded an audio app."

"*Ti amo*, Summer."

"*Ti amo*, Ren."

I wrap my hands around his hard length and slowly pump him up and down. He hisses out a breath. "If you keep doing that, it will be a disappointing ending for me as I'm about to come all over myself like a teenager."

I laugh, but quickly sober, as he puts on a condom and guides himself into me.

"Wait," I say, feeling suddenly panicked. "Are you sure this is what you want?"

"Summer, I don't know if you've figured this out yet, but I'm not letting you go." He rocks into me slowly, and I feel every damn inch of him. I arch my back as his thumb draws tight little circles over the sensitive bundle of nerves at my apex. He moves faster, and I want to savor this feeling, but I can't stop the tidal wave from crashing down around me.

I wrap my legs around his waist and meet his thrusts. He speaks to me in Italian, and I explode into a thousand pieces as I cry out his name. He increases his speed, his pace becoming erratic, his muscles straining as he holds himself over me. I squeeze his tight, toned ass and scrape my nails down his back.

"*O dio!*" he shouts as he comes. We lie there motionless for a moment as we try to catch our breaths, tangled in each other's limbs. He smiles down at me and kisses my lips. "*Incredibile.*"

"What were you saying to me when I orgasmed?"

His cheeks pink. "Just some silly Italian words. It was nothing."

I grin. "My interest is now piqued, Mr. Rossi. Spill it."

"Don't make me say it out loud, *tesoro*. I was in the moment."

I walk my fingers across his chest. "But I love when you talk dirty to me in Italian. What did you say, Ren? I can always ask Nonna—"

He side-eyes me and sighs. "*Lo adoro quando vieni sul mio cazzo.* I love when you come on my cock."

"*Molto bene.*" I grin. "Was that so difficult?"

"Only when you bring Nonna up during sex."

I laugh and throw the sheets off. "I've missed you, Lorenzo Rossi."

He grabs me from around the waist and I squeal as he pulls me back to bed, smothering me with kisses. He brushes his nose gently against mine. "I've missed you more, tesoro."

We clean up and brush our teeth, grinning at each other in the mirror like a pair of loons, before climbing back into bed. Lorenzo holds me in his arms while I trace small circles on his chest. We both stare at the painting hanging across from us.

"How come you didn't tell me you were an artist?" I ask.

He shrugs. "It's not something I tell many people. I stopped painting when my grandfather died. I had to take over my father's position and Nonno's. I didn't have the time or desire."

"That's right around the time you and Gabriella broke up, too, isn't it?"

He squeezes me. "*Sí.* She was angry my father was taking a step back from the company, but he was having stress-related heart issues. He didn't have a choice. I need you to know…" I look up when he pauses, and he visibly swallows as he tries to control his emotions. "The olive farm is my heritage, Summer. I will admit, I wasn't fair to Gabriella. I knew who she was when I started dating her, and that I wouldn't be able to give her everything she wanted, but I was hoping we could meet in the middle. That love would be enough for her.

"At the time I had the weight of the world on my shoulders. I felt like I had to prove myself to my father, brother, and Nonna that I could run the business. The farm consumed me. Late nights, long hours…I wasn't much of a doting fiancé. I chose the olives over Gabriella. After we broke up, I swore to myself I'd never do that again if I met the right woman."

"Perhaps the right woman wouldn't ask you to choose," I murmur.

"Mm…I'm afraid in business, it always comes down to a choice…a decision to be made which takes you away from your family." He gently grabs my fingers, kissing them. "It's different with you, *tesoro*. I found myself rushing to be done with work so I could get home to you. I started taking walks during phone meetings in the hopes I might run into you." He smiles that coy smile. "I never wandered down to the shop before you started working there. I was…I *am* completely smitten with you. I don't want to lose you again. *Ti amo, piccola gatta randagia.*"

I snuggle against his chest, feeling the happiest I've ever felt. "There's that *randagia* word again."

"My little stray cat." He kisses my head, and I smile.

Afraid to ruin this moment but needing answers, I shift up onto my elbow and gaze down into his smoky gray eyes. He looks exhausted, but I won't be able to sleep a wink if I don't ask.

"Ren, where do we go from here?"

His eyes slide to the painting. "I made my choice, Summer. I chose you and I'm here. If that means running the California farm, then so be it."

My breath catches, my heartbeat accelerating. "But that would mean you would give up the farm? Give up Italy?"

"*Sí*, not give up per se, but hand it back over to my father and Gio to run."

"But your father—"

"He's already agreed, *tesoro*." His gaze shifts back to me. "I know what I'll be leaving behind. This is what I've been working on since you left. You are more important to me than the olives."

I trail my fingers down his chest. I should feel elated, but I don't. My heart is heavy. He'd be willing to give up his birthright, his legacy, to move here for me? He would leave his family, his home, and the beauty of Italy all for me. And what would I be giving up? I think of my job I no longer enjoy. I think of my mom who, despite being sober for four months now, still struggles with addiction. I think of Cara and Damien, who I would miss terribly, but realize that being a constant third wheel isn't ideal for their marriage. They have their own life together. I have my townhome, but the view in Italy is way better.

"No, Lorenzo."

"No? You don't want me here?"

"No." I shake my head. "I can't let you give that all up for me."

"*Cara mia—*"

I press my finger to his lips. "You are too important to me. I'd never ask you to give up the olive farm, to give up Italy, to give up your promise to your Nonno Rossi. I know what it means to you. These past few months, I've been walking around, a shell of my former self. I don't feel like I have a purpose anymore, and that terrifies me more than anything."

"But if I'm here with you, that will make you happy, *sì*?"

"No. If you're here with me, that means you gave up everything, and I would feel incredibly guilty. You have so much more to lose than I do." I sigh and shift, giving us some space. "There are some things I haven't told you. My mom—"

"I know about your mom, *tesoro*."

"How do you—"

"Nonna told me she's an alcoholic."

"Yes," I breathe out, relieved to have it out in the open. "The reason I had to return to the States so quickly was because she was involved in a drunk driving accident. She's been in rehab, but was recently released back into my care. It hasn't been easy, but we're navigating it together. I was embarrassed to tell you."

"Why?"

"Because your family is so wholesome and good and…mine is a mess."

"I'm so sorry you felt that way, *tesoro*. You are the only thing that matters to me. I could have been here for you. I thought…*Gesù, non vuoi sapere cosa ho pensato.*"

"No, tell me. I want to know everything."

"I thought you were making excuses to leave Italy. That we were moving too fast, that I was too intense."

I caress his cheek with my fingertips. "No, never. I was falling apart at the seams. Our relationship was the only thing holding me together. I needed your comfort and strength, but I was ashamed. Your family is so strong and united. Barbara and I are the exact opposite."

He sits up on his elbow and runs his fingers through my hair. "What happened with the accident?"

"Thanks to Cara, we had an excellent attorney and lucked out with a lenient judge. Because it was her first offense, he gave her probation and community hours. Her sponsor helped her find a job bagging groceries at a local market. It hasn't been ideal, but she has to start somewhere. She and I have always been a million miles apart, running in opposite directions, but we're trying to meet in the middle."

"I'm glad she's trying."

"Me, too. I think the accident really scared her."

"I'm not leaving you again, *tesoro*. I'm staying right here."

"No." I take a deep breath, gathering courage for what I've known since I left. "I want to be with you, Ren, but not here in California."

He's silent for a beat. "What are you saying?"

The decision feels scary, but also comforting. "I'm saying I'll move to Italy. I'm not sure what I'm going to do there, and I'll probably have to figure things out with Barbara after her probation period is over, but—"

I yelp as he lifts me into his arms and kisses my lips. "You've just made me the happiest man on earth, *tesoro*."

I smile down at him. "I'm so happy you're happy. *Ti amo*, Lorenzo."

"*Ti amo*, Summer." He brings the comforter over our heads, hiding us from the world for just a little longer as we make love again, our connection unbreakable.

# Chapter 35

I SHOOT OUT of bed at the sounds of pots clattering in my kitchen. It takes me a second to orient myself, my gaze falling on the empty side of the bed. Last night's events rush back. Lorenzo is here, and we're moving to Italy together. I'm so happy, nothing could push me off this cloud. I'm finishing up in the bathroom when I hear a loud cackle.

"No! No, no, no," I cry, throwing on a bathrobe.

"Oh, Lorenzo, aren't you *so handy* in the kitchen," Barbara purrs while she sips her coffee at the kitchen table, eyeing Lorenzo's butt in his pajama bottoms. She looks up and winks when she notices me standing in the doorway. "You didn't tell me you have an Italian boyfriend, Summerita."

"I thought you weren't supposed to be home until tomorrow?"

"Lois was called into work today. She dropped me off about ten minutes ago. And what a surprise to walk in to find this Italian gladiator standing in your kitchen." She waggles her eyebrows.

'*Stop!*' I mouth to her and widen my eyes, trying to convey to her I will strangle her in her sleep if she continues. She grins like a Cheshire cat.

Lorenzo turns from the stove and winks at me. "*Buon-*

*giorno, tesoro.* I'm sorry I didn't wake you. I wanted to surprise you with breakfast. Barbara was telling me all about the time you got your braces stuck to Chad McMillan's retainer on your first kiss."

"Seriously? That's the first story that comes to mind?" I glare at my mother before I cross the kitchen and kiss Lorenzo. She shrugs innocently as she sips her coffee.

"I am so sorry," I whisper in his ear.

"*Non precoccuparti, tesoro. Tutto va bene.*"

I huff as I translate the Italian in my head. *Don't worry, everything's fine.* He hands me a cup of coffee.

"I'm making eggs, nothing fancy. Sit down and relax."

I begrudgingly sit down next to Barbara, who's grinning from ear to ear. "Oh Summerita, not only is he sexy as sin, but that accent…no wonder you were keeping him a secret! The apple doesn't fall far from this tree."

I roll my eyes and smile behind my coffee cup. Barbara may be sober and trying her hardest to be responsible, but some things never change.

She watches him with hawk-like eyes over the brim of her coffee cup. "Is he rich? He looks expensive," she whispers.

"Will you shut up?" I hiss, praying to the Italian gods he doesn't hear her.

Barbara sits back, pantomiming zipping her lips, giving me a smug smile. I wouldn't blame Lorenzo one bit if he decided not to take me to Italy with him.

"Does he have any brothers? Maybe a devastatingly handsome uncle?" she asks, breaking the code of silence. "Lorenzo, Summer tells me you're in the olive oil industry. Is that a lucrative business?"

"Barbara," I groan, scrubbing my hands down my face. I chance a peek in Lorenzo's direction. His lips twitch as he scrambles the eggs.

"Rossi Olive Oil does quite well. We're the number-one imported olive oil in the United States."

"That sounds really fancy." Barbara winks at me while I laser her in half with my eyes. "What? Lorenzo doesn't mind, do you, honey?"

"I don't mind. Your mother is charming." He smiles lazily at me.

"Anyone who thinks Barbara is charming needs to have their head examined."

"You know, Summer, I *can* hear you." She turns her attention back to Lorenzo. "Lorenzo, say something in Italian."

Lorenzo looks over at me, his gaze locking on mine. "*Voglio passare il resto della vita con te.*"

"What does it mean?" she asks.

"I want to spend the rest of my life with you," he says quietly as he lays a plate down in front of me. He sweeps a gentle kiss across my cheek.

"Such a romantic. You should marry her, Lorenzo."

"Oh my God, please stop," I grumble.

"What? What did I say wrong now?" She swats my arm playfully. "You're not getting any younger. Someone has to give you a little push."

"I want to die."

"She's always been so dramatic, Lorenzo. Ever since she was a baby and would refuse to fall asleep without her raggedy stuffed cat, she called Roy Roy. She still has it."

I close my eyes, rubbing my temples, hoping this is a bad dream. I open them back up to find Lorenzo grinning at me. He lifts an eyebrow. "Your lovie was a cat?"

"Oh, she carried that thing everywhere. Pretty sure it's missing its tail and an eye. That grubby old thing is hiding around here somewhere."

"Roy Roy is not grubby," I say huffily.

The doorbell rings, saving me from any more humiliation. I open the front door, and Cara and Damien are there with a box of bagels. "Surp—"

"Oh, thank God you're here," I cut Cara off, pulling her into the foyer. Damien looks contrite as he follows behind. He hands me the bagels.

"Sorry, Summer, I tried to stop her, but she wanted to make sure you were okay."

"I'm relieved you guys are here. Barbara's embarrassing the crap out of me. I think she's trying to play catchup for all the times she wasn't there to humiliate me when I was a teenager."

"I can't believe he's here. Is everything okay between you two?" Cara whispers as we head to the kitchen.

"*Molto bene.*" I squeeze her hand. "So good."

She pulls back, stopping me before we enter. She looks into my eyes. Her lips slowly curve into a smile and she squeezes my hand back. "*Molto bene*, Summer."

I bring her and Damien into the kitchen and interrupt Barbara, who is asking Lorenzo about the financials of Rossi Olive Oil.

"Lorenzo, I'd like you to meet my two best friends, Damien and Cara Stevens."

Lorenzo wipes his hands on a towel and shakes their hands. "I've heard so much about you two. It's nice to finally meet you."

"Wow, it smells incredible in here. What are you making?" Cara asks, beelining for the stove.

"It's an Italian dish called Purgatory eggs," Lorenzo says.

Cara groans, lifting the lid of the saucepan and I have to bite my lip to keep from laughing when Damien scowls at her.

"She never acts like that when I'm cooking," he bellyaches. Cara makes a quiet, strangled noise as she replaces the lid on the pan. "Excuse my wife. She's acting like she hasn't had a home-cooked meal in years. Anyway, it's a pleasure to meet the infamous Lorenzo. Summer has been moping around here for months." Damien shakes Lorenzo's hand.

"Yes, well, hopefully that will change from here on out." He smiles, gathering me into his arms. Cara sighs and slaps Damien's stomach. "How come you never look at me like that?"

"Like what?"

"Like I'm the only one in the room."

"What are you talking about, woman? I look at you all the time like that at home."

"Yeah, because I'm literally the only one in the room."

I laugh, happiness spreading through my veins, making my heart feel full. My friends sit down at the table and we laugh and share stories over Purgatory eggs and bagels. I don't even mind Barbara's embarrassing Roy Roy stories. A peaceful calm washes over me as Lorenzo wraps his arm around my shoulder and talks sports and cooking with Damien. Cara fans herself when they aren't looking, making me giggle. I didn't realize how badly I needed my family's approval.

# Chapter 36

CARA SITS DOWN in the booth across from me and settles her purse on the seat beside her. She agreed to meet me for an early dinner while Lorenzo had a meeting at the Rossi California headquarters. She was all smiles at breakfast, but knowing Cara as well as I do, I know she's concerned.

As soon as the server takes our drink orders, she leans in. "So…are you going to tell me about your hot Italian stallion or what? He was gorgeous in the pics, but so much better looking in person."

"The one picture you saw him in, he was wearing a paper coat and hairnet." I arch an eyebrow.

"True, and he pulled that off. The man has amazing bone structure."

I decide to rip the Band-Aid off quickly. "Cara—"

"I know what you're going to say, Summer. It was written all over your face this morning." She breathes deeply and reaches for my hand. "I need to say my peace."

I squeeze her hand and nod for her to continue.

"I've always felt a bit overprotective of you. You are the sister I never had, my best friend. I'm not gonna lie, my emotions were swinging all over the place when you said you wanted to go to Italy. I was excited for you—you needed to let loose a little. But, I was scared too. What if you got hurt?

What if you didn't want to come back?" She shakes her head and straightens her silverware. "I can't believe I'm about to admit this, but when you called to tell me Barbara had been in an accident, I was strangely relieved, because it meant you had to return. It was extremely selfish of me, and I…I'm sorry. I hope you can forgive me."

"Aw, Cara…"

"You weren't the same person that left at the beginning of summer. Between Barbara and your job, there was a light missing from your eyes. I see that light missing every day in my clients, and I felt responsible for it happening to you. I convinced you to leave Italy when it was clear you weren't ready. Damien told me to butt out of your business, because you were a grown woman who could take care of herself. You were back at work, and life was the way it should be, but it wasn't right."

I open my mouth, but she holds up her index finger to stop me.

"No, let me finish. I felt sad for you, and I didn't know how to undo it. Seeing you this morning, it opened my eyes. I knew you were miserable, but I didn't realize to what degree. I'm so happy you found your forever person, Summer." A tear trickles down her cheek. I get up and go over to her side of the booth and wrap her in a big hug. "Can you forgive me?"

"Of course. It's all going to be okay."

She sniffles and releases me. "You're special to me, Summer."

"You're special to me, too. You were right, you know. I had to come back and take care of Barbara. She's my responsibility, not yours. I could have tried harder with Lorenzo, told him I loved him, and we could somehow make it all work, but I was scared and unsure of where our relationship was going. It was so new. As Damien likes to say, it was a recipe for shit pie."

A laugh bubbles up from her. "He does like to say that. Okay, enough tears. Tell me what happened last night."

"I'm sorry I left without trying to find you. I was barely holding myself together. After I bumped into that creep Kevin and dumped my drink on him, I ran out of the bar and drove home. I pulled into my driveway and there was Lorenzo, waiting for me. He told me he was willing to give up the farm in Italy to move here and be with me."

"He did?" Cara dabs her eyes with a tissue.

"Yes." I bunch my napkin in my hands and smooth it out again. "But I can't make him give that all up, Cara. If you saw how he talked about the business in Italy, how much it means to him, you'd understand. I can't ask him to leave his family behind."

"I think any guy who intends to give up everything for you is worth taking a chance on."

"Am I crazy?" I laugh, swiping fresh tears off my cheeks.

"Nah, not crazy, just a woman who finally found her man. A woman who's ready for whatever life throws at her."

I twist the gold shaped horn dangling from my neck. "I have. We were written in the stars."

Cara groans. "Tell me this isn't a line from *Under the Tuscan Sun* or some bullshit."

I giggle. "It's not. Just something a wise woman once told me."

She takes a sip of her iced tea. "Have you told work yet?"

"No, we just made this decision last night. I'm going to turn in my resignation on Monday. Jeremy has been blowing up my phone all weekend asking for finished chapters. I think it's time to move on from this job."

"What are you going to do about Barbara?"

"I'm not sure. She still has six months left on her probation. She's too fragile to be left on her own." I shrug and sit back as the server brings out our salads. "Lorenzo said he's willing to wait."

Cara sets down her fork. "You're willing to put your life on hold *again* for Barbara?"

"Barbara has been trying really hard. I promised I'd meet her halfway. I don't know. I'll have to feel it out at our next therapy session."

"How long is Lorenzo here for?"

"He's overseeing business at the California farm this week, and then it's Christmas. Probably after New Year's. If I can get Barbara situated, then I might go with him."

"I only have a few weeks left with you?" she cries.

"I'm not dying, Cara. You know, there are such things as airplanes that will deliver you right to me. Besides, I'll have to return to ship the rest of my things, tie up loose ends, I have to figure things out with Barbara and my townhome."

"I know, I know…it's just not the same. Promise me we'll video chat once a week so I can see everything going on in your life."

"I pinky swear. Ren asked me to help in the marketing department for the farm. He wants me to design a new logo for Rossi Olive Oil and finish the ads I had been working on before I left."

"That's amazing! Finally, your talent isn't being wasted on college textbooks."

I smile. "Promise me you'll come visit."

"I've already booked a ticket." She smiles sheepishly.

"What?" I laugh. "When?"

"Well, okay, I haven't booked it *yet*, but I'm going to. I want to give a week of cooking classes to Damien for Christmas. Lorenzo gave me his sister Fiore's information this morning when Damien was in the bathroom."

"That's so perfect." My head feels fizzy as everything comes together. "I'm happy, Cara. Really happy."

"Then I am too, and will support you one hundred percent. But I will always look out for you."

"Thank you. That's means everything to me."

# Chapter 37

DR. RICE SMILES as she sits down in the armchair opposite me. Barbara is on the couch, fiddling with her blouse. Dr. Rice's private office, outside of the rehab facility, is decorated in warm grays with white accents. Colorful watercolors hang on the walls, complementing the light gray furniture and chairs. On the coffee table is a lit citrus-scented candle next to a box of tissues and a mini Zen garden. It's a tranquil atmosphere, immediately putting me at ease. Barbara has continued seeing Dr. Rice weekly since she's left the rehab facility, and I have been joining her every other week for family therapy.

Dr. Rice opens her memo pad to a fresh page and clicks her pen. "It's nice to see you again, Summer. How have you been?"

"I've been good." I smile, clasping my hands in my lap.

"Barbara shared with me you have a friend who came to visit from Italy."

"Yes." I uncross my legs, shift and cross them again, uncertain of how this will go. "Um, that's what I wanted to talk about today, if that's okay?"

Dr. Rice smiles, tilting her head and fixing her gaze on Barbara. "Barbara, are you okay with talking about Summer's friend?"

"Sure. He's quite the catch. If I were ten years younger—"

"Mom…" I groan.

"Summer, why don't you tell us about him?" Dr. Rice interrupts, jotting down a note. "Is he still here? Is he staying at your place?"

"Yes, his family owns an olive farm here. He's been working there all week, and yes, he's staying with me." I shift in my seat, worried about how Barbara will take my announcement. "I met Lorenzo while I was in Italy this summer. We were…*are* romantically involved. He's asked me to move to Italy with him."

"How wonderful." Dr. Rice smiles warmly. "Is that exciting for you, Summer?"

"Yes, very much so. I'd like to go, but I'm worried. I don't want to leave Barbara."

"What worries you about leaving Barbara behind?"

I cast an anxious glance at my mom. "I'm worried she'll slip back into her old ways without me around. She's been doing so amazing these past few months, I don't want to interrupt her progress by moving thousands of miles away. This summer when I went away is when everything fell apart."

Dr. Rice nods. "Barbara, do you want to respond?"

Barbara shakes her foot at a manic speed. "Summer, I'm a recovering alcoholic. It's something I have to live with every day. I'm trying to survive this. I *want* to survive this. I don't want to be the person I was before the accident." She looks over at Dr. Rice, who nods her head, reassuring. "I think it's a good idea for you to move to Italy. You need your freedom and I need to learn how to be independent...from you."

"But Mom—"

"I'll be alright, Summer. For God's sakes, stop acting like you're the glue holding me together—"

"But that's just it! I *have* been holding you together...for years. Making sure you don't crack again. Do you know how stressful that has been?"

My knuckles are white from clasping the armrests. The elephant in the room slowly makes a lap between us.

"The truth is, you're stifling me," she says.

I glance at Dr. Rice, my mouth parting in disbelief before my gaze returns to Barbara. "I'm stifling *you*?"

"Yes. Ever since the accident, you've been smothering me. I'm surprised you don't make me take daily breathalyzer tests."

"Well, excuse me for caring."

"I know you care! You care *too* damn much. I don't deserve it."

"Barbara, why do you feel you don't deserve it?" Dr. Rice asks.

"Because I haven't been a good mom to her. I haven't been a good person."

My anger dissipates like morning mist. She looks so frail, hunched over on the couch. "You're my mom. Despite all the awful shit, I still love you and care about you."

Barbara pulls out a few tissues, unable to meet my gaze.

"Summer, are you worried that if Barbara slips back to her old ways, you'll feel guilty and blame yourself?"

"Yes." I shift in my seat, focusing on the Zen garden.

"That's a lot to carry on your shoulders. Barbara, how

does that make you feel?"

"Like I wish I had a cigarette right now," she grumbles, looking up at the ceiling. "Sometimes the pressure and scrutiny I'm under from her makes me want to backpedal."

"Whoa, wait a minute." I hold up my hands. "I'm in your corner. I just want you to get better."

"And I want to get better, I do. But Summer, you have to give me a chance. I've seen the difference in you since Lorenzo arrived. You're softer, more thoughtful…happy. I know I'm holding you back. I *want* you to go to Italy. I will be okay here."

"Summer, do you trust what Barbara says?"

"I trust she wants to be a better person, but I don't believe she'll be okay here without me."

"Oh, for Pete's sake, you're not my fucking savior, Summer," Barbara snaps.

Dr. Rice holds up a hand. "Summer, Barbara is right. You can't keep her from slipping or making a mistake. Only Barbara can do that. She has a great support system here, and we will continue therapy. You've been her conservator long enough. I think independence will do wonders for her growth and recovery. She has given you her blessing to go to Italy, and I support that move as well."

Barbara moves over closer to me and holds out her hand. I hesitate a few seconds, before placing mine over her upturned palm. Sadness and regret are etched in the fine lines around her eyes. "I'm sorry I haven't been there for you. Let me be the one to stand in your corner for once. Go to Italy, Summer. Be happy for once in your life."

I squeeze her hand before pulling away. I unclasp the

golden horn from around my neck and lay it in her palm. "For protection, Mom. Wear it for me. *La mia famiglia.*" I wipe a tear from my cheek, finally putting my past to rest. Free from the cage that has trapped me my whole life.

# Chapter 38

I SQUEEZE HIS hand and tug him to stop. "Wait."

He turns and lifts his fingers to graze my cheek. "What is it, *cara*?"

"I'm nervous."

An infectious grin spreads across his face. "*E la tua famiglia, tesoro.*"

"What if they're mad at me for leaving?"

I gaze into his smoky gray-green eyes flecked with gold before I'm swept up into his arms. He kisses my lips, his touch lingering. "I promise they are not. If they're mad at anyone, it's me for taking so long to bring you back." He touches his forehead to mine. "I will never let anything happen to you."

The door flings open, and we jump apart at the sudden interruption. Noise from the party spills out onto the front stoop.

"*Felice anno nuovo!* I thought I heard you out here. *Benvenuta a casa*, Summer!" Stella pulls me into a tight squeeze. "*Ci sei mancata così tanto.*"

I laugh as I hug her back. "I've missed you so much, too. Happy New Year."

She releases me and steps back, wiping a tear from her cheek, waving us forward. "Come in, come in, everyone is here."

"*In bocca al lupo, tesoro,*" Lorenzo says from behind me.

"Why are you wishing me luck—"

"She's here! *Felice anno nuovo!*" Fiore screeches, launching herself at me as I cross over the threshold, knocking her brother to the side.

"Oof. Fiore, I can't breathe," I wheeze.

"I'm so happy you're here," she cries. "There's so much to catch up on."

"I've missed you too." I laugh as she clings to me. "*Felice anno nuovo.*"

"*Basta!* Let her breathe," Nonna Rossi gripes from behind her. Fiore's arms release from around my neck. Nonna Rossi looks me over from head to toe. "*Hai bisogno di mangiare. Sei troppo magra.*"

"Happy New Year, Nonna Rossi."

"I see you still haven't learned Italian," she grumps.

I smile slyly at her. "You said I was too skinny."

Her eyes twinkle with delight. "Ah good, so you agree. *Come una gatta randagia.* Let's eat and start fattening you up." Nonna, festively dressed in a satin green tunic and palazzo pants, pulls me through the living room and shoves a platter of antipasto into my hands. "*Mangia.*"

"Uh...okay." I glance down at the plate and pick up an olive. "I'm sorry I didn't get to say goodbye—"

"Bah, you're here now. That's all that matters. You've come back and are here to stay, *sí? Per coltivare le radici come un albero.*"

"*Sí*, I'm here to stay and grow roots like a tree."

Nonna shuts one eye as she peers at me, assessing.

"*Bene.*" She leans in and kisses my cheek, her familiar rose perfume bringing me back to warm summer days in Italy.

"I've missed you, Nonna," I whisper against her hair.

"I've missed you more *stellina*, my little star. I knew you would find your way back."

"Nonna, can I borrow Summer for a moment?" Lorenzo asks.

"*Non te la meriti. Sei proprio un asino.*" Nonna lifts her nose in the air and grabs the plate out of my hands, before storming off to the kitchen.

"Did she call you an ass?"

Lorenzo sighs. "Sí. She said I don't deserve you and that I'm an ass."

"Oh no, Ren, I'm so sorry."

"Actually, this is progress." He chuckles. "She told me before I left, if I couldn't convince you to come back to Italy, I shouldn't bother showing my face around here again."

"What?" I laugh. "Oh my God, Harrison was right…Nonna Rossi is wicked scary."

"I'm just glad you said yes." He bends to kiss my lips.

"Me too."

"Well, I guess it's true. You're back," Nina's nasally voice comes from behind me. I turn around and she pushes her hand in front of my nose. "I'm engaged."

"Oh, congratulations, Nina. Engaged to…"

"Angelo, of course. Who else would it be?"

"Oh, I…" I stammer. Lorenzo covers his laugh with a cough.

Nina squints. "How long are you staying this time, Summer?"

I turn, gazing into Lorenzo's eyes. "I'm staying for good this time, Nina."

"*Interessante. Benvenuto*, Summer," she grumbles, before walking away.

"*Sí, molto interessante.* I think she's softening." Lorenzo grins as he circles an arm around my waist and kisses my lips. "Welcome home, Summer Andrews."

# Chapter 39

LYING ON OUR backs on a quilt underneath the old tree lit with fairy lights, I thread my fingers with his. It's been about six months since I moved back to Tuttoscano, and I miss nothing about my old life, except for Cara and Damien. I wish they lived closer. I've flown back a few times to pack up some stuff and to check on Barbara. She and her fellow AA friend Lois are renting my townhome from me, which worked out really well for everyone.

Barbara slipped about four months ago when she ran into her old friend Janice, but she reached out to her AA sponsor. With help from her friend Lois and Dr. Rice, they got her right back on the sober track. Dr. Rice wasn't discouraged like I was. She said even though Barbara fell off the wagon, she was heartened by the fact she immediately reached out for help. It helps to identify her triggers and Janice is definitely one of them. This isn't a sprint to the finish line, she reminded me. It's a lifelong slow jog. Barbara and I aren't perfect, but we try to meet each other in the middle.

I lay my hand on my stomach and moan. "Remind me to yell at Fiore for the strawberry shortcake. She was under strict instructions, no sugar or carbs until I lose ten pounds."

Lorenzo turns his head and grins. "No one held a gun to

your head, *tesoro*. The strawberry shortcake was for me."

"Yes, but that was torture listening to you moan while you ate it. I have zero self-control."

"Good to know." He snickers, bringing my hand to his lips, kissing my fingers as we stare up at the sky. "You know what today is?"

"Thursday?"

"No—"

I sit up suddenly. "Oh God, is it Friday? How did I miss a whole day? Shit, that means I forgot Razzo's vet appointment today. I gave him his last sedative for nothing? There's no way in hell I can shove him into a carrier without meds."

"Summer, you're ruining this moment."

"Oh, sorry." I scrunch my forehead, worrying about how I'm going to capture the feisty little shit. "What were we talking about?"

"Today *is* Thursday, June twelfth...not tomorrow, when Razzo's appointment is." He smirks. "Today is our one-year anniversary of when we first met."

Relief floods through me that I hadn't missed the cat's appointment. I lay back down and thread my fingers with his.

"Aw, it is? That's when you fell madly in love with me when I tried to steal your house right out from under you?"

His chest rumbles with laughter. "*Randagia*, I *let* you have the house."

"You *let* me? That's funny, because I remember Nonna reaming you a new one, making you run out of the house with your tail between your legs."

Lorenzo scoffs. "*Inconcepibile.*"

"Totally conceivable, but go on. Sorry, I'm ruining your moment again."

"I'm not sure I want to continue."

I laugh and sit up on my elbow and gaze down at him. He's grinning like a little kid on Christmas. He tucks a lock of loose hair behind my ear. "*Ti amo, tesoro.*"

"*Ti amo*, Ren."

"Do you ever regret moving back here with me?"

"Not for a millisecond. You make me so happy, Ren." I lean down and tenderly brush my lips against his. "I love the daily hugs I get from Nonna, and Fiore and I have grown so close. She told me she opened up to your parents and Nonna that she's gay. She said you were there right beside her, holding her hand through it all."

"*Sí*, she was trying to get everyone's attention off my woes and she felt she was finally ready. I'm really proud of her. Mom and Dad were a little shocked, but they're coming around. I thought Nonna would have been the one to give her the most grief, but she told Fiore, *l'amore si presenta in molti colori diversi*. Love comes in many different colors."

I smile and squeeze his hand. "Once again, Nonna surprises us all. And of course, she's right. I'm happy Fiore can be true to herself and not have to pretend to be someone she's not."

"Me too. It took a lot of courage for her to come out."

"On another note, Fiore won't stop trying to fatten me up. Nonna mentioned in passing I was too skinny to conceive a baby, so they've been shoving pasta in my face every time I turn around."

"Meddling family. I'll tell them first thing tomorrow to

quit their antics."

I press my finger to his lips. "I don't mind. I've never had family care about me the way yours does, not since my Grams. And if it gets too much, I'll unleash my big, bad beast on them, but for now, I can handle it."

"I like it when you call me your big, bad beast."

"I was referring to Razzo."

He laughs and pulls me under him, kissing my lips. "You know what else I like? Having you down the hall from me at the office. Now I don't have to wander the property looking for you."

"As if you didn't have enough on your plate."

"I'm enamored by the beautiful American woman." His eyes dance with happiness as he sits back and holds out his hand, helping me into a sitting position. "Run away with me?"

"Where do you want to go?"

"I never got a chance to take you to the sea. There's a beautiful, quiet beach called *Spiaggia Rosa* in Sardinia."

"Sounds beautiful. What's the special occasion?"

"Well, we'll need somewhere to go for our honeymoon." He holds up the most beautiful diamond ring glittering in the fairy lights. Exhilaration courses through my veins like fizzy champagne bubbles. I've dreamt of this moment since the night of the falling stars, but it's better than I imagined. It's everything. "*Mi sposi*, Summer? Will you marry me?"

I swallow past the tears and nod vigorously. "*Sí*, Lorenzo. *Sí*." He slips the ring on my finger. It fits perfectly. "It's so beautiful," I whisper.

"It was Nonna's. She wanted you to have it. She gave it

to me the day I met you at the house. I laughed and told her she was crazy."

"But you kept it?"

"Nonna has a way of making you do things you don't want to do."

"Oh, how well I know." I grin goofily, admiring the diamond.

"I kept it in my safe, but I knew the night of San Lorenzo, as we watched the stars, I was going to ask you to marry me."

"That's when I knew you were it for me." I sigh and hold up the beautiful round diamond surrounded by a ring of little diamonds, the twinkling lights making them sparkle. "These diamonds look like little stars."

"*Sí, scritti nelle stelle.*"

"Written in the stars," I whisper.

"I want to make you happy, *tesoro*." Holding my face, he gently kisses me.

"You already do, Ren."

We stay under the old tree, making love until the stars fade.

# Chapter 40

MY LEGS BURN as I push the pedal down. "Why on earth am I in this circle of hell again?"

"It's a beautiful day, *cara mia*," Romeo shouts as he glides by, giving me a thumbs-up.

I glance to my left. Lorenzo smirks as he catches my expression. I shake my head. "This was a bad idea."

Lorenzo grins, looking cool as a cucumber on his bike, while I probably look like I had a fight with a racoon.

I groan, my legs protesting, muscles I haven't used in a year burning.

"I thought you enjoyed biking, *tesoro*."

"I hate it."

"Then why are we doing this day tour?"

"Because it turns out I'm a sentimental idiot, and I thought it would be fun for all our friends. I know you could easily be at the front of the group," I pant. "Just go."

"I'd never leave you behind, Summer." He smiles cheekily. "Besides, I enjoy looking at your fine ass."

Harrison and Daniella whiz by on their electric bikes. Harrison starts to sing "Eye of the Tiger," and I give him the middle finger. He laughs and waves.

"I'm pretty sure Romeo chose the hardest route," I gripe. "Why didn't we opt in for the electric bikes again?"

Lorenzo laughs like he's not dying on this hill from hell. "Because this is a better workout. Keeps you in shape for other activities…such as sex."

"We get plenty of exercise doing that."

"Oh Jesus, Mary, and Joseph, when is this hill going to end?" Lynnette cries out from behind me.

I peer over my shoulder and grin at her sparkly blue *Be Happy* visor. Her skin is lobster red as she huffs and puffs alongside her boyfriend, Gary. They met in the grocery store a few weeks after she got back from Italy. They reached for the same bottle of Chianti, and it was love at first sight. Gary said he fell in love with her blue eyes. Lynette thought he had a nice smile. It was serendipitous. If she hadn't gone to Italy, she never would have started drinking Chianti and never would have met Gary.

I watch Daniella throw her head back and laugh at something Harrison says. Lorenzo and I grin at each other. I never would have thought those two would mesh, but they've been inseparable since we introduced them at dinner on Harrison's first night back in town. Daniella's father is a plumber and she, too, is terrified of birds. It's a match made in heaven, if you ask me. We've become good friends since I moved back. She, Fiore, and I are pretty much inseparable. Perhaps she can convince Harrison to move here, too. Toilets are a universal product, after all.

Cara and Damien are ahead of us. They are avid Peloton riders and keep ooh-ing and ah-ing over the picturesque landscapes while they chat with Romeo. Damien is super excited to get back to the villa, though, because Fiore has promised him a cooking lesson while she prepares for a big feast tonight at the Villa Rossi. This could be the beginning of a beautiful friendship…for Damien *and* for Cara.

Lorenzo's brother, Emilio, and his wife, Caterina, are up in front with Harrison and Daniella. They both welcomed me into the family with open arms. They have three adorable daughters who are currently tearing up Stella's shop while she watches them for the day. Emilio shared over cocktails last night that he never thought his little brother would marry. He's ecstatic Lorenzo found someone who appreciates the family history and how important the farm is to the family.

After a group picture overlooking the town, Romeo guides us onto a side road that leads us back down into Tuttoscano. "Hey Harrison," I call out. "Remember this spot? This is where you dislocated my thumb. If it hadn't been for you, I never would have moved here!"

He peeks back over his shoulder and smiles. "Somehow, Summer, I think you would have found a way to stay. An American lost in Tuscany."

"True, I was determined to find something here."

"Did you?" Lynnette shouts from behind me.

I look around at all my friends, who jumped on the first flight here when I said I was getting married to the most amazing man in Italy. I'm surrounded by family, laughter, and a hot guy who thinks I've hung the moon.

I turn to Lorenzo, my heart completely full. He returns my smile with a wink, and I thank my lucky stars that led me to him.

"*Sí*, Lynnette. I found it."

# Chapter 41

FIORE HANDS ME a champagne flute as Stella buttons the back of my dress. "*Bellissima, sorella.*"

I smile and take a sip, hoping the bubbles will calm my nerves. "*Grazie*, Fiore."

"I've always wanted a sister."

I smile and squeeze her hand. "Me too."

She clasps a pearl bracelet on my wrist. "I'm just so happy for you both. Mamma and Papà gave this to me on my confirmation day. Something borrowed *per mia sorella per sempre*. For my forever sister."

"It's beautiful, thank you." I lean in and kiss her cheek. Stella fusses for me to stop moving.

Cara smiles at me from her chair, where she's sipping champagne and taking pictures.

Nonna claps her hands once Stella finishes. "Everyone out, I need to speak to Summer alone, *per favore*."

Cara kisses my cheek. "I need to go check on Barbara, anyway. When I last saw her, she was asking Great-Uncle Giovanni if he preferred blondes or brunettes."

I laugh. "Oh God, some things never change."

"Great-Uncle Giovanni?" Fiore's face scrunches. "Ugh, no. Get that image out of my head, Cara!"

I give Cara a grateful smile as she shuffles Fiore out the

door. Stella gives me a wink before the door closes with a soft click.

The older woman fluffs out the back of my dress and inspects her handiwork. Thousands of seed pearls have been sewn into the bodice and skirt of the dress. It's breathtaking. She's wearing her signature tunic and palazzo pants in oyster-gray silk with seed pearl embroidery along her neckline. She looks elegant and stunning as always. She picks up a navy velvet rectangular box and hands it to me.

"This is from Renzo. He asked me to give it to you."

I open it up and gasp. A delicate gold chain holds three stars made of diamonds. The note attached reads:

> *Tesoro, a star for you, a star for me, and a star for what will come to be. You are making me the happiest man in the world today. Eternamente tuo, eternally yours, ti amo, Ren*

I turn toward the mirror and Nonna helps me put the necklace on. It glitters against my skin.

"You're just missing one more thing, *stellina.*"

She opens my palm and places a diamond pin of an angel holding a sapphire star.

"Oh, Nonna, it's beautiful."

"*My* nonna gave it to me on my wedding day, and Stella wore it on hers. I know you are missing your grandmother today, and that she would have wanted to be here on this special occasion. This is my way of saying she's here with you in spirit." She hands me a tissue. "Now, don't cry and ruin your makeup. This is a happy day."

I wrap her in a hug. "*Grazie*, Nonna, for everything…but especially for giving me wings to fly and roots to grow. For giving me a chance."

She takes the pin from me. "*La famiglia é la casa del cuore.* Family is here, Summer." She points to her heart. "Always remember that." She lifts the skirt of my dress and pins the angel to the inside. "*Che gli angeli benedicano te e* Lorenzo *con una lunga e felice vita insieme.* May the angels bless you and Lorenzo with a long and happy life together."

"*Grazie*, Nonna."

"No, thank you, Summer, for making this old woman's heart a happy one."

"Lorenzo told me about the ring. You always knew we'd end up together, didn't you?"

"From the moment I opened the door and saw you standing on my front step. I was so worried about Renzo taking the house and turning it into another project that would consume his time. I thought, he's never going to produce great-grandbabies for me if he works all the time. You may be small, but you have good birthing hips."

I bite back a laugh as she lays my skirts back into place.

"I knew Nonno had sent you to me. *Un segno.* And your wish came true, *sí*?"

"My wish?"

"The one you asked for on the night of San Lorenzo."

*I wished for Lorenzo to be mine.* "How did you know?"

Nonna's eyes twinkle. "A wish made on the night of the falling stars always comes true."

I eye her dubiously, and she chuckles. "I also might have read your journal you kept in your bedroom drawer."

"You mean my *diary*?"

"Journal, diary…eh." She shrugs.

Oh my God, I'm pretty sure I wrote about Lorenzo's sexual talents in there. I want to vomit. "Nonna, that was personal!"

"You shouldn't leave things lying around."

"It was in a drawer next to my bed!"

"*Basta*, let this sentimental old woman remember what it's like to be young and in love again, looking for adventure."

"Nonna, your English is perfect, isn't it? The day I met you, you told me you only spoke a little. You could understand everything Harrison and I were saying, couldn't you?"

She grins like Razzo when he watches me scream after he drops a mouse at the back door. "*Sí*, I understand it and can speak it perfectly."

"Nonna!"

"What? I get bored from time to time." She gently pats my cheek. "You're the best stray cat I've ever taken in, *piccola*, besides Nonno Rossi, of course."

Laughter bubbles up inside me. I should be angry with Nonna for reading my diary, annoyed by her impertinence, and upset she lied about her English, but I can't find it in me. If it weren't for her, I wouldn't be standing here right now, about to marry the man of my dreams.

"Shall we head down to the courtyard?" I ask, gathering my skirts.

"Change of plans."

"Wait, what do you mean a change of plans?"

"Lorenzo has a surprise for you." Nonna motions for me to follow. "Come with me."

She leads me out of the back door of the villa to a waiting car.

"Nonna, where are we going? I don't like surprises."

"You'll see."

She helps me tuck my dress into the car and climbs in after me. The driver pulls away from the house. He should turn left around the farm to where Lorenzo and I are supposed to get married, overlooking the trees and hills, but he takes a right down the hill to the old house. Thunder rumbles in the distance. I glance wearily at Nonna. "I hope the events staff covered everything with tents. It wasn't supposed to rain today."

"*Pazienza*, Summer. It will be alright." She pats my hand. The driver pulls up to the front door of the old house. Harrison and Damien are waiting for us out front in suits, looking dashing.

"Why are we here? Why are *they* here? Everyone's supposed to be at the farm! Wait, Lorenzo said this house is under construction!"

Nonna peers back at me over her shoulder before she exits the car, cackling. "He lied."

"Nonna Rossi, lovely as always." Harrison bows slightly as he helps her out. His jaw drops as I try to scoot out of the limo behind her. He helps me to my feet. "Wow, Summer. You're stunning!"

Despite my confusion of why we're here, his compliment makes me smile. "*Grazie*, H."

"Did you see smoking-hot Daniella? She looks like a goddess. Not as pretty as you, of course."

"Of course," I deadpan. "Do you call her smoking-hot

Daniella to her face?"

Harrison's cheeks bloom pink. "Sometimes? I can't help myself. She's freaking smoking hot." Nonna clears her throat and Harrison ducks his head. "I gotta go. Nonna scares me."

Damien whistles as he lends me his hand. "You look beautiful, Summer. He's a lucky man."

My cheeks heat. "Thanks Dame." I smooth out my dress while we wait for Harrison and Nonna to slip inside the house. "Okay, tell me what's going on."

"You don't know?"

I jab him in the side. "You know I don't. Spill it."

"Sorry, I made an oath to Nonna. She threatened me with bodily harm."

"You're seriously scared of an eighty-eight-year-old woman?"

"Yes," he chuffs and looks at his watch. "Forget about Nonna. Summer, you know you've always been like a sister to me. Cara and I are going to miss you so much, but you deserve all the happiness in the world. We love you. And Lorenzo's a cool dude, too."

"Oh damn, Damien, don't make me start crying now." My nose burns, tears threatening to spill. I wave my hand in front of my face.

"Shit, my bad."

I laugh, my emotions swinging like a pendulum. He looks at his watch. "It's time." He opens the front door.

# Chapter 42

GOLDEN LIGHT SPILLS down the hallway, making the freshly sanded and stained wood floors gleam. Harp strings pluck softly from somewhere in the house. I glance to my left, where a wall used to be. In its place is an archway framed in brick leading into the kitchen. I pause, my mouth hanging open as I quickly take in the remodeled kitchen. I knew the house was being worked on, but Lorenzo wanted it to be a surprise.

"Oh my God, do you see this?" I wander into the new kitchen. I'm in complete awe, it's gorgeous in here. "It's a Viking stove!"

"Come on, Summer, you're going to get me in trouble," Damien whispers.

"But it's all brand new! Did you see the marble counters? Stunning."

"Focus, Summer. You're about to get married."

"Right, sorry. I'm a little nervous and excited."

He steers me down the hall. Two large glass lanterns with candles and flowers flank the entrance to the open living room. We pause and everyone seated turns in our direction. All the furniture is gone, except for the gold wedding chairs for the guests. We only wanted immediate family and close friends, so it's a small affair. Everyone else will greet us afterward at the reception at Fiore's café.

Airy cream linen curtains float in the breeze of the open French doors. There are so many candles in cream and gold that the room looks incandescent. White gardenias, roses, and peonies flank the chairs. Cara steps forward with tears in her eyes and hands me my bouquet with matching flowers. She kisses my cheek, before she and Damien send me on my way down the aisle toward Lorenzo. He looks heart-achingly sexy in his midnight-black tuxedo that fits him like a glove.

"This is a surprise," I whisper as he takes my hand.

"I wanted to marry you in the place where we first met. Where you fell madly in love with me."

I throw my head back and laugh. "*Perfetto.*"

We turn to the priest, hand in hand, as he begins the ceremony.

Thunder rumbles overhead and lightning flashes. A brown animal streaks through the open doors. I close my eyes, praying its Razzo. Signor Rossi quietly closes the French doors as the raindrops bead on the windows. I glance at Lorenzo, but his attention is on the priest, who starts the vows in Italian and then repeats them in English. "Lorenzo." The priest nods. Lorenzo turns toward me.

"*Io*, Lorenzo Raffaelo Rossi, *prendo te*, Summer Elizabeth Andrews, *come mia sposa e prometto di esserti sempre fedele, nella gioia e nel dolore, nella salute e nella malattia, e di amarti e onorarti tutti i giorni della mia vita.*" He slips the diamond band on my left ring finger.

"I, Summer Elizabeth Andrews, take you, Lorenzo Raffaelo Rossi, as my husband and promise to be faithful to you always, in joy and in pain, in health and in sickness, and to love you, honor you, every day for the rest of my life."

I slip the platinum band on his finger. Something sizzles behind me. Lorenzo's gaze wanders over my shoulder, his brow furrowing. His attention returns to me, and he smiles as the priest says a blessing in Italian.

The steady beat of rain against the windows continues as we stare into each other's eyes, grinning like we just won the lottery.

"*Con il potere conferitomi, dalla Chiesa e dalla Repubblica Italiana, vi dichiaro ora marito e moglie. Puoi baciare la sposa.* You are now husband and wife."

Everyone cheers as Lorenzo dips me back and kisses me. He pauses and eases me up before he looks up at the ceiling. Candles not in lanterns flicker before they completely snuff out. I stare up at the ceiling as a drop of water splashes on my forehead.

"I take it you never got a new roof put on?"

"No, not yet. I had some interference…"

Several guests look up as drops hit them as well.

"*Sposa bagnata, sposa fortunate!*" Nonna shouts, grinning with delight. "A wet bride is good luck! *Un segno!*"

I turn to Lorenzo and laugh. "Nonna and her damn *segnos*."

He cradles my face in his hands. "You make me so happy, Signora Rossi. I love you." He softly kisses my lips while everyone whoops and hollers. Drops of water splash all around us. "Now let's get out of here before the whole roof caves in. Oh, and prepare yourself, *tesoro*. You're about to be bombarded with flying pasta."

It may not be the water pouring out of the faucet in

*Under the Tuscan Sun*, but it's pretty damn close.

"ON THE COUNT of three."

"Uno, due, tre!" people holler behind me. Blindfolded, I stumble through the crowd as people cheer and shout, gently pushing me in different directions. It's disorientating, and I can't help but giggle. It was my idea, after all. Instead of doing the traditional bouquet toss, which I've always despised, the first person—woman or man—that I stop in front of and hand my bouquet to will be the next to marry.

An internal voice tells me to stop, and everyone cheers. I pull off the blindfold and stand in front of a blushing Fiore. I laugh and smash my bouquet into her arms as we hug. She takes the flowers and kisses my cheek. "*Grazie*, Summer."

"I can't wait to meet the lucky lady," I whisper before Fiore is pulled away by Fredo.

Lorenzo gathers me into his arms as we dance under the star-laden sky. I try to straighten his bow tie, but it has chunks of material cut from it. Another Italian tradition I had never heard of where the groomsmen cut the groom's tie and sell pieces of it at the ceremony. "How much money did Emilio, Fredo, and Gio get for your bowtie?"

"A couple hundred, I'm sure."

"Oh good, we could use a new roof."

Lorenzo laughs and swings me around. "*Sí*, I'm sorry about that, *tesoro*. Fiore and Nonna insisted the kitchen should be done first since it's the heart of the home. Bad luck and all that stuff. You know how pushy those two can be. Obviously, the roof will be next." He smiles tenderly, caressing my cheek with his thumb. "Have I told you lately how much I love you?"

"Yes, but you can say it again."

He touches his nose to mine and closes his eyes, breathing me in like the first time he smelled my perfume. "I love you, Summer Rossi."

"I think I might love you just a little more, Lorenzo Rossi."

"*Impossibile.*"

Twinkling lights and candles sparkle against the tables as guests drink and dine on Fiore and Fredo's fabulous cooking. The rain stopped soon after we left the house and thank goodness our wedding coordinator insisted on tents. Angelo sits sullenly at a table next to Nina. The honeymoon phase ended quickly after Nina found out she was pregnant three months ago and Angelo had to trade in his yellow Ferrari for a non-descript gray SUV. Despite Nina's sour disposition in the beginning, she's matured since my return, and I now enjoy her company at work.

Nonna sits with her best friend Elena and some other women, gossiping and drinking grappa. I've never seen her so animated and happy. I'm glad we brought her such joy today, and she didn't have to curse anyone or go *pazza* to get it.

I scan the crowd for Barbara and see her on the dance floor behind us. Cara has been monitoring her tonight. I've been anxious that the flowing alcohol this weekend might cause her to relapse, but she's been okay, checking in with her sponsor every day. She said this day was too important to miss because of alcohol, which made me cry. I shake my head and chuckle, catching her eye. She winks at me as she dances way too close to Gio. I groan, burying my face in Ren's neck.

"Are you okay, *tesoro*?"

"Barbara just squeezed Gio's butt out on the dance floor. He's half her age."

His chest rumbles with laughter. "Gio likes the attention."

"So does Barbara."

"Then they suit each other perfectly." He tilts my chin up and we sway as one. "You look so beautiful tonight, *amore*. I've been dreaming about this day since San Lorenzo. That was my wish, you know. I can tell you now that it came true. I wished on that night you would become my wife."

"Funny, because I wished you would be mine forever."

He gently kisses my lips, and I sigh. He smiles down at me and holds me tighter. "I've been thinking about Casa Rossi. It would be a shame to fix it all up and let other people stay in it."

"I saw a glimpse of the kitchen. It's beautiful."

"*Sí*. It will take a while with some major overhauling, but I thought we could move in when it's done. Make the master bedroom larger with a door that won't cave in. Perhaps I could convert a room into an art studio. Would you want that?"

"Does Razzo come with it?"

"I'd be too scared I'd lose my arm if I tried to remove

him."

"Then yes, I want it." I smile tenderly, curling my fingers up into his hair and luxuriating in this moment that he is mine, and this is real. "Wait, can we put in a pool?"

Lorenzo snorts and looks into my eyes. "*Sí*, Summer, if that will make you happy, we can put in a pool."

"Ren?"

"Summer?"

"Are you laughing last?"

He arches an eyebrow in confusion.

"When we first met, you said, *Ride bene chi ride ultimo.* He who laughs last, laughs best."

He shakes his head, grinning. "No, *tesoro*, I think you got the last laugh. You own me—heart, body, and soul."

"You should know, I never like to lose a challenge."

He dips me and smiles against my lips. "I never doubted you for a second."

Nonna was wrong. My adventure doesn't end here. It's just begun.

# Epilogue

I PICK UP two plates of lasagna and watermelon and slip two bottles of water into my dress pockets. I search the crowd for Lorenzo and grin when I spy him chatting with Fiore and Daniella.

"*Auguri e figli maschi*, Summer!"

"*Grazie*, Alberto." I nod at the couple who lives in our apartment building. People keep stopping me every two feet to wish me well and congratulations. It's nice everyone is so happy for us, but I really just want to grab my husband and find a quiet corner away from the town.

Lorenzo looks so handsome, the wind ruffling his dark hair. His white linen button-down glows against his deep tan. I want to take him back home and spend the rest of the night making him say naughty things in Italian, but I can't. It's the Feast of San Lorenzo. It's tradition to watch the stars.

We came back a day early from our honeymoon because of it, which made Lorenzo incredibly grumpy. He wanted to camp out under the old olive tree and watch the stars from there, but I insisted we go into town for a bit to say hello to everyone, and to eat the scrumptious food.

"I snagged some lasagna!" I waggle my eyebrows and kiss Fiore and Daniella's cheeks.

He smiles at me, and it takes my breath away. He'll take

my breath away for as long as I live. "I swear, the only reason we came back early was for the lasagna."

"You know, Summer, I can make it for you whenever you want," Fiore teases.

"I know, but there's something special about lasagna on the night of the falling stars." I wink at Lorenzo.

"I was just telling Fiore and Daniella about our trip."

"I can't believe you guys stayed on a private yacht and met the Clooneys. *Sono così geloso*," Fiore grumbles.

"Don't be jealous, little sister. If you play your cards right, perhaps you can become my personal chef and work on my yacht."

"I already am your personal chef. *Idiota*." She rolls her eyes and slaps him in the stomach. "Go away."

"You don't have to tell me twice." Lorenzo grins and motions with his head for me to follow. "*Sei pronta, bella?*"

"I'm ready. Same place?" I ask as he takes my plate.

"*Sí.*"

We climb the cobblestone hill and walk to the blessedly empty courtyard at the top, sitting down on the stone wall. I immediately dig into my lasagna, moaning as I devour it.

"Hungry, *tesoro*?" Lorenzo stares at me in wonderment, chuckling as I inhale the pasta.

"Starving. I've been dreaming about this lasagna for a year."

"That's a long time."

"You have no idea."

We finish our food, and he cradles me in his arms. We gaze out over the town with its twinkling lights, music, and laughter surrounding us like a warm hug from home.

I sigh in contentment. "I hope we can do this until we're old and gray."

He kisses the shell of my ear. "What are you going to wish for tonight?"

I turn my head slightly, gently elbowing him in the ribs. "I can't tell you that. It's bad luck."

"Hmm."

"Why? What are you going to wish for?" I ask.

"All my wishes came true, *cara mia*."

"All of them? What if I could grant you one more?"

"So now you're San Lorenzo's genie?" He grins goofily down at me.

I trace his lips with my finger. "Lean down and find out for yourself."

He looks at me curiously and bends his head down. I whisper in his ear and he rears back. "Are you sure?"

Laughter bubbles up. "Of course, I'm sure."

He squeezes me tight and drops a tender kiss on my lips as the stars fall from the sky. "Make a wish, *mi amore*."

Like a little kid, I squeeze my eyes shut, my fingers grasping the diamond stars on the necklace he gave me. I wish for a lifetime of love and happiness with this man. I open my eyes to find him watching me with a tender expression.

"Did you make a wish?" I ask.

"*Sí.* I wished for…lasagna every night." He winks.

I throw my head back and laugh, love making my heart grow twice its size. He grabs my hand, threading my fingers with his.

"*Ti adoro, tesoro.* I'm so glad you got lost in Tuscany."

"I'm so glad you found me." I lean in and kiss his lips.

I'M SIGNORA ROSSI of *L'Azienda Olivicoloa Rossi.* Wife to this beautiful man, daughter to Barbara, Stella, and Raffaelo, sister to Fiore, Cara, Damien, Emilio, and Caterina. Granddaughter to Nonna Rossi, and now a mother to the little miracle growing inside me. *La mia famiglia.*

Fine.

# A Note from the Author

If you or a loved one are having issues with drugs or alcohol,

please contact the Substance Abuse and Mental Health Services Administration's (SAMHSA) National Helpline www.samhsa.gov/find-help/national-helpline

at 1-800-662-HELP (4357). Or text 988.

You are important, you are loved, and you are worth it.

# Acknowledgments

Man, this book took a serious village and two years to see the light of day. A huge thank you to everyone who helped bring it to fruition. I wouldn't be here writing this without your love and support. To my core group of die-hard readers who make these books possible, I adore you. Thank you from the bottom of my heart for loving my stories. To my sister Allison, thank you for always being my sounding board. I appreciate you and love you. Stephanie and Nel, thank you for offering to Beta Read and take the time to give me feedback. Words can't describe how much I appreciate and value you. To Lucia Scarano and Anneliese Schultz for your amazing help with the Italian. *Grazie dal profondo del mio cuore.* To Lisa for always being my cheerleader, thank you. To Addie, thank you for not only being one of my beta readers, but for always being in my corner. I appreciate you. To Jaspen, thank you for giving me the appropriate weightlifting number for Gary. Hey look, you're in a book! ;) To Holly, thank you for your honesty and help editing this book in the beginning. It helped me to become a better writer. To Michelle, thank you for understanding my humor and polishing my sentences. You understand what my characters are trying to say better than I do. I am forever grateful for you, and your support means everything to me. To my family, for your love and support and insisting on reading my books, thank you and I love you. To my husband and ids for putting up with my inability to get anything done while I'm in book launching mode, I appreciate you more han you'll ever know. Thank you for letting me do my dream. Your patience made this book happen. To Josephine and Richard, thank you from the bottom of my heart for all your love and support.

# Other Books by Sophie Sinclair

The Coffee Girl Book Series

*Coffee Girl – Coffee Girl Book 1*

*The Makeup Artist – Coffee Girl Book 2*

*The Social Hour – Coffee Girl Book 3*

*Last Call – Coffee Girl Book 4*

The Love Series

*Lindsey Love Loves*

*Patrick Loves Love*

The Greyson Gap Series

*Where The River Takes You – Greyson Gap Book 1*

# About the Author

Sophie Sinclair lives with her husband, two daughters, a boxer-mix named Dunkin Donuts, a chi-pit named Moki, and a cat named Pickles in Davidson, NC.

You can find me on my website:
www.sophiesinclairwrites.com

Social Media:

Instagram:
@sophiesinclairauthor

Facebook:
Sophie Sinclair Writes

Twitter:
@authorssinclair

If you enjoyed this book, please leave a review!

Thank you,
Sophie

www.ingramcontent.com/pod-product-compliance
Lightning Source LLC
Chambersburg PA
CBHW032141190726
48290CB00005BB/1354